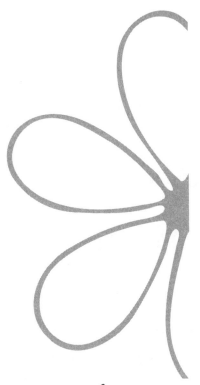

soul searching

Shannon Guymon

Bonneville Books
Springville, Utah

ISBN: 1-55517-872-3
v.1

Published by Bonneville Books,
an imprint of Cedar Fort, Inc.
925 N. Main Springville, Utah, 84663
www.cedarfort.com

Distributed by:

Cover and book design by Nicole Williams
Cover design © 2005 by Lyle Mortimer

Printed in the United States of America
10 9 8 7 6 5 4 3 2 1

Printed on acid-free paper.

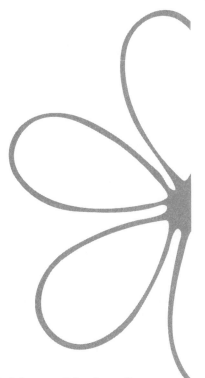

For my children—Skyler, Savannah, Jessica, and Kaleb—the joy of my life.

chapter one

Micah sat down in the back row with her two room-mates, Lisa and April. She smoothed her long linen skirt over her knees and concentrated on not crossing her legs. She tucked the blond wisps of hair that had come loose from her clip behind her ears and took a deep, calming breath as she looked out over the large congregation of beautiful people. She hated going to church.

She felt her body tense up as it always did and concentrated on the perfection of her fingernails. She might have her problems, but at least there were no chips in her fingernails. *That has to count for something,* she thought. She'd had the lady at the nail salon paint them a light shade of mauve. Not too bright, not too pale. Her father would surely approve.

Micah looked up as the opening song ended and waited for the bishop to approach the podium. She liked Bishop Nielson. He was always polite and courteous to her. And as long as he didn't call her in for any kind of interview, she would like him a lot.

Testimony meeting. Great. Micah felt her stomach clench into an even tighter ball of nerves and automatically reached for her purse. If she didn't have a roll of Tums, then she might as well lie down and die. Her fingers searched the bottom of her purse and finally clutched around the half-eaten tube of comfort—the only comfort she would be getting that morning anyway. Her father had told her just last week that he was expecting her to bear her testimony soon. He was disappointed that she hadn't been given a calling yet. *Embarrassed* was the word he had used. He had gently suggested that by bearing her testimony, she would give the bishop a good impression of her.

She hated bearing her testimony. What was a testimony anyway, except people getting up and crying about how wonderful their roommates were, or how hard going to school was but they made it through because they worked so hard? *Blah, blah, blah.* And today it would be her. She felt all cold and clammy inside at the thought. She always wondered how these girls could get up every fast and testimony meeting and cry their eyes out about the dumbest things. Every time the bishop got up and talked about how strong the Spirit had been in a certain meeting, she felt so confused. Couldn't he hear how pointless they all sounded?

If her father hadn't been expecting her for lunch today, she would have gotten up and walked out right then. Using the excuse of feeling ill and staying home could only be used so often though. *I could always lie.* She could tell her father she had borne her testimony and he would never

know. Except her father had a bad habit of always checking up on her—accidentally running into her bishop at the
bank or calling up Brother Harris, the first counselor, for
tax advice.

Her father wasn't stupid. He'd just pack on the guilt until
she cracked. Until she'd do anything for him to stop—stop
what? What was it exactly he did? She paused and thought
about it as the bread was passed to her. He sucked the life
out of her. That's what he did. She frowned at the disloyal
thought. Surely, a loving, dutiful, and grateful daughter
wouldn't think something so awful of her father. Would
she?

Micah threw all thoughts of her father out of her mind
and focused on her game plan: getting through the next
hour. What could she bear her testimony about? What?
Think, think, think. What would impress the bishop so
much that he would have no choice but to make her the next
Relief Society president? *As if.* But her father just wouldn't
give up hoping. He kept reminding her that if she would
just mention the fact that her great-great uncle had been a
General Authority, she would see some results. What her
father didn't seem to understand though, was that Bishop
Nielson had a way of looking right through you. He didn't
see all of the superficial stuff she had been throwing at him.
He saw her soul. She, Bishop Nielson, and God all knew
there wasn't much there worth talking about. Too bad her
dad didn't understand that.

She looked around desperately, wishing for any kind of
inspiration. But all she could see were perfect, happy people.
It made her sick. She couldn't imagine being one of them.
She always felt as if she were outside looking in. Or to be
more exact, inside looking out—inside a prison and looking out into a world where people were happy. Where it
was possible to be somebody wonderful. Where you didn't
always feel so . . . broken.

If she could just steal a little bit from each person. Not much, just a little. If she could just take a little of Erin's confidence, snatch a small portion of Julie's glow, or take a teeny bit of Carly's sense of humor, then she'd be okay. She would be normal then. Okay, so she would be some kind of soul snatcher and would go to hell, but for just one day, wouldn't it be worth it? All of these girls in her ward had something that she didn't have. She wasn't sure exactly what that was, but she knew it, just like she knew her own name. They had this inner glow that made people swarm to them. People wanted to be near them. People *enjoyed* being with them. Micah winced as she realized that there was no one swarming to be anywhere near her.

Micah glanced over at her roommates and smiled gratefully. At least she had two roommates to sit by. And these two girls were actually nice. They weren't exactly girls approved of by her father, definitely no one she could bring home for dinner. But still they tried hard to include her, even when she had spent the better part of the summer trying to ignore their existence. They always insisted on dragging her to ward activities or to the movies. She had to admit it was kind of nice. She almost felt normal when it was just the three of them. Too bad Lisa was at least twenty pounds overweight. Her father was very critical of people who were even slightly overweight. And April. She *really* liked April, but she could just imagine her father's comments about her. Micah thought April was so cool. She had ultra-black hair and super-thin plucked eyebrows, and her choice of makeup was, well . . . interesting. She was very much into the primary colors. Her T-shirts and jeans looked like she purchased them from garage sales. Yep, her dad would have a field day with April. Better to leave well enough alone.

Every time her dad questioned her about her roommates, she would act as if she despised them and the only reason she was staying was so she could set a good example for them. Her father would always beam at her approvingly when she would say stupid things like that. And she knew her secret was safe. She was happy in her little apartment with her unlikely roommates. And no one would ever have to know.

chapter two

Bryce looked over at Micah Rawlings and studied the sharp lines of a headache creasing her forehead. *What is it with her? Why is she always so tense?* She looked so cold and stuck-up all the time. He'd spent the best part of spring and summer term studying her and trying to figure out exactly why she was so cold—and could only come to the conclusion that that was just the way she was. She was born that way.

Too bad she was also gorgeous. Yeah, her hair was kind of old fashioned and she dressed like his mother, but there was just something about her. He couldn't put his finger on it, but she intrigued him like none of the other girls did. He remembered when he had first moved into the ward, she had actually smiled at him a few times. But just when he had made up his mind to ask her out, she gave him the cold shoulder and pretended he didn't exist anymore. He had written her off as strange after that, but he still couldn't stop trying to figure her out. It had to be her brown eyes. They always looked so sad. Even when she was at her iciest, they looked sad.

He shook his head. She was just a tall, good-looking blonde like practically every other girl on campus. Except she wasn't. Bryce sighed. Her face was art. The graceful cheek bones and the wide mouth that hardly ever curved into a smile. The high, arched eyebrows that were always raised in a question. And her nose. Her nose was perfect. That had to be it. He couldn't get Micah Rawlings out of his mind because she had the one perfect nose in the world. Well, at least he had figured it out. Finally.

He felt his little sister Jenny pull on his earlobe and grinned down at her. Jenny hated it when he stared at Micah. Jenny couldn't stand the sight of Micah. At the last ward picnic, Jenny had tried to strike up a conversation with Micah but had been given the cold shoulder. And that had been that. Jenny had made up her mind that Micah was a witch, and there was no way she would allow her big brother to be trapped by such a demon.

Bryce tapped his little sister on the nose gently and whispered, "Mind you own business."

He went back to staring at Micah, but she had disappeared. He looked at the exits, but she was nowhere. Man, she was fast.

"Good morning, brothers and sisters . . ."

Bryce's mouth went slack. No way was Micah Rawlings bearing her testimony. He couldn't even imagine it. Okay, he was being judgmental, but come on! He still wasn't sure she had a heart. He watched her stumble over her words and stutter on about the Book of Mormon and couldn't help wincing. She was trying, he'd give her that. But what exactly was she trying to do? He couldn't really call it a testimony. It was more a recital of events than a testimony of belief. He noticed the strained look on her face and the panic in her eyes and sat up straighter. What was going on here? There was something strange about Micah. Why—oh why—did he have to love mysteries?

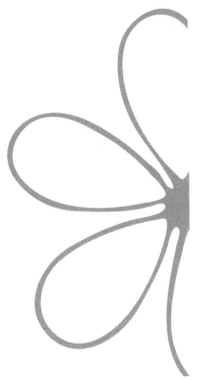

chapter three

Micah walked quickly back to her row and sat down, not looking to her left or her right. She'd made a complete fool of herself. What an idiot she had been. Next time her dad suggested she bear her testimony in order to get a prominent calling in her ward, she would flat out tell him no. She could just picture it in her mind now. *No, Dad, I don't think so. If you feel like hearing a testimony, bear one yourself.* Her already clammy skin grew paler at the thought, and she let out a breath. Her father could freeze anyone at five paces. His cold blue eyes could cut quicker than even words. On second thought, maybe she would just sign up for a drama class for the fall semester. If she could learn how to speak in front of people and maybe learn how to shed a few tears tastefully, she could try this again. But until then, uh-uh. No more public humiliation for her. From now on she would leave the podium to those who wanted it. And there were plenty of them.

Micah took five more mind-clearing breaths and then peeked up to see who was bearing their testimony now. Hopefully it would wipe everyone's memory clean of her shattering disaster of a performance. Jenny Jorgenson. She was one of the girls that Micah envied the most. She was petite and feminine and utterly adorable. The guys in their ward seemed to swarm around her like bees to the brightest and most beautiful flower. She had dimples on *both* cheeks and possibly the most sincere smile she had ever seen. Last month, when she had borne her testimony, she had announced her intention of going on a mission. Jenny's eyes had glowed at the prospect as she shared her love for the whole world and especially for those people whom she would have the chance to teach the gospel to someday.

Micah had rolled her eyes at this, since Jenny had just barely turned nineteen. She was betting that Jenny would be engaged by the end of the year, if anything. The only thing that awaited Jenny was a big diamond ring and years of dirty diapers.

Micah tried to focus on exactly what Jenny was saying. Maybe she should take down notes so that next time she was coerced into walking up to the microphone, she could say something normal. All she would have to do is change every sixth word and it would be legal. She searched in her purse for a notebook but looked up when she caught Bryce's name. Micah glanced over to where she instinctively knew Bryce was sitting. She couldn't help the pain she felt in her heart every time she looked at him. She tried hard *not* to look at him. He was so beautiful. He was at least six inches taller than she and had the physique of a basketball player, although she knew he preferred football. He had long, tapered hands that fascinated her. And he was always using them to shake somebody's hand, or to hug his sister, or to pat someone on the back. He was very touchy-feely. She remembered the first time she had met him at a ward movie night, out on the lawn in front of their apartments. He had come over to introduce himself to her and her roommates, and had reached over and pushed the hair out of her eyes as if he had known her forever.

She remembered looking up into his face and catching her breath as if she had been waiting her whole life for him to do just that. He had a beautiful face. A classically thin, sculpted mouth, a long aristocratic nose, and deep green eyes that were always crinkled up in a grin. She was obsessed with his hair though. Sometimes when she was supposed to be studying, she would daydream about running her fingers through his wavy brown hair.

But her father had said no.

Micah reached up and massaged the place where her heart was supposed to be. She remembered typing up Bryce's profile. She had been so careful with every detail. She had done her research. She had talked to his roommates and had done the background check as well as she could from the Internet. She had done everything her father had required of her. But in the end, Bryce hadn't passed the test, and she didn't know why. Everyone she had talked to seemed to love him. Her father had said something about getting involved with a would-be journalist was no way to live the good life. That and the fact that his parents were divorced were two strikes against him.

Micah glanced over at Bryce again and wished with what little soul she still had that she could have had him. Good life or not. She couldn't imagine what life would be like with someone who smiled at everyone with laughing acceptance. She couldn't imagine Bryce's green eyes ever looking at her coldly or disapprovingly. Was what she'd had growing up with her father the *good* life? Micah frowned. It hadn't felt very good. Ever.

Micah turned and looked at the man sitting two rows ahead of Bryce—Corbin Larsen, the blond-haired, blue-eyed law school student. The man her father *wanted* her to go after. She'd never submitted a profile on Corbin to her father. Her father had submitted Corbin's profile to her. She didn't even like him. He was so stuffy and serious. His face always looked pained whenever he had to talk to someone who wasn't his intellectual equal. He had given a talk last month on the allegory of the olive tree. She shuddered at the memory. He had talked as if he were the only one capable of understanding all of the symbolism and he was doing a great favor to everyone to try and bring it down to their level. He'd mentioned only three times that he was going to law school during his talk.

She couldn't imagine being married to Corbin. He was the mirror image of her father. She felt her stomach clench in another spasm and reached for the Tums again as she remembered her second assignment from her father: talk to Corbin this week and make it understood that she was available and interested in him. She studied his weak chin and sloped shoulders and shuddered. Bear her testimony in church—yes, she would do that. Sacrifice her happiness and sanity to be married to a successful lawyer just like her father? No! She just couldn't.

Micah glanced over at her roommate Lisa and felt an idea pop into her head. She could report back to her father that she had talked to Corbin and had tried. But what she didn't have to tell her father was that she would try to set her roommate up with him.

Micah reached for a piece of paper from her purse and scribbled a quick note on it before passing it to her roommate. *What would you think about going out with Corbin Larsen?*

Lisa read the note curiously and then reached for her own pen. *He's adorable—go for it.*

Micah read the note and winced. She'd have to be more specific. *Would YOU like to go out with him???* She passed the note back to Lisa and waited for her reaction. Lisa blushed a bright red, making her plump cheeks look rosy and charming. She looked like a little Danish girl. All she needed were clogs and braids and she would be a postcard. Micah couldn't help grinning at her. April noticed the interplay going on between her roommates and grabbed the note. She snorted quietly and grabbed Lisa's pen out of her hand and scribbled something before passing it back to Micah.

Excuse me! If you're in the mood for setting someone up, HELLO! I haven't had a date in years!

Micah grinned at her ultra-cool and modern roommate and scribbled again on the note before passing it back. *I didn't think Corbin was your type.*

April sighed and shrugged, turning her attention back to the meeting. Lisa, however, grabbed the poor note and wrote one last sentence on it. *If you can set me up with Corbin, I will love you forever.*

Micah read the note and for some reason felt an odd tightening in her throat. Lisa would love *her* forever? The last time she had heard someone say they loved her was before her mother had died when she was nine.

Micah cleared her throat and blinked a few times before winking at Lisa. She had a mission today, and she would set up her roommate if it was the last thing she did.

chapter four

Bryce watched his sister walk back down the aisle toward him and grinned at her. He loved his sister; she was a constant inspiration to him. She was so pure and good and kind and beautifully naive. But he loved that about her too. He put his arm around her and reached over to kiss her forehead, when his eyes fell on Micah. She was grinning at one of her crazy roommates. *Grinning.* For the second time that day, she had surprised him. He couldn't ever remember seeing her grin. Ever. He felt his stomach drop to his knees and all breath leave his body. And he knew he was going to figure her out. Somehow he knew that if he didn't, he'd regret it forever.

At the end of sacrament meeting, Bryce watched Micah out of the corner of his eye while he talked to his roommate, Joel. He was going to talk to her today. But he was going to be suave about it. She'd have no choice but to divulge all of her secrets to him by the time he was done with her. His constant curiosity about life was why he'd chosen journalism as his major. Well, that and he wanted to be a writer like his dad. She would be putty in his hands. He slowly followed Micah and her roommates down the hall toward Sunday School. She was sure taking her time. She looked like she was on the prowl herself. Bryce's eyebrows drew together at the thought. Who was she going after? He watched as she nervously adjusted her purse strap on her shoulder and knew for sure she was up to something. She walked up to Corbin Larsen—the idiot!—and tapped him on the shoulder. *Brother.* Anyone interested in Corbin Larsen could not possibly be anyone Bryce could be interested in.

Bryce felt his shoulders sag in disappointment and walked faster, hoping that in his stupidity he hadn't lost his chance of getting a good seat. As he walked past the happy couple, he couldn't help overhearing though.

"Corbin, what would you say to being set up with one of the most beautiful girls you'll ever meet?"

Bryce paused at the door and looked back over his shoulder at Micah. Her eyes were sparkling, and she was grinning again! Why hadn't she ever grinned at him like that? This was totally out of character for her. Someone who practically hyperventilated during her testimony didn't have the guts to go up to some idiot and tell him about herself. Did she?

"Uh, well, if she looks like you I'd be interested," Corbin said with what was almost a leer.

Micah's smile faded instantly, and her eyebrows snapped together. Bryce felt his disappointment fade away just as fast as he realized what she was doing. She was trying to set up her roommate! *Yes!* He quickly took his seat next to his sister in Sunday School and tried to figure out which one. April was a neat girl but not someone he could picture being interested in Corbin. Her hair was so black it glowed. He could just see Corbin sneering now. Now, Lisa was a different story. Lisa was lovely. Yeah, she was a little heavier than all the walking skeletons drifting around the campus, but if it had been thirty years earlier, she would have ruled the social scene. She had long, reddish brown hair and cute little freckles on her nose. Yeah, she was all right. If Corbin turned down a date with Lisa, he was more clueless than Bryce had thought.

chapter five

Micah stared at Corbin and felt her skin crawl. *Please no.*

"Umm . . . well. Actually she's a lot prettier than I am. Definitely your type. And I happen to know that she thinks you're kind of cute."

Corbin looked surprised by this, and his eyes narrowed in curiosity.

"Who is it?" he asked.

Micah cleared her throat nervously and looked into the Sunday School room, noticing that Lisa was staring at her. No pressure.

"Her name is Lisa Marchbanks. She's my roommate and

she's really cute and the nicest person you'll ever meet. I was just thinking you two would make a really awesome couple. Maybe you guys could go out to the movies or something? Just get to know each other a little bit, what do you think?"

Micah felt her stomach tense up again and had to control the urge to reach for the Tums. If he said no, she would have to go and tell Lisa. She hadn't thought that far ahead in the plan. That wasn't something she wanted to do.

Corbin tilted his head and looked around Micah into the Sunday school, scanning everyone until his eyes fell on Lisa. Lisa quickly looked away, blushing even brighter than before.

Corbin frowned as he considered Micah's proposal and then shook his head. He looked Micah up and down, smiling grotesquely.

"I think you're more my type actually. Lisa is cute, but . . ." Corbin let his sentence drift off as he raised his eyebrows at her.

Micah gritted her teeth. *No.* She would not let this happen.

"Oh, that's too bad, Corbin. What a shame. I mean, here's Lisa who thinks you're the coolest guy in the whole ward. And she was just telling me how much she would love to go out with you. And me? Well, I'm kind of already in love with someone else. I couldn't possibly go out with you. Looks like you're dateless."

Micah finished her sentence as she turned away and started to walk toward the door. Corbin's arm reached out quickly and grabbed her shoulder.

"Wait a second. You're in love? I don't buy it. You ignore all the guys here like they're less than dirt. You don't look like you're in love. Hold on, do you have a missionary you're waiting for?"

Micah's face turned pale at Corbin's words. She could

easily say she had a missionary. She could make up some fake name and some strange country, but BYU was a small world. Everybody knew everybody. There was a big chance she'd get caught in a lie. No, she'd play it straight.

"No, I'm not waiting for a missionary. The man I'm in love with doesn't even know I exist, to be honest. So what do you say, should I tell Lisa you're on for Friday?"

Corbin shook his head at her, still frowning.

"The best way to get over someone you're in love with is to hit the dating scene hard. I'll take your mind off this guy."

Micah's temper started to flash, and she realized that maybe Lisa was too good for Corbin. Corbin was an idiot.

"Look, I don't *want* to get over him. I'm sorry, Corbin, if you thought *I* was trying to get a date with you. I only started this conversation with you to set up my friend. Obviously you're not interested. So fine. See ya around."

"Stop," Corbin said with authority.

Micah was so used to that tone of voice, she automatically obeyed. She turned around again and stared at Corbin expectantly.

"One condition. We double and I want to see this guy you're in love with."

Micah's mouth dropped open in shock. He had to be kidding. She turned around to look at Lisa, who was still staring at them hopefully, and remembered Lisa's promise to love her forever. But did she really want her friend to get involved with this jerk at all? Not really. And her dad! Her dad would expect a report this afternoon. All she would have to tell him was that Corbin was seeing someone else. Ugh!

"I think we can work out the double dating thing, but the man I'm in love with won't be there. Sorry. That's the deal breaker."

Corbin took a minute to consider and then shrugged.

He hadn't gotten his way. But he did have a date for Friday night. Why not?

"Go ahead and tell your roommate we can hook up. Have her call me tonight after six. And don't forget. You'll be there too," Corbin said and then walked away coolly, as if he had just done her the biggest favor in the world.

Micah watched him walk away from her and felt like chucking something at the back of his head. What an arrogant jerk! What a complete . . .

"Excuse me, Sister Rawlings, unless you're thinking of someone else to set up on a date, I'd like to get to Sunday School."

Micah turned quickly to see the bishop standing right behind her. He didn't look too mad. As a matter of fact, his eyes were twinkling, and he was smiling kindly down at her. She let the breath she had been holding out and stepped aside quickly.

"I'm so sorry, Bishop. Please go ahead."

The bishop took her by the arm and escorted her through the door.

"Ladies first, my dear. By the way, I'm glad you've taken up matchmaking. I've always felt that matchmaking should be an official calling in every singles ward. Good job."

Micah went to take her seat next to Lisa and April and felt a ball of warmth fill her stomach and dissolve the tension. The bishop had told her good job. Why did that feel so good? Possibly because she hadn't heard it very often.

Micah looked down as Lisa rammed a pen and a piece of paper into her hands. She grinned at her roommate and wrote down the pertinent details. As she watched Lisa read the note and the smile that exploded on her face, she had to agree with the bishop. Matchmaking felt like heaven.

chapter six

As Sunday School ended, Micah picked up her scriptures and headed for the door. Relief Society was next and if she waited around in the girls' bathroom long enough, the secretary would never have a chance to ask her to give the opening *or* closing prayer. She had her system down perfectly, and she'd gone almost two years without getting caught.

"Micah, dear?"

Micah turned around at the sweet voice she didn't recognize and couldn't believe it was coming from April. She hadn't known April could even make her voice sound like that.

"What?" Micah asked nervously.

"Do you hate me? Do you just not care at all? What is it about me that you just can't stand? I'm curious, really. Please tell me."

Micah reached out and grabbed April's black-lace-clad arm and felt her migraine come back full force.

"April, why would you say that? You know I don't hate you, you're, like, one of the only friends I—"

April started cracking up at Micah's reaction, and Micah shut her mouth slowly.

"Micah, you are so easy it's pathetic. I only meant, why are you trying so hard to set up Lisa? I think it's only fair that if you set her up, then you automatically *have* to set me up too. If you don't, then there will be hurt feelings, and who knows how long I can pull off an icy silence? Really."

Micah smiled at her roommate and sighed.

"April, if you can set me up with someone, then I'll set you up with someone. Corbin says that we have to double-date this Friday. So now that I've done my good deed for the year, I have to pay for it. I have no clue what to do. I can't stand the thought of asking a guy out. I haven't done that since the eleventh grade, and I still haven't gotten over the humiliation of being turned down."

April crinkled up her forehead as she thought about it.

"This could be fun, you know. I'll find someone for you, and you'll find someone for me. Five dollars to the one who can get a date before church ends."

Micah felt her shoulders sag in immediate defeat. It had just about killed her to get Lisa a date. Now she had to get a date for April too.

"Hey, don't look so pathetic. You're acting like it would be a major miracle to get me a date."

Micah smiled wanly at April but knew in her heart that this time she wasn't kidding. April really hadn't gone on a real date for a long time. She was being dead serious.

"I will do my best. But as far as my date goes, please be kind. Remember all the times I brought you home brownies and chocolate cake? Have some compassion. I'm fragile."

April's grin reappeared as she scanned the emptying room.

"I know just the guy. He would be absolutely perfect for you. He's tall, dark, and way too handsome. For me anyway. I like a few sharp edges, myself. But for you, it would be like the missing puzzle piece. Where did he go now?"

Micah felt her stomach churn and clench and she sat down quickly and massaged her temples. Why did her life have to be so stressful?

"Ah ha! I'll meet you in Relief Society. Save me a seat." April said and practically sprinted away.

Micah raised her head, too scared to even think of who April thought would be perfect for her. It was probably Robert Wood. He was Corbin's twin, except he was taller and darker, and even more dorky. Or it could be that new guy—Jason something? She didn't know much about him, except that he liked to answer every single question asked in Sunday School, talking for such long periods of time that the teacher didn't even get to finish the lesson. Definitely right off his mission. No thanks. But it would be for just one night. She could survive anyone for three hours. Hopefully.

Now, who would go out with April? Who would enjoy her dark hair and her crazy sense of fashion? April said she liked sharp edges—who did that describe in their little student ward?

Micah got up and walked out of the now empty room and began her prowl. Almost everyone was still in the halls, but they would disappear quickly. She walked quickly down the corridor, looking from her left to her right. *No . . . no way . . . uh-uh . . . holy cow, no! Nope, not him . . . nooooo.* Micah reached the end of the hall and looked to her right one last time—and her eyes fell on Joel Hughs. She paused and tilted her head as she considered. He really was nice. She'd never seen him wear a suit; he preferred the white shirt and tie. He had longish light brown hair and deeply tanned skin. She knew he must have had his ear pierced at one time, but she'd never seen an earring in his telltale hole. He never said much at church, but he was always the first one there for service projects. Well, his edges didn't seem too sharp, but that was probably a good thing. He would do nicely.

Micah walked casually up to Joel and leaned up against the wall.

"Hey, Joel, how's it going?"

Joel looked down at Micah and smiled slowly.

"It's been interesting, I'll say that."

Micah had no idea what he meant by that, so she ignored it and pushed on.

"Joel, I've been thinking, if you're not already seeing someone, would you be interested in being set up?"

Joel looked heavenward and closed his eyes, as if asking for help. Micah frowned and couldn't help biting her fingernail.

"It's not an eternal commitment or anything—it would be just one little tiny date. This Friday."

Joel opened his eyes and looked suspiciously down at her.

"You girls are up to something here. Corbin's already bragging to everyone that you set him up on a date for this Friday. And April just took off with—"

Micah whipped her head around, looking for April. How embarrassing could this get!

"With who?" Micah demanded. "Who did April take off with?"

Micah was suddenly curious whom April had found for her.

Joel raised his eyebrow at her reaction and smiled.

"I seem to have forgotten, but if I were a logically thinking person, should I guess that it's April that you're trying to set me up with? I mean, that would make sense, right? Then your whole apartment would have a date this Friday."

Micah turned back to Joel and frowned.

"It's not what you think, and there was no planning involved. It's called an avalanche with a little guilt thrown in. But yeah, it's April, and before you say anything, April is extremely nice once you get to know her, so don't go judging—"

"Hold on a minute," Joel interrupted her. "Who's the one judging here? Why would you assume that I wouldn't want to go out with her? As a matter of fact, I was thinking just the other day that April would be a lot of fun to hang out with."

Micah felt her shoulders lift and a grin of relief spread across her face. *Victory!*

"You know what? You should do that more often. A lot more often," Joel said.

Micah shook her head. "What do you mean?"

Joel smiled down at her. "Smile. You're beautiful when you smile. And tell April that Friday would be great. I'll call her tonight."

chapter seven

Bryce stared down at April and shook his head in exaggerated confusion.

"Excuse me?"

"A date, hello! Haven't you ever tried it before? You get set up with someone, you go out with them. It's so easy. No big deal, really. Come on, just say yes."

Bryce shook his head firmly. "No."

April glared up into Bryce's green eyes and squared her shoulders. There was no way she was coming up with five bucks for Micah. She was dead broke. And she needed this date thing to happen. It was either start dating again or starve to death.

"Why not? Are you already seeing someone? I know you're not, so don't bother lying. Just do it. Please."

Bryce let out his breath slowly and smiled at April apologetically.

"Sorry, no."

April grabbed Bryce's shoulder before he could walk away and jumped in front of him.

"Look, this means a lot to me. And besides, I happen to be a very observant person. I happen to know that you want to go out with her. I've seen how you stare at her. I don't know why anybody else hasn't caught on yet."

Bryce glared down at April and took back every nice thing he'd ever thought about her.

"Fine. You got me. Does she know you're setting her up with me?"

April unclenched her hands from Bryce's shirt and stepped back.

"No, of course not. Why? You think she'll say no when she finds out it's you? What's going on between you guys anyway? There's little crackles of tension and electricity every time you pass each other in the hall. I don't know why you haven't just asked her out yourself to begin with. Coward."

Bryce glared at April and felt like strangling her. *Brat!* But as he saw the twinkle in her hazel eyes, he relaxed and laughed. She definitely had a way of getting under his skin.

"Now I have no choice, do I? If I say no, then I'm a coward. If I say yes, then my honor is safe and my reputation as a man is preserved. Fine, April. You win. Set me up with Lisa."

April grinned, then choked.

"Lisa! You idiot! We're talking about Micah. Where have you been?" April sputtered.

Bryce grinned and shook his head.

"I thought you said you were very observant. Who is Micah?"

April reached over and pinched Bryce hard on the arm.

"Ow! I was just kidding," Bryce said as he rubbed his injured arm.

April shook her head at him.

"Maybe I was wrong about you. I know ten guys who would die to go out with Micah. Forget it, Bryce. It's like throwing pearls before swine. Have fun doing your laundry Friday night."

It was Bryce's turn to grab April's shoulder this time.

"Look, all kidding aside, I would be happy to go out with Micah. Have her call me tonight, and we'll set up the details."

April sneered at him. "Uh, excuse me, *you'll* be the one calling her. Don't forget, you're a gentleman."

Bryce watched her walk away and sighed. What had he just gotten himself into? He had just promised himself today that he wouldn't rest until he had figured Micah out. And now here was her roommate, shoving a date with her down his throat. *Ask and ye shall receive,* he thought. He rubbed his arm one more time and walked slowly toward priesthood with a smile on his face. He couldn't wait to tell Joel.

chapter eight

Micah rammed her car into drive and sped down the street. *That rotten April!* Her dad wouldn't care why she was late though. It was always *her* fault and *her* lack of consideration. Forget the fact that April had set her up on a date with Bryce Jorgenson! If she had even known for one second . . . *OHHH!* She could kill April. And after all the cookies and brownies she'd fed that ungrateful little . . .

Micah almost smiled, though, when she remembered April's reaction to finding out whom she had set her up with. April had acted more surprised than she had. April had even blushed—and Micah had to admit, she never would have taken her for a blusher.

Micah was starting to wonder if there was any way she could use her matchmaking talents in a career situation. She should start an Internet business setting LDS college kids up. Micah could just see her dad's face now though. *Purple* described it. She giggled to herself and shook her head. *Nah.* Actually knowing the people made it way more fun. She had walked out of her apartment, ten minutes late, leaving April looking shocked and Lisa glowing. Not too bad. Except for that part where she had to go out with Bryce.

Micah's frown returned full force. She couldn't go out with him. Her father had flat out told her she was forbidden. And if she did go out with him, and he turned out to be wonderful, then it would just be all the harder to let him go. Then she would have to do something drastic, like move. No, tonight when he called her, she would just tell him that something had come up and she wouldn't be able to make it after all. Too bad, but she had already promised Corbin she'd be there with a date. She could come up with someone . . . maybe. But then, Joel was Bryce's roommate. They were all going out together, and he would be sure to tell Bryce that she had been there with someone else.

Micah sighed and stopped at a stop sign. She was stuck. She would just have to harden her heart against him. She would have to encase herself in stone before the date. She wasn't sure how to go about doing that, but she'd have to. One date and that was it. Forever.

Micah drove her car up the little road that led to her father's home high up on the Provo bench. The one thing she liked about her father's home was the view. The rest she could do without. It was an all-white, stucco, two-story mini-mansion full of glass and steel. It shouted, *Hey! Look at me!*

She remembered one time going over to her Laurel adviser's home when she was seventeen. Sister Beckstrand— she was the coolest teacher ever. But it was her home that stuck in Micah's mind the most. She still remembered the time her whole Laurel class had been invited over to bake cookies and watch a movie. The house had smelled so good, like scrubbed floors, family dinners, and fresh flowers. And there had been color—tons of it everywhere. Pictures of their children all over the place. Fluffy, overstuffed cushions of all sizes and colors. A big L-shaped couch and two huge beanbag chairs big enough for Goliath. It was a home that shouted, *Kids live here!* But it was also a home that whispered, *Love.* After the cookies had been baked and cooled, she had been the first one to grab a beanbag and had snuggled down with two cookies. And she had wished—with all her heart, she had wished that this had been her home.

She hadn't wanted that night to ever end. But it had, and she had gone home to her cold house and to her stern father. In her heart though, she had known that if her mother had lived, things would have been different. There would have been color in her life. There would have been love. Micah didn't want to think about her mother though. When she was nine years old, Helen Rawlings had died giving birth to her little brother, Jefferson. And her whole world had disappeared. Well, not really disappeared. Sucked down a black hole, more like it. Thrown into another dimension where nothing was the same and everything was different. No, she didn't want to think about that.

Micah sighed and parked her car. If her dad was in a good mood, he would only scold her for being late and give her a short lecture. If he was in a bad mood, then she was in for it. Maybe she should have just set herself up on a date with Corbin? A little good news would go far with her father. Micah squared her shoulders and walked in the front door. She would face the lecture gladly.

chapter nine

"Micah! Come into my office please, I've been waiting," Phillip Rawlings commanded in a clear, deep voice.

Micah shut the door and laid her purse on the table bought especially for that purpose. She felt like walking slowly, but the sharp, quick sound of her heels on the tile would let her father know that his order was being obeyed—kind of like the little bark a dog gives after receiving a command.

She walked into her father's office and immediately felt as if the sun had set. The whole room was covered in dark mahogany wood. Even the ceilings were dark. The combination of books and wood was very masculine. At least that's what her father's interior decorator had told him. If masculine meant depressing, then she had hit it on the mark.

"Sorry, Father. My roommates were having a crisis, and I couldn't in good conscience leave them while they were so distraught," Micah said guiltily.

Phillip inclined his head royally, accepting her explanation.

Micah's eyes widened in surprise. Where was the guilt trip? Where was the insult?

"I hope someday your roommates realize what an incredible person they had to teach them true gentility, true breeding, and refinement."

Micah frowned. Something odd was going on. Something definitely wasn't right.

"Umm, okay. So, how have you been, Father? I hope that your Sabbath has been restful."

Phillip smiled warmly at her and held out a hand.

Micah gawked at him. What did that mean? Did he want to shake her hand? Did he want to inspect her manicure?

"Father?" Micah questioned timidly.

"Come, come. I want to talk to you. We only have about ten minutes or so, since you're late, but there's something I need to tell you," Phillip said, still holding his hand out for her.

Micah walked around her father's large desk and over to where he was sitting in his large leather chair. She placed one of her now clammy hands in his and raised her eyebrows questioningly.

"What's going on, Father? You seem . . . happy?" Micah said but couldn't really believe it. She hadn't seen him like this, well . . . ever.

Phillip chuckled and took both of her hands in his.

"Micah, of course I'm happy. Why wouldn't I be? I have a beautiful home, an accomplished daughter, a successful practice. I'm a very blessed man. Yes, I've worked very hard for those blessings, but it was all worth it. All of it. And look at you. You're everything I've wished for in a daughter: beautiful, kind, devoted, and intelligent. Life is almost perfect. Do you know what I've been missing all these years though?" Phillip asked.

Micah swallowed and thought hard. *A heart?*

"Umm, a Mercedes?" she said instead.

Phillip paused and considered that. "Well, actually, that's a good idea, but no. That's not what I meant, although now that you mention it, it's about time, isn't it? My Lexus is a year old. Anyway, moving on. I've been missing love, Micah. Love."

Micah's mouth dropped. He had finally admitted it. Since her mother had died, he hadn't shown her an ounce of affection. He hadn't shown her fatherly love in so long she couldn't even remember what he'd been like before her mother had died. But now he had realized his mistake! Now they could have the loving relationship she had been longing for, for so long.

"I'm so happy to hear you say that," Micah whispered, with tears in her throat. She threw her arms around her father's neck and hugged him tightly.

Phillip froze at the outward show of affection and quickly grasped Micah's arms and pulled them down firmly.

"Micah, control yourself. Finding out that you're going to have a new mother is no reason for an emotional outburst. Honestly, if I'd known you would react this way, I would have started dating a long time ago," Phillip said, sounding flustered.

Micah straightened up slowly and reached up to massage her temples automatically.

"Excuse me? Did you say I was getting a *new* mother? What exactly are you talking about?" Micah said in a high, thin voice.

Phillip flicked an imaginary piece of lint off his Italian

silk tie and looked at his watch impatiently. He had obviously grown bored with the conversation.

"Exactly what it sounds like, Micah. There's no need to be dense. Her name is Katherine, and she's a wonderful woman. When you get to know her I'm sure you'll understand why I've decided to marry again."

Micah felt as if the air had been knocked out of her. *Marriage? A new mother?* This was too unreal. Katherine. Katherine. She sounded like some old English queen. She was probably old, rich, and cold. Like her father.

"So I get to meet her today? Is that why you keep looking at your watch? You scheduled ten minutes to give me the good news and then an introduction. You couldn't have mentioned this last week? Last night, even? What was the point in throwing this at me with no time to even catch my breath?" Micah demanded almost hysterically.

Phillip raised his eyebrow at her tone of voice and stood up.

"Because I didn't want to deal with any tiresome, female emotions on your part. Like now. I knew if you met her, then that would be the end of it. You would like her, you would understand the logic behind my decision, end of story."

Micah walked back around the desk and stood, willing her heart to slow down. Willing her heart to stop breaking. Again.

"Well, I look forward to meeting her. I'm sure you've picked a wonderful woman to be my stepmother," Micah said woodenly, only because that's what her father expected of her.

Phillip smiled and looked out the window.

"I knew you'd handle this in a mature fashion. I had faith in you, Micah. Good. Now, she's just pulled up. I think it would be nice to meet her at the door. Come."

Micah followed her father out of his office and toward the foyer. She had to admit she was curious. Her father had such strict regulations for his daughter, she couldn't imagine the woman he had picked for his wife to be anything less than perfect.

The doorbell sounded and her father actually rushed forward. Micah's mouth fell open slightly. *He must really be in love*, she thought. Phillip opened the door to reveal Micah's new stepmother.

Or was it step*sister*?

"Darling! So glad you made it safely up the hill. Please come in and meet my daughter, Micah. I've told her so much about you. She can't wait to meet you."

Micah blinked at the outright lie and then locked gazes with her father's idea of the perfect woman. She was maybe twenty-two or twenty-one. Almost a foot shorter than her father. Long, long hair, highlighted in five different shades of blond and red. Her eyes were a bright green that Micah had never seen before, obviously contacts. And her father must have met her at a tanning booth because she'd never seen anyone quite that bronze. As for the rest of her, Micah didn't want to judge her plastic surgeon harshly, but he wasn't going for the natural look at all. But it was the fingernails that really got her. The fingernails were killing her. Long, very long and deep, bloody red. She glanced down at her own classy nail polish, chosen because of her father's strict rules on what became a woman.

Micah was looking at the exact opposite of everything her father had told her *she* must be. She forced a smile.

"It's such a pleasure to meet you, Katherine." Micah held out a cold hand to grasp Katherine's surprisingly strong and warm grasp.

Katherine grinned back at Micah, showing perfect, super-white teeth.

"Call me Kathy. I can't believe I'm finally meeting you. Phillip has kept you hidden away like a secret treasure or something," Katherine said as she expertly sidestepped

Micah and reached up to kiss Phillip on the mouth. Micah looked away, deeply embarrassed.

Katherine giggled and wiped her smeared lipstick off of Phillip's mouth. Micah looked to see if her father was embarrassed by this awkward public show of affection. He was smiling! He was staring down at Katherine as if she were the most beautiful woman he'd ever seen.

Micah shook her head in shock. She had just walked into a nightmare. That was it. She'd wake up soon, and this would all be gone. She took a few breaths the way April had been teaching her to, and then pasted a bright smile on her face. Nightmare or not, she would make it through this.

"Well, let's eat, shall we? I don't want you losing any more weight. You're too thin, Katherine," Phillip said in an attempt to flatter her.

Micah silently followed the couple into the dining room, where Marcy, her father's housekeeper, was just now bringing in all of the dishes. Marcy had gone all out. There was no way she had done all this herself. Her father must have catered this! Micah swallowed a large knot in her throat and took her seat.

Phillip glared at her coldly, and Katherine smiled pityingly.

"Micah, sweetie, I believe you're sitting in my seat. I wouldn't mind, of course, but Phillip is such a stickler about decorum. Aren't you, honey?"

Phillip smiled quickly at his fiancée, and then motioned for Micah to quickly move. Micah pushed away from the table and the seat where she had sat for the last twelve years of her life and took another. She watched out of the corner of her eye as Katherine sat across from her father and preened. She was gloating! Micah smiled blandly at her father and her future stepmother and then took a sip of water from her glass. Her whole life was changing in a matter of minutes, and she didn't know what to do. Should she laugh? Should she yell and scream? Or should she just get up and walk out the door? That's what she really wanted to do, but she knew her father would be furious with her. *Hmmm.* But did that matter anymore? The thought took her breath away. Now her father's hypocrisy was apparent, did she really have to get an ulcer if her hair wasn't done the right way or her clothes weren't the appropriate style?

Micah glanced at the clothes Katherine had chosen for Sunday dinner and wondered if miniskirts and tank tops were the new standard. She glanced at her father, who was back to staring at Katherine, and realized that obviously they were. As Katherine blew Phillip a kiss across the table, a new emotion enveloped Micah: pity. She smiled again at Katherine before taking another sip of water, and what she felt for her was altogether different. No, she knew this feeling—she'd felt it about herself for so long. It was loathing. She knew she loathed this woman totally and completely.

Life was going to be interesting from here on out. She might as well get as much information as she could because her father never thought he needed to tell her anything.

"Katherine, it's obvious you two are so in love. Tell me, how did you two meet?" Micah asked sweetly.

Katherine took her gaze off Phillip, and her smile faltered for a fraction of a second.

"Micah, I don't see why that's any of your business. Katherine, don't feel that you have to answer her questions. She's always been too curious," Phillip said rudely.

Micah felt as if ice had hit her in the face, but as she watched Katherine's reaction, she decided not to back down. Her father couldn't bully her anymore. Not now.

"I assume when you two are married you will have a reception. What do you think everyone in the line will be asking you? It's a normal question, isn't it? Unless you're embarrassed about it," Micah added.

Her father's face turned red, and he glared at her as if he

wanted to yell at her, but he didn't dare in front of Katherine. She had him.

Katherine tilted her head as she thought about it.

"You know, she's right, Phillip. I hadn't thought that far ahead. But sooner or later everyone will know. I don't see why Micah shouldn't know. I mean, she is an adult. She's older than me, for heaven's sake. Besides, it's not like it's some secret or anything. It's sweet."

Micah choked on her water. "How old are you exactly, Katherine?"

Katherine laughed and showed Micah her new diamond ring on her right hand.

"Twenty pretty little diamonds for all the years I've been on earth. I think Phillip told me you were about a year older than me. Isn't that right?"

Micah shook her head silently and looked over at her father. Not only was he getting married to someone young enough to be his daughter, he was getting married to someone *younger* than his daughter! She was starting to see him in a completely different light. She was starting to see that maybe he wasn't the man she had thought he was. Or at least the kind of man he had always told her he was.

"I do hair. I had just barely graduated from beauty school, and it was my first day at Tres Belle Salon. Well, your father came in one day for a trim, and I was so nervous I totally messed up his hair. I thought I was going to be fired, so I started to cry all over him, and he was so sweet about it. He wasn't mad at all. He told me his heart went out to me. So he took me to dinner that night, and we fell in love over a shrimp cocktail. Can you get more romantic than that?" Katherine asked as she winked at Phillip.

Micah felt the migraine she had been fighting all day explode in her head and felt instantly nauseous.

"Wow, that is *really* romantic, Katherine," Micah managed to say.

Marcy ladled all sorts of food onto Micah's plate, but she knew she wouldn't be able to eat it. Marcy patted her shoulder sympathetically.

To cover the fact that she wasn't eating, Micah continued to ask questions. That and causing her father to turn a deeper shade of red was starting to feel enjoyable for some strange reason.

"Where are you guys planning on getting married? The Salt Lake Temple? I love the Mount Timpanogos Temple myself. I know, you guys should fly to Hawaii and be married there," Micah said in false happy tones.

Phillip cleared his throat, and an awkward silence followed. Micah looked from Katherine to her father. They were both looking down at their plates.

"Micah, Katherine isn't a member of our church. We won't be getting married in the temple, I'm afraid. We'll be getting married in Las Vegas this Tuesday. Of course, you're welcome to come to the ceremony, but with your classes and your hectic schedule, I really don't see that you have to be there if you'd rather not. It's going to be a small affair really. Katherine's mother and stepfather will come, of course. We just want to keep it small and intimate. We'll be flying to Jamaica for a month afterward, so we'll tell you all about it when we get home."

Micah shook her head in disbelief. Her father was getting married in Las Vegas next week, and she wasn't even invited. This could not be happening.

"I see," was all Micah could manage to say.

Phillip looked down at his plate guiltily but didn't say anything else.

Katherine realized that the atmosphere was tense and started eating with gusto. Marcy came in a few minutes later.

"Sir? You're wanted on the phone. It's Bishop Wesley."

Phillip looked pale and tense as he stood up.

"Please continue eating, my dear, this should only take a few minutes."

Katherine smiled but didn't say anything, since her mouth was full.

Micah turned to her future stepmother and shook her head in disbelief. This wasn't a nightmare. This was really happening.

"This must be a real shock for you, Micah. Are you okay? And if you really want to be at the wedding, I can have a talk with Phillip. I told him that you should be there, but when he gets an idea in his head, he can be very stubborn."

Micah blinked in surprise. Was it possible her new stepmother was trying to be kind to her? Not likely.

"Of course I'm okay, but thank you for asking. I do have a question for you though. Are you in love with my father? I mean really in love with him?"

Katherine took a sip of water and tilted her head as she thought about it.

"The thought that popped into my head when I first met your father was that he looked like a sad little puppy dog, all lonely and adorable. I just wanted to take him home and feed him and cuddle him, you know? I do love your father. He needs me. He needs someone to take care of him. I think all men do. Don't you?"

Micah had absolutely no clue what this woman was talking about. Obviously she was on drugs or something. She could have been hit on the head when she was a child. Lack of brain cells could explain a lot here. *Her* father, cute and vulnerable? Not even possible.

"Uh, sure, Kathy. Well, I know you two will be very happy, I'm sure. And don't worry about me being at the wedding. Just take lots of pictures," Micah said lamely.

Katherine smiled brightly at Micah and reached for another roll.

"Phillip said you were a darling. He was right. You're so easygoing. You know, I've never had a sister. A couple bratty brothers, but no one to talk to about boys and hair and clothes. This will be so fun."

Micah reached up to rub her head again and closed her eyes as she wondered if she could make it through another fifteen minutes of this. Her stepmother, as of this Tuesday, thought she could talk to her about boys and clothes. And she was being serious.

"Well, that's one way to look at it. So how long, exactly, have you known my father?" Micah asked, knowing her father could walk in at any second and put an end to the interrogation.

Kathy sipped her water and looked guiltily at Micah, as if she'd rather not say.

"Don't tell Phillip I told you, promise?" she pleaded

Micah felt her stomach tense up as she felt like a big bomb was hanging over her head. What else could this woman say? What could be worse than this? So she nodded in silent agreement.

"Well, to be honest, I've only known your dad a few months. But the fact is, I'm pregnant, and when I told your dad the news, he did the honorable thing, of course. He asked me to marry him. Look, don't worry! I know for sure it's your dad's baby. I broke up with Brad a week before I met your dad. Trust me."

Micah pushed away from the table and moved toward the entryway. She was going to have a mental breakdown any second, and she'd prefer not to do it over dinner and in front of her soon-to-be stepmother.

"Hey, Micah! I didn't mean to upset you. Are you mad or something?" Kathy said as she followed her.

Micah felt blinding pain envelop her eyes, but she took her last ounce of strength and turned around.

"I'm sorry, Kathy. Please don't be offended by my reaction. Sometimes I get bad migraines, and for some reason, I got one today. I need to get home and take some medication. Please tell my father that I had to go but that I wish him all the happiness in the world. And congratulations on your good news. Call me when you two get back into town so I can hear all the details. Okay?" Micah finished in almost a whisper.

She didn't even wait for a reply but wrenched open the front door and stumbled out into the fresh, clean air. She paused to get her bearings before walking down the concrete steps. Falling and busting her head open was not something she wanted to do. Making a quick getaway was the only thing that mattered.

She reached her car unsteadily, but as she shut her door and leaned her head against the steering wheel, her migraine seemed to lessen. She would have to take a pill when she got home, but at least now she knew she would make it there. She turned the key and slowly pulled out of her father's driveway, past the red convertible Miata parked beside her with the license plate that read HOTTIE.

chapter ten

Micah felt so much better when she got home that the pain behind her eyes had even receded to a bearable ache. She went right for the medicine cabinet and reached for her medication, though. She hated going to the emergency room for a shot. Taking a pill before things got too bad was much better. She took one last breath and looked around her little apartment in relief. This was her home. Here, she could let her guard down. Micah broke down into harsh, soul-racking sobs and leaned her head against the fridge. Her life as she had known it was a huge lie. Her father had molded her into some strange translation of perfection, and she had let him do it. She hadn't rebelled at all. Sometimes, growing up, she had thought about it. She'd thought about breaking free from her father's relentless control, but she never could. He had lost his wife. He had lost his baby son. She was all he had. She couldn't bear to let him down. But now that he had turned her into this creation, he had betrayed her. He had abandoned her. And she was all alone . . . with this person she hated.

Micah walked into the bathroom and stared at her tear-soaked face and hated what she saw: long, dark-blonde hair, always curled as her father specified. Modestly applied makeup—*we wouldn't want to give men the wrong impression.* Clothes that were bought at the only store her father approved of. Yes, it was a store geared for the wealthy middle-aged woman, but her father knew what was best for her—didn't he?

Micah groaned and turned away. She hated herself because she didn't even know who she was anymore. She walked into her bedroom and shut the door. Her roommates were probably at a fireside. She was glad. She wouldn't know what to say if they asked her what was wrong. *Everything* was wrong. Her life was a joke, and she didn't know where to go from here.

Micah fell onto her bed and rested her arm over her eyes. She would show him! If what he really liked were women who dressed like hookers, then she could do that. That would spite him. And when he asked her why, when he got mad and blew up at her, she would just point to Kathy. *See, Dad! I'm following my new role model. Don't I look great?*

Micah smiled, just picturing her dad's reaction. He would see through all of his mistakes then. He would realize what he had done. He would beg her to forgive him. He would get rid of Kathy and everything would go back to normal. Micah's smile disappeared as she remembered that normal wasn't all that great. She wasn't very happy with normal. And besides, Kathy was pregnant. Did she really want her father to abandon his baby? Not really.

Micah sighed and rolled onto her side, pulling her knees up and closing her eyes, wishing she had some answers, wishing she knew where to go from here.

"Knock, knock! I thought I heard you come in. Are you okay?"

Micah sat up quickly. She had thought she was all alone! April was home. Now what was she going to do?

"Um, yeah, April. I'm fine, just a little tired. I think I'm going to go to sleep now though. I'll talk to you tomorrow."

April opened the door anyway. Micah groaned. She wasn't up to this.

"Look, Micah, I was on the phone with my dad when you came in. But I'm not deaf. I heard you crying. Something is wrong, and you need to tell me what it is. I won't go away until you do."

Micah glared at her roommate. *How rude.*

"Where's Lisa? Why aren't you at the fireside?" Micah demanded.

April sat down next to her on the bed and stared at her seriously.

"Oh, I don't know. Probably because I was having a mental breakdown because my roommate, instead of setting me up with some jerk who would be happy to buy me dinner and then send me home, set me up with the one guy I have a thing for. Out of eighty-five guys, you pick the one you're not supposed to."

Micah giggled unexpectedly but then started to cry again.

"Sooorry. I guess I just mess everything up," Micah said through her tears.

April frowned but then reached over to pat her back.

"Okay, so everyone has their faults. What's really going on? Spill it."

Micah looked up into April's concerned eyes and felt like doing just that. She felt like laying her burden on someone else's shoulder. It was too big for her. She couldn't deal with it anymore.

"My forty-eight-year-old father is engaged to be married this next Tuesday to a twenty-year-old beautician who is not a member of the Church and who is very pregnant. And no, I'm not invited to the wedding," she said quickly and without any emotion.

April whistled and shook her head in awe.

"You have got to be kidding me. That is so typical of a midlife crisis. This is unreal," April said.

Micah interrupted April before she could say anything else.

"That's not the worst part. If you haven't noticed, I'm this carbon copy of my father's ideal Molly Mormon. He's made me into this person that *I* don't even like. And there's no point in trying to please him anymore. He's abandoned me, and now I don't even know who I am anymore. Who am I, April? Because I sure as heck don't know."

April smiled pityingly at Micah.

"Look, young lady, if you're going to use words like *heck* around here, I'm going to have to leave," she said seriously.

Micah threw her pillow at April but did crack a small smile.

April took in a deep breath and grabbed Micah's two hands.

"Listen, chick, you are at a crossroads in your life. You've been forced down this one road for a long time. But now you're *here*. You can keep going as you have been, but to be honest, you're not happy going there. Or you can spite your father and go in the opposite direction. You could go through this wild rebellious phase and shock everyone and get thrown out of BYU. Or you can take option three. The road over there. The road undiscovered. You could actually find out who the *heck* you are. What do you like, Micah? What's your favorite color? What is your favorite food? What kind of clothes do you like? What kind of hairstyle makes you feel good about yourself? What makes you— *you?* Who is Micah Rawlings? That's the question."

Micah flicked the tears off her cheeks and closed her eyes. She had no idea.

"Help me," she whispered.

"Honey, you're asking the wrong person. For that, you need to ask your Father."

Micah's eyes flew open and she glared at April.

"That's been my whole problem! Haven't you listened to a word I've been saying?" she asked incredulously.

April smiled and pointed toward the ceiling.

"I'm talking about a father who loves you, Micah. A father who loves everything about you. He knows you, even if *you* don't. Your Father in Heaven."

Micah blinked twice and let her head fall into her hands.

"I haven't talked to him in a while. I don't think he'll remember me."

April laughed and gave Micah a hug.

"Micah, take it from someone who knows. *He remembers.* But if it makes you feel any better, I think I will help you out a little. This might be fun. Actually, now that I think of it, this could be a blast. Kind of like *My Fair Lady* in reverse. Why don't we start tomorrow, after your last class? I have to work tomorrow for a couple hours at the gym. I'm scheduled to teach a yoga class tomorrow afternoon, so we'll start by having you come over and try that out. You'll love it. Then, after work, I'll take you to this little place I know. I know this girl Charlotte who is a wizard at hair. Then we'll go to the mall. It's going to be a huge job trying to figure out who you are, but getting the outside right will be easy. It's always the inside stuff that's so hard. So get a good night's rest and we'll hit life hard tomorrow. Okay?"

Micah nodded her head slowly. Yeah. This might be okay.

"Thanks, April. I don't know why, but you're a good friend to me. Thanks."

April nodded with a grin and walked out the door.

Micah looked at the closed door and thought about all of the doors that were now getting ready to open for her. She'd felt so closed in practically her whole life. She had been encased in resentment for as long as she could remember. She resented her mother for dying. She resented her baby brother for taking her mother away from her. She resented her father for taking out all of his hurt and pain on her. She resented God for letting it all happen. And she resented herself for not making her father happy enough.

Maybe it was time to stop resenting everything and everybody and start living. Micah closed her eyes and smiled. If it was like April was saying, that maybe this was a new rebirth for her, then maybe she owed Kathy a thank-you note.

chapter eleven

As she closed the door behind her, her smile slipped a notch. Micah didn't know what she was talking about. Micah had called *her* a good friend. April was sure that wasn't even a possibility. If Micah even had a clue what kind of person her roommate was, she would have run back to daddy's house a long time ago.

April sighed and opened the fridge door. Micah hadn't brought home any dessert from her dad's. *Great.* She had been looking forward to something chocolate all day. She didn't get paid for another week, and she was already dangerously low on food. April moved the food around the fridge, looking for something her two roommates wouldn't miss too much. *Ah hah!* Tupperware. Nobody ever looked in those things. Micah had thrown out so much food last month when she was cleaning out the fridge that it had taken April biting on her cheek not to yell at her, "Hey, you idiot! Can't you tell I'm starving here?"

As April heated up somebody's leftover stroganoff in the microwave she thought about Micah's dilemma. Here Micah was twenty-one years old, and it was like she was just starting her life over again. *Weird.* April frowned and wished for a moment that she was in Micah's shoes. What she wouldn't give to start her own life over again. April was still trying to get over what had happened three years ago. She took her meal out of the microwave and went and sat on the couch with her knees pulled up. It was so ironic. Here was Micah trying to break this mold she'd been poured into and *she, April* was the real Molly Mormon. She'd been the real thing. No forced dress code. She had loved being perfect. That was just who she was. And then she had messed everything up. She'd not only ruined her life, but her best friend's life and Mark's life and her parents' life, and on and on and on.

April felt her head grow hot and her chest constrict and fought back the tears that seemed to always be so close to the surface. It was hilarious. She was a stake president's daughter from Idaho and everybody thought she was some skater chick from California. Nope, she was a fraud. What a joke. She was telling Micah to find out who she really was, and all April wanted to do was hide from her true self. She'd died her light golden-brown hair jet black and had bought the biggest eyeliner pencil she could find. Add some crazy clothes from the DI, and—*ta da!*—the new April. If she was going to be a bad person, she might as well look the part.

April sighed and chewed on the rubbery noodles, which had been sitting in the fridge for at least a week and a half. She didn't care. It wasn't as if she deserved any better. She had started out *so* good too. The perfect family, loving parents, and great brothers and sisters, good grades, Laurel president, honor roll—everything. And then she had shown her true colors. Her senior year of high school, she had purposely gone after her best friend's boyfriend. She had planned it out, and she had done it. Jennifer had been her friend from kindergarten. But in the end, it hadn't mattered. She had betrayed her. She had gone after Mark and had taken him away from Jennifer. And it had only taken a month. April sighed and wondered why she was going over all of this in her mind. It wasn't going to do her any good. It would only depress her like it always did. But her pain was nothing compared to Jennifer's.

Jennifer had found out at school, of course, and had had a complete mental breakdown. She'd had to drop out of school and take some serious counseling sessions. Mark had felt so guilty that he'd dumped April immediately and gone back to Jennifer. And Jennifer had flat out refused to ever speak to her again. After high school graduation, Mark and Jennifer had gotten married. They'd invited the whole world, it seemed—everyone but April and her family. It had torn the two families apart. Jennifer's mom and dad had been *her* mom and dad's best friends. Now they wouldn't even shop at the same grocery store.

So she had left home. She'd ruined so many lives in her home town, she might as well find a new crop of people to torture. She'd left her family and what few friends she had left and had moved to Provo. And for three years now, she'd been in school, working when she could and starving most of the time. At least that didn't leave much time for causing other people pain.

April groaned and finished her dinner quickly. Maybe when she took Micah in to Charlotte for a new do, she'd have her fix *her* hair color. She was tired of looking like a vampire, anyway. Besides, no one here really cared what she had done in her past life. And she hadn't run in to anyone from Rigby in years. She wasn't really impressing anyone with how evil she was. If guys looked at her at all, it was mostly with pity. The ones who looked like she did always thought that she'd be interested in the same things they were. She hated heavy metal, and she'd never smoked pot in her life. Not a lot of common ground. Maybe it was time for her and Micah to find out who they were together. Maybe she wasn't the total Molly Mormon she had always thought she was, but she wasn't exactly a wild and crazy rebel either. It was time to stop pretending. Of course, fixing her hair had nothing to do with the fact that she had a real date with Joel. April grinned to herself and put her bowl in the sink. Who was she trying to kid? It had *everything* to do with Joel.

chapter twelve

Rrrrrrrrrring! Rrrrrrrring!

Micah opened her eyes and looked at the clock. It was almost nine. She'd been asleep for two hours. Where was April? Micah heard the shower and groaned. What use were roommates if they couldn't get the phone? Micah wondered for a second if it was her dad, calling to check up on her, and quickly grabbed the phone.

"Hello?" she said quickly.

"Uh, hi, Micah. It's Bryce. I thought I'd give you a call and um, see if you'd like to go out this Friday. April mentioned that there was a group of you guys going out and that maybe you and I would have fun together. What do you think?"

Micah felt all the blood leave her head, and she slumped back down in her bed. She'd totally forgotten about their dates this Friday!

"Oh, umm yeah. April told me that she had talked to you about a date. Um, listen. I know she put you on the spot and everything and if you want to back out, it's totally okay. I'll understand," Micah said lamely, feeling her skin grow clammy and wishing that April had been the one to get the phone.

Her migraine was better, but it was still sitting at the back of her head, making her weak and useless. She just wasn't ready for a stressful social situation, even if it was on the phone. Actually, she was never ready for those.

"Look, if you don't want to go out with me, just say so. Next time, just give April a list of guys you do and don't want to go out with. I'm sure that will make it easier for everyone involved," he said with a touch of impatience in his voice.

Micah winced and knew she had offended him.

"Bryce, I'm sorry. I didn't mean it that way. Of course I want to go out with you. Um, how about you pick me up around seven?"

There was a long silence on the other end of the line, and Micah wondered if she should just hang up.

"Okay, you got yourself a date. I'll see you Friday," Bryce said and then hung up the phone without waiting for a reply.

Micah replaced the phone in the charger and closed her eyes, completely exhausted. He was mad at her for some reason. *Great.* Dating was nearly impossible for her in the first place. Starting out a date with a guy who was already irritated with her was . . . well, typical. What was one more bad date in a string of disastrous, embarrassing, boring, horrible dates?

Micah looked at the clock and whimpered. Now that she

had taken a nap, she wouldn't be able to go back to sleep. *Men!* Micah got up and put on her long, white, puffy robe. She slid her hair into a scrunchie and went into the kitchen to see if April was out of the shower yet. No one. Micah looked in the freezer. If she didn't have any Ben and Jerry's left, she would cry. Today was a day for ice cream like no other. Yeah! Her favorite flavor too. It had everything in it: peanut butter cups, chocolate-covered almonds, Heath bar bits, and chunks of white and dark chocolate. Heaven in a carton. It was the closest she'd get to heaven anyways.

"If you give me a bite of that, I promise you my firstborn son. No joke," came a voice from behind her.

Micah smiled and turned around to see April with a towel wrapped around her head.

"Is that *all?* Well, since you're going to be helping with my transformation, I'll give you a whole carton. I think there's a Cherry Garcia shoved in the back. I forgot I had it."

April's eyes lit up like the sun and she full-out ran to the freezer.

"You are the best, Micah. Forget all of those horrible things I said about you. You are divine," April said as she ripped the top off and actually licked the lid.

Micah blinked in surprise but went back to her own ice cream. Everybody had their passion in life.

"I would have offered you the ice cream before, but when you got that job as a yoga instructor, I thought you had to swear off all unhealthy food and sugar and stuff like that."

April shoved a gargantuan spoonful of ice cream into her mouth and tilted her head back, closed her eyes, and then held up her hand for a moment. Micah had to put her spoon down and stare. She'd never seen anything like it.

"I may be into yoga, but that's because my body is a temple. I'm also into Ben and Jerry's because my body is a temple. I know what my temple likes, and I try to keep my temple happy. *Comprende?*"

Micah was confused but nodded her head in agreement. The front door opened suddenly, and Lisa walked in, looking happy and breathless.

"If you don't put that poison away, I'm suing you both for mental anguish and emotional distress."

April turned her body so Lisa couldn't see but kept on shoveling in the ice cream as if her life depended on it.

Micah smiled guiltily but didn't put hers away either. She loved Lisa like a sister, but not even for her own sister would she stop eating the ice cream. She'd had a rotten day, and Ben and Jerry's was the only Band-Aid she had handy.

"Sorry, Lisa. How was the fireside? Did you sit by Corbin?" Micah asked.

Lisa put her purse on the counter and got a low-fat, low-carb snack bar out of her cupboard.

"No, I didn't. I sat by Jenny and Cary. But he did come up to me afterward and talk to me for a little bit. We talked about what we might want to do Friday night. I tried to talk him in to country dancing, but he said *no way*. So I suggested dinner and a movie, but he said he didn't really want to spend that much money. I guess he put himself on a budget or something. So I suggested a picnic and video at our place, and he said he'd think about it. He is *so* cute. I just love the way his eyebrows come together when he's talking," Lisa said.

Micah shot April a look of disbelief at Lisa's comment. Micah could not for the life of her see what Lisa saw in Corbin—but to each her own.

"Well, that takes care of you, Lisa. What about you, Micah? I thought I heard the phone ring when I was in the bathroom. Was that Bryce or your dad?" April asked with her mouth full.

Micah swallowed a big chunk of Heath bar before answering.

"Bryce. And I guess we're on for Friday too. That just

leaves your phone call, April. Joel said he'd call you tonight. Was he at the fireside, Lisa?"

Lisa jerked her gaze away from the almost empty carton of ice cream and focused guiltily on Micah's face.

"Um, yeah. He was. He was sitting two rows ahead of me. You know, April, I was thinking. Joel is really cute and all, and he's supposed to be really smart too, but I just don't know. I mean . . . I heard some of the other girls talking and everything and I don't think he's even gone on a mission, and he's, like, twenty-five or something. And everyone can tell he's had earrings in his ears. Sometimes those holes never close up. I mean, he could be some crazy wild guy. If it were me, I'd be a little careful," Lisa said.

April put her spoon down and looked seriously at Lisa. Micah raised her eyebrows; she sensed a storm brewing. She was an expert at storms. Her whole life had been nothing but rain.

"Lisa, would you look at me? Do I look like I should be judging anyone? No one is perfect, and yeah, I have noticed his ears and I've heard how old he is and the whole story. No, he did not go on a mission. Does that mean that everyone should avoid him or not date him? Should we start stoning him now?" April asked in a testy voice.

Lisa looked to Micah for backup, but Micah held up her hands and shook her head. Lisa was on her own on this one. Personally, she thought Joel was one of the nicest guys in the ward.

"April, don't get so defensive. I'm just trying to look out for you. You know I love you, and I wouldn't say anything to purposely offend you."

April put another bite of ice cream in her mouth and nodded.

"I know, Lisa, that's why I'm not kicking your rear right now. I'm just trying to point out that maybe it's too soon to start judging any of these guys we have dates with. For all we know, Joel might turn out to be a General Authority someday, and Corbin could be in jail for insider trading. Who knows? Let's just plan on having fun Friday. But only if Corbin says we can."

Lisa glared at April but didn't say anything as the phone started ringing. Micah walked over and picked up the phone.

"Hello? . . . Hi, Joel . . . Yeah, she's right here, hold on."

Micah handed the phone to April and watched as her roommate turned pale and nervous. April put her ice cream down and took three deep breaths before putting the phone to her ear.

"Hello? . . . Yes, I would love to go out Friday. . . . A dinner and a movie? That's sounds fantastic. I would love to. I just talked to Lisa about Friday, though, and she said that Corbin might not have enough money to do something like that. She said he might want to just do a video or something. . . . Really? Bryce does too? . . . Okay, well, I'll let you guys work it out then. . . . Yeah, I'm looking forward to it. . . . See you then, bye."

April put the phone back in the charger and turned around with cheeks almost as rosy as Lisa's.

"I love Joel," April said and flopped onto their ancient brown couch.

Micah laughed and Lisa gasped. April tilted her head back on the couch and smiled with her eyes closed.

"He said that videos were not for first dates. He wants to take me to the Macaroni Grill. I've heard the food there is yummy. I told him about Corbin, but he just laughed. He says Corbin has money coming out of his ears, and that we're going out to dinner. I just love that man," April said and looked up with a grin.

Micah couldn't help smiling back at her. This group dating thing was starting to sound fun. Just watching April stuff her face all night was going to be a blast.

"Well, that's real nice for you, April, but what if Corbin says no? What if he refuses to take me out to dinner?" Lisa said in a very worried, small voice.

April's smile slipped and she looked to Micah for help. Micah shrugged but walked over to Lisa and slipped an arm around her shoulder.

"Lisa, all I know is that Corbin is way lucky to be going out with you. There aren't any girls in the ward nicer than you. So if he backs out, then that's his loss. *Big time.* And if he does, then we'll just have to set you up with someone who will treat you like a queen and jump at the chance to take you out to dinner."

Lisa looked up at Micah doubtfully.

"It's because I'm overweight, isn't it? I don't think he really wants to go out with me, Micah. I saw you talking to him at church. You looked like you were getting mad at him."

Micah cleared her throat, wondering what she could say now.

"Well, I don't know why I looked mad. Maybe I was looking nervous? Sometimes nervous and mad look a lot alike. But about being overweight. I think you look just fine. I mean, not everyone can or should be ultra skinny. For most people, it's not their natural body weight and it's unhealthy. But if it bothers you, why don't you come down and do yoga with me tomorrow afternoon? April's teaching a class, and I'm thinking of trying it out. April and I were talking earlier, and this whole week we're going to concentrate on transforming ourselves, right, April?"

Micah looked to April and widened her eyes, trying to get her to go along. April's eyebrows shot up and she gave a large nod.

"Yeah ... um, yeah, Lisa. I've been thinking of trying a new look for a long time, and now that Micah's life is in an uproar—sorry Micah, but she'll find out anyway—she wants to do a whole Micah makeover. So join the crowd, Lisa. Join the club, literally, and try out yoga. I think it would be great for you. It's not like aerobics or weight lifting or running or anything like that. It's all about getting in touch with your body. Focusing on the inner you. I absolutely love it. And Micah needs it like no other. Talk about a stress case. But as far as exercise, it's gentle and it's not competitive. You'll love it. Trust me."

Micah glared at April. *Ingrate!*

"That is the last Cherry Garcia I will ever give you! Stress case! You're calling me a stress case!" Micah practically shouted.

April and Lisa both smiled at her and nodded. Micah frowned.

"So why's your life in an uproar, Micah?" Lisa asked.

April jumped in before Micah could even draw a breath to answer.

"Her dad is getting married this week to someone younger than she is. And she's going to be a big sister in about seven months. Just a *little* uproar."

Lisa's mouth dropped a foot, and she stared at Micah as if she had never seen her before.

"Wow, that is an uproar. I would die if my dad did anything like that. Holy cow," Lisa said sympathetically.

Micah shrugged and scraped the rest of the ice cream off the bottom of the carton.

"Enough of my problems. So are you in? Are we all in this together? I want yoga, I want a new hairstyle, I want a new wardrobe, I want a new me," Micah said.

Lisa looked between April and Micah as if she weren't sure if she could believe them. April rolled her eyes.

"Look, I'll make a deal with you. If I fix my hair and change my style, then you have to promise to do yoga three times a week for the next six months. It's up to you," April said.

Lisa frowned and looked down at her feet. Micah wondered what was going on inside her head. She knew Lisa hated exercising more than anything. But she also knew Lisa had been wanting April to change her style for a long time.

"Okay. I'll do it. On the condition that you don't criticize me if I don't lose weight and that you don't compare me to Micah and that you don't laugh at me when I can't do all of those weird positions that you do all the time."

April smiled and got up off the couch and gave Lisa a huge hug.

"Honey, you just made the best decision of your life. And if you think I'd criticize you or compare you or anything like that, then you don't know me very well. Besides, most of the ladies in my yoga class are middle-aged moms who weigh twice as much as you. Remember, I said that yoga isn't competitive. It's about getting in tune with your body. You'll see. You'll be so in to what your body is doing that you won't even care what anyone else looks like."

Lisa gave April a small smile but looked doubtful.

"Six months, right? And you better look like a Relief Society president tomorrow night, or it's off. Got it?" Lisa said.

Micah laughed and April groaned.

"I think you got the better deal, Lisa. Now I'm starting to worry," April said.

Micah laughed at both of her roommates' expressions.

"Well, if you need a wardrobe that would make a Relief Society president proud, then you're in luck. I've decided to donate my whole closet to the DI. Why not just give my stuff to you and save myself a trip?" Micah asked April.

They were the same size, so it would work, if April agreed to it.

April looked shell-shocked. Micah wondered if free ice cream and free clothes were too much for April. Maybe her heart just wasn't in it.

"Are you serious, Micah? Are you really, really serious? I mean, I'm not trying to talk you out of it or anything, but your clothes are worth a bloody fortune! And you just want to give them to me? Are you insane?" April demanded.

Micah grinned and threw her empty carton into the garbage can.

"Yep. I'm totally and completely insane. Come on, let's go through my stuff. You too, Lisa. After April is through with you, you'll be able to fit into anything I own easily."

April and Lisa ran past Micah toward her room. Micah laughed and then stopped. What was that she had just felt? What was that? She knew it had a name. She hadn't felt in a long, long time, but she recognized it. Yeah . . . she knew it. It was happiness. Micah shook her head as her smile grew wider. That would be the first step in her transformation. Being happy. Micah hurried to catch up to her roommates. She hadn't told them about her shoes under the bed yet. They would love those.

chapter thirteen

Micah turned over in her bed and looked at her alarm clock. It wouldn't go off for another fifteen minutes, so she rolled back over and snuggled down into her warm sheets. She had three classes this morning, but then she was free. Summer term was practically over, and then she would have to face the new year. She loved going to school during spring and summer terms. It was less hectic, less crowded, and just more her style. It made facing classes easier.

Micah's eye's popped open. She had just realized she had one more thing to transform. Her father had insisted that she get a degree in business. She hated business. She hated everything about it. Micah sat up straight in bed. She only had one year left to get her bachelor's degree, but what if she switched majors? What if she actually got a degree in something she enjoyed? What if she were able to do something that made her feel alive?

Micah jumped out of bed, turned off her alarm, and quickly got dressed. She was going to do something she had never done before. *Ever.* She was going to skip her classes. Just for today though. Instead of going to class, she was going to the library on campus and do a little research. She was going to figure out what she wanted to do with her life. She already had a pretty good idea. All the daydreaming she had done hadn't been for nothing. But she wanted to find out more. And today was the perfect day. Today was definitely her day to change everything. If she was lucky, she could even see about getting an appointment with the head of the department and get some career counseling. Anything and everything was possible today.

Micah rushed out of her apartment without even stopping for breakfast. April and Lisa were still sleeping, and she didn't want to talk to them yet. She wanted to surprise them later that day when they met up for yoga. She could just see their faces now when she told them that she was no longer a business major. Nope. Micah Rawlings was soon to be a psychology major.

Micah giggled to herself as she put her car in reverse and drove out of the parking lot. She felt good just thinking about it. She remembered taking a basic psychology course her freshman year and how much she had loved it. But the real reason she wanted to go into psychology was because of Dr. Hawkins. When her mom had died, Dr. Hawkins had been called in by the hospital as their grief counselor. He had sat down with her and talked to her. Her father had been busy with paperwork and funeral details, so he hadn't pulled her away. She still remembered the counselor's kindness to her. He had held her hand and talked to her about where her mom was right then. He had told her that it was okay to be sad and mad and everything in between. He had also given her his card. She had kept it, hidden in her Book of Mormon so her dad wouldn't find it. But she had never called.

She could be like Dr. Hawkins. She could help little kids who had lost their parents, or help parents who had lost their children, or people who just needed to talk to someone. She could help people be happy again.

Micah felt her heart start to beat faster, and she felt her mouth turning up. Again! She was feeling that feeling again. She was feeling good. Micah looked into her rearview mirror and blinked. She hardly recognized the person looking back at her. This person had eyes that sparkled with a bright light. Her face looked clear and open, not dark and heavy. This person looked hopeful. Micah shook her head in wonderment. Her dad's midlife crisis was possibly one of the best things that had ever happened to her.

chapter fourteen

April changed into her yoga clothes and pulled her hair back into a ponytail. She carefully folded her new pants and shirt, given to her by Micah the night before, and gently placed them in a locker. She quickly headed for the small room on the west side of the gym. It wasn't large, but it had high ceilings and lots of windows. Her classes weren't too big, so it was the perfect spot for yoga. She walked over to the CD player and picked a soothing instrumental to put on. She could feel the pounding of the bass and the frantic beat of the music coming from the aerobics room down the hall and wondered why people would rather work themselves into exhaustion than stretch themselves into a new level of energy. She smiled at some of the ladies walking in who were regulars and wondered where her roommates were. If Micah didn't show up, she was going to be ticked. If Lisa didn't show up, then she would be immensely relieved. This little deal they had of turning her into a Relief Society president look-alike in exchange for a little exercise wasn't sounding fun anymore.

She had tried on most of Micah's clothes the night before and had loved them all. The knit sets and the white button-up shirts with pearl buttons. The wool pants with silk lining and the leather shoes with small, demure heels. The long skirts with matching tops. She had tried it all on and had been in heaven. She remembered trying on a dress with a lace collar and looking in the mirror as Micah and Lisa had laughed—and had almost cried. She had once had a dress almost exactly like the one she had on. It felt as if she were slipping back into her old skin.

And it had scared her. She had felt so good in those clothes, as if she were coming home—but she knew she was a fraud. Girls who stole their best friend's boyfriends and ruined people's friendships didn't deserve to look like Relief Society presidents. That wasn't who she was anymore.

Or was she? April paused and looked out the window at the high mountains and the blue skies. Nobody was perfect, even Relief Society presidents. In her heart, she knew that everyone was here to make mistakes and repent. But it was so much easier to believe that for other people. April had always held herself up to a higher standard than others. Maybe that was why she was having such a hard time forgiving herself and getting over what had happened. But maybe these new clothes were a sign. A sign from God, even? Maybe it was time to let it go and move on, and be who she really was. April sighed and then smiled. Everybody deserved second chances—even her.

April caught a glimpse of herself in the mirror and

looked hard at the girl staring back at her. Thin, tall, with a know-it-all look about her. Large blue eyes that looked harder than they should. And a stubborn chin. Crazy black hair that looked so out of place. But Charlotte had already told her that that was no big deal. Hair could be changed as easily as clothes. Was she still April underneath everything? It was time to find out. April smiled at herself and stepped onto her sticky mat. It was time to begin.

April called the class to their mats, and began with a simple side stretch to limber up and warm the body. She grinned as Micah and Lisa walked in, looking out of breath and excited.

Maybe she could scare Lisa off? April grinned and went into a sun salute before lowering into chair position. Nah, that wouldn't be nice at all. For someone trying to turn over a new leaf, being mean on the first day wouldn't help things.

She noticed Lisa frown slightly and knew she would stick to her regular routine. Lisa was going to have a hard enough time as it was. Making it worse would only make Lisa swear off exercise for the rest of her life. This transformation stuff wasn't going to be easy for any of them—she might as well help Lisa out as much as possible. It was her turn next, and she needed all the help she could get. Especially from her friends.

After ten minutes of warming up, April flowed down into a downward facing dog position. Micah, who had no upper body strength to speak of, groaned out loud. One of her regulars chuckled and gave Micah some encouragement. April grinned and began her soothing spiel of encouraging words along with her instructions. Empowering words always made you work harder than you had planned on or stretch further than you thought you could. Words were so powerful, April wondered if that was why reading the scriptures daily was so important. Because Heavenly Father knew that as well.

April instructed her students to move into the dolphin pose. After showing them what she wanted, April walked around to all the ladies, helping them, adjusting them, and encouraging them. When she came to Lisa and Micah in the very back, she grinned wickedly down at them.

"Give up, Lisa?" April asked quietly so that none of her other ladies would hear.

Lisa looked up at April with sweat beading on her forehead and her arms quivering.

"Never. I'll never give up, April. But if you want to call off our deal, I'll understand. Looking normal for some people is a real stretch," Lisa said, and then laughed at her own yoga joke.

Micah frowned at her two roommates.

"Hey, guys. We're not supposed to be trying to get each other to quit. We're trying to help each other. We love each other, remember?"

April leaned down and pushed the hair out of Lisa's eyes.

"Lisa knows I'm just kidding, Micah. The way she is, she's probably going to be better than I am in a few months and go after my job. Look at her, Micah. She has perfect form, and this is the first time she's even tried this pose. Amazing."

Lisa rolled her eyes and Micah smiled at her.

"Excuse me? I'm not hearing any praise about my form. Maybe I want your job," Micah said.

April laughed and adjusted Micah's elbows.

"There you go. Now you're perfect too."

"Um, I know I'm doing really good and everything, but how much longer is your class?" Lisa asked.

April smiled. "Only thirty more minutes."

April left her friends and walked back to her mat at the front of the class.

"Okay, remember your breathing, ladies. All the way

in and all the way out. Deep, cleansing breaths. Keep your stomach muscles working and your knees drawn up. Now, let's move into warrior position."

April stretched and worked with the class until their time was up. She walked around to all of the women, thanking them for coming and answering questions about yoga and diet.

As the class emptied out, she was left with Lisa and Micah lying, comatose, in corpse position. She walked over and nudged Micah's leg with her toe.

"Come on, guys, it wasn't that bad. You both did wonderful."

Micah turned on her side and sat up. She looked over to Lisa and frowned.

"You've killed her, April. Is that any way to start off your transformation? I thought yoga was all gentle and rejuvenating. I feel like a worn-out old shoe."

April felt a little guilty as she noticed Lisa still hadn't moved.

"You'll feel rejuvenated in about twenty minutes. This is your first time, so you might be a little sore tomorrow, but if you keep coming three times a week, you'll just get more and more limber and stronger and stronger. Give it some time. The energy is going to flow into your body and you won't be able to live without it. I promise. Are you going to come tomorrow?"

"You bet your yoga mat we will," Lisa said out of the blue, making Micah and April jump.

Lisa opened her eyes and slowly stood up.

"I'm so loose I don't think I'll be able to walk to my car," Lisa said proudly.

Micah put an arm around her shoulder.

"Come on, Lisa, I'll help you. At least you get to go home and soak in the tub. I've got to go get my hair done and do some shopping at the mall still."

Lisa's eyes snapped open.

"You guys are going shopping too? I want to come! I'm not going to sit at home while you two have all the fun. Let's go," Lisa said and walked quickly out of the room.

Micah and April exchanged grins and followed their roommate.

Tonight was going to be fun.

chapter fifteen

Micah drove her car into the parking lot of a tiny little cinder block building, with a sign in the window that said Hair Gone Wild. Micah turned around to pierce April with a glare.

"Is this who does your hair now? Because I have to tell you right now, I don't think finding myself has anything to do with mohawks, spikes, or fluorescent pink hair."

April stuck her tongue out at Micah.

"Look you little ingrate, Charlotte is awesome at hair. I know her from my sculpting class. She just graduated from beauty school. She's cutting hair to support herself. She showed me some pictures of the mannequins she's done. I was amazed. *Really*. But the best thing about it all is that, since we're going to be her first customers, she's only going to charge us ten dollars for a cut. She's going to charge me more for changing my hair color, but with all the money I saved on my new wardrobe, who can complain?"

Micah felt her stomach clench up nervously.

"Why don't I drop you two off? I'll meet you at the mall in about an hour and a half," Micah said with a nervous smile.

April sighed and closed her eyes. Lisa looked as nervous as Micah felt but kept silent.

"Just because you're not spending sixty dollars on a haircut doesn't mean it won't be a good one. You're being a snob, Micah. Now come on, Charlotte is peeking out the window, wondering why we're not getting out. Don't embarrass me," April said and got out of the car, slamming the door.

Micah looked at Lisa and raised her eyebrows questioningly. Lisa winced but nodded her head.

"All for one and one for all," Lisa said and quickly followed April.

That left her. Micah watched as April and Lisa disappeared inside the small, dark building. What was she going to do? True, she hated her hair, but did she really need to punish it? *Ugh!* Micah banged her head on her steering wheel and cringed at the thought of giving a complete novice control of her hair. April was doing it. Lisa was doing it. But if they jumped off a cliff, would she? Micah bit her fingernail and tried to think of an excuse.

She couldn't. Micah opened the door and stepped out of her car. She took in a deep breath and straightened her shoulders. *This must be what a caterpillar feels like*, thought Micah. She'd never thought about it, but the process of metamorphosis couldn't all be pleasant or easy.

She walked slowly toward the old, rusted steel door and opened it slowly. She peeked around the corner and waited until her eyes adjusted.

"Hey! We're over here. Come on, don't be shy. I'll be very gentle with you."

Micah looked over to where the voice was coming from and saw a petite, brunette with short spiky hair. She knew there would be spikes somewhere. But at least they weren't flaming red, white, and blue. It was kind of cute on her. Micah stepped around the door and shut it firmly.

"Sorry, just a little last-minute jitters is all. Nothing personal," Micah said feebly.

Charlotte winked at Micah and motioned for her to sit down in a chair beside Lisa.

"No problemo. Changing our appearance is sometimes one of the hardest things we can do. Check out April. She's not so tough either. She's so nervous she's about to hyperventilate."

April glared at Charlotte but leaned her head back and breathed loudly through her nose. Micah giggled and sat down in the chair and waited her turn for a shampoo.

"Now, I want you two girls to sit over here under this dryer for about ten minutes. The heat will open up your follicles and let more of the conditioner in. You'll love how your hair feels. I'm just going to get April started. She's got a lot more going on than you guys do. We have to strip her hair, add back color, and do some major conditioning. I hope you brought your camera though. You're all going to be amazed."

Micah felt herself relax as she tilted her head back and let the warm air flow over her plastic-wrapped head. This wasn't so bad. This was actually kind of . . . nice.

"Here, take one of these. I haven't had a haircut in about seven months. I don't know if I just want a trim or something more drastic," Lisa said.

Micah opened her eyes and took the magazine shoved under her nose. Lisa might have a point. What was she going to tell Charlotte she wanted done with her hair? She had no idea. Kathy's multicolored streaked hair came to mind, but Micah quickly pushed that image aside. She didn't want any thoughts of her father—or her father's new wife—intruding on today's events.

What did she like? Micah thumbed through the pictures in the magazine and hoped that Charlotte would take all the time she wanted with April. Micah glanced over at Lisa and noticed that Lisa was staring hard at a picture of a beautiful model with long hair almost the same color as Lisa's. But instead of straight and long, it was slightly layered with light waves running through it. It was a beautiful look.

"You know, that would look great on you, Lisa," Micah said.

Lisa looked over at her, frowning.

"Do you really think so? I mean, I've had the same haircut since I was in the seventh grade. I've never had bangs before. I wouldn't know how to style my hair or anything. It looks kind of complicated."

Micah looked over at Charlotte, who was hard at work on April, and smiled.

"Lisa, I think we have an expert here who will tell you exactly what to do. Why not go for it? Picture yourself looking like that for your date Friday. You'll be smashing," Micah said with a grin.

Lisa smiled back. "Okay. Yoga, a new hairstyle, maybe a new outfit. I'll be a whole new person. Cool."

Micah frowned at Lisa. "Lisa, you might be able to change the way you look on the outside, and that's fun and everything, but you're practically perfect on the inside. That's the real you. You don't want to change that at all."

Not like me, Micah added to herself. She needed an extreme overhaul on the inside *and* the outside.

Lisa smiled even bigger. "Thanks, Micah. You're sweet. So, which hairstyle did you decide on? You'd look good in any haircut."

Micah groaned and turned the pages more quickly, feeling that her time was about to run out.

"I don't know, Lisa. Help me look. Look in your magazine and show me ones that you think would work."

The two girls had raced through their magazines and the other three on the rack when Charlotte walked over to them.

"Okay, April has to sit for a while. Who's first?"

Micah blurted out quickly, "She is!"

Charlotte laughed and led Lisa over to a stall on the other side of the room, leaving Micah to herself. She watched as Lisa explained what she wanted and then Charlotte grabbed her scissors. Micah watched, fascinated, as feathery wisps of hair floated down to cover the floor. Then Charlotte grabbed a long razor blade and started running it over sections of Lisa's hair. Micah shook her head in wonder. She'd never seen anyone use a razor blade to cut hair. Then Charlotte rubbed something liquid all through Lisa's hair and blew it dry with a large round brush. Lastly she used a huge curling iron to curl only certain sections of hair. She finished it off with a light spray and then handed the mirror to Lisa.

Lisa's giggles and shouts of happiness reverberated throughout the small room.

Micah laughed along with Lisa's happiness. Maybe this wasn't going to be so bad after all.

"Now it's your turn," Charlotte said, motioning for Micah to come over.

Micah gulped but got to her feet and walked slowly toward Charlotte. Lisa had walked over to show April her new look, so it was only the two of them.

"Don't look so excited. Come on, have a seat."

Micah sighed and sat down gingerly in the chair and waited as Charlotte wrapped a drape over her.

"So what's it going to be? A trim? A new style? A new color?" Charlotte asked as she lifted Micah's hair, studying it critically.

"Well, I really don't like my hair the way it is. I don't know if April explained what we're doing, but we're all kind of going through a transformation thing. I really would like to just look like me. Sometimes I look in the mirror and I don't see me. You know?" Micah said.

Charlotte tilted her head to the side and looked at Micah through the mirror. She smiled.

"I totally understand. So do you know what you would like or do you want to be really brave and put yourself in my hands?"

Micah blinked and thought about it. Could she do it?

"If I did, and I'm not saying that I am, but if I did put myself in your hands, what would you do to me?" Micah asked timidly.

Charlotte grinned and walked slowly around Micah tilting her head this way and that.

"I know exactly what I'd do. It would be very different from what you're used to. It would be fun and young and stylish. It would be you. If that sounds like something you might want, just say the word and I'll do it. I'm not good at explaining things, but I could show you," Charlotte said with a gleam of excitement in her eyes.

Micah looked over to her two roommates, who were listening in to their conversation. They both gave her the thumbs up.

"Yes. Let's do it," Micah said firmly and nodded to Charlotte.

"All right! We've got ourselves a winner here, folks. Buckle up, hold on, and get ready for some serious change, girls," Charlotte said and walked quickly into the back room. She brought back some bottles, brushes, foil, and some other things—Micah didn't even know what they were.

"We're going to add just a few highlights around your face to lighten things up. You won't have to touch up roots for at least three or four months," Charlotte said as she began to mix this and that as if she were a mad scientist. Micah cringed when she realized Charlotte wasn't exactly measuring anything. Was her hair going to fall out? She'd never had her hair colored—ever. Great, she *was* going to turn out looking like her new stepmother. Micah felt her stomach muscles re-tense and started to pray silently. Charlotte began painting the liquid onto sections of her hair and wrapping the foil around them. It only took about twenty minutes, but in the end, she looked like some beauty school experiment gone terribly wrong.

"I thought you said you were going to do only a few highlights? This looks like a ton," Micah said with only a small tremor in her voice.

Charlotte snorted as she set a timer.

"You've got to be kidding me. Where are you from?"

Micah frowned and decided to be quiet the rest of the time.

Charlotte placed a magazine in her hands and told her to relax. She went over and started rinsing April's hair. And then she went through the same process with the foil and the color as she had done with Micah. Micah didn't even look at her magazine as she watched Charlotte work quickly to cover April's entire head with foil. She'd never seen anything like it in her life. She glanced at her own head and realized she *had* sounded like a complete idiot. April looked like a foil monster. Micah glanced at April's face and realized she wasn't the only one having a hard time transforming. April looked terrified. Micah suddenly felt much, much better.

"Okay, it's rinse time. Let's go," Charlotte said to her.

Micah got out of her chair and walked over to the sink, letting Charlotte rinse her hair. She headed right back to her stall and watched as Charlotte expertly combed her hair. It was wet, so she couldn't really tell what her new highlights would look like. She was curious though. Her natural hair color was a dark blond with lighter and darker shades here and there. She hoped she didn't end up with orange hair. That had happened to a girl she had known in high school who had gone crazy with Sun-In spray.

Charlotte grabbed her scissors and without even telling Micah what she was going to do, began cutting huge sections of hair off. Micah gasped as she realized what was going on.

"You're cutting all my hair off! What are you doing?" Micah yelped in outrage.

Charlotte shook her head in exasperation but kept going.

"Look, Micah, you look like an eighth-grader with all this hair. Let's bring you into the twenty-first century. I'm not hacking off *all* your hair, just the parts I don't like."

And then she laughed.

Micah felt like crying, but instead of falling apart, she watched the mirror. She barely even blinked as she saw a different shape begin to appear to her hair. Charlotte was cutting a lot of layers into her hair. Micah wondered what it was going to be like looking like a boy. She'd never really wanted to look like a boy. Micah felt her throat tense up and realized that she was probably going to start crying. Charlotte grabbed a bottle and spritzed her head with something, and then began blow-drying her hair.

Micah closed her eyes and concentrated on not having a nervous breakdown. She could wait until she got home for that. But could she walk around the mall looking for new clothes like this? Micah felt her shoulders sag as she realized that looking ugly really hadn't been in the plans of her transformation. New, better, *yes*. Ugly, *no*. What was Bryce going to think? Micah groaned softly.

"Okay, open your eyes scaredy-cat," Charlotte said.

Micah opened her eyes slowly and stared at the person in the mirror. The person in the mirror didn't have short hair.

She didn't look like a boy. She looked fantastic!

"Yeah!" Micah yelled, twisting her head this way and that. Charlotte had chopped a ton of hair off but had kept most of the length in the back. The layers weren't everywhere like a boy's, they were chunky layers that added volume and shape.

"This is fantastic," Micah whispered as tears did come to her eyes.

Charlotte laughed again and took Micah's drape off, twirling the chair around and helping her out.

"Do you like the highlights?" Charlotte asked.

Micah stood in front of the mirror, running her hands through her hair. She looked at the strands of hair that had been lightened and grinned. She didn't look tacky; she looked natural, and fun.

"You are getting a big tip, Charlotte. Big," Micah said with a grin.

Charlotte grinned back.

"I'll take that to be a yes."

Micah continued to touch and look at her hair as Charlotte went back to April, rinsing her hair and putting her through the exact same thing that Micah had just gone through.

"Let me do it, April. Come on. I've been dying to get my hands on this hair ever since I've met you. Just give it a chance. And if you don't like it, you can always grow it out."

April rubbed her temples and closed her eyes.

"I've never had short hair, Charlotte. I don't think I'll like it."

Charlotte continued combing April's hair as she frowned.

"Most of it's dead, anyway. There's a lot of damage from all that junk you put on it. What I'm thinking of doing will give your hair a new start. It will look good as your natural hair color grows back in. It's not going to be as short as mine. Come on, you can't let your two roommates show you up. They're going to think their big, tough friend is a little priss-pot."

"You're such a bully, Charlotte. Fine, hack my hair off, but you're not going to get a tip," April said stiffly.

Charlotte smiled kindly at April and tilted her head down and began cutting. Micah gasped as Charlotte whacked off seventy-five percent of April's hair. Micah rubbed her hands through her hair thankfully and felt her heart go out to her friend. April was literally cringing in her seat.

Micah walked over and grabbed April's cold hand to give her some support. Lisa walked over and grabbed April's other hand. Micah had been so worried about herself, she hadn't realized that what April was going through was a lot tougher than what had been dealt to her.

As April's pile of wet hair on the floor grew bigger, her grip on Micah's hand grew harder and tighter. Micah prayed that Charlotte would stop cutting soon. She didn't think her circulation could take any more constriction.

Ten excruciating minutes later, Charlotte lowered the scissors and smiled. She spritzed April's hair with a leave-in conditioner and then rubbed some gel on the ends. She grabbed her blow-dryer and a large round brush and went to work shaping April's hair with heat and air.

Micah studied April's hair in the mirror and wondered what she was going to think. Would she like it? And if she didn't, would she be in a bad mood for the next six months? It really wasn't as short as she had thought it was going to be. It was cut to just under April's chin, with light layers that Charlotte was flipping up. *It was kind of cute.*

Micah smiled as she saw the light brown and golden honey-toned highlights that were appearing in April's hair. Before Micah's eyes, April was going from pale and washed-out to alive and glowing with color. Her blue eyes were now popping, and the faint dash of freckles across her nose was now more noticeable. And her cheeks looked like they had been brushed with peaches. *Wow.* Take away all that bleak, black hair and April looked like a completely different person. Micah grinned as she realized April was really pretty. And yes, April had lost a lot of hair, but from where she was sitting, that was a good thing. April looked, young, trendy, and very cool.

"Charlotte, you are some kind of genius," Micah said as Charlotte turned off the blow-dryer and ran her fingers through April's hair, fluffing it out here and there.

"Glad you think so, Micah. But I want to know what April thinks," Charlotte said worriedly.

April studied herself in the mirror and silently held her hand out for Charlotte's handheld mirror. She turned herself around so she could see the back of her head. She twisted this way and that way, rubbing her hand over her hair.

Micah winced as she realized that April was not smiling. She was frowning and her eyes looked red and her forehead seemed pinched. *Uh oh.* This was not going to be good.

"April, I think you look beautiful. It's a whole new you," Micah said softly, hoping to head off any fireworks.

April shook her head and covered her eyes with her hands. And then started sobbing hysterically. And then Charlotte began sobbing hysterically. Micah and Lisa exchanged panicked looks. What were they going to do now?

"April, what's wrong?" Lisa asked as she put her arm around her shoulders. "Do you not like the color? I think it looks fantastic. It looks like what your natural hair color should be. But if you don't like it, maybe Charlotte could make it darker, or something."

April shook her head and cried harder.

"Well, is it the cut? I know you've been used to long hair, but this is *very* stylish. It makes you look like a million bucks, seriously," Micah added quickly.

April shook her head and lifted her eyes to Micah's

"I . . . love . . . it." And then she sobbed harder than ever.

Charlotte stopped crying and stared at April. Then she punched April in the shoulder and stalked off to the back room.

Micah looked at Lisa and at April's stunned faces and burst out laughing.

"April, you idiot! If you like something, you don't cry like it's the end of the world. You jump up and cheer and shout hallelujah!"

Lisa giggled helplessly and sat down in a chair beside April.

"April, you are one loco chick, you know that?"

April reached for the tissue that Micah was holding out to her and wiped her tears.

"I'm *me* again. This is the real me. I haven't been me in so long, I don't know what I'll do. I don't know if I'm ready to try my life again. I messed it up so badly. What if I mess up again?" April said.

Micah's eyes widened as she realized that April was sharing something with them that she never had before. April never talked about her life before college. Something traumatic must have happened to her to make her want to hide from herself. She was just plain scared of *being* herself.

"April, tell you what. Why don't we go give Charlotte a huge tip, and then I'm going to treat you guys to the best Chinese fast food the mall has to offer. And then I want you to tell us what's really going on. You've been keeping a few secrets, and if today is the beginning of our transformation, then we all need to start fresh. No looking back."

April looked up at Micah and Lisa and nodded.

Micah grabbed Lisa's hand, and they headed in the back to find Charlotte. She couldn't wait to find out what April had been holding back from them. Micah smiled as she realized that her trip to self-awakening wasn't going to be lonely at all.

chapter sixteen

"You stole your best friend's boyfriend?" Micah asked, raising her eyebrows questioningly.

April nodded, not looking her in the eyes.

"Yeah, pretty much. I don't know if you'd really call her my best friend though, you know? I mean, her parents and my parents are, I mean *were*, real best friends, and since they were always doing stuff together, we were always thrown together, sort of. You just have to understand Jennifer. She's kind of different. When she started going out with Mark, everything was great, but I think she got bored or something. She would constantly flirt with other guys, in front of him too, just to make him jealous. And he would always cry on my shoulder. I'd tell her to knock it off because she was hurting this great guy who loved her, but she would just laugh and say something stupid, like it was good for him. After a while of this, me and Mark started getting closer. And so I made a decision. I decided that if she didn't appreciate what she had, then she didn't deserve him. So I decided to steal her boyfriend. One night, he came over to study with me and I looked at him and he looked at me and then he kissed me. And I kissed him back. And then my whole life fell apart."

Micah took a bite of her mandarin orange chicken and mulled over what April had just told them. Lisa choked on her soda and started sputtering. April reached over and pounded her on the back and kept going.

"Well, Jennifer found out the next day because Mark called her that night and broke it off with her. She had a complete mental breakdown. And when her parents and my parents found out, they had a huge fight. It was like the whole world took sides. And to be honest, there weren't too many people on my side. I don't even think my own parents were on my side, to be honest. I think the whole state of Idaho hates me to this day. Anyway, after a few weeks, Mark started acting funny and all depressed. Who could blame him though? Jennifer would call him every day and cry her eyes out. So we broke up, but things weren't the same. My parents are still social outcasts. My name is mud. And I haven't been home in almost three years. I feel so guilty about everything that I won't even let my parents pay for college. They insist on paying for my apartment, but that's it. Which is a good thing because I love having my own room, and there's no way I could afford our place on my own. I'm starving as it is. By the way, thanks for dinner."

Micah nodded her head and speared a chunk of broccoli with her fork.

"You know, April, I hate to say this, but do you think

that maybe you're blowing this whole thing out of proportion? I mean, leaving home, changing your whole look and persona just because of a bad breakup? In my high school, if something crazy didn't happen every day, then something was wrong. What do you think, Lisa?" Micah asked.

Lisa took another sip of her soft drink and wiped the tears from her eyes, from all the coughing.

"April, why didn't you tell us this sooner? I mean, why hold all of this inside you? If you'd told us your big, dark, secret sooner, we could have saved you a lot of pain and guilt. Number one, you're acting like you single-handedly destroyed the Garden of Eden or something. Number two, Jennifer sounds like an evil witch who deserved a wake-up call. If those two were meant to be together, then now she won't take him for granted so much, will she? You probably did them both a favor. Number three, your parents are adults—they can handle their own problems. You don't need to take the weight of their problems on your shoulders. If Jennifer's parents are good people, they'll move on and won't blame your parents for someone else's decisions. Holy cow, what a soap opera," Lisa said and took one more sip.

April stared at Lisa, open-mouthed and unblinking.

"What?" Lisa asked with her mouth stuffed full of egg roll.

"You should have your own talk show or something. You have a lot of common sense. It's a good thing we have you around," Micah said.

Lisa turned red and blushed at the compliment.

"Do you think she's right? Am I acting stupid over this? Am I not as bad as I thought?" April asked, almost hopefully.

Micah pretended to consider the question thoughtfully but ruined it by laughing.

"April, you goof. You're not perfect. There was only one person on earth who was. And if the worst thing you've ever done is to steal the handsome prince away from the wicked witch, than you're a lot better than me."

April looked stunned.

Micah and Lisa exchanged grins. April was going to be all right.

"Are you guys serious? I mean, tell me the truth, are you just saying this because you're my roommates and you feel sorry for me, or do you really think maybe I could still be sort of a good person?" April asked quietly.

Micah sighed and set her fork down.

"Are you like one of those girls who gets a cheap thrill by going around and stealing everyone's boyfriend?"

April glared at her. "Of course not, who do you think I am?" she asked angrily.

"Are you some hormone-crazed woman who cares more about men than a good friendship?" Lisa asked with a straight face.

April slammed her hand down on the table and stood up.

"I am not! I did what I did because of special circumstances. My mistakes are not *who I am*. I am a good person!" April practically shouted.

Lisa and Micah laughed up at their roommate.

"Good. Then shut up and eat your dinner, it's getting cold."

April sunk down into her chair and laughed weakly.

"I've been an idiot, haven't I?" she asked.

Micah laughed and reached over to give her a hug.

"Yeah, but aren't we all? I think that's why God invented roommates," Micah said.

Lisa smiled and patted her mouth with her napkin.

"If life were just that easy. Heck, if I told you half the stuff I've done, you'd be shocked. Who would have thought our scary, tough roommate was really Molly Mormon? I still can't believe you're a stake president's daughter. Unreal,"

Lisa said, shaking her head with a smile.

April frowned at Lisa. "Excuse me, *I'm* Molly Mormon? Who are you then, Lisa, the Laurel president?"

Lisa laughed. "Not likely. Even chubby little me has made some mistakes. I used to steal money out of my dad's pants at night and go to the store and buy candy bars when no one was looking. How sad is that?" Lisa asked with a frown.

April laughed. "Sorry, but stealing quarters compared to stealing boyfriends is no comparison. Hands down, I win."

Micah frowned at both of them.

"Look, if this is a contest to see who's been the worst, then I'm afraid you both lose. No one can beat me," she said sadly.

April and Lisa's head's swiveled to Micah.

"You guys are hilarious, sitting here comparing your dark and murky pasts. The rebellious daughter of a stake president who hasn't even done anything wrong but has punished herself for years anyway. And the princess of her family, who feels guilty for taking her dad's change to buy herself a treat. Yeah, I'm really shocked here. I shouldn't even be sitting with you guys. You're too good for me," Micah said and surprised them all when a tear slipped down her cheek.

April and Lisa scooted their chairs closer to Micah's and looked expectantly at her. Micah sighed and reached for a napkin to wipe her eyes.

"I don't think I have a testimony of the Church," she said and then started to cry in earnest.

Lisa's mouth dropped open a foot, and April frowned and reached for Micah's hand.

"I just don't know what to believe anymore. I mean, look at my dad! He's not exactly temple worthy, is he? I'm getting the feeling that his testimony isn't so bright and shining.

They'll probably excommunicate him or something. I mean, what happened to 'families are forever'?" Micah said through her tears.

Lisa closed her mouth and looked at April with her eyebrows raised. April took a breath and patted her friend's hand.

"Micah, you aren't responsible for your dad's mistakes, just like my dad isn't responsible for mine. Your dad's testimony might not be what it should be, but that doesn't have to affect you or your testimony. There's nothing stopping you from having a strong, firm testimony of the Church. It's all up to you and whether or not you want it bad enough. Do you believe in God, Micah?" April asked.

Micah looked surprised by the question but nodded.

"Yes, I do," she said simply.

"Do you believe that Jesus Christ lived and that he died for us and was resurrected?" April continued.

Micah nodded her head firmly.

"Of course," she said.

April took a breath and asked her last question.

"Do you believe that Joseph Smith was a true prophet of God?"

Micah frowned and lowered her head as she thought about it. She had taken seminary in school and had gone to church almost every Sunday. She knew the story, and she had read the scriptures. But did she honestly believe that some young kid had seen an angel? Did she really believe that a fourteen-year-old boy had seen God and Jesus?

Micah closed her eyes as more tears slipped through her eyelashes.

"Sometimes yes, sometimes no," Micah said quietly.

April smiled and lifted Micah's chin up.

"Then that's a good start. We're set on refurbishing your outside and your inside—we might as well include your spiritual side too. Makes sense," April said.

Micah tried to smile back at April and Lisa, but her heart was still sick at what she had just voiced. It wasn't a new thing for her. She had lived with her doubts for so long that she was used to them. But what would it be like to really know? She wanted to know, for once and for all. She wanted to be free of the doubts.

"Well, so where do we go from here?" Micah asked.

Lisa grabbed the fortune cookies and passed them around the table.

"Start where I always start when I have a problem, with the priesthood," Lisa said and broke open her cookie.

April nodded in agreement. "She's right, Micah. You need to ask the bishop for a blessing. When you need help, you have to ask for it. This Sunday is the perfect time to ask. And, if you both agree, I think we should hold nightly scripture study together. We used to do it at home before I left. After dinner, we'd all gather around the table and read the scriptures and talk about it. What do you say?" April asked nervously.

Micah frowned. Scripture study? *Ugh!* The scriptures always put her to sleep. Why did she have to open her big mouth?

"Um, yeah, I guess so. If you really think that will help," Micah said doubtfully.

April grinned at Lisa. "Yeah, I think it will help."

Lisa nodded her head in agreement. "Yeah, Micah, that's, like, mandatory if you want a testimony."

Micah tried not to groan out loud. She wanted to change the subject before they came up with any other wonderful ideas on how to help her.

"Hey, what did your fortune cookie say?" she asked Lisa

Lisa held hers up and read it.

"'You will find happiness and success just around the corner.' What's yours?" she asked.

Micah broke her cookie open and read hers out loud.

"'You will find happiness and success just around the corner,'" she said and laughed.

April grinned and broke hers open.

"'You will find happiness and success just around the corner.' I think they got a good deal on these fortune cookies, what do you think?" April said, giggling.

Lisa laughed and grabbed all the little papers from her roommates. "What if it's true, for all of us? I'm going to frame these with a picture of us. We're all looking pretty good tonight, let's go hit that little photo booth. We can all squeeze in. My treat."

The girls threw away their trash and followed Lisa to a small photo booth on the second level of the mall and squeezed in, smiling and giggling. Micah had never done this before. It was kind of fun. Five pictures were taken quickly as the three girls giggled and smiled and posed for the camera. Five minutes later they had the snapshots in hand.

"Hey, we're gorgeous!" Lisa said in a surprised voice.

"Yeah, we're not so bad, are we?" April said, sounding stunned.

Micah took the pictures and looked at the three smiling girls critically. They did look pretty good.

"What did you guys expect?" she asked. "We are young, smart, attractive women. Now let's go find something cute to wear for our dates Friday," she said and walked off without looking back. Lisa and April ran to keep up with her. Micah grinned at her two roommates as they devoured the mall. She was starting to think that maybe it wasn't an accident that she happened to have these two girls as her roommates. Maybe Heavenly Father had something to do with this. She smiled and grabbed a shirt off the rack and followed April and Lisa into the changing room.

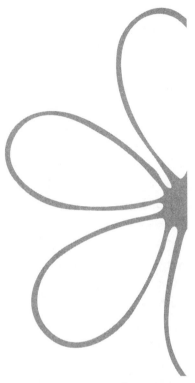

 chapter seventeen

April said good night to her roommates and walked into her room, shutting her door quietly behind her. She had told Micah and Lisa that she was tired, but what she really wanted to do was think. She put her purse on the dresser and walked over to her bed. She lay down and plumped up her pillow beneath her head. She looked up at the picture of Jesus that was hanging on the wall to her left and focused on it. She felt immediately peaceful and calm. She closed her eyes and took a deep breath.

Why had just sitting down and talking to her roommates about what had happened back home made her feel so much better about herself? Why did she feel so cleansed and so free, as if she had just been let out of prison? And why was it her roommates instead of her parents who had done the freeing? Why hadn't her parents ever sat her down even once and told her that she was okay . . . that even though things had gone bad, that didn't make her a bad person?

April frowned and reached up to massage her temples. Was it because they thought she was bad? They'd never gone to any trouble to help her think otherwise. The heaviness of the guilt she had been carrying around for the past few years had been so tiring and painful. She felt so different tonight. She felt like a new person—or like the person she remembered she always was.

April sighed and turned over on her stomach. She didn't want to think bad thoughts about her parents. She was so tired of blaming herself, she didn't want to turn around and start blaming other people now. But the thought that maybe her parents had kept her in her own little prison of guilt for some strange reason was causing her heart to hurt in a new way. And she was tired of hurting, *period*. She needed to talk to her parents. She wanted to be done with this once and for all.

April turned on her side and reached for her cell phone. She quickly dialed her home phone number and waited.

"Hello?"

April smiled, it was her younger sister, Karen.

"Hey, Kare, it's April. Is Mom or Dad around?" April asked.

"Yeah, Mom's right here. Hold on," Karen said.

April waited nervously as her little sister got her mom on the phone. How should she even go about this?

"Hello, honey! How are you?" said April's mom.

"Hey, Mom. I'm doing good. Actually that's why I'm calling, I just kind of wanted to touch bases with you guys and tell you what's been going on in my life." And to check up on their lives, while she was at it.

"Oh, good. We were just talking about you at dinner and wondering what you were up to. We're so bored here, hopefully you have more of a social life than we do."

April took a breath and closed her eyes.

"Well, I have a date this Friday night with a really nice guy. I'm kind of excited about it. It's kind of the first real date I've had in a while," April said, leaving it open for any comments on the past her mom might want to make. There was a slight pause on the other end of the line.

"Well, honey, that's wonderful. I bet you'll have a lot of fun. Is this boy of yours, like . . . I mean, does he dress like, um . . . you?" her mom asked diplomatically.

April smiled and leaned back on her pillow. "Well, you haven't seen me in a while, Mom. I look kind of like I used to. My hair is a little bit shorter, but it's kind of cute and flippy now. It's brown with shades of amber and honey in it, and I just love it. And my roommate, well, she's kind of well-off, and she just decided to buy herself a whole new wardrobe and she gave me all of her old stuff, so I'm actually dressed better than I've ever been. But this guy I'm going out with, he's just so cool, Mom. I wish you could meet him, so you could see for yourself," April said, sounding like a teenager going out for the very first time.

"Oh. Well, that's so generous of your roommate. She must be a really nice person to do that. But this just doesn't sound like you, honey. What's going on?"

April frowned. *What was that supposed to mean?*

"What doesn't sound like me, Mom? What am I supposed to sound like?" April asked. There was another long pause on the other end of the phone.

"Well, you know, dear. Ever since everything fell apart here, you've been on your own little path. Are you saying you're ready to come back to the straight and narrow? Have you repented?" her mom asked.

April felt as if every good feeling she had felt during the

last few hours had been immediately sucked out of her soul.

"What exactly do I need to repent of, Mom? Be specific now because sometimes I'm a little slow," April said with a touch of steel in her voice.

"Well, ruining our relationship with the Johnsons, of course. You know what happened, April. Why do we need to go over all of this again? You know what you did. I don't want to get in a fight with you, I was just asking whether or not you've decided to change."

April covered her eyes with her hands and put the phone on her chest for a moment. This was why she hadn't been home. This was why she wouldn't accept money for school from her parents. But did she have to put up with it any-more? If her roommates were listening to this, what would they say? April said a silent prayer in her heart and put the phone to her ear again.

"Are you there, April? Are you there?" she could hear her mother say on the other line.

"Yes, Mom. I'm right here. Look, I think I need to set you straight. You're under the misconception that you have a prodigal daughter. I let you believe that, for the reason of the guilt that you so readily heaped on me. But I'm kind of over feeling guilty now. Three years is plenty for anyone. What happened between me and Mark was a mistake. But that mistake had nothing to do with my testimony, or whether or not I'm a good person. I happen to believe that *I am* a good person. You don't know all the details of the situation, so I'll give you a little break. I know this affected your relationship with your friends and neighbors, but that's something that as adults you need to deal with and move on. I can't take responsibility for your social life anymore. If you can't make up with them, then for heaven's sake, go find some new friends. Sitting at home moaning about how it used to be is old and depressing. Pick yourself up and move on because life is passing you by. And further, I plan on coming home for Christmas. I haven't seen my little brothers and sisters in too long, and it's time. If that's too embarrassing for you, then tough. I'm your daughter. I should matter more to you. Good-bye."

And she hung up on her mother. April stared at the phone in her hand and burst into tears. Why hadn't that gone better? Why couldn't she have stayed cool and calm? Now what would her parents think of her? April groaned and buried her face in her arms. She had been feeling so good about herself. Why did five minutes on the phone with her mom have to always devastate her?

chapter eighteen

Micah spread out some of her new clothes on her bed and looked them over with a grin on her face. They were so cool and fun and young. She had been waiting her whole life to wear clothes like this. And now she could. She hated to think what her dad would say if he saw what she had purchased—with his money—but since his wife's choice in attire was so far on the opposite side of the spectrum, she couldn't picture him having the guts to voice any objections.

Now, which outfit would she wear Friday to go out with Bryce? She looked over her selections, smiling. There really wasn't a bad choice. The faded denim capri pants with the simple lime green T-shirt, or the long denim skirt with snaps up the front and the white tailored shirt with the large cuffs? No, definitely the white cropped pants with the bright red T-shirt.

Micah laughed softly as she looked at every color of T-shirt she had bought that night. It looked like a rainbow on her bed. She hadn't worn a simple T-shirt in so long, she was actually excited about it. She didn't know what her dad had against regular T-shirts, but she had practically been forbidden to wear them. Her father hadn't wanted her to look too casual or sloppy. He was always going on and on about giving people the right impression. Micah grabbed an armful and hugged them to herself. She felt good—she felt so good for once in her life. She quickly laid the clothes down and folded them neatly to put them away. She wanted to change into the new pajamas she had bought that night. They were so cute. They were a soft, brushed cotton with clouds and angels splattered across them. They were so young and fun—something she had never been. But now that was going to change. Micah quickly put the rest of her clothes away and was just slipping the top to her pajamas on when there's was a quick, hard tap on her door.

"Micah? There's someone at the door for you. Um, I think you should hurry," came Lisa's voice through the door.

Micah slipped the bottoms on and whisked her fingers through her hair. She opened her door and walked into the family room to find Lisa looking nervous and kind of . . . what? *Scared?* What in the world?

"Hey, Micah. Well, Kathy said you were a looker, but I didn't believe her. She says that about our grandma too. I'm Rod—your new uncle. I thought I better come over and get acquainted. Man, am I glad I did."

Micah felt all color drain from her face as she turned to see a large, tall, dark man—at least thirty—who was standing in her family room, staring at her as if she were a piece of candy and he was a hungry trick-or-treater. His dark hair was worn long and feathered back. *Ick.* And his five o'clock shadow was at least a day old. He was wearing tight jeans and a tank top, a gold pinky ring, a gold necklace around his neck, and two earrings in his right ear. His name was Rod, and he was her new uncle. *Please—please!—no,* she thought wildly.

"Um, hi, nice to meet you. Kathy didn't mention you, Rod. Was she supposed to call me and let me know that you were coming over? Because I wasn't exactly expecting anyone. I was kind of going to bed," Micah said in a voice that shook only slightly.

Rod walked closer to her and grabbed her hand.

"Nah, Kathy didn't know I was coming over. She's already in Vegas. I took it on myself as part of your new family to come and welcome you into the fold. You should be glad I got here before Mike. If he comes sniffing around here, you tell him I got first dibs. You got that? Hey, why don't you go get changed and we can go get something to eat and get to know each other a little better?" Rod asked, moving even closer and grabbing her other hand.

Micah heard a squeak to her left and whipped her head around to pierce Lisa with a look begging for help. Lisa scrambled down the hallway toward April's room. Micah hoped that April would come quickly. She had a presence and a strength about her that made people stop and take notice. Hopefully she had enough presence to kick this guy out of their apartment because she wasn't sure she did.

"Um, Rod, I'm sorry, but I don't think so. And as my new uncle, I really don't think that that would be appropriate. I'm pretty sure my father would not approve of this," she said, hoping that using her father's name would put some distance between them.

Rod laughed and dragged her toward the couch, where he pulled her down to sit beside him. She tried to scoot away, but every time she moved, he moved too. She was starting to get scared.

"Old Phillip doesn't care about anything right now except Kathy. And that's the way she likes things. I don't think that's going to change for a long, long time. And in the meantime, I say, we have some fun. Just you and me," Rod said with a look that was supposed to be sexy but just turned Micah's stomach to acid.

"No. I'm telling you no. I don't want to get to know you any better, and as a matter of fact, I want you leave right now. I'm going to bed—I have an early class tomorrow, and I just don't have time for this. Good-bye, Rod," Micah said in the firmest voice she had ever used in her life.

Rod tilted his head to the right and studied her as if he were trying to figure out if she were bluffing or not. She pulled her fingers out of his hands and stood up, quickly moving back from him.

"Now, that's not very friendly, Micah. I don't think Kathy would like to know that her new stepdaughter was being rude to her favorite brother. Nope, I don't. She'd probably complain to your daddy about your bad attitude. And what Kathy doesn't like, your daddy doesn't like. Am I right?" Rod asked, frowning menacingly at her.

Micah stared at him in horror. Was this for real? She felt rather than saw Lisa and April take their places on either side of her.

"Well, then, Rod, it's a good thing Micah isn't her daddy's little girl anymore, isn't it? Phillip has his own life and Micah has hers. And you don't have a place in her life at all. And I really don't think Micah's boyfriend *Bryce* would approve of some guy coming in here uninvited and trying to pressure Micah into something she obviously doesn't want— *you*. Now, I just called Bryce to come over. So if I were you, I'd hit the road—now," April said in a voice much firmer and stronger than Micah's had been.

Micah watched Rod take in everything April said, and

since he got up off the couch and moved to the door, he had obviously made the decision that April wasn't bluffing. He reached for the doorknob and looked back at Micah, sneering and obviously very angry.

"Don't think you've seen the last of me. Kathy found her jackpot, and so will I—you're it. You better start getting used to it."

Rod swung the door open, looking left and right for any angry boyfriend who might be coming, and left as quickly as he had come.

Micah rushed to the door and slammed it shut, locking both locks and checking them twice.

"Oh, my heck!" she said in a weak voice, sagging on the floor and looking up at Lisa and April in shock. "Did that really just happen? *To me?*" Micah asked.

April walked over to the window and pulled the curtain aside to see if Rod had really gone.

"I think we should call the police and make a report. If he comes back we can apply for a restraining order. That guy was insane. And he obviously really liked you. Not a good combination," April said, still looking intently into the dark.

Lisa patted her heart with her hand. "I've never been so scared in my life as when he barged into our apartment. I thought we were all goners. I can't believe he's your *uncle*, Micah," she said weakly.

Micah shook her head and started to laugh almost hysterically. "My uncle. That was my new uncle, thanks to my dad. Thank you, Dad!" she shouted to no one.

April looked over at Micah still sitting on the floor and gave her a crooked grin.

"Micah, you may have your problems, but at least you're not boring."

Micah smiled and pushed herself up. "Same at ya," she said, making April laugh.

A loud knock on the door made all three girls scream.

"It's him, you guys, call the police!" Micah squeaked and ran to the other side of the room, looking under the cushions for the phone.

April walked quickly over to the door and looked through the peephole. "Relax, it's Bryce. I really did call him." She quickly opened the door to Bryce and Joel and moved over to let them in, running a hand nervously through her hair.

Micah walked slowly over to the two men, feeling very awkward and even more embarrassed.

"Wow, you guys came over to help. That's, really . . . really nice," she said lamely.

Bryce and Joel exchanged unsmiling looks and looked around the apartment suspiciously.

"What's going on, Micah?" Bryce asked, staring at her.

Micah shifted on her feet and cleared her throat.

"Well, I'm sure April told you over the phone, but we had a guest here who was unwelcome and didn't really want to leave. But April was able to finally get him to go. He, um, well, he's gone now. So thanks guys, you can leave now. Everything's okay."

Joel, who had been staring at April, tore his gaze away and focused on Micah.

"I don't think so. Some guy came over here and wouldn't leave? Something's going on here. Who was he and what did he want?" Joel asked.

Lisa stepped into his line of vision and clasped her hands nervously.

"His name was Rod and he wanted, um . . . he wanted Micah to go out with him, but she didn't want to, and he didn't understand that. I think," she said and then moved to sit down on the couch.

Micah looked down at her bare feet, even more embarrassed now. Lisa had made it sound like she had a stalker or something. *Great—now what is Bryce going to think?*

"Well, actually, he's my new uncle. My dad is getting

remarried tomorrow and his new wife's brother came over to introduce himself, and he just kind of—um. He just sort of acted a little funny. We were kind of worried and that's why April called you," Micah said, sounding unsure.

Bryce frowned and walked over to the bar stool by the kitchen bar and sat down, folding his arms over his chest. Joel, who had gone back to staring at April, still stood in the entryway. April was looking down at her feet now, her cheeks very red. Micah smiled at the picture the two of them made. It was kind of funny to see some cool guy knocked off his feet by a cute girl.

"Micah? I asked you a question. What exactly did he say to you that upset you?" Bryce asked in an irritated voice.

Micah frowned. He was acting like some policeman or something. He was supposed to be sympathetic and comforting. He obviously wasn't knocked off his feet by *her* makeover.

"He said something about wanting to hit the jackpot like his sister did with my dad and that we should go get something to eat and get to know each other better. I told him no, but he didn't believe me or something. He acted like he wanted to go out on a date. It was kind of creepy," she said, being completely honest.

Bryce frowned even deeper and looked to Joel. Joel was no help at all.

"How old was this guy? Did he act like he would get physical with you? Did he touch you or try to pressure you at all?" Bryce asked, continuing with the interrogation.

Micah sighed and rubbed her arms. Just thinking about what happened made her feel gross.

"He was probably around thirty, and yeah, he did touch me. He kept grabbing my hands and trying to stand right next to me or sit down really close to me. He didn't seem to want to listen to me when I told him no. It was like he was going to get his way, and it didn't matter what I thought or wanted. He was pretty scary. April thinks we should call the police and file a report. But the thing is, my dad is getting married tomorrow! I can't cause problems with his new family. He'd kill me. Putting a restraining order on my new uncle is no way to start a relationship with my new stepmother," Micah said.

Bryce raised his eyebrows in surprise and rubbed his hand through his hair as he thought about her situation.

"He said he wanted to hit the jackpot like his sister did with your dad. So he came over for the money, but when he saw how pretty you were, he changed his mind. Now he wants the money *and* you. This doesn't sound like a man you want to get involved with, Micah. I think you *should* file a report with the police. Or better yet, call your dad and have your dad put a stop to this," Bryce said, looking worried.

Micah shook her head quickly. "No way. My dad's getting ready to go on his honeymoon. He won't even be back for a month! And like I said, if I file a report, my dad will kill me. Rod will probably say something like he came over to be nice and get to know me and make *me* look like the bad guy. No. I can't do anything yet. But at least April scared him. I should be okay. And if he does come back, then I'll think about calling the police. I promise," Micah said firmly.

Bryce rubbed his hand over his mouth and shook his head.

"If you were my sister, I wouldn't like this one bit. He could grab you on your way to the parking lot. He could be dangerous, Micah," Bryce said, and stood up.

Joel took his eyes off April and swiveled to Micah.

"So, what exactly did April say to scare this guy off?" he asked curiously.

Micah blushed even brighter than April and walked over to the kitchen area to get a drink of water.

"Oh, I can't remember," she mumbled, hoping he would let it go.

"April told him that she had called Micah's boyfriend and that he was coming over right now. She told him that the boyfriend wouldn't like some guy trying to pressure her to go out with him. And that's when he left," Lisa volunteered helpfully.

Micah groaned softly and turned the water on, leaving her back to the group standing in her family room. Why was this happening to her? She had been having such a nice day.

"Boyfriend, huh?" Bryce said, sounding amused.

Micah frowned but kept drinking the water as if her life depended on it.

"That wouldn't happen to be *me*, would it, Micah?" Bryce asked, walking up behind her.

Micah turned slowly to face him. He was teasing her, she knew, but she wasn't used to being teased, and she just didn't know how to handle it. She was just too embarrassed to even think straight.

"Well, of course you're not my boyfriend. I mean, we have a date Friday, but that doesn't imply a commitment on your part by any means, and I wouldn't want you to feel like I thought you *were* or anything. I mean, of course not. No, you're not my boyfriend. I don't know who April meant," she finished, turning even brighter red as everyone turned to stare at her.

Bryce laughed and took the water glass out of her hands, placing it on the counter.

"Relax, Micah. I'm glad she called me. And I want you to call me if this guy comes back. No matter what. Promise?" Bryce asked, still smiling at her.

Micah gulped and stared up into Bryce's laughing green eyes and felt wonderful again.

"I promise," she said softly.

Bryce reached a hand out and moved a wisp of hair out of her eyes, just like he had done the first time he had met her.

"I like what you did with your hair. It looks really good

on you," he said, still smiling down at her.

Micah couldn't help smiling back at him.

"Thanks. We all got a makeover today. I think Lisa's hair turned out pretty too, but April's makeover was the best I think."

Bryce turned to look at April and did a double take.

"That's April? I thought that was some other roommate of yours or something. April? I don't believe it," Bryce said, walking over to where April was still standing by the front door.

April, if it was possible, blushed an even deeper shade of red.

"Yeah, it's me. The real me, anyway. I guess I needed a change or something," she said, trying to sound nonchalant.

Joel leaned on the wall next to her and smiled.

"I love what you did with your hair. I mean, I always thought you were pretty, but now, you're just . . . beautiful," he said sincerely.

April's mouth dropped open as she stared back at Joel.

"That's the nicest thing anyone's ever said to me. Thank you," she said, still looking shocked.

Lisa got up off the couch and walked over to join the group.

"She is beautiful, huh? We are going to have too much fun Friday. Aren't we?" she said enthusiastically.

Joel and Bryce turned to smile at Lisa and nodded their heads in agreement.

Bryce reached for the door.

"I'm definitely looking forward to Friday. Unless we hear from you sooner, we'll see you then," he said and opened the door.

Joel followed Bryce out the door but turned back around to smile at April one more time.

"Bye, gorgeous," he said and walked out.

April shut the door behind the two men and turned to

look at her two roommates, looking awestruck and slightly confused.

"Did he just call *me* gorgeous? *Me?*" she asked.

Micah laughed and sat down on the couch, pulling her feet up and putting her arms around her knees.

"Of course he was talking to you. He didn't even look at anyone else in the room. I've never seen a man's tongue hang out like that before. I believe Joel is smitten. What do you think, Lisa?" Micah asked, still grinning.

Lisa joined her on the couch and grinned over at April too.

"I would have to say that April is going to have a very romantic date this Friday. Joel couldn't take his eyes off her. It was so sweet," she said, laughing at April's stunned expression.

"No one's ever looked at me that way before. He called me beautiful. He called me gorgeous. The man has to be either blind or insane," she said, clearly hoping he was neither.

Micah laughed and Lisa snorted.

"You idiot. Haven't you looked in the mirror? You look like Jennifer Aniston when she had short hair. *Of course* Joel is blown over. And the neat thing about him is that he always thought you were pretty. Did you hear him? He's always liked you, but now he *really* likes you," Micah said.

Lisa frowned. "Great, you guys are going to have a wonderful time Friday. I still don't even know if Corbin is even going to show up. And even if he does, I bet you a million dollars he won't fall all over himself at the sight of me, or look at me like I'm the only woman in the world, like Bryce does to Micah. It's kind of depressing," she said frankly.

April and Micah exchanged a quick look. Micah sat up straighter and grabbed a pillow to hug.

"Look, Lisa. Friday is just one date. Maybe Corbin isn't the man for you. But let's just get through this date, and then we'll focus on finding someone who can't live without you."

Lisa rolled her eyes and looked to April. April smiled encouragingly at her.

"Friday is going to be fun, whether Corbin shows up or not. Who needs a man to have fun, anyway?" April asked.

"That's easy for you to say, but I'll relax. If it happens, it happens. If not, then I'll just keep looking. And in the meantime, I'll keep doing yoga and doing that diet you told me about. Things are going to change around here," she said and then got up from the couch, waving good night to April and Micah.

Micah frowned as April sat down beside her.

"If Corbin ruins this for her, I'm going to have to kill him," Micah said.

April nodded in agreement. "We can always set her up with Rod if Corbin backs out. I think he's in the market."

Micah giggled and shook her head. "Lisa has better taste than that, I'm sure."

April sighed and leaned her head back against the couch. At least she had been so busy during the last hour that she hadn't thought once about her conversation with her mom. And Joel's reaction to her hair had made her feel like a million bucks again. But her heart still hurt. Maybe it always would.

"Can you be happy and sad all at the same time, Micah?" she asked

Micah looked closely at her roommate before answering.

"I know you called your parents. Were they mean to you again?" she asked bluntly.

April's eyes widened in surprise. How could Micah know that?

"What do you mean?" she asked, trying to divert the question.

"Look, April, every time you get off the phone with your parents you're depressed. I've seen it all summer long. I guess it's none of my business though."

April smiled weakly. "Well, you might be right. But since we're doing this whole transformation thing together, I guess part of my transformation will be trying to figure out how to not let my parents' low opinion of me affect my opinion of myself. I'm pretty sure that's impossible though," April said sadly.

Micah frowned and brushed the hair out of her eyes.

"I kind of have your same problem. I guess what we have to do is maybe try to see ourselves through Heavenly Father's eyes and forget what everybody else thinks. Maybe his opinion is the only one that should count," Micah said.

April grinned over at her. "Well, for someone who has a shaky testimony, you just hit one out of the ballpark."

Micah grinned back at April and stood up.

"Maybe I'm not as shaky as I thought. Maybe you're not as bad as you think, and maybe we're both a whole lot more awesome than anyone's ever thought before. But I think before this year is out, we're going to surprise everyone."

April got up off the couch and did something she had never done. She gave Micah a hug.

"You are one great roommate, Micah. Good night."

Micah watched April go into her room and smiled. In one week, she had gained a new mother, a new hairstyle, a new wardrobe, and watched two roommates turn into two good friends. Disasters and blessings were starting to look strangely similar.

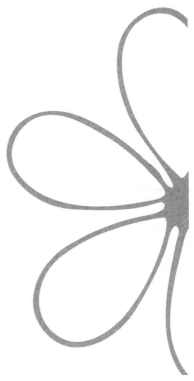

chapter nineteen

Micah turned around in front of her mirror and frowned at the image looking back at her. She was really going on a date. And not just any old boring date her dad had set up for her. No, she was going out with Bryce. The one guy she had been wanting to go out with ever since she had met him. Would he like the new Micah? He had certainly seemed to like her new haircut. But would he like the inside stuff too? She frowned and knew she had no idea.

Well, tonight was the night she'd been waiting all week for. She had gone to class, done yoga, ate dinner, studied— everything. But it was all something that she'd had to do to get to this point. She hated that she was looking forward to this date so much. There was no way Bryce would really like her or anything—just the hope that *maybe* he would made her feel nervous—and wonderful and horrible all at the same time.

Micah put on some lip gloss, shook her hair out with her hands, and turned away from the mirror. She was tired of analyzing herself. He either liked her or he didn't. Either way, she was going out for a nice dinner, and she hadn't done that in a long, long time. Besides that, she would have Lisa and April with her, and she always had a good time with them. So there was really no way she could have a bad time. She smiled as she mentally patted herself on the back and walked out into the family room to wait with her room-mates.

"Hey, guys, how much time do we have?" she asked April and Lisa.

April put the book down that she had been reading and glanced at her watch.

"About ten minutes unless they're early. You look nice. You're going for the natural, 'I'm too good-looking to have to try that hard' look, huh? I went for the 'please fall madly in love with me' look—red lip gloss and perfume. Lisa is going for the 'I'm me, proud to be me, and I don't want to look like you' look. I think we're all stunning," April said with a smile at the two girls.

Lisa smiled hopefully back. "Really? I look good? Thanks, April. I think you both look beautiful. And I was going to wait to tell you guys later, but I weighed myself today, and guess what? I lost three pounds! Can you believe that? I really do feel thinner. It's amazing," she said with a giggle.

Micah walked over, hugged Lisa, and sat down beside her on the couch.

"That is so awesome, Lisa. Most people gain weight at first because they're gaining muscle and muscle weighs

more than fat, so you must really be sticking to your diet.
I'm so proud of you," she said.

Lisa looked stunned and even happier as she took in
what Micah had said.

April nodded her head in agreement. "Yep, you are one
determined person, Lisa. Truly impressive."

Micah grabbed an old magazine and thumbed through
it without seeing anything. She was just so nervous! What
was she even going to say to Bryce? He would probably be
bored to death with her.

"Stop worrying, you idiot. You're going to have a fun
time tonight. Relax," April said without looking up from
her book.

Micah laughed and put the magazine down. "I know. I
really need to relax, but it's like the first date I've been on
where I might actually like the guy. Imagine going out on
dates with these strange guys that your dad is always setting you up with. Dating to me has always been about being
very uncomfortable, very bored, and very disappointed.
And just the fact that Bryce is so nice and wonderful and
good-looking just scares me to death—plain and simple. I'm
scared to death," Micah said honestly.

April put her book down and looked at Micah.

"Well, at least you have something to compare it to,
even if it's bad. I've never even been on a date. I would invite
Mark to come over and study at my house and sometimes
he'd stay and eat dinner with my family, but he never took
me to the movies or out to dinner. He was always scared he'd
run into someone who would tell Jennifer. This is officially
my first date. How pathetic is that?" April asked, sounding
as scared as Micah.

Lisa looked at her in surprise.

"You mean, I've been on more dates than both of you?
You mean you didn't even go to prom? I can't believe it,"
Lisa said.

Micah's eyebrows went up in surprise. "You have got to be kidding me. I mean, why? You are so cute and smart and funny. What about before Mark? Didn't you date before him? I thought that all happened in your senior year—what about your junior year?" she asked curiously.

April frowned and leaned her head back against the couch.

"Being the stake president's daughter, I had to set a good example for everyone. I went on a few *group* dates with some friends, but it wasn't like I was with a certain boy. I felt that if I waited until I was eighteen to single-date, then that would be appropriate," she said.

Micah and Lisa exchanged looks before erupting into giggles.

"Sorry, April, but this is just so weird. All this time I thought you were some wild biker chick or something, who had a drug problem or morality issues, and you're like a nun," Micah said, still laughing.

Lisa wiped tears from her eyes. "Appropriate? You wanted to be appropriate? April, you are something else. I don't think Joel has any idea what he's got himself into. He thinks he's going out with some reformed rebel. He doesn't know what he's in for. Wow, is he in for a surprise!" she said.

April glared at her roommates and stood up. "Look, guys, you don't need to laugh at me. I was just being honest with you. And if you say anything to embarrass me tonight, I'll kill you both. Got it?" she said menacingly.

Micah smiled up at April. "Now that's the real April. Tough as nails and as kind *and* as good as anyone you'll ever find. Don't be nervous about tonight, April. We'll be with you," she said.

April's shoulders sagged, and she sat back down. "Easier said than done. But—"

Ding-dong.

The girls jumped as the doorbell sounded.

Lisa looked at her nervous roommates and walked over to open the door.

"Honestly, you guys have got to get a grip. This is just a date," she said and opened the door.

Corbin was standing on the doorstep, frowning, with his hands in his pockets. Lisa smiled hopefully and opened the door wide open.

"Hi, Corbin. Come on in. Bryce and Joel aren't here yet."

Corbin looked up at Lisa and did a tiny double take. His frown lessened fractionally as he tilted his head and studied her like he would a petri dish.

"Have you done something different, Lisa? You look . . . you look kind of good," he said lamely.

Lisa frowned at Corbin's compliment and stepped aside so he could walk in.

"Well, we all had mini-makeovers a few days ago. I got a new hairstyle. Do you like it?" she asked, turning around in a circle to show off her wavy new hair.

Corbin walked into the apartment and looked her up and down. Lisa blushed and looked to Micah and April in embarrassment.

"Well, yeah. I think you look great. I wasn't really expecting . . . I mean, yeah. You look great," he said and smiled at her.

Lisa thought about it and then smiled back. Micah and April shared a look of surprise with each other—and then the doorbell sounded again. This time, they knew it was for them. Since Corbin was right there, he reached over and opened the door. But it wasn't Bryce and it wasn't Joel. It was *Rod.*

Micah felt her skin go cold and clammy almost instantly. April's smile turned to a quick snarl, and Lisa stepped quickly behind Corbin.

"Hey, Micah, I see you're ready for our date. Perfect. Let's go," he said, shouldering past a stunned Corbin. April even looked too shocked to say anything.

Micah looked around at her friends and then squared her shoulders. This was her first real date, and she wasn't about to let this loser mess it up for her.

"Rod, *please* leave. I'm getting ready to go out," she said as firmly as she could.

Rod looked Corbin up and down with a sneer and puffed out his chest menacingly.

"*This* is the guy you're turning me down for? You've got to be kidding me," he said, his voice turning into a growl.

"No, *I'm* the guy she's turning you down for," Bryce said from the doorway, with Joel standing right next to him. They both looked mean and ready to do whatever it took.

Rod's eyebrows shot up, and he held his hands up innocently. Although Rod was more muscular, he had to tilt his chin up to look Bryce in the eyes. He didn't like that.

"Hey, guys, no problem. I was just leaving. I came by to ask Micah if she wanted to go do somethin', but obviously she has other plans," he said.

Rod shot a dark look at Micah and then walked toward the door. Bryce and Joel didn't budge.

"The problem is, you just don't get it. She shouldn't have to tell you more than once that she's not interested. Now get it through your head—don't come back," Bryce said without blinking.

Rod laughed in his face. "You think you're that tough, huh? I don't think so. You want to start something, go ahead. Let's see what you got. And after I'm done with you, we'll see who Micah thinks is the better man," Rod said, bunching up his hands into tight fists.

Bryce shouldered past Rod and reached for the phone on the kitchen bar. He dialed 9–1-1 smoothly and turned to smile at Rod.

"Yes, hello. I'm at my girlfriend's house, and this guy who has been asked on more than one occasion to leave, *won't*. We would like to file a complaint and a restraining order if possible. And can you please send a squad car over? He's still here."

Micah felt her mouth drop open and turned to see the look of horror on Rod's face. He was just as shocked. He turned quickly and ran for the door, shoving past Joel.

Joel clapped his hands theatrically and grinned. "Well done, bro—effective but not messy."

Bryce hung up the phone and turned to smile at the three girls, still staring at him.

"I didn't really call. Micah said she didn't want to upset her dad. But at least Rod will think we did. Hopefully just the threat of a restraining order will scare him off. If not, then we'll have to do the real thing. But at least this gives him the chance to wake up."

Micah closed her mouth and smiled at Bryce. On the phone he had said *his girlfriend's house.* This was the best date she'd ever been on.

"Come on, you guys, let's go. We have reservations in fifteen minutes," Joel said and took April's hand in his, pulling her out the door.

Micah smiled and grabbed her purse off the stool. She followed Lisa and Corbin through the door.

"Hold up, Micah. Why don't you lock your door? I don't think we should chance it," Bryce said.

Micah's smile slipped a notch as she took her keys out and locked the dead bolt. She turned around and looked up into Bryce's eyes. Her worry disappeared as he smiled down at her.

"Don't worry, Micah. He's gone now. By the way, you look great tonight," he said and clasped her hand in his, pulling her toward the others.

Micah felt her face go warm, and she hoped she wasn't

blushing like April. He was holding her hand! She'd never even held hands with a boy before. It felt so nice. Bryce had large, strong hands. After a few seconds though, she forgot about being embarrassed and concentrated on keeping up with Bryce. She took two steps for just one of his.

They caught up with the others quickly and squeezed into Joel's bright yellow Hummer. As they drove out of the parking lot, Micah thought she saw the large, menacing form of Rod walk quickly behind a tree, but she quickly put it out of her mind. She was just being paranoid. If he was smart, he was long gone by now. Besides, it was time to have fun now. She didn't want to waste one more second of her life on Rod.

Micah cleared her throat in embarrassment as she was squeezed up tightly against Bryce's side. She tried to scoot closer to the window to give him more room, but there was really nowhere to go. She glared at Corbin, who was hogging more than his share of the space. Bryce put an arm around Micah's shoulder and turned her chin, so she was forced to look up at him.

"Are you okay?"

Micah tried to relax, even though she was squished and just happened to have Bryce's arm around her.

"Well, he does make me a little nervous. But every time he's come over, I've had people with me. I'm kind of worried about what he'll do if he catches me by myself," she said, voicing her real concern.

Bryce frowned and pulled her in closer to his chest.

"Micah, I'm serious, if he comes around even one more time, you have to file a complaint. I don't care what your dad says or does—your safety should come first."

Micah sighed. She could just picture her dad coming home early from his honeymoon *just* because of her. Besides which, he'd see her new hairstyle and her new clothes, and he might even find out about her change in classes at school.

Nope, her dad would not be happy.

"Hey, don't worry about it. Let's forget about Rod. Let's just have fun tonight, okay?" Bryce said, smiling down at her.

Micah tried to smile back but felt nervous all of a sudden, and it didn't have anything to do with holding hands. Her dad was going to come home eventually. Would she ever be ready for that? Micah turned away from Bryce's stare and looked forward at April and Joel. The two front seats were bucket seats, but Joel still had April's hand locked in his, happily swinging away. Micah smiled; she could tell by the side of April's face that she was grinning her head off. Micah smothered a giggle.

"They're great together, huh?" Bryce said, leaning down to whisper in her ear.

Micah smiled at Bryce. "Yeah. They're the perfect couple."

Bryce leaned down again. "What about you and me? I thought we were the perfect couple."

Micah gulped and looked up to see if Bryce was joking. He looked serious. How could he be serious? This was their first date. But wouldn't that be nice? To be part of a couple. She'd never been a part of anything.

"Um, well, I don't know. Why don't we see how tonight goes, and then if you want to go out again . . ." she said, letting her sentence drop as she noticed Bryce's eyes were twinkling. He had been kidding her! *Oh, how embarrassing.* She dropped her eyes and groaned inwardly. Only she would be such an idiot.

"Of course we're going out again. This is only one of many, many dates you and I are going on. I have a good feeling about us, Micah. Very good," Bryce said and clasped her hand firmly in his.

Micah melted into a large pool of bubbly happiness. She was in heaven.

* * *

After making it to the restaurant, the three girls excused themselves to the restroom while the guys waited to be seated. After shutting the door, all three girls looked at each other and started giggling.

"I'm sorry, but tell me Joel isn't the most gorgeous man in the whole world. Did you see him hold my hand! I'm dying of happiness. Oh, I can't believe it," April said, patting her cheeks and trying to calm down.

Micah walked around to the back of April and fluffed her hair in places, making sure it looked just right.

"Joel is cute, April. *Definitely*. You deserve this. Just don't get anything stuck in your teeth during dinner," Micah said, still laughing.

Lisa checked her makeup in the mirror and smiled sadly at the two other girls.

"Umm, April wasn't the only one holding hands," she said.

Micah blushed as April turned and stared at her.

"No way. Bryce held your hand? That is so awesome. Do you like him, Micah? I mean, really?"

Micah pretended to fix her lip gloss but couldn't stop from grinning.

"Yeah, I've always liked him. My dad didn't approve, but now that my dad's out of the picture, I'm sure things are going to work out. My life will finally be my own," she said to April and Lisa.

April beamed at her and Lisa frowned.

"Wow, you guys are, like, in love already or something. That's so . . . neat," Lisa said dully.

Micah and April turned and looked at Lisa in concern.

"Aren't you having fun with Corbin, Lisa? Don't mind us, we're just acting crazy because we haven't dated like you have," Micah said.

Lisa laughed in a strained sort of way and looked at her feet.

"Oh, just forget it. I mean, I like Corbin, but he sure isn't acting like Bryce or Joel. Although, he did seem to like my new makeover and everything, but I can tell something's just not right. I don't know if it's me, or him, or what it is," she said.

Micah gave Lisa a quick hug, and April pulled the door open for them to go through.

"Lisa, if anything's wrong, it's *not* you. I'm not going to say it's Corbin, but maybe he's just not the right one. Regardless, let's go get the best Italian dinner these guys can buy us," April said and ushered the girls through the door.

chapter twenty

Bryce smiled at Joel and waited until Corbin walked over to study the menu.

"Wow, that April sure turned out to be cute. Who'd have thought that under all that goth makeup and strange clothes, she was so normal?"

Joel frowned at Bryce and held up a hand of protest.

"Stop judging her, Bryce. She's been hiding under all that junk. I knew it the first time I saw her. She's been an angel from the very beginning. I was just too stupid to wait this long to ask her out. When I make my first million I'm sending Micah on a cruise to the Bahamas as a thank-you," Joel said seriously.

Bryce smirked at his friend. No *way* was he being serious.

"*What?* You have got to be kidding me. All this time you knew April was cool and you never did anything about it? And now that we're all on this group date, all of a sudden you're planning your fiftieth wedding anniversary. Sorry, man, but this is too much. What happened to my tough 'I don't need anyone, especially a girl' roommate?" Bryce asked.

Joel rubbed his hands through his hair impatiently.

"Don't you get it, Bryce? This is it. I felt it that night we went over to see if they were okay. I've been in some strange cocoon or something for the last few years. But when I saw her, it was like lightening struck and I felt alive again. I think this is the girl for me, Bryce. No kidding, just deal with it," Joel said.

Bryce shook his head, still dumbfounded.

"And I think it's real funny that you're giving me a hard time. I saw you in my rearview mirror. I wasn't the only one feeling electricity," Joel said with a grin.

Bryce smiled sheepishly. "You know, Joel, there's just something about Micah. I can't put my finger on it, but there's just always been something there that has pulled me toward her, like a magnet or something. When this stupid blind date thing happened, I wasn't sure at first, but I think it's the best thing that's ever happened to me. And then she changed her hair and clothes, and it's like she was made for me or something. It's weird, but I'm going for it."

Joel laughed and punched his friend in the arm.

"You hypocrite! You just said the exact same thing *I* said, but for some reason, it's different because it's you. You are such a dork. Shut up though, here they come. Look at her, man, isn't she gorgeous?" Joel asked, staring at April.

Bryce's eyes locked onto Micah walking toward him and simply nodded his head. The waitress walked up and escorted the group to a large circular table at the far end of the restaurant. The lighting was dim and romantic and the soft music playing added to the mood. Bryce pulled out Micah's chair for her and couldn't help noticing that Joel did the same for April. He watched Corbin sit down while Lisa blushed in embarrassment and felt like kicking the idiot. He quickly walked over and pulled Lisa's chair out for her and smiled at her brightly, wondering which one of his friends he could set her up with instead of this jerk.

Corbin looked up at Bryce as Lisa was seated and frowned as if Bryce had been the one to do something wrong. Lisa saw the frown, and her face dropped immediately. Bryce walked back over to Micah and sat down. He'd just ignore Corbin as much as he could. He wasn't going to let him ruin his first date with Micah. No way. He'd been waiting too long for this.

"What do you guys feel like?" he asked to everyone in general as he opened his menu.

The conversation opened up, and even Corbin talked to Lisa and made her smile a couple times. Bryce ordered appetizers for everyone, and since he knew their waiter from one of his classes at school, their drinks were never down below half-full. Bryce studied Micah carefully as she ate and talked to everyone. He'd never seen her so relaxed—or so happy. She'd always seemed so uptight and stressed whenever he'd watched her before. But with her roommates, she was an entirely different person. You could tell she'd been brought up going to nice restaurants because she was so proper and polite. His mom would love that. He wanted to know more about her—her parents, her home, her brothers and sisters. He wanted to know who she really was.

Just then Micah looked over at him as she was telling a story and smiled just for him. Bryce felt a shock of that electricity Joel had been talking about and leaned over and grabbed Micah's hand in reaction. Micah smiled even brighter and squeezed his hand. That did it; Bryce was in love.

"Well, surprise, surprise. I didn't expect to see you here tonight, Bryce."

Bryce let go of Micah's hand immediately and turned with a frown to see his sister, Jenny. This could not be good. He gritted his teeth and stood up. He loved his sister, but this was his life and he was going to make up his own mind about who was right for him. Jenny, for some reason, thought that job was hers. He gave his sister a warm hug and a quick kiss on the cheek.

"Hey, guys, you probably already know Jenny, my little sister. Jenny, this is Micah, April, Lisa, and you know Joel. Oh, and that's Corbin," he said, pointing out everyone for his sister.

Jenny smiled at everyone but Micah. Micah, who had been smiling happily, frowned slightly at the cold shoulder Jenny had just shown her. His arm, which was still around Jenny's shoulder, dropped off as he turned and frowned at her, his look warning her to behave.

"Well, it's nice to meet everyone. This is my date, Jake. He just got off his mission from Russia. Do you mind if we join you guys? It looks like you're just about finished, but if you guys order dessert, than we can still have a nice, *long* chat," she said and grabbed a chair from the next table before anyone could say anything.

Bryce looked over at Joel, but his friend just smiled and shook his head. Joel knew all about Bryce's overprotective little sister. He loved her like his own sister, but when she wanted something, there was no stopping her. And right now, it looked like she wanted to disrupt the romantic date going on.

Everyone scooted their chairs closer together as the two new guests squeezed in and ordered quickly from the menu.

Bryce frowned as he watched Micah go from a dazzling, happy person to a quiet, reserved, almost shy person. Jenny was in trouble.

"Wow, I'm stuffed. I just don't think I can eat another thing. I think we're going to have to bail on you guys. We've still got plans for tonight, and we don't want to be late," he said, motioning to his waiter that he wanted the check, quick.

Corbin shook his head, grabbing everyone's attention.

"Sorry, Bryce, but if you're the one paying the bill tonight, I'm ordering dessert," Corbin said with a sly grin.

Bryce and Joel exchanged a quick look. *The jerk!* Corbin had been trying to weasel out of the date, and they had told him that if he would just come along, they would pay his share of the tab. But they hadn't wanted Lisa to find out. Bryce looked at Lisa, but she was staring at her lap and frowning. *Great.* She knew.

"Perfect! Now we can all have a fun little chat," Jenny said with a cold smile.

"Micah, that is such a pretty name. Is it some form of Michelle?" she asked innocently.

Micah cleared her throat nervously and shook her head.

"Um, I don't think so," she said.

"Strange. It sounds so similar. But that reminds me, Bryce. Have you heard from Michelle lately? I just got a letter yesterday from her. I can't believe it's been almost eighteen months. The time goes by so quickly, doesn't it? She was saying how excited she was to see us again. She's the sweetest girl, Micah. I'm sure you'll meet her when she comes up to see Bryce in a couple weeks. Aren't you guys still planning on a Christmas wedding?" Jenny asked innocently, although her eyes had gone a hard, concrete gray.

Bryce looked coldly back at his sister and wished she was far, far away in Alaska.

"What wedding would that be, Jenny?" Bryce asked in a voice his sister had rarely heard from her loving older brother.

Jenny frowned, unsure now that she could see how mad he really was. But there was no way she was going to watch her brother fall in love with a cold-blooded snob whom she would never be able to like.

"Well, that's what people who are engaged do, don't they? They get married. It's all Michelle can talk about in her letters. She can't make up her mind if she wants to get married in the Salt Lake Temple, the Logan, the Manti, or the Mount Timpanogos. Mom is *so* excited about it. She's already planning the wedding dinner," Jenny said firmly.

Bryce couldn't help but notice that even Joel looked stunned by this news. He looked quickly at Micah, and her face had gone almost completely white. Her hands were clenched tightly in her lap, and she looked almost exactly the way she did when she was sitting in church—*miserable.* He was going to stop Jenny's verbal rampage right now.

"Jenny, this was really tacky of you. To make my date feel like dirt in front of everyone is just inexcusable. I think you and your date should leave," Bryce said quietly.

Jenny glared at Bryce but got up from the table.

"Come on, Jake. Let's go." She stormed away from the table and practically ran out the front door.

"Maybe you should go after her," Micah said softly to Bryce.

The whole table was completely silent. Bryce looked around at everyone, still frowning, and nodded his head. He got up to follow his sister but turned around before walking away.

"I'll be back in five minutes. Just order dessert and wait for me." He walked quickly away.

By the time he reached the parking lot, Jenny and Jake were getting into Jake's old Dodge pickup.

"Wait a second, little sis," Bryce commanded.

Jenny turned around slowly and stared at her older brother broodingly.

"*I'm* tacky? I'm the one who's tacky? *You're* cheating on your fiancée with the weirdest girl in Utah, and I'm tacky. That's just perfect," Jenny said, going on the offensive.

Bryce walked up to his little sister and stared down into her upturned face.

"That's exactly what I call someone who deliberately makes someone I care about feel bad. Especially when they're lying," he said fiercely, putting his hands on his hips.

Jenny looked quickly at her date. Jake was just two weeks off his mission, and even the hint of sin would have him running in the opposite direction. But she knew when her older brother had her in a corner.

"Lying? You gave her a ring, Bryce! Admit it," she demanded.

Bryce shook his head in frustration.

"You're ruining my chances with Micah over a stupid little promise ring I gave to Michelle my senior year in high school? That was before I even went on my mission! A lot has changed in four years, Jenny. Now, since you're having a hard time understanding the situation, I'm going to spell it out for you. I am *not* engaged to Michelle. I am not in love with her. I never have been. Is that clear?" he asked.

Jenny frowned up at her brother and clenched her teeth in frustration.

"But why her? Why Micah? She's horrible! I can't stand her! If you end up marrying her, I'll never forgive you. Never!" she practically screamed, with angry tears running down her cheeks now.

Bryce threw his hands in the air in exasperation.

"You know, Mom has spoiled you rotten. I love you, but you are something else. Since when is who I marry any of your business? This world does not revolve around you,

Jenny. I know you think it does, but believing that is just going to turn you into one disappointed, bitter little girl. Now go home. And mind your own business," Bryce said, and turned around and walked back to the restaurant, not waiting for a reply.

The conversation was over if he had anything to say about it. Finally, a date with Micah, and his little sister, the bulldog, had to show up and chew everything to bits within seconds. She needed a spanking, the little brat.

Bryce reached the door and paused, taking in a breath of air and counting to ten to regain his cool. Now he would have to face Micah. What were they all thinking of him? He knew what he'd think if he were in their shoes. Nothing good, that's for sure.

chapter twenty-one

Micah cleared her throat in embarrassment as she watched Bryce hurry out of the restaurant. Why was she even surprised? She should have known it just wasn't possible for her to have one decent date with one decent guy. She looked at the food still on her plate and felt ill. No dessert for her tonight. And no romance either. Micah felt a catch in her throat and clenched her hands even tighter. She would not cry—not here. Not in front of Bryce's best friend. She wouldn't give him that satisfaction. She would just wait for him to come back and when he did, she would demand that he take her home immediately. She might have her problems, but at least she didn't date guys who were already engaged. At least she wouldn't from here on out. Micah blinked back a tear that was threatening and focused on looking at her lap.

The rest of the group of friends took turns looking at each other. The night had been ruined, and nobody was having much fun anymore. April broke the silence.

"Joel, is it true? Is he really engaged to a girl getting home from her mission soon?" she asked solemnly.

Joel took a sip of water and shook his head.

"Listen, guys, I've been roommates with Bryce for the last year and a half, and I've never heard one word about Michelle. I really don't know what is going on here, but I do know this. Bryce is a good guy. He wouldn't be going out with Micah if he was engaged. Jenny is a sweet girl, but she is very protective of Bryce for some reason. I love her, but I think she's gone off the deep end on this one. So let's just wait to hear Bryce's side of the story before we make any assumptions, okay?" Joel said to April, although he was looking at Micah.

Micah refused to look at Joel but nodded her head anyway. She felt a soft, comforting pat on her knee and knew Lisa, who was sitting next to her, was trying to help her through this. If her roommates hadn't been there, she would be running hysterically for the door. She squeezed Lisa's hand in response and took a deep breath. She would get through this. She would. It wasn't as if she had any other choice.

The table sat quietly, except for Corbin, who was noisily enjoying his dessert.

"You guys are missing out! This cheesecake is the best I've ever had. Come on, Lisa, try just a little bite," he insisted.

Lisa frowned at Corbin and shook her head.

"No thanks, Corbin. I don't think so," Lisa said quietly.

April cleared her throat loudly, trying to get Micah's attention.

"Oh look, here's Bryce now," she said.

Micah looked up and watched sadly as Bryce walked quickly toward them. What could she possibly have to say to him? What was one supposed to do in a situation like this?

Bryce walked around the table and over to Micah. He kneeled down beside her, ignoring his chair and pulled her into a comforting, gentle hug. Micah remained stiff and unyielding in his arms, but as she felt his warmth and kindness seep into her, she relaxed.

"I am so sorry for that, Micah. I would never want to hurt you. Jenny is spoiled, and her behavior was inexcusable. You'll love her when you get to know her, she has a good heart—but she went too far tonight. I'm sorry you're upset. But I want you to know there was no truth to anything she said. I am not engaged. I am not in love with another girl. Michelle and I are just friends as far as I'm concerned. Do you believe me?" Bryce asked earnestly.

Micah pulled back from Bryce and felt the tears she had been holding back slip down her cheeks. She couldn't say anything. She wiped the tears from under her eyes and nodded her head, trying to hide her face from the staring eyes of everyone.

Bryce pulled her back into a hug and kissed her cheek gently.

"I know you were embarrassed by this and hurt. I'll make it up to you. I promise," Bryce whispered into her hair.

Micah relaxed into his arms and sniffled, wishing she had a tissue. Not only was she embarrassing herself by crying, she was going to make a mess of Bryce's shirt. She pulled back and reached for her napkin. She took a moment to wipe her eyes and her nose and looked Bryce in the eyes.

"It's okay," she said. And she meant it. She believed him. She didn't know why Jenny had said what she had said, but she was going to trust Bryce. The alternative meant never seeing or going out with Bryce again. And that she didn't want. She wanted to be with Bryce—someone who cared enough about her to hug her in public, in spite of what other people were thinking, was someone she could believe in.

Bryce kissed her cheek again and then sat back down in his chair. He looked seriously at everyone at the table and put his hands on the table.

"Please don't hold that little scene against my sister. I love her, and I wouldn't want her judged harshly because she acted badly tonight. Okay?" he said, talking mostly to April and Lisa.

Micah's two roommates looked at her first before they nodded in agreement.

"Good! Now that the fireworks are over, let's enjoy the rest of our evening. There's *no* reason not to," he said, and took Micah's hand, holding it for everyone to see.

Micah smiled and felt the last bit of tension she was holding onto leave. Everything was going to be okay. Bryce was hers. Micah sucked in her breath and felt her eyes go wide with the realization. She wanted Bryce for her own; that's why what Jenny had said had hurt so much. She looked over at Bryce, and as he smiled kindly into her eyes and squeezed her hand, she knew it was true. This was the man she wanted. She smiled back at him. She would enjoy the rest of the evening. She was with Bryce.

chapter twenty-two

Joel dropped everyone off after the movie, saying something about wanting a little more one-on-one time with April. Corbin had grabbed Lisa's hand almost immediately and said something about going on a little midnight walk. So it was just the two of them.

Micah felt her hands go clammy as Bryce walked her to her front door. She had been fine at dinner, even after Jenny's sabotage. She had been great during the movie when he had put his arm around her shoulders the entire time. She hadn't been nervous at all. But this was it. This was the big good night.

Bryce was naturally very affectionate. With *everyone*—

his sister, his roommates, his friends, *her*. She knew he was going to kiss her. What he didn't know was that she had only been kissed three times in her entire life. The boys brave enough to kiss her, even though her dad was watching them from a side window, hadn't been allowed to ask her out again. And even then they were just little pecks. Nothing like the kisses she'd watched in the movies.

When she had moved on to college, things hadn't changed much. Her dad would grill her so much about boys or dictate whom she *should* date, that she hadn't gone out much at all in the last two years. She could have sneaked around. She could have done a lot of things. It was just the mountains of heavy, suffocating guilt she hadn't wanted to deal with. Being the perfect daughter had always been so much easier. But now things were different. Her dad had chosen his path, and now she was choosing hers. She was choosing to be who she really was. She was choosing Bryce—which put her right here, with him, getting ready to be kissed.

"Hey, what's the matter? You've gone all quiet on me. You're not still thinking about what Jenny said, are you?" Bryce asked, pulling Micah in closer and putting his arm around her shoulders as they walked.

Micah laughed softly.

"No, I believe you, Bryce. I'm not thinking of that. I guess I'm just nervous. I'm not used to dating much, and I don't think I'm very good at this good-night stuff," she said, looking at her feet nervously.

This was where he was going to laugh at her. She knew it. What normal, twenty-one-year-old woman didn't date like crazy if she was going to BYU? She must sound so strange to him.

Bryce rubbed his hand up and down her arm and pulled her even closer, so they were walking hip to hip.

"That is so cool, Micah. I guess when you see a girl as

beautiful as you are, you just assume that they've dated a lot. Do you mind me asking why?" Bryce asked curiously.

Micah looked up at Bryce and smiled.

"Well, it wasn't really my decision. My dad is—*was* very protective of me. I have a feeling that his getting married is going to give me a lot more freedom. But he pretty much controlled who I was allowed to see and who I wasn't. And in the end, I wasn't allowed to see too many guys. Especially ones *I* liked," she said.

Bryce smiled down at her.

"Is that why you went from the girl of my dreams to the ice queen? Did your dad tell you I wasn't appropriate dating material?" Bryce asked.

Micah squirmed a little.

"Well, yes. This is going to sound so strange to you, but if there is a guy I'm interested in, then I have to type up a profile of him and submit it to my father. If he says yes, then I can date him; if he says no, then it's just no." She frowned as she realized just how pathetic that sounded.

Bryce came to a standstill and dropped his arm from her shoulder. "Are you serious? You're telling me that you basically haven't been allowed to have a social life? What is up with your dad? He sounds a little mental—no offense."

Micah pushed the hair out of her eyes and refused to look at Bryce.

"I know, it's weird. It's not like I've enjoyed sitting back and watching everyone have fun and fall in love and be normal. It's just the way life is—or *was* for me. You see, my mom died when I was really young, and so it was just me and my dad. He kind of went overboard with the rules and regulations because he was trying to be a good father. It hasn't been very fun, to be honest," she said, finally looking up at Bryce.

Bryce reached over and pushed the hair out of her eyes, trailing his fingers down her cheek.

"Your dad was wrong, Micah. I think a good dad is one who loves you no matter what," Bryce said.

Micah smiled sadly. "Do you have a good dad, Bryce?"

Bryce shoved his hands into his pockets and looked up at the stars before answering.

"Well, in some ways, yes. He does love me no matter what. And he's the kind of dad who hugs you and kisses you all the time. He's a great guy. But to be a really great dad, I think you have to have a strong moral commitment. You have to stick around and really be there for your kids. Micah, my dad is fun and nice and cool—but at least your dad didn't leave your mom with two kids to raise by herself and go to Hollywood to be a screenwriter. He's on his fifth marriage now. He's well on his way to becoming an alcoholic, and who knows what else. But when he comes to town, he's a lot of fun. If he had stayed with my mom and the Church, I think he would be just about perfect. So, there you have it," Bryce said and looked sadly at Micah.

"It looks like we're on opposite sides of the spectrum," she said, taking his hand.

Bryce smiled and reached for her other hand.

"No problem. We each learn from our parents' mistakes and have a wonderful, happy life. How about it?" he asked.

Micah laughed. "What are you asking me, Bryce?"

Bryce laughed too and then bent down and kissed her on the lips. Micah went still with surprise and then tried to figure out what she was supposed to do. Bryce seemed to know what was going on, so she left it to him and just tried to enjoy herself. She realized that those three kisses hadn't prepared her for Bryce. *This was kissing.*

Bryce pulled back and smiled down into her eyes.

"There. Nothing to be nervous about now. Right?" he said.

Micah blinked a few times and smiled.

"Um, yeah. Nothing at all."

Bryce pulled her toward her door.

"That's our first kiss, Micah. Now I want you to go in and write it down in your journal. Someday our grandkids are going to want to hear all about it," he said.

Micah did laugh then. "You are crazy, Bryce. This is our first date! There are no grandkids anywhere yet," Micah insisted.

Bryce tilted her head up. "Look up at the heavens, Micah. See how the stars are twinkling down at you? Those are your grandkids, jumping for joy that you finally ignored your dad and went with your heart."

Micah smiled and looked at Bryce. "That was sweet, but we'll see. Maybe I haven't made my mind up about you yet. Maybe it will take a few more dates for that to happen."

Bryce reached over, slid his arms around her back, and slid her into a deep dip, while looking into her eyes. He kissed her again playfully.

"Okay, okay," Micah said, pushing him away. "You're right, we're meant for each other, and no one else." She laughed.

Bryce set her on her feet and hugged her close.

"Are you asking me to marry you, Micah? It's a little early for that. What would your father say?"

"Oh, I think he'd say something like, 'You better get your hands off my daughter,'" said a deep, cold voice coming from the doorway.

Micah and Bryce let go of each other immediately and stared into the gloom. Phillip Rawlings walked out from under the small porch of Micah's apartment.

"How long have you been standing there?" Micah demanded, horrified at the thought of what she and Bryce had been discussing.

"Not too long. You two were so loud, you couldn't even hear the door open," Phillip said.

Micah looked up at Bryce and saw that his face had

turned to stone. Not a good way for the two men in her life to meet.

"So, Dad, why are you back so early from your honeymoon? I thought you were going to be gone for a month," Micah said, trying to divert her dad's attention away from her being on a date with Bryce.

"Kathy wasn't feeling good. She wanted to come home early and see a doctor. She's fine, she's fine. But that's why I came over tonight. There's something I need to talk to you about. There's something you need to know," Phillip said, almost nervously.

Micah smiled. Her dad hadn't realized that Kathy had already told her they were expecting a baby. Now it was her dad in the hot seat. She was curious as to how he was going to explain his behavior.

"Okay, Dad. Why don't you go back into the apartment, and I'll be right there. I want to say good night to Bryce."

Phillip looked Bryce up and down and frowned. He walked back inside without saying another word.

Bryce waited until the door shut firmly with a click.

"Between my sister and your dad, I think we have an uphill battle," he said seriously.

Micah frowned and turned toward Bryce, forgetting about her dad for the moment.

"Does that change your mind about all of those grandkids?" she asked sadly.

Bryce grinned and pulled her into another hug. "Nah, it just means we're going to Hawaii for Thanksgiving dinner and going skiing for Christmas," he said with a laugh.

Micah laughed too, so relieved by his answer she felt almost faint.

"Good." She hugged him back fiercely.

"Listen, since you have your dad here, tell him about Rod. He needs to do something about it. If not, we need to go to the police."

Micah grimaced but nodded her head. "Okay. I'll talk to him about it." *Along with everything else we have to talk about,* she thought gloomily.

"Well, I better go. Have a fun chat with your dad. I'll be up for the next hour if you need me for anything," he said and let her go.

Micah smiled warmly. "Okay. Thanks for taking me out tonight, Bryce. In spite of everything, it was the best date I've ever had," she said honestly.

Bryce grinned and walked backward.

"And they're only going to get better and better. Hey, I was just wondering, how many profiles have you submitted to your dad?" Bryce asked seriously.

Micah blushed and looked at her feet.

"Oh, I don't know. Why?" Micah said, backing up toward the door.

"Be honest, Micah. I really want to know," Bryce said firmly.

Micah groaned and looked up at the stars, still twinkling down at her.

"Just one. Yours," she said quietly.

Bryce ran back to her, and kissed her quick and hard on the mouth.

"That's all I wanted to hear. Bye, sweetie," he said, walking backward.

"Bye!" She was caught off guard by the term of endearment. She'd never been called *sweetie* in her life. Not ever. It felt marvelous.

She turned and walked into her apartment, grinning her head off. As she turned and saw her dad standing by the window, she frowned though.

"Were you spying on me?" she demanded in surprise.

Phillip raised his eyebrows at her tone. "Watch your mouth with me, young lady. You know very well that I told you not to go out with him. He did not receive approval. You were forbidden to socialize with him. And what have you done with your hair and your clothes? You look like some low-class, trashy teenager. You have disobeyed me, Micah. I want an explanation right now," Phillip said in curt, cold sentences.

Micah stepped backward, crossing her arms defensively against her chest. She felt like she was ten years old all over again. And she didn't like that.

"Look, Dad, I'm twenty-one years old now. You don't have a right to tell me who I should or shouldn't date. It's none of your business. Just like who you date—*or marry*—is none of my business. Right?" she said, just as coldly as her father.

Phillip looked at his daughter in surprise. He hadn't been expecting that.

"You're *my* daughter, you will always be my daughter, and I will always be your father. You *will* do as you're told. You always have and you always will. My marrying Katherine doesn't mean that you're free to throw yourself at the first loser that comes along. It's immature to try and get back at me for finally finding some happiness in my life," Phillip said, raising his voice in irritation.

Micah shook her head in frustration.

"First off, don't talk about Bryce that way, and I *didn't* throw myself at the first loser to come along. If I had done that, I would be on a date with Rod, your new brother-in-law. He's been coming around trying to intimidate me into going out with him so he can 'hit the jackpot' just like Kathy. I went out with Bryce tonight because I want to find some happiness in my life too," she said sincerely.

Phillip frowned. "Rod? What are you talking about, Micah? Who's Rod?"

Micah walked over to the couch and flung herself down. "You don't even know your in-laws, Dad? Holy cow. Rod is Kathy's older brother. He came over here Monday night.

April had to call Bryce to come over before he would leave. He's pretty much stalking me. Everyone wants me to file a restraining order, but I didn't because I didn't want you to start out *your* new life with *your* new wife on the wrong foot. But now that you're back, please do say something to him because he was here tonight again, before my date. If you don't, I *will* call the police," she said firmly.

Phillip rubbed his hands over his face and looked older than his years. He looked pale under his tan, and worried.

"I'm sorry, Micah. I seem to remember Kathy saying something about a wild older brother. I had no idea this would happen. I'll have a talk with him immediately. You have my word on it. But I didn't come here to fight with you tonight. I came here for an important reason. I need to tell you something, and I don't know how you'll feel about it," he said nervously.

Micah almost smiled. She was so grateful that Kathy had already let the cat out of the bag.

"What, Dad? What do you need to tell me?" she coaxed.

Phillip cleared his throat nervously and turned to stare out the window again.

"Kathy and I are expecting a baby. In about seven months, to be exact. I—we—just thought you should know," he said.

Micah looked down at her lap, embarrassed for her father.

"Congratulations," she said simply.

Phillip turned around and stared at her in surprise.

"That's it? Congratulations? That's all you have to say?" he demanded.

Micah sighed and got up off the couch, going to the kitchen to get a glass of water.

"What did you want me to say, Dad? Do you want me to say, '*Gee, what in the world has gotten in to you?*' Do you want me to say something like, '*Gee, Dad, what in the world are you doing, marrying someone younger than your own daughter?*' Do you want me to ask you what has happened to your testimony? Because I'm pretty sure the prophet has said something about not having premarital sex," she said, turning to stare her father in the eyes.

Phillip dropped his eyes to the ground and sighed.

"Yes, that's what I was expecting. I should have taken the congratulations and been grateful. Look, I'm not perfect. I tried to be, for you, but to be honest, I've been absolutely miserable since your mother died. When I met Kathy, I went a little crazy, I'll admit that. But now that she's having our baby, I feel like I can start over. I mean, look at you. You're twenty-one, you don't need me anymore. I could fall over dead, and no one would even care. But now I have Kathy and the baby. I know, I know—I've made mistakes. Things happened that shouldn't have happened. But I'm sure that Kathy will join the Church someday. You'll see, it's all going to work out in the end," Phillip said, almost pleadingly.

Micah set her water glass down and looked at her father. What had happened to the cold, controlled man who was her father? He looked almost human, standing here in her family room. She could almost see a heart beating in his chest. Why had he waited this long to be human? Why had he waited until she finally didn't need him anymore?

"I'm sure you're right, Dad. Look, let's make a deal. You live your life and I'll live mine. I won't judge you and your relationship with Kathy, and you don't judge me and my relationship with Bryce. Deal?" she asked, holding out her hand.

Micah watched as emotion after emotion flashed by on her father's face. Fear, dread, anger, resolve. He didn't even have to say a word. There would be no deal. She let her hand fall limply to her side.

"Judge me all you want to, Micah, but I don't want you

seeing that boy again. He's not for you, and that's final."

"And Corbin Larsen is? *He's* the one that's right for me? I would rather die than be with him. He's a complete jerk, oblivious to other people's feelings, and someone I could never love. Thank you very much, Dad, but when it comes to picking someone to spend my life with, I'll be the one who makes that decision. Not you."

Phillip's mouth dropped open at the fierceness of his daughter.

"I don't think you've ever talked to me that way before. And I *won't* have it. I am still your father, and if you want your nice apartment, food, clothing, and schooling paid for, you'll do what you're told. And that includes listening to me when it comes to boys. I might be open to discussion about your hair and wardrobe, but that's as far as I'm willing to compromise. End of discussion," Phillip said, and turned to the door.

"Oh, and Kathy said she wants your help decorating the nursery. You'll do everything she asks you to. Understood? I don't want her upset. If anything happens to this baby . . ." Phillip didn't finish his sentence. He let himself out the front door and shut it firmly.

Micah stared at the spot her dad had been standing in. He was gone, but his commands were still floating in the air like noxious fumes. Her dad wasn't backing down. But then again, neither was she.

chapter twenty-three

April watched her roommates and their dates get smaller and smaller as she and Joel drove quickly away. Now she was starting to worry. What did Joel expect from her? Did he think just because she used to dress wild that she *was* wild? What if he was taking her to some make-out spot? April gulped nervously. She'd never made out in her life. What if all the girls in their ward were right and he *was* some sex-crazed maniac who would kick her out of the car and make her walk ten miles home out of revenge if she said no? April started paying attention to what direction they were going. They were still in the city limits, but they were heading toward the mountains—classic make-out territory.

What was she going to do?

"What's going on in that mind of yours, April? I can see you thinking a mile a minute," Joel said, looking over at her.

April jumped nervously.

"Nothing. Nothing. I'm just wondering where we're going. You said back there that you wanted some one-on-one time with me, and um . . . I just don't want you to think that something is going to happen tonight, um, physically, if you get what I'm trying to say," she said bravely.

Joel laughed and grabbed her hand, kissing it.

"You are so strong, April. I love that about you. You are so up-front and honest. Why didn't I meet you five years ago? I think my life would be very different. But put your mind at ease. I'm not hijacking you to some mountain cave to do immoral and sinful things. Although I am looking forward to a good-night kiss," he said, grinning at her.

April laughed in relief and relaxed. She was so paranoid!

"Sorry, I get a little ahead of myself sometimes. Don't take it personally, I just haven't had a lot of one-on-one time with anybody," she said, looking out the window happily.

Joel looked over at her in surprise and smiled.

"Wow, you are unique, April. But if you're wondering why I wanted some one-on-one time with you, it's because I wanted to talk to you without any roommates overhearing. There's something I need to tell you if this relationship is going to go any further," he said, suddenly serious.

April frowned and looked at the side of Joel's face. He looked tense all of a sudden and very subdued—not like himself at all.

"What is it, Joel? Is it something I did? Is it because of the way I used to look? What?" April asked, nervous all over again.

Joel looked quickly over at April and shook his head.

"Of course it has nothing to do with you. You're practically perfect. No, this is about me," Joel said and then drove in silence the rest of the way.

April wasn't surprised to see that Joel had driven up to a small overlook in the Provo canyon. Well, she had guessed his location correctly but not his intentions. What in the world could he possibly want to tell her?

Joel turned the car off and pushed his seat back as far as it would go. He turned and looked at her and took both of her hands.

"April, I'm not like all of these other guys in the ward. I haven't gone on a mission. I haven't always chosen the right path. I've made a *lot* of mistakes in my life, and I need to be up-front with you about that."

April smiled at Joel and felt her heart melt.

"Please don't, Joel. I don't think you should have to confess every bad thing you've ever done to me. That's what the Atonement is all about—wiping the slate clean. Nobody in this world is perfect; that was part of the plan. What's important now is the future and where you're headed right now. I know you're a good guy. I know you have a good heart. I've listened to you bear your testimony in church. I can tell how strong you are now. Please don't feel like you have to explain yourself to me," April said seriously.

Joel's eyes went wide with surprise.

"April, you're just as beautiful on the inside as you are on the outside. You're making this way too easy for me. Okay—well, I won't go into the dark side then. I wasn't looking forward to that anyway. But there still remains one part of my life that I do have to tell you about if our relationship is going to go anywhere. I have to tell you about Garrett," Joel said, looking very determined and serious.

April tilted her head quizzically. Garrett? He took her all the way up this mountain to tell her about some guy named Garrett?

"I couldn't go on a mission because I have a son. He's about two and a half now, and I love him more than my life," Joel said simply, and then sat back and waited for April's reaction.

April stared at him in shock. *Joel has a son.* Joel was a father? Okay, now what?

"You have a son named Garrett, and he's two and a half years old. I really wasn't expecting to hear that," April said and tore her eyes away from Joel and looked out at the city lights, trying to catch her breath.

Joel sighed and leaned back in his seat, letting her hands drop. He rubbed his hands through his hair and closed his eyes.

"Yeah, I know you weren't. I was living the prodigal life, and my girlfriend of the minute tells me she's pregnant. She was only eighteen at the time and not ready for motherhood. *At all.* Amy's not LDS, and she wanted to get an abortion. I convinced her to have the baby and to let me have custody. He lives with my mom and dad in Bountiful. They're pretty much raising him until I can get my degree and find a . . . um, a wife," Joel said and glanced at April quickly. She was still staring out the window but blinked quickly at the word *wife.*

"I go and see him every weekend. It's hard, but he's still so young, he just knows he's loved a lot. My little brothers and sisters spoil him rotten. But I am his dad, and he knows it. And I take that responsibility very seriously. This is my last year of school. I graduate in the spring. I'm going to take care of my family. Whoever that ends up being," he said, and turned his head to look at her.

April looked over and caught his eye. She reached for his hand and held it tightly.

"The last few years must have been very hard for you. Do you still see Amy much? Does Garrett get to see his mom?" she wondered.

Joel shook his head sadly. "No, I haven't seen Amy since the day she delivered Garrett in the hospital. She took off and moved to California with a bunch of her friends. It's a good thing she's not around though. I heard from some of my old buddies that she's heavily involved in the hard drug scene down there. But everyone needs a mom. A good mom," Joel said.

April groaned in sympathy for Joel and his son.

"Oh, that breaks my heart. A little boy growing up without a mom. And here you are working so hard to get to a point where you can take care of him. You're amazing, Joel. You know how many guys your age would just shirk their responsibility? Is that why you changed your life around? For Garrett?" she asked curiously.

Joel smiled and nodded his head. "Yep. My mom and dad had everything set up to where they were going to have Garrett placed with the LDS Family Services to be adopted into a family. And that's when I woke up. I wanted my son. I promised them that I would stop doing drugs, drinking, and everything else, and go back to church if they would help me keep Garrett. They made a deal with me that if I could pass weekly drug tests then they would support me. So when they saw what a change Garrett was causing in my life, they realized I was serious. And I was willing to do whatever I had to, to be worthy of being Garrett's dad. They had faith in me that I would make things right. And I'm still trying."

April shook her head in wonder. She was amazed at what Joel was telling her. And here she had been thinking he was taking her up here to seduce her.

"Oh, Joel, you are one good guy, you know that? I'm sorry I thought you had making out on your mind," she said, and started to laugh.

Joel leaned his head forward onto his steering wheel and laughed along with her.

"So, you're not going to run screaming back to your roommates? You're not going to pretend I don't exist and refuse to go out with me? I think that's the usual protocol in these situations," he said.

April reached over and patted Joel's cheek, still smiling.

"You picked the wrong girl then. Going out with a good-looking guy who takes his responsibilities seriously and has a firm grasp on the gospel is not something I would run away from," she said, smiling at him.

Joel shook his head in wonder. Then he opened his car door, walked around to her side, and opened her door for her.

"Would you join me for a little moonlight please?" he asked, holding his hand out for her.

April shrugged and grinned at him, as he helped her down onto the ground. Joel shut the door and walked with her to the edge of the cliff.

"I have a rule now about not kissing a girl while sitting down. It's not going to happen. But if you wouldn't mind, I'd really like to kiss you right now. No making out, I promise. Just a kiss," he asked.

April swallowed nervously. Things were going so good. Kissing wasn't her area of expertise. What if he kissed her and then took her straight home and never called *her* again? Should she say no? She looked up at him, frowning. Joel smiled down at her and cupped her face gently in his large, rough hands.

"Remember this night, April. This is the night that I fell in love," he said and leaned down and kissed her very, very softly on the lips. She smiled and put her arms around his waist and moved in to where her head fit right below his chin. She looked out at the starry sky and closed her eyes in happiness. She finally felt at home.

chapter twenty-four

Micah turned on her side and groaned. How could it already be morning? She peeked at the clock on her side table and groaned again. She had promised April and Lisa that she would go to a yoga class this morning with them. They were probably already up and dressed, waiting on her. It was their fault though. She had tried waiting up for them but had finally given up and gone to bed, too tired to care anymore.

She rolled out of bed and managed to get herself dressed clumsily and then walked out into the bright, sunshine-filled family room. April and Lisa grinned at her happily and opened the front door.

"We knew you'd rise from the dead eventually. Come

on, we have to hurry now. The class starts in fifteen minutes," Lisa said, patting her on the shoulder.

Micah raised an eyebrow at her two perky roommates and groaned again.

"How can you guys go to bed later than me and be little Miss Mary Sunshines the next day? It's not right," she said, following everyone to her car.

April handed Micah her car keys and pushed her into the driver's seat.

"Falling in love fills you with energy, Micah. I absolutely recommend it," she said, laughing at Micah's expression.

Micah grinned at April and looked to Lisa, who had climbed into the backseat.

"So what's your excuse?" she demanded playfully.

Lisa buckled her seat belt and tried to look innocent.

"Well, I know you guys don't like Corbin all that much, and he really is kind of clueless when it comes to women. But when we went on our walk last night, he was really honest with me, and told me that now that I had lost some weight, that he could really see himself being with me. And then he kissed me. A lot," she said, turning a bright red.

Micah caught April's eye. April frowned slightly at her and nodded. Corbin was still an idiot.

"But, Lisa, he's already making his feelings for you conditional upon what you look like. Maybe that's not the best way to start a relationship? I still say we look around for another guy for you," April said gently.

Lisa frowned and looked out the window. Micah drove out of the parking lot and wondered what she could say. She completely agreed with April, but Lisa looked so happy.

"April, you just don't understand. You weren't there, and well, you're not me. When he was kissing me, I felt something. And since I'm doing yoga now and eating right, I am losing weight. I'm only going to look better and better for him. Just be happy for me please," Lisa pleaded.

April turned around in her seat and looked at Lisa. Micah grimaced, wondering what April could possibly say to that.

"Well, who am I to judge? You're a big girl now, Lisa, you have to make your own decisions. And even though I wouldn't make the decisions you make, you probably wouldn't make the decisions I make. So I guess I'll just say good luck," April said with a smile.

Micah's mouth fell open. April had let it go just like that? April—the "chew 'em up and spit 'em out" defender of all underdogs—had just let it go. Micah shook her head in disbelief. Well, maybe she would be the one to not let it go then. Lisa was her friend too, after all.

"Lisa, let me just say one thing and then I'll mind my own business. You know I love you, and I don't want to say anything to hurt you. I'm just worried about you. I know you had a good time last night and everything, but you've kind of already set a pattern for your relationship. You do a good job, and he rewards you. You look good, and he treats you well. So, what if everything goes perfectly and you two get married someday? Well, I'm sure Corbin wants children, and say you gain a little weight with the baby. What is Corbin going to say then? How is he going to treat you when you don't look as good as you do now? And then you have your children to worry about. Are they always going to be worried about being good enough for their dad?"

Lisa and April stared at her in openmouthed surprise. Micah blinked, embarrassed.

"Sorry, I just have a dad who's a lot like Corbin."

Lisa shook her head and sat up straighter.

"You don't really know Corbin at all, Micah. You just think you do. I'm sorry your dad's like that, but that doesn't mean Corbin is. Just wait until you get to know him better."

Micah looked at Lisa in her rearview mirror and nodded. She would keep silent for now and hope she was wrong.

They reached the gym in a few silence-filled minutes and walked inside with their yoga mats tucked firmly under their arms.

"You guys are going to love Yvette. She teaches the advanced class, and she is awesome. I'm not as good as she is yet, but she's been teaching me some new things. Hopefully there's still room for us. She's very popular," April said and started to walk faster.

Micah winced at the word *advanced.* She had barely survived the intermediate class April had made her take last week. Lisa looked determined and followed April, who was practically running now. Micah groaned again. Saturday mornings were supposed to be relaxing and fun. She picked up her pace and followed April and Lisa into a large room, already full of women dressed in anything from leotards to old sweats to the newest line of yoga wear. She looked down at her sweats and shrugged. It didn't matter what you wore. April was one of the best, and she wore an old T-shirt and pajama pants to do yoga in. That's the one thing about yoga that all of the other kinds of exercise didn't have—acceptance. It didn't matter who you were, what you wore, or even how good you were. You just had to do the best you could.

Micah smiled and laid her mat next to April's. April grinned at her. Lisa put her mat down and walked over to talk to a girl she knew from one of her classes.

"We're at the back, but that's okay. If you have trouble with a pose, I'll help you," April said.

Micah rolled her eyes and sat down as she waited for Yvette to start.

"So how did it go with Bryce last night?" April asked as she took off her shoes and socks.

Micah smiled and leaned back on her hands.

"Well, I'll say two things. There was talk about future

grandkids, and he kissed me. More than once," she said, and caught herself giggling like an idiot.

April laughed and punched her in the shoulder.

"I knew it. You two were made for each other. All we have to do is keep his little sister far, far away, and life will be perfect."

Micah frowned and nodded. "I know. She does kind of worry me. I have to win her over or Bryce might rethink those grandkids. I know he loves Jenny a lot. Family is very important to him."

April leaned over and laid her face on her knees, wrapping her hands around the soles of her feet. Micah sighed and concentrated on trying to touch her toes.

"Well, in case you're wondering, which I guess you're not because you haven't even asked, Joel and I had a good time last night too," April said, and blushed.

Micah laughed and sat up.

"How good are we talking here? Was there any kissing involved?"

April sat up and crossed her legs.

"Yes, there was. But *no* making out. We talked a lot about his son, Garrett," she said, watching Micah's reaction closely.

Micah coughed and whipped her head around to stare at April. "Did you say *son?*"

April gave a half smile and nodded. "Yes. He has a two-and-a-half-year-old son named Garrett. The mom is out of the picture, living in California, and Joel's mom and dad are taking care of him until he can. But he goes to see him on the weekends," April said, still studying Micah closely for her reaction.

"Wow, April. That's why he's so mature. He's *had* to be," Micah said, still in awe.

April sighed in relief at her friend's reaction and smiled. "Yeah, that's why he's so great. I really, *really* like him,

Micah. But do you see me as a stepmom some day?"

Micah rolled her head around on her shoulders and thought about it.

"Well, I think in some ways, you've had to grow up pretty quick too. You're a loving, kind person who is the first one in line to stick up for anyone. I can't see you passing up a little boy without a mom. It's almost as if you were made for this situation," Micah said honestly.

April pinched the top of her nose and closed her eyes, surprising herself and her friend when tears came to her eyes.

"That's what I thought too. I just wanted an outside opinion to confirm it. This could be serious."

Micah smiled and shook her head at her friend. "Oh, you're not out of the woods yet. What will your mom and dad think about you having a relationship with a man who hasn't gone on a mission? Joel has a past and already has a son."

April went pale at the thought and frowned.

"Well, if they think I'm bad and all I did was go out with someone who should have been off-limits, then I don't even want to think about it," April said sadly.

Micah frowned and straightened out her yoga mat.

"Well, at least you have some time until they find out. My dad came over last night while you guys were on your drive, and he saw me kissing Bryce. He gave Bryce the cold shoulder and then he told me that I wasn't allowed to see him anymore and that if I did, he'd stop paying for my clothes, apartment, and schooling. And Bryce is an RM and going to school. I just don't know why my dad won't approve of him," Micah said.

April grimaced on behalf of her friend. "I think we both have a fight on our hands. But don't you think our guys are worth it?"

Micah smiled and watched as Lisa took her place and

Yvette started the music for the work out. "Unlike some other guys I could mention, I think they're very worth it," she whispered to April as she thought of the way Corbin treated Lisa. There were a lot worse guys out there to be had. She'd fight for hers.

chapter twenty-five

Micah almost jumped out of bed Sunday morning. In just two hours she would see Bryce again. Would it be weird, or would it be wonderful? She couldn't wait to find out. She took extra time with her hair and makeup and picked out a new outfit for church. It was nice but a lot more relaxed than the blazers and heavy skirts she was used to wearing. The shirt was a spandex-cotton blend with lots of bright colors. It had a scooped neckline and short sleeves. It tapered at the waist and went perfectly with the long, khaki skirt she had fallen in love with at first sight. Her father would die if he knew what she was wearing. But what her father didn't know couldn't hurt her. She walked out and noticed Lisa and April were already eating breakfast.

"Hey, come join us. Let's read some scriptures before we go to church. What do you say?" April said, opening up her Book of Mormon.

Micah sighed but nodded her head. *Isn't three hours of religion enough for one day?* she wondered sulkily. April and Lisa were on a quest to strengthen her testimony, and every time she turned around they were reading the Book of Mormon or the *Ensign* to her. It was starting to get on her nerves.

But she kept her thoughts to herself as she joined them and mindlessly munched away at some cold cereal. She noticed that Lisa and April had taken some extra effort with their usual Sunday routine as well. They all looked pretty good for going to church. She tried to pay attention to what April was reading, but her mind kept zoning out. Lisa even kicked her under the table a couple times to get her attention. When April finally finished twenty minutes later, Micah was ready to shout hallelujah.

Lisa then suggested they kneel for prayer together before going to church. Micah couldn't remember ever kneeling down to pray with anyone before. It was kind of embarrassing. But when Lisa asked her to give the prayer, she almost said no. What was this? Religious boot camp? She bowed her head and thought about what she could say. At night, if she didn't fall asleep first, she'd just lie in bed and say a quick prayer. This was a lot different.

"Dear Heavenly Father, um, we're thankful for this day and, um, we're grateful that we can go to church and, um . . . uh, please bless us that we'll have thy Spirit to be with us and, um, in the name of Jesus Christ, amen," she said, grateful to be done.

Lisa and April exchanged a look between them that Micah couldn't decipher, but she shrugged it off. After all, she hadn't grown up with a stake president for a dad. She hadn't grown up like Lisa with the typical large, loving

LDS family, either. Nope, she was what she was, and if that wasn't good enough for Heavenly Father, then oh well. Too bad.

They walked the three blocks to church almost in silence, each deep in her own thoughts. Micah glared at the backs of her roommates' heads. Next time they asked her to pray, she would just pray for less obnoxious roommates. That would get them.

They reached the building and walked quickly inside, all three of them looking for a particular person. Micah frowned when she didn't see Bryce. And from Lisa's and April's expressions, they hadn't been successful either. The three girls headed for their usual spot, far in the back.

Micah felt a gentle tap on her shoulder and turned her head with a bright smile. She knew Bryce would want to come sit by her in church. But it wasn't Bryce. Micah looked up into the serious gaze of the executive secretary, Brother Jansen.

"Sister Rawlings, the bishop would like to speak with you right after sacrament service in his office."

Micah gulped, at a complete loss.

"Oh. Really? He wants to see me? Did he say what it's about?" she asked him.

Brother Jansen's mouth flickered in what might have been a small smile.

"No, Sister Rawlings. That's between you and the bishop. Will you be there?" he prodded her.

Micah knew April and Lisa were listening in with every ounce of nosiness they had. She glanced at them, and they nodded their heads in encouragement.

"Um, okay. I'll be there," she said in a scared, small voice.

He nodded and walked quickly away. Micah turned to April and Lisa with a helpless expression on her face.

"Holy cow! What did I do? Do you think Jenny turned

me in for going out with her brother? Maybe it was my dad? Do you think he would have the bishop yell at me for going out with someone he doesn't approve of?"

April and Lisa both shook their heads. Lisa looked over at the bishop and smiled.

"I don't think so, Micah. You know, it didn't occur to me until now, but with fall semester starting next week, I bet he's trying to fill some callings that are empty now, with people graduating and moving on. Relax, Micah. You're not in trouble; I bet you're being called to something. I hope it's a fun one," she said wistfully. It was no secret that Lisa's secret fantasy was teaching gospel doctrine. It was her favorite class, even though she was too shy to raise her hand and participate.

Micah stared at Lisa in horror. A calling? *Her?* It was a ridiculous thought! The one girl in the ward with a testimony as shaky as a palm tree in a hurricane should not be given a calling.

April patted her knee consolingly. "Don't worry, Micah. Hopefully you're just in trouble for something," she said, joking.

Micah didn't laugh. She honestly would rather be in trouble than be given a calling.

"Hey, beautiful. What's the matter?" Bryce said, leaning over the bench and giving her a light kiss on the cheek.

Micah's frown disappeared immediately as she turned to smile at Bryce.

"Hey! I was wondering where you were. Have a seat," she said, and moved over to make room for Bryce, who squeezed past Lisa and April. He sat down and immediately put his arm around Micah's shoulders. Micah blushed a little but felt good all the same.

"So what's going on? You look like you just saw a ghost. Has Jenny been over here bugging you?" he asked, looking at Micah searchingly.

Micah frowned, but relaxed into Bryce's arm. It didn't seem so bad now that Bryce was here, for some reason.

"No, of course not. Brother Jansen just asked me to meet with the bishop right after sacrament meeting. Lisa thinks he wants to give me a calling. It just caught me off guard I guess," she said, trying to smile.

Bryce smiled down at her and rubbed her arm bracingly.

"You'd be great at anything, Micah. I wouldn't worry about it if I were you. He probably just wants to tell you what an amazing person you are. That's what I would say if I were him."

Micah laughed and leaned her head against Bryce. "Right now, I wish you were the bishop."

Micah and Bryce talked for a few more minutes while they watched all of the other people walk in and find seats.

"Where's Joel?" Micah asked after a few minutes. She had noticed April's head craning back and forth, searching for him. He was really running late.

Bryce sat up quickly and turned to April.

"That reminds me. Hey, April, Joel wanted me to tell you that he's with Garrett today but that he wanted to see you later this afternoon, so stick around," he said.

April relaxed and smiled. "Oh, well, that's good. I was kind of wondering where he was. Thanks, Bryce," she said, smiling now.

Micah was calm as church started, but every second that came closer to the meeting being over had her more and more nervous. Bryce held her hand and kept whispering funny things in her ear, but even that didn't help. As the closing prayer was said, she felt her heart begin to race. She gave herself a mental shake and told herself to relax. But she wasn't listening to herself any more than she was listening to Bryce, April, or Lisa. She was a wreck. She followed everyone out of the chapel after the meeting and didn't even notice the angry glare Jenny gave her as they walked by. Bryce did, though, and put his arm around Micah's shoulders protectively.

He walked her to the bishop's office and waited with her until the bishop arrived. He squeezed her hand and walked quickly away.

"Well, Sister Rawlings, I'm glad you came. Please come in and have a seat," he said warmly, and ushered her in.

Micah walked into the office and noticed immediately pictures of Jesus feeding the multitude and Joseph Smith. She stared into the kind eyes of the prophet and for a minute felt as if he were looking back at her encouragingly. She knew that wasn't possible but felt better all the same. She watched as Bishop Nielson walked behind his large desk and sat down. He shuffled some papers to the side and then clasped his hands together and looked at her seriously. She really liked Bishop Nielson. He reminded her of someone's grandpa—balding, with gray hair and twinkling, bright eyes, and a little bit overweight. He looked like Santa Claus on a mission.

"Sister Rawlings, I know you're wondering why I asked to meet with you today. Let me put your mind at rest immediately. You're not in trouble, so stop looking so scared," he said with a chuckle.

Micah tried to laugh too, but she knew if she wasn't in trouble, that left the only other option: a calling.

"The Lord is extending you a wonderful opportunity to serve today, Micah. We are calling you to be the next Relief Society president. How do you feel about that?" he asked gently.

Micah reeled back in her chair, in complete and total shock. *Me, a Relief Society president?* This could not be happening—her father's fondest wish and her worst nightmare.

"Sister Rawlings? Are you okay? Would you like a drink

of water?" the bishop asked in a concerned voice.

Micah shook her head, still in shock. She couldn't say anything. What could she say—no? She definitely couldn't say yes. The bishop must have gotten his inspiration mixed up. She would just have to set him straight.

"Um, Bishop, I'm sorry, but I really, *really* think you have the wrong person. There is no way *I* could ever be a Relief Society president. You just don't know me very well. If you did, you would realize that I really shouldn't have a calling like that. Relief Society presidents are people who are really strong and spiritual and—oh I don't know—um . . . organized! I'm not organized at all. It's just a mistake. A simple mistake," she said in a pleading, desperate voice.

Bishop Nielson looked at her gravely and straightened his tie. He stood up and walked around the desk and pulled a chair from the wall over to where she was sitting. He leaned toward her and spoke very softly.

"Dear, dear Sister Rawlings. I don't know you very well, that's true. But I know someone who knows you better than even you know yourself: your Heavenly Father. And he told me that you were meant to lead and serve the sisters in our ward. You might not think you're strong, but Heavenly Father knows you are. You might not think you're spiritual, but Heavenly Father knows your spirit, and it's a good one. Accepting this calling will take a lot of faith on your part, but if you do accept, I promise you that you will grow in so many wonderful ways. You'll be a better person for it, a better woman, a better wife and a mother. Saying yes will bring happiness, joy, and peace into your life. But you do have your free agency. Take a moment and think about it."

Micah shook her head in confusion. Out of all the incredible, glowing, strong girls in the ward, why in the world would he want her? She clenched her hands in her anxiety and shook her head again. The bishop couldn't be serious.

"Bishop, please, try to understand. I love Heavenly

Father, and I would never want to tell him no, but I just don't think I'm the best one for the job. You see, my testimony isn't as strong as it should be. My roommates are trying to help me, we even read our scriptures this morning and they made me pray, so I am trying, but why don't you call me to do the newsletter? I'm pretty sure I could handle something like that," she said, smiling brightly.

The bishop smiled back at her but shook his head.

"Micah, you need to know right now that the Lord does not make mistakes. If he called you to be Relief Society president, then he knew you were up to the job. So if he thinks you're the best one for the job, and I think you're the best one for the job, that just leaves you. Will you accept this calling?" he asked softly.

Micah felt tears fall from her eyes, but as she looked past the bishop at the picture of Joseph Smith, she knew there were probably times that he didn't feel up to the job either. But he accepted his calling and did the best he could. What in the world was she getting herself into?

"Okay, Bishop. I accept the calling," Micah said. She bowed her head and cried softly.

The bishop reached over and patted her back comfortingly.

"Don't worry, Micah. I'll set you apart and you'll be blessed. You'll be blessed—you'll see."

Micah was ushered out of the bishop's office. She wiped her eyes and looked up to see Bryce staring at her very seriously. He looked upset.

"Bryce! What are you doing here? It's almost time for priesthood to start," she said with a sniffle.

He walked over to her and put his arm around her shoulders, but instead of walking toward Sunday School, he turned her in the opposite direction and walked outside with her. There was a beautiful old maple tree in front of the church, and he steered her toward that. He sat down on the ground in the shade and pulled her down to sit beside him.

"I guess it's none of my business, but when I see my girl crying her eyes out as she leaves the bishop's office, then it worries me. Are you okay? Is it something you can talk about?" he asked gently.

Micah grimaced. "Well, April was right. But I don't know if I'm supposed to tell anyone because I haven't been set apart yet, but if you promise not to tell, I'll tell you. I was just called as the Relief Society president."

Bryce just stared at her. He looked as surprised as she felt. She laughed at his expression and felt some of the stress lift from her shoulders.

"Oh, come on. You too? I hope the whole ward doesn't apostatize," she said, still giggling.

Bryce blinked a couple of times and grabbed her hands. "Are you serious, Micah? Really? I mean, that's a really big calling. Of course you'll be great at it—you're so sweet and wonderful—but that is one big job," he said seriously.

Micah leaned back in the grass and rested her head on her hands. "I'm being set apart next Sunday. Will you raise your hand to sustain me, Bryce?" she asked.

Bryce turned on his side and looked into her eyes. He stared at her for a moment before answering. "Yes, Micah. I will always sustain you. I think you're going to be wonderful. Are you okay though? I mean, you came out of there with tears all over your face," he said.

Micah looked up at the leaves and the light shining down through them and felt a warm breeze drift over her face. If the bishop were right and Heavenly Father knew her and thought she was up to the job, then maybe—just maybe—she was. Wouldn't it be wonderful to finally do something good for once?

"I was shocked, Bryce, really. I didn't know what to say or what to think when he asked me. But he talked to me for a long time, and we said a prayer together. I think it's going to be okay," she said, feeling better and better about her decision to accept.

Bryce relaxed and smiled down at her. "I'm impressed, Micah. I have to say, you're turning out to be the biggest and best surprise I've ever had."

Micah smiled back up at him. "Thanks."

Bryce started picking long strands of grass and making a pile of it on her arm.

"So how did it go with your father after I left? I don't think he likes me very much. Did he say anything about dating me?" Bryce asked.

Micah frowned, feeling some of the glow leave as she thought of what her father did say about Bryce. She still hadn't figured out what do without her father's financial support.

"Well, it didn't go all that well. I'll be honest with you, Bryce, my father has something against you, and I just don't know what it is. He told me that if I continue to see you, then he'll stop paying for my schooling and apartment and food and clothes. He seemed pretty upset about seeing me with you. I just don't get it though. He didn't even give me a reason," Micah said and turned over on her stomach, sending Bryce's grass pile flying.

Bryce picked up his little pile of grass and started rebuilding it on Micah's back.

"Well, Micah, you have too much to worry about right now with this new calling. You just worry about the spiritual things for now, and let me worry about your father. I'll come up with a solution for us. I promise. Okay?"

Micah stared up at him with a smile. "Sounds good to me. I'm tired of thinking about it. I was going to go down to the bank tomorrow and fill out a student loan application. But if you can come up with another solution, then I'm all ears," she said, pushing the hair out of her eyes.

Bryce grinned down at her and took his grass pile and

flung it up into the air. Micah laughed and shook her hair. She was going to have to go into Relief Society covered in grass. She loved it.

"A girl who would take out a loan for me. You're amazing, Micah. Did I mention how all of our grandkids are very happy with you right now?" he said, leaning down and kissing her on the cheek.

Micah grinned and sighed in happiness. Forget the grandkids. She was thrilled to pieces.

chapter twenty-six

After church, he drove Micah home, kissing her quickly on the cheek and promising to call her later. He had something he needed to take care of. He jumped up into his jeep and drove broodingly down the street toward Micah's home. He was going to confront Phillip Rawlings. Parents had always jumped at the chance to have their daughters date him. He was an RM and an honor student; he had never treated any of his dates dishonorably. And he was a nice guy! Bryce frowned darkly; if Phillip was going to forbid Micah to see him, then he wouldn't leave until he had the truth. There had to be a reason.

Ever since his date with Micah, and the way her father

had told him to take his hands off her, he had been planning on having a nice little chat to reassure Phillip that his intentions were honorable. But threatening to take everything away from his daughter just because she was going out with him completely mystified him. No, he would get to the bottom of this.

Bryce drove up to the address he had written down that morning and stared at the large, imposing mini-mansion. Micah was definitely used to the finer things in life. No problem—being a journalist, he would make sure she had nice things.

Bryce grimaced, *who was he kidding?* Journalists weren't exactly at the top of the food chain. But money shouldn't matter when it came to love. If he and Micah were meant to be together, then everything would work out in the end. He parked the car in the driveway and got out, walking slowly to the front door. He was here to fight for his chance with Micah. If she was willing to do whatever it took to be with him, the least he could do was be a man and stand up to her father.

Bryce rang the doorbell and waited. A few minutes later, the door was opened by a pretty little blond with a pert nose and freckles. This had to be Micah's new stepmom.

"Hi," the girl said with a grin.

Bryce smiled winningly and held out his hand.

"Hi, Mrs. Rawlings. I'm Micah's boyfriend, Bryce. I was wondering if Micah's dad was here. I just needed to talk to him," he said.

Kathy giggled with glee when she heard the word *boyfriend* and grabbed his hand, pulling him inside immediately.

"You're Micah's boyfriend! Oh, that's just fabulous. And I could have sworn she wasn't seeing anyone. I'm calling her tonight. We'll have to go out to lunch, and she can give me all the details. And you're just gorgeous, the lucky thing," she said with a wink.

Bryce laughed at her exuberance and held up his hands.

"Well, we've only been going out for a very short time. I don't think there's that many details to give," he said.

"And it's a good thing," came Phillip's angry voice from the stairs.

Bryce's smile quickly disappeared as he looked up and saw Phillip glaring down at him.

"Phillip, honey, you don't understand," Kathy said with a laugh. "This is Bryce, Micah's *boyfriend.*"

Phillip walked down the stairs slowly, staring at Bryce the entire time with a cold, mean glare.

Bryce swallowed and began to sweat.

"I've come to talk to you in private, Mr. Rawlings. I hope that you can spare me a few moments of your time," he said as bravely as he could in the face of that icy disdain—something he'd never faced before, not even on his mission.

Phillip frowned and looked like he was going to say no.

Kathy walked over to Phillip and took his clenched hand in hers.

"Oh, come on, Phil. He just wants to talk to you. I know Micah would want you to. *Oh.* Oh, my goodness," Kathy said and grabbed her stomach while turning green.

Phillip's glare turned immediately to concern as he ushered his new wife to the guest bathroom, where Bryce couldn't help but overhear the wretched sounds of a good case of morning sickness. When Phillip appeared in the doorway, it was to ignore him as he led his exhausted wife to the back of the house, where Bryce hoped she would lie down. Ten minutes of loud, explosive vomiting would bring anyone to their knees.

Phillip returned moments later, still grim but without the glare.

"Well, Katherine insists that I see you, so I will. Please follow me. My office is down the hall," he said and walked quickly away.

Bryce knew this was his chance, so he walked quickly after Phillip. *Now, what in the world am I going to say?* He followed Phillip down the hall and into a large room, covered in wood and beautiful paintings. Bryce couldn't help but stare in awe. His mother's kitchen, dining room, and family room could fit in here easily. The clearing of a throat brought Bryce quickly around though.

"What do you want?" Phillip asked, not wasting any time.

Bryce straightened his shoulders and looked Phillip in the eye.

"I want to know why," he demanded, not backing down.

Phillip raised an eyebrow at Bryce's directness.

"I assume you want to know why I forbade Micah to see you again. As if you didn't know? You should have known immediately that Micah was out of your reach. Micah is special. She's not meant for someone like you."

Bryce felt his temper flare but tried to remain calm.

"Someone *like me?* What exactly am I, then? As far as I know, I'm a returned missionary with a 3.5 GPA. I'm a loving son and good brother. Whatever it is you think I am, I know that I will treat Micah with nothing but respect. My intentions are completely honorable," he said slowly and clearly.

Phillip sneered at Bryce and shook his head.

"You forgot to mention one thing about yourself Bryce. Your father. When Micah brought me your profile, I did a background check on you. Micah is my only daughter. She means the world to me. Do you think I would let my daughter be involved with the son of a man who writes scripts for rated-X movies and articles for pornographic magazines? Your education is being paid for by the money earned off of anything from child pornography to the latest gay porn movie. It sickens me—your father sickens me!—and I won't have my daughter anywhere near him. Do you understand me? Do you?" Phillip asked, almost shouting now.

Bryce felt all blood leave his face and his hands begin to tingle. He couldn't breathe. He could not believe it. His father involved in pornography? No! It couldn't be. *Please, no. Don't let it be true*, he thought wildly. Bryce backed up and sat down on a green leather chair; his legs had lost their strength. Phillip had to be wrong.

"What? You look surprised. You must have known," Phillip said sternly.

Bryce shook his head silently. He'd had no idea. None.

Phillip cleared his throat almost guiltily as he watched the tortured feelings pass over the young man's face.

"Well, now that you know, you have to understand that you just cannot have a relationship with my daughter—ever. I won't stand for it. The idea of your father even being in the same room with Micah makes my skin crawl. Now, please understand, I know that your father left you and your sister when you were quite young, so I'll concede that you probably aren't involved in that filth. But what if you two got married? She would carry your last name—the name in the credits of all these disgusting movies and on all the articles that man writes. No, she has carried an honorable name for more than twenty years. I won't let her exchange it for yours," Phillip said proudly.

Bryce felt as ill as Micah's stepmother. He had to get out of there. He had to digest this information. He had to find out for himself if it was true. He couldn't sit there for another second and let this awful man belittle his father and his family name. He stood on shaky legs and tried to look Phillip in the eyes.

"Look, Mr. Rawlings, I don't know if what you say is true or not. I'll be finding out for myself today from my father. But I will say this. Every man has to pay for his *own* sins— *not* his father's. If what you say about my father is true, then I feel sorry for him and the choices he's made. But let me be very clear. I am my own man. I make my own choices, and my last name is one to be proud of because *I* honor it. And someday if I'm lucky, and Micah agrees to be my wife, then she'll be proud to take my name because she loves me. Telling her that you'll take away funding for her schooling and living expenses if she sees me won't work. She already has plans to take out a student loan. You'll lose her if you make her choose between you and me. If you love your daughter, you'll let her make her own choices and accept me for who *I am:* a good man," he said clearly and with every ounce of conviction he had.

Bryce looked Phillip in the eye one last time before turning and walking out of his office. As soon as he was out of Phillip's eyesight though, his shoulders sagged and he quickened his pace. He reached the door and let himself out, practically running for his jeep now. He turned the key and peeled out of the Rawlings's driveway as quickly as he could without turning his Jeep over. He headed north, toward his home. As old as he was, he needed his mother right now. His home was all the way in Bountiful, but he could use a good drive. He needed to sort this out.

Bryce got quickly onto the freeway and grabbed his cell phone. He dialed his dad's number and listened to it ring. On the fifth ring, it was finally picked up. It was a girl's voice who answered. Bryce gritted his teeth and asked as civilly as he could for his dad. Less than a minute later, he heard his dad's voice on the line.

"Hey, Bryce! My boy! I'm so glad you called. I've been thinking of you lately. I want to come down soon and take you guys out on the town. I've got so much to tell you. I just signed a contract with a cable station to write for a new sitcom they're putting on. It's the deal of a lifetime. Even if the show gets cancelled, I still get the money. Bryce, the good times just keep coming," he said with sharp laugh.

Bryce felt his stomach churn and wondered if it were

true, or if it was just another lie to cover up what he really did for a living.

"Look, Dad, I've got to talk to you about something serious. Do you have a few moments to talk in private?" he asked, thinking of the young woman's voice he had heard.

"Of course, son. Go ahead, what's going on? Do you need money for anything? I already paid your tuition for fall, and your apartment's paid up until next spring. Is it your car? Are you finally going to give the heave-ho to that piece of crap and let me buy you a real car?"

Bryce winced, replaying Phillip's words in his mind. His education was paid for by child pornography. Bryce felt a surge of anger at his father.

"Dad, you won't believe it, but I was just told that I was forbidden to see a girl that I'm in love with. Do you want to know why, Dad? Do you?" Bryce asked in a strained voice.

The line was silent for a moment.

"Why, son? What's going on? Do you need me to have a talk with this guy, set him straight?" his dad asked, suddenly serious.

Bryce had to swallow before he could say the words.

"Phillip Rawlings did a background check on me to see if I was worthy of his daughter. He found out that *my* father is a great and glorious writer of pornographic movies and magazines. He told me that I wasn't good enough for his daughter and that he would never let his daughter take on such a dishonorable name as mine. Can you believe that, Dad?" Bryce said, choking on his words.

The silence on the other end of the line was answer enough for him. He hung up on his father and turned his cell phone off. He surprised himself when tears began trickling down his face. He wiped them viciously away as he concentrated on just getting home. He had to see his mom. She would know what was going on. She would tell him the truth.

chapter twenty-seven

Phillip watched discreetly from his window as the young man tore out of his driveway as if he had a devil on his tail. He frowned and shut the blinds, walking back to his desk. The young man had actually stood up to him. He had looked him in the eye as an equal and had thrown all his information in his face as if it didn't matter one bit.

Phillip winced. It had mattered. He had crushed the kid. He had shattered him with just a few words. And he wasn't feeling very good about it right now for some reason. Could it be possible he was wrong? Could this young man be right for Micah? He certainly had enough backbone. His background check hadn't come up with one bad thing about Bryce—just his father. Could Phillip live with that? He shuddered at the thought. But what if he didn't have a choice? What if Bryce was right and Micah would choose him over her father's wishes? Phillip frowned and watched as the door to his office slowly opened and his new wife walked slowly and tiredly toward him.

"Hey, sweetie. What did Bryce want to talk to you about? Isn't he darling? He'd be perfect for Micah. And if they get married soon and have some babies like we're doing, they could grow up together. Then we'd be a real family, Phil. Wouldn't that be nice?" Kathy asked with a sweet, hopeful smile.

Phillip smiled at Kathy gently and walked over to her as she sat down gingerly on a chair.

"Katherine, you're a romantic darling. To be honest, I just don't think he's right for Micah. But don't worry, she'll find the right man soon," he reassured his wife.

Kathy just smiled at her new husband.

"Oh, Phil, he looked just like you did when you fell in love with me. Would you have let anything stop you?" she asked with a grin.

Phillip stood up and looked away. Kathy was right. He wouldn't have let anything get in the way of his marrying Kathy. And if Bryce was the same—and he was beginning to think so—then he would have to rethink his strategy. And fast.

chapter twenty-eight

April stared out the window, impatient for a glimpse of Joel coming around the corner. Bryce had told her to stick around, so that was what she was doing. *And nothing else,* April thought ruefully and sighed. This was ridiculous. She'd always made fun of girls who sat all day by the phone, just waiting for it to ring. It was less funny now that she knew what it felt like.

She glanced at Lisa and Micah, who were sitting at the table doing their nails. Now that the summer semester was over, they only had a few days of freedom until fall semester started. April looked forward to it. At least then she'd have something to think about besides Joel—and his son. April frowned. Was she really okay with the fact that Joel already had a child? She kept telling herself she was. But deep down, she wasn't sure. What if Garrett hated her? April massaged her forehead and got up. She had to do something before she went crazy, just listening to her own thoughts.

"Hey, guys, I'm going to make some cookies. Does anyone have any chocolate chips, flour, sugar, and butter I can borrow?" she asked hopefully.

Micah looked up from her nails and smiled. "Go for it. You know where everything is. But I get to eat most of them," she added seriously.

Lisa frowned at April. "You know I'm on a diet, April. Do you have to make cookies now? Can't you wait until I'm gone tomorrow or something?" she asked.

April paused as she took the flour down from the shelf in their pantry.

"Lisa, it's one thing to be on a diet, but even healthy, thin people eat a cookie once in a while. I've been watching you and all you eat anymore is salad and fruit. You're completely forgetting about good carbohydrates and good proteins. I'm impressed with how good you've been, but one cookie won't kill your diet. I promise," April said seriously.

Lisa glared at her as she twisted the fingernail polish lid on tightly.

"You're the one who sat down with me and told me what to eat. I've lost five pounds, April. I refuse to put it back on. And you're just torturing me when you eat junk food in front of me. You're being cruel," she said and got up from the table.

April's mouth dropped open. She glanced at Micah, but her mouth had dropped open too. Was this hormones or was Lisa being serious?

"Lisa, you need to calm down, sweetie. Whenever I eat something, it's because I'm hungry. It's not to be cruel to you. I'm your friend, I wouldn't do that to you. Look, I'm sorry making cookies offends you, but eating healthy doesn't mean saying no to everything all of the time. A cookie or an ice cream cone every once in a while is allowed," she said slowly and calmly.

Lisa's mouth drooped down in a pout, and she didn't look happy at all.

"Well, I'm going to my room then. Do what you want," she said and walked briskly away.

April shook her head in wonder. "Holy cow. I got chewed out over making cookies. That's never happened before."

Micah let out the breath she had been holding. "Wow. She is really taking this new lifestyle seriously. She's been doing yoga every day, sometimes *twice* a day. She goes for walks, and she barely eats anything anymore. I wonder if she's taking this too far."

April frowned as she measured ingredients into the bowl.

"Well, actually, I'm glad she's being serious about her diet. Losing a good twenty pounds is the healthiest thing she can do for her body right now. So going overboard right now is probably okay. If she starts getting too skinny though, then we'll have to worry. She just needs to find the right balance of exercise and diet. She'll be okay. I think she's grumpy because Corbin didn't sit by her at church. He barely said hi to her," she said.

Micah leaned back, holding her hands up to blow on the newly painted nails. She'd chosen a bright metallic blue.

"Good. The sooner she realizes he's not worth her time, the sooner she can meet someone who will treat her good."

April smiled at Micah. "Good point."

April and Micah talked and laughed for the next forty-five minutes as they waited for the cookies to be done. As April removed the last cookies from the baking sheet, the doorbell rang. Her heart jumped as she ran to the door to answer it. She didn't even bother looking through the peephole. She practically flung the door open with her exuberance.

"Hi, April," Joel said, grinning at her. "I've brought someone special to meet you," he said, pulling a shy little boy from behind his legs.

April's eyes went wide in surprise. She hadn't expected this so soon. Joel hadn't even warned her. But as she studied the little boy, who was looking up at her curiously, she felt a smile bloom inside. He was adorable. He was dressed just like his dad, in jeans, tennis shoes, and a T-shirt. His hair was a slightly curly light blond. And his eyes were bright blue. His chubby cheeks were sticky with something. Joel had probably given him a sucker.

April kneeled down to be on Garrett's level and held out her hand to him.

"Hey, Garrett. Your dad told me all about you. But he didn't tell me just how cute you are. You are one tough-looking kid," she said with a grin.

Garrett looked up at April curiously. "I am tough. Just like my dad. I can run real fast too. Do you want me to show you?" he asked hopefully.

April tilted her head to the side, thinking about it. "Well, I have an idea. Why don't you come try one of my cookies I just baked and have a glass of milk and then we can go for a walk. There's a duck pond just down the road, and we can go feed the ducks some bread and have a few races. Does that sound good?" she asked, still on her knees.

Garrett smiled at her, took her hand, and shook it hard.

"Deal. Where's the cookies?" he asked, walking around her and into the apartment.

April laughed and stood up. Joel was smiling sweetly at her; he leaned over and kissed her lightly on the lips.

"I had a feeling you two would hit it off," he said.

April smiled and pulled Joel into the apartment, shutting the door firmly behind him.

"Of course we did," she said, as one of the worries she had been gnawing on all day disappeared. She and Garret would be just fine.

chapter twenty-nine

Amelia Jorgenson pushed the curtains out of the way so she could look out the window. She was in her early forties with light brown hair that fell just below her chin in a bob. Her slight figure and gentle eyes were what people remembered most about her. But she was stronger than she looked. Being a single mom was a refiner's fire that had turned a naive young girl into the woman she was today. But was she tough enough for what lay ahead?

She had just gotten off the phone with Bryce's dad, Troy, and didn't look forward to this conversation. She had spent most of her life making excuses for Troy, and she was tired of it. Bryce was old enough to know the truth about his dad.

But how could she break her son's heart? She frowned sadly as Bryce pulled into her driveway and got quickly out of the car. She opened the door before he could pound on it in his anger and hurt.

"Hi, baby," she said and opened her arms to her son.

Bryce felt broken as he let his fist drop to his side. He let his mom envelop him in a warm hug and was saddened when that didn't automatically make him feel better. There was nothing that could help him take away the stain of his father's life—not even his mother's love.

"Come in, honey. I just got off the phone with your dad. We need to talk," Amelia said and gently pulled her son into her home. She walked him toward their old, comfortable couch and waited until he sat down before she let herself join him.

Bryce looked at his mom and shook his head in utter misery.

"How? How could somebody who was raised in the Church, who went on a mission and was married in the temple, end up making pornographic movies?" he asked bluntly.

Amelia bit her lip and dropped her eyes. She had only found out herself six months earlier. But even that wasn't long enough to prepare her for this.

"You're asking the wrong person that question, Bryce. I don't know. I've spent many, many years trying to figure out why your dad makes the choices he does. But I will say that whatever choices your father has made in his life are *his* choices. They don't have anything to do with the fact that you are a good and honorable man. You are not your father. You never will be, thank heavens," she added sincerely.

Bryce groaned and leaned his head back on the cushions, closing his eyes and willing himself not to cry again.

"You're wrong, Mom. Dad's life has everything to do with me. Do you want to know how I found out? It certainly wasn't from you or Dad, that's for sure. I found out from the father of the girl I'm in love with. He doesn't want me to have anything to do with her and when I asked him why, he told me. He doesn't want his daughter tainted with my last name," he said, lifting his head to look at his mom.

Amelia gasped and put her hands to her mouth in distress.

"Oh, no," she moaned.

Bryce felt some of the anger that he had directed toward his mom for not telling him disappear. His dad's actions weren't his mom's fault. She didn't deserve this.

"Yeah. Nice way to start things off with the in-laws, huh?" he said, trying to make a joke out of it.

"Well, what did your girlfriend say? Does she care? She won't hold this against you, will she?" Amelia asked, almost frantically.

Bryce jumped up from the couch and pounded his thigh with his fist.

"I don't know! I haven't told her yet. I just barely found out myself. But I can just imagine her reaction. It's been nice knowing you, Bryce, but you're just not my type," Bryce said bleakly.

Bryce stopped his pacing and leaned up against a wall, shoving his hands in his pockets.

"What do I do, Mom? I've been halfway in love with this girl since the day I met her. And now that we're finally going out, I just know that she's the one for me. I want to marry her. I want to start a life with her and have children with her. It was all so perfect. But no—it's not going to happen. Her dad has already told me to back off, and as soon as I tell her the truth about our family, she'll be gone. And I'll never be happy again," he said, closing his eyes and wishing with everything he had that his dad was someone different. Someone he could be proud of.

Amelia grabbed a pillow and hugged it tightly. "Bryce,

honey, maybe you aren't giving your girl a chance. Let's not judge her too harshly. Let's give her the benefit of the doubt, and if she loves you as much as you love her, then she won't hold your father against you. Don't give up just yet."

Bryce walked back to the couch and slumped down next to his mom.

"I can't stand the thought of Jenny knowing about Dad. It would kill her. Can you imagine what would happen if she gets engaged and Dad's skeletons come out of the closet? This could destroy her, Mom. Why is it that Dad is the one who has committed all these sins and does all these evil things, but we're the ones who have to pay for it? It's just not fair. I wish . . . I wish he wasn't my dad," Bryce said emphatically.

Amelia shook her head at her son's venomous feelings but couldn't hold them against him. She had felt the very same thing at one time.

"Honey, you need to know something. Your father may have tainted his name, but your name will never be tainted. Think of your heritage as a long chain of links going back forever. Your father, because of his decisions, has taken himself out of that eternal chain. But you haven't. You won't. You are linked to your Grandfather Jorgenson, who was one of the most honorable and gentle men I ever knew. You are linked to him, and his name is one to be proud of. Don't ever be ashamed to be a Jorgenson. Ever."

Bryce looked at his mom, and quickly blinked the unshed tears out of his eyes. If only he could believe what his mom said. If what she said was true, then there was hope for him. There was hope for Micah and him and their future.

"Sorry, Mom. You don't need this. This is between me and Dad. You shouldn't have to suffer every time something he does comes out into the open. It's not fair to you," he said quietly.

Amelia patted her son's knee and got up from the couch.

"That's what moms are for. Why don't I make us some popcorn, and we'll sit down at the kitchen table and figure out how to break it to your girl? We'll work through this together. You'll see. Everything is going to be fine. By the way, what's you're girlfriend's name? I should at least know what my future daughter-in-law's name is," Amelia said with a smile.

Bryce smiled back up at his mom. She was the best.

"It's Micah, Mom. Your future daughter-in-law's name is Micah."

The two walked into the kitchen hand in hand.

chapter thirty

April sat and watched Garrett feed the ducks little bits of bread and laughed at the happiness she saw on his face. He was loving it. And she loved to just look at him. It was amazing to her that part of Joel was in Garrett. What a beautiful little boy. And to think that maybe, just possibly, this little boy could be hers someday. April grinned at the thought. And he was already potty-trained. Bonus!

"What in the world are you thinking about to put that smile on your face, April?" Joel asked as he lay back in the grass, resting his head on his hands.

April looked back at Joel and smiled at him.

"I was thinking about Garrett and how lucky you are to

have him. He's amazing," she said.

Joel sat up and grabbed her hand, pulling her over to sit by him.

"Do you really think so, April? Are you being completely honest with me?" he asked seriously.

April frowned at Joel.

"Of course I'm being serious. Why would I lie? He's standing right there. Anyone with eyes can see what an adorable little boy he is. Why would you ask me that?" she asked curiously.

Joel sighed and looked up at the sky.

"Sorry. It's just that when it comes to Garrett, I'm very careful. I have to be. The choices I make affect my son. And I'm determined that my son will have a good life, that he'll be happy and . . . loved. He needs to be loved," Joel said.

April's frown disappeared, and she looked back at Garrett, still giggling over the ducks.

"Joel—I know we haven't been going out for very long, so you don't know me very well. But I want you to know something about me. I don't lie. If I say I love someone, it's the truth," she said.

Joel's frown turned into a happy grin.

"Um, I didn't say anything about love, April. What are you trying to say? Are you saying you love Garrett, or are you saying you love *me*? Which is it?" he asked, laughing at her expression.

April blushed a deep, deep red and turned her face away from Joel, mortified at the slip she had just made. Had she really just said that?

"Fine, I won't press you. But it's good to know. It's so good to know," Joel said, still smiling.

The two watched Garrett for a little while longer and then walked back to the apartment hand in hand. As they reached the parking lot, April's smile slipped a notch as she saw a car that looked just like her dad's car—with Idaho license plates exactly like her dad's. It *was* her dad's car. Her dad was here. April came to a complete stop.

"What's the matter? Are you okay? You just went white," Joel said, grabbing her other hand and looking closely in her face.

April shook her head quickly and tried to smile.

"I'm fine. Really. It's just that I think my dad's here—at my apartment. I didn't even know he was coming. He never has before. It's been a long time. But, um, would you like to meet him?" she asked nervously.

Joel looked curiously at April before grabbing Garrett's hand.

"Well, of course I want to meet your dad. Let's go," he said and walked quickly ahead of her.

April rubbed her hands over her face and took in a deep breath for courage. She wasn't sure why, but she didn't feel good about this. This was scary. She walked behind Joel and Garrett, and then waited as he opened the door for her. She and Garrett walked into the apartment together with Joel close behind. And the first face she saw was her father's. He wasn't smiling.

"Hi, Dad. What a nice surprise," she said quietly and then walked quickly over to her dad and gave him a quick hug and kiss on the cheek.

Adam Bentley looked down at his daughter, still not smiling but hugged his daughter in return.

"You look beautiful, April. It's amazing what people can do when they make the right changes in their life. Your roommates have been kind enough to entertain me while you were gone for your walk. Why don't you introduce me to your friends?" he said, cutting his eyes to Joel and Garrett.

Joel's friendly smile faded to a polite smile as he held his son's hand firmly in his. April looked over to Joel with pleading in her eyes. If her parents were going to give her such a hard time for the mistakes she had made in her life, what would they think of Joel—and Garrett?

"Dad, this is my boyfriend, Joel Hughs, and his son, Garrett. Joel and Garrett, this is my dad, Adam Bentley."

She watched her father stiffly shake hands with Joel, but when he came to Garrett, he crouched down on his knees in front of him and held his hand out solemnly to the two-and-a-half-year-old. Garrett looked at him curiously but shook his hand anyway.

"You're April's dad? I like April. She makes good cookies," Garrett said.

April grinned at his words and looked to Joel for his reaction. He smiled back at her but still didn't say anything.

"Well, this is interesting. I come down to visit my daughter, and I find out she has a boyfriend who has a *son*. Obviously, you're not a returned missionary. April, I don't understand. You always told me while you were growing up that you planned on marrying a returned missionary in the temple. I thought you had more conviction, April. I never thought you'd give up your dreams. Why am I just now finding this out, April? Would you have *ever* told me if I hadn't come down and surprised you?" he asked accusingly.

Joel frowned at Adam Bentley and walked over to April.

"April, I'm going to leave you to have a visit with your father. I don't want Garrett getting home too late. Thanks for a great afternoon. Call me tonight," he said and kissed her lightly on the lips.

He walked over to April's dad. "It was nice meeting you, Mr. Bentley. I'm sure we'll be getting to know you much better in the future." He walked out of the door with Garrett in his arms. Garrett looked back at April over his dad's shoulder and waved at her.

April shut the door softly and turned to face her father. Micah and Lisa had disappeared magically, leaving just her and her dad. Alone.

"Did you really have to act that way in front of Garrett? I don't care what your assumptions of the situation are, there was a little boy here who means a lot to me, and you acting this way is not something he should have to witness. What are you even doing here?" she asked angrily.

Her father glared right back at her.

"Well, I thought I'd come down and try to talk some sense into you after you yelled at your mother on the phone the way you did. But I can see I'm going to get the same treatment. What in the world are you doing, involving yourself with a man who has a child, April? Even you have more sense than that. At least, I had always thought so until now," he said with his hands on his hips and his voice raising.

April winced at what her roommates were hearing but didn't know what else to do.

"I don't feel the need to justify my actions to you. I won't. But I will say that Joel is an honorable man. He honors his priesthood, and the fact that he has a beautiful son is not something that I or he should be ashamed of. And he didn't need to be given the cold shoulder by my father. I'm ashamed of you," she said passionately.

Her father's eyes went wide and his shoulders slumped at the hurt and anger he heard in his daughter's voice.

"Then I guess there's no reason for me to stay then, is there?" he said, looking at her and waiting.

"If the only reason you came down to Utah was to scold me for telling Mom the truth and to treat the people I love badly, then no. There is no reason for you to stay. However, if the reason you came down to Utah was to see your daughter, whom you haven't seen in three years, because you love her and miss her, than stay. I'd like that."

April and her father squared off, neither one blinking an

eye. Her father was the first one to give in.

"I'm staying in town for business for the next couple of days. Go to dinner with me tomorrow night and hopefully we can talk some of this out. It will give us the night to think things over. And hopefully we can have a polite and calm conversation."

April let her hands fall from her hips and knew this was the best she could expect.

"Okay, Dad. That sounds good."

He walked over to the counter and grabbed his suit jacket off the back of the chair. He walked to the door and opened it.

"I do love you, April," he said and walked through the door, shutting it firmly.

April stared at the now empty room and felt the tears fall quickly from her eyes. What a way for Joel and her father to meet! This was horrible. She had seen the anger in Joel's eyes. He was mad at her dad. She couldn't blame him. What a mess! She continued to cry but lifted her head when she felt a pair of arms encircle her from behind.

"Oh, April. It'll be okay. It will," Micah said gently.

April blinked and held back a sob. "I don't think so. I don't think it will. How could it?" she asked desperately.

Micah walked around to the front and pulled April toward the couch.

"Listen, if I can overcome my father, then you can overcome yours. It's called making your own decisions and living your own life. I've been trying it for a few weeks, and I have to say I love it."

April snorted. "Okay, your dad forbids you to date Bryce, who is just about perfect in every way. A returned missionary, smart, good-looking. What's not to like? He'll have your dad won over in no time. Now, my situation is a little different. Joel is good-looking and smart and a great guy, but he hasn't been perfect and he has a son. I just don't see my mom and dad accepting that. They can't even accept *me*," April said miserably.

Micah wrinkled her nose as she thought of it this way. But before she could say anything in response, Lisa walked in the room and looked accusingly at the both of them.

"Joel has a son, April? I can see why you didn't tell your family. *I* sure wouldn't. But why didn't you tell me? Micah obviously knew. Were you embarrassed?" Lisa asked.

April's eyebrows shot up in the air at Lisa's tone.

"I guess because I knew you'd react the same way you are now. You didn't want me to go out with Joel in the first place. You tried to warn me away from him and that was before you even knew about his son. You're just like my father—completely intolerant of other people," she said hotly, glaring at Lisa.

Micah stared back and forth between her two room-mates, wondering how she could diffuse the situation. She had no idea, so she decided to be quiet.

Lisa's eyes narrowed at the attack, but she didn't back off. She walked farther into the room, glaring at April the entire time.

"I don't even know why I care. I was doing you a favor by even being your roommate. Everyone told me that you were some wild druggie and that I should stay as far away from you as I could. But I didn't listen to them. I gave you a chance. I think that's called tolerance. And finally, because of *my* good example, you eventually decided to look more acceptable. Well, hallelujah! But before I can even enjoy having a normal roommate, you go and start dating a guy who has a son. You have got to be kidding me!"

April tilted her head back on the couch and closed her eyes, praying for patience.

"If being my roommate is such a strain on your daily allotment of tolerance than maybe you should find a differ-ent apartment. I wouldn't want to make you uncomfortable with my lifestyle choices," April said wearily.

Lisa's face fell a fraction, and her eyes dropped to the floor.

"Well . . . I guess . . . um, maybe so. Maybe that would be the best thing for everyone," she said and turned to walk out of the room.

April and Micah watched Lisa walk away from them quietly. April shook her head sadly.

"Micah, maybe you should go and talk to her."

Micah shook her head firmly. "No way. If she thinks that you are too wild and crazy for dating Joel, there's no telling what she'll do when she meets my stepmother. She doesn't even realize that you're more normal than me," Micah said with a slight laugh.

April tried to smile but couldn't.

"I'm going to go take a bath and try to relax."

Micah watched April walk tiredly out of the room and felt her heart break for her friend. She really didn't deserve this—from her father or from Lisa. Maybe she would go and talk to Lisa.

Micah walked quickly down the hall toward Lisa's room and knocked hard on the door.

"Come in," she heard Lisa say. So she opened the door and walked in. She was shocked to see Lisa eating a Snickers bar with a box of doughnuts opened beside her, half of them gone.

"What's going on here, Lisa?" asked Micah carefully.

Lisa ignored Micah and reached for a doughnut as she shot the Snickers wrapper into the waste basket with the other hand.

"I'm taking a break from my diet. I wasn't very happy with it, anyway. All these restrictions, all these things I can't do. I'll start again tomorrow. Maybe," she said without any emotion.

Micah pulled Lisa's computer chair out and sat down,

facing Lisa on the bed.

"What's going on really, Lisa? I mean, you're yelling at April, you're being mean to everyone. This isn't you. You're sweet and kind, and we love you. What's happening?" Micah asked.

Lisa finally met Micah's eyes and then broke down crying. She threw the doughnut down and grabbed her pillow, sobbing loudly into it.

"You just don't understand. Your life is so perfect. You look perfect, you have a skinny body, great clothes, a rich dad, a gorgeous boyfriend who loves you and wants to be with you. Heck, even April's whacked-out boyfriend can't wait to see her. But me—nothing! I'm fat, and nothing I can do will change that. The more weight I lose, the harder it gets. And Corbin acts like he doesn't even know me," Lisa said in between sobs.

Micah nodded her head in understanding. So this *was* about Corbin. April had been right.

"Have you ever thought that maybe—just maybe—you shouldn't want to be with Corbin? Yeah, so what, he's like your dad. Why not pick someone who *isn't* like your dad? There are thousands and thousands of guys on campus. One of them might be the one that's right for you. If it were me, I'd never pick Corbin. Never in a million years. He's cold, he's not kind, and anyone who can go out with a girl and then ignore her in front of his friends at church isn't worth it. He's not. So the sooner you realize that, the happier you'll be. Keep going on your diet. It's okay to give yourself a break every now and then. Remember, April said that one day a week, you can eat anything you want. So let's pick today for that, and tomorrow you can go back to your diet and yoga. Everything is going to be okay, Lisa. Just don't take everything so seriously," Micah pleaded.

Lisa pulled the pillow down from her face and stared at Micah searchingly.

"You're right. It's just so hard to see you and April so happy, knowing that there isn't a guy in the world that will give me the time of day. I really thought Corbin liked me, you know? And then when I realized he didn't today, it just, oh . . . I don't know, it hurt me, really bad. And I took it out on you and April. I'm sorry, Micah. Will you forgive me? Will you let me stay and still be your roommate?" Lisa asked with more tears in her eyes.

Micah smiled at her. "Of course. But I think you should talk this out with April. I think she's hurting too," Micah said honestly.

Lisa frowned but nodded. "After she gets out of the bath, I'll talk to her."

Micah got up from her seat and walked to the door but turned before walking out.

"We're all here searching for our bit of happiness, Lisa. It's just a lot nicer when you're searching with the help of your friends," she said and walked out.

Lisa stared at her and then threw the other doughnuts in the trash. She had a lot of searching ahead of her. And none of it was going to be easy. Soul-searching never was.

chapter thirty-one

Bryce drove home from Bountiful in complete silence. He didn't want any music to distract him from his thoughts. He was going straight to Micah's apartment and having it out. He knew he couldn't stand the stress of wondering if they had any future together. It was better for both of them if she found out now, especially if it was from him and not her father. That's what his mom thought anyway. According to his mom, a relationship with secrets wasn't a good relationship. And that's what he wanted: a good relationship. *No, forget that*, he amended silently. He wanted a great relationship. He wanted an eternal relationship.

Bryce felt nauseous again and turned the air conditioning

on high, hoping the air would cool his hot forehead. He just hoped he could keep his lunch down when he was talking to Micah. He could just see it now. *Hi, Micah, my father is heavy into the porn scene down in Hollywood. Would you like to get married?* And then him throwing up in the bushes and her laughing all the way to her front door before she slammed it on him. Yeah, he was really looking forward to this.

Bryce groaned out loud as he reached his exit. In less than ten minutes he would be at her front door. How could he do this? How could he tell Micah something so sick and vile about his family? About his father?

Bryce realized he couldn't do it alone. He pulled off into an empty parking lot and took a few breaths. He needed his Father for this—his Father in Heaven. Bryce bowed his head and said a short prayer for courage. He leaned his head against his steering wheel and hoped with all his soul that Micah would see past his father to him. If she couldn't, then he would have to deal with that. But there was no backing out now. Bryce put his Jeep into gear and headed down the street. As bad as he had it, he felt worse for his mom. She had convinced him to tell Micah, and he had convinced her to tell Jenny. *Oh, man.* He wouldn't trade shoes with her for a million bucks. Jenny was so emotional and so proud of her family. This was going to kill her.

Bryce frowned, wondering at the power one person had to cause so much damage and pain. It just wasn't right. He blinked a few times as he realized he had pulled into Micah's parking lot. This was it. No going back.

Bryce got out of the car and walked slowly toward Micah's front door. But before he could knock on it, she was pulling it open for him with a smile.

"I was just looking out the window and saw you pull up. I'm so glad you came over," she said, reaching up to hug him and kiss him sweetly on the cheek.

Bryce smiled sadly down at her and kissed her back.

"Hey, why don't you take a walk with me? There's something we need to talk about," he said, taking her hand.

"Sure," Micah said, and closed the door behind her.

They walked in silence for the first block or so. Bryce looked curiously down at Micah. His sister, Jenny, would be dying to know what he wanted to talk about. But Micah was just walking calmly along, patiently waiting for him. He loved that about her. She was strong. She could take this—he hoped.

"Micah, after I left you this afternoon, I went over to your dad's to confront him about why he didn't want you to go out with me. He told me he didn't want his daughter having my last name. It wasn't good enough for you. I just couldn't believe it. But I guess he did a background check on my dad and turned up some pretty horrible information about him. Stuff I didn't know about. He told me that my father was not a writer for sitcoms down in Hollywood, like I've always thought. He's a writer for pornographic movies down in Hollywood. He's done it all. Think of the most horrible, vile, disgusting filth out there, and my dad writes the scripts for it," he said, looking away from Micah in desperate shame.

Micah stopped in her tracks and looked up at Bryce. He looked almost broken. And her dad had done this to him. *Her* dad.

"I'm sorry you had to find out something so sad from my father. That wasn't right of him. He shouldn't have done that. I know he's protective of me, but that's going too far. I'm sorry," she said, squeezing his hand.

Bryce looked at Micah in surprise. "What? No, look, Micah, you don't understand. If we take this relationship further, you're going to have to decide if you can handle the possibility of your last name being Jorgenson. According to your father, you're better than that. This is serious. If you make a commitment to me, I just want you to know that I would never let you feel demeaned or shamed by carrying my last name. I would want you to be proud to be my—"

Bryce stopped walking and looked down at his feet. *What was he doing?* Was he trying to tell Micah the truth or was he proposing? Man, he was losing it.

Micah looked up at Bryce with a twinkle in her eyes. "What, Bryce? What are you trying to say?" she asked patiently.

Bryce looked Micah in the eyes and reached for both of her hands.

"I guess what I'm saying is, that if you can accept me, despicable father and all, than that's someone who I'd want to be with forever. That's what I'm saying."

Micah grinned up at Bryce.

"Oh, Bryce, if you can get past my father, I'll get past yours," she said and started walking again.

Bryce's mouth dropped open. He ran to catch up with her.

"Hold on," he said, grabbing her arm. "Are you saying that you don't even care that my dad writes scripts for pornographic movies? Are you kidding? That's not even normal, Micah. You're supposed to run screaming back to your apartment and change your phone number or something. This is weird. This is so not what I was expecting," Bryce said, shaking his head in confusion.

Micah stopped walking and grabbed Bryce's hand.

"Hey, now, don't freak out. I'm sorry I don't react the way most people do to most things. I just react the way *I* react. Did you *want* me to run screaming back to my apartment?" she asked with a frown.

Bryce smiled at her and shook his head.

"Hey, this isn't some weird plan to get rid of me so you and your sister missionary can hook up, is it? Because I'm not buying. You'll have to flat out tell me that you don't like me and don't want to see me again to get rid of me. If not, then you're stuck. I'm yours," she said.

Bryce felt the large lump that had been sitting in his throat slip down into his stomach and dissolve. How could he be so lucky?

"Micah, I absolutely adore you," he said, putting his arms around her. He held her tightly, not patting her back or rocking back and forth. He just stood there and quietly held her.

Micah held him as hard as he held her, knowing he needed a moment.

"Now that that's settled, what will your dad do when he finds out you still want to be with me in spite of my father? He's going to flip out. You really are going to need a student loan. He's going to totally disown you," Bryce said seriously.

Micah grabbed Bryce's hand, and they turned to walk back to the apartment.

"Who knows, Bryce? I don't even want to waste my time thinking about it. All I want to think about right now is that you totally adore me. Let's just forget everything else for today. Okay?" she asked, smiling up at him hopefully.

Bryce grinned down at her and pulled her closer to his side.

"Sweetie, you have a deal. Let me take you back to my apartment, and I'll make you dinner. You look like you could use some lasagna and French bread. Am I right?" he asked, still smiling.

Micah nodded her head happily. "How did you know?"

Bryce turned her toward the parking lot and his car.

"Oh and by the way—my mom wants to meet you. I told her I'd wait and see if you could handle the family skeleton, but she told me you'd be fine. And she was right. But she wants you up to dinner next week sometime," he said, helping Micah with the door.

Micah looked surprised but agreeable. "Sure, Bryce.

I'd love to meet her. But, um, is she like Jenny?" she asked before sitting down.

Bryce laughed and then leaned down and kissed her quickly on the mouth.

"Complete opposites," he said.

Micah took her seat and let him shut the door. Bryce got in the car and drove to his apartment. He knew he was smiling. And for some reason, for the life of him, he couldn't stop.

chapter thirty-two

Micah and Bryce were just sitting down to their dinner when the doorbell rang. Joel, who was sitting on the couch, motioned Bryce to sit back down.

"I'll get it," he said and opened it to see Jenny standing on the doorstep with tears running down her red cheeks.

Joel's mouth fell open, and he turned to look at Bryce. Bryce frowned and got up from the table, walking slowly toward his devastated sister.

"Bryce," was all Jenny said and ran into her brother's open arms. She sobbed noisily into her brother's shoulder, not caring who was looking on.

Micah felt the warm feeling she'd had all afternoon

dissolve into a cold, hard knot of anxiety. Her father was the reason Jenny was crying and Bryce was so stressed out. Well, Micah amended, actually, it was *their* father that was originally to blame for choosing an immoral lifestyle, but her father didn't have any business dredging it up and smearing it in their faces. Micah's eyes fell to her lap. Okay, yeah, she knew her father was very protective and strict. She knew why he had done what he'd done. But he wasn't the one sitting here listening to Jenny cry her eyes out and seeing Bryce speechless and aching. It just wasn't right. None of it. *Why couldn't he have let everything alone for once?* she wondered silently. Micah got up from the table and walked over to Joel, who was still looking on in disbelief.

"Joel, could you give me a ride home? I think Bryce and Jenny need some time alone," she asked quietly.

Joel nodded his head. Bryce turned around as Joel and Micah headed out the door.

"Micah, I'll call you later. Sorry about this, but this needs to be dealt with once and for all. Okay?" he said.

Micah nodded and gave him a small, sad smile before disappearing out the door.

Joel walked silently beside her and opened the car door for her.

"Wow," Joel said as he sat down and started the engine. "I knew Jenny was emotional, but she looks like the world has just ended."

Micah grimaced and knew, in some ways, for Jenny it had. Her heart went out to the young girl, even though she knew Jenny didn't like or approve of her.

"It's probably a personal family matter or something," Micah mumbled, hoping Joel would change the subject. And he did.

"Personal family matters. Those three words sure say a mouthful, don't they? I guess you heard April's dad this afternoon. I don't think I'm going to get his blessing to see

April," he said and frowned darkly.

Micah looked over at Joel's profile. He really was so good-looking and nice. So he had a son. Micah couldn't think of anyone else who would treat April so well.

"Don't worry, Joel, April is strong. She's been on her own without her family's help for a while. So what if they don't approve of you? She does. She really likes you—*and* your little boy. If you're really worried about it, why not pray about it?" she asked on impulse.

Joel smiled and looked over at Micah.

"Hmmm. You're sounding like a Relief Society president, Micah. Watch out, or the bishop will find out," he said, trying to make a joke.

Micah's face paled, as she had totally forgotten about her calling. She needed to submit names for two counselors and a secretary to the bishop within the next week. How could she have forgotten?

"Hey, I was just joking! Stop looking like you're going to faint," Joel said quickly.

Micah sighed and knew it was probably a good thing she had gone home when she did. She had a lot of thinking to do. The bishop said that choosing the right counselors was very important.

"It's okay, Joel. It's just been a long day. And don't worry about April's dad. Dads can moan and groan all they want, but when it comes down to it, it's the daughter who makes the final decision about who she wants in her life," Micah said as Joel pulled up to her apartment.

Joel smiled at Micah. "Thanks, Micah. I'm glad April has you for a friend. You're very wise."

Micah opened the door and got out but leaned down to see Joel's face.

"You know, I wouldn't want to go back to the apartment if I were you. I bet Jenny's still crying. Why don't you come in and see if April has any cookies left?" she asked.

Joel didn't need to be asked twice. He was out and joining her on the sidewalk within seconds. April opened the door with a frown, but when she saw Micah and Joel, she grinned and threw her arms around Joel.

"I knew you wouldn't be scared off by my dad. I knew it," she said, hugging him tightly.

Joel laughed and winked at Micah. "Did you think I was a wimp? Besides, he hasn't pulled his shotgun out yet. Um—*does* he own a shotgun?" Joel asked, in a worried voice.

April laughed and pulled Joel inside. Micah left April and Joel in the family room. She grabbed a couple cookies and headed to her room. She flopped on her bed and grabbed the ward directory the bishop had handed her just that morning. What was she going to do? How in the world could she be the next Relief Society president?

She munched on her cookies and tried to think of something else. Just thinking about it made her ill. It was much easier to think about what she was going to say to her father. Better yet, why not call him and get it over with?

Micah reached for the phone and dialed her dad's phone number.

"Hello?" answered a soft, feminine voice.

Micah sat straight up. *Kathy!*

"Uh, hi, Kathy. This is Micah. Is my dad there? I need to talk to him," Micah said carefully.

"Oh, Micah! I'm so glad you called. It's been too long since we've talked. You promised we'd go out to lunch too. And I'm just in the mood to take you up on that tomorrow. Oh, and I've been craving Mexican food like crazy lately. You have no idea. Why don't we go to Los Hermanos tomorrow at one o'clock? It'll be fun. I can pick you up," Kathy said, all in one breath.

Micah massaged her forehead and wondered why it was she always seemed to get a headache every time she talked to her stepmother.

"Umm, gee. I don't know about that. The new school semester starts tomorrow, and I need to meet with my professor after my last class for a little counseling session. And then I have to do some Church stuff," Micah said, trying to sound very busy.

"Oh, it's just lunch, Micah. Even a busy college girl like you needs to eat. Tell you what. I'll pick you up in front of the Wilkinson building at one. Don't make me wait, Micah. See ya!" Kathy said and hung up.

Micah looked at the phone in her hand in shock. *What just happened there?* she wondered. She could swear she had called and asked to speak to her father. Instead of her father, she had gotten a lunch date with her younger stepmom. No way was this happening!

"Ugh!" Micah screamed into her pillow. *Now what?* Micah asked herself. She sighed and lay back down on her bed. It served her right. Next time she'd just wait until her dad came to her. In the meantime, though, she was in for chips and salsa with Kathy.

Micah groaned again and turned her head into her pillow. Maybe a good night's sleep was the best thing. Tomorrow would get here soon enough.

chapter thirty-three

Micah walked out the large glass doors in front of the Wilkinson Center and stood, looking morosely at the passing cars. She sighed and glanced at her watch. It was so interesting that Kathy had insisted that *she* be there on time and yet she was nowhere to be seen.

A loud retching noise from the bushes had all of the passing students looking to their right. Micah's eyes went wide at the horrific sound the person was making. It sounded like someone was seriously ill. She walked over to the bushes to see if the person needed help.

"Um, hi. Are you okay in there?" Micah asked, stepping even closer to the bush.

Kathy's long blond hair appeared first, and then her green face appeared next, matching her green contacts. Micah gasped and ran to her stepmother, grabbing her by the shoulders.

"Are you okay, Kathy? Do you need to go to the doctor? We need to call my dad," Micah said quickly, letting go of Kathy's shoulders to reach for her cell phone.

Kathy smiled weakly and let her hair fall as she wiped her mouth on a tissue she pulled from her purse.

"Oh, please don't, Micah. I don't want your dad worrying. It's just this darned morning sickness. It happens all of a sudden, and I'm running for the nearest bush. It's so embarrassing. Sometimes when I stand for a while I get really sick. I would have waited in the car, but I didn't want to miss you," Kathy said, looking weak and ill.

Micah immediately felt guilty for her annoyance at Kathy for making her wait. Kathy had an interesting habit of surprising her. Micah was determined to make her into a wicked stepmother, but Kathy just refused to fit the mold.

Micah smiled and held out a hand to Kathy.

"Hey, I know what would make you feel better. A nice big plate of enchiladas. Let's go get something in your tummy. My little brother is probably starving," she said kindly.

Kathy looked up at her in surprised delight and took Micah's hand. The two girls walked to Kathy's car in the parking lot without saying a word, but both were feeling that this might be the beginning of something.

Micah insisted on driving and pulled in front of Los Hermanos within ten minutes. They were seated right away, and Micah told the waiter to put a rush on their order since her stepmother was ill.

The waiter looked surprised and did a double take of the two girls but hurried away without saying anything.

Kathy smiled sweetly at Micah and put her water glass down.

"You know, Micah, you're a lot like your dad. You take care of people. You take charge, and you take care. That's why I fell in love with Phillip. I'd never met anyone like that before. But you're the same way. I think that is so wonderful."

Micah stared at Kathy for a second before taking a sip of her own water. *Her?* A take-charge kind of person? Right.

Micah cleared her throat softly. "So, Kathy, tell me how you've been doing. Obviously you've been pretty sick. Did the doctor say if it's going to go away soon?" Micah asked curiously.

Kathy bit into a chip and groaned.

"It is supposed to go away next month, but my doctor says that sometimes it never does. I might be throwing up my entire pregnancy. You know, I've always wanted a large family, but if this is the way it's going to be, then I told Phillip I would only have a few children. Forget having five or six. This pregnancy stuff is harder than I thought. And I don't even want to think about the delivery," Kathy said worriedly.

Micah winced, not wanting to think about it either, and decided to change the subject.

"I'm sure it will be okay. Um, the last time I talked to Dad he mentioned you might like some help with decorating a nursery or something. Have you thought much about it?" Micah asked and took a chip to nibble on.

Kathy went from night to day within seconds. Micah smiled at the change in her stepmother.

"I've thought of nothing else! And when Phillip told me that you insisted on helping me with the nursery, I just knew everything was going to be perfect," Kathy said, yanking her purse up off the floor and grabbing a large envelope out of the side pocket.

Micah's eyes widened in surprise as Kathy showed her swatch after swatch of fabric and samples of wallpaper. After

Micah laid them all out on the table, she looked at them critically. She'd always been good with color and design. She'd even wanted to go into interior decorating until her father had laughed her out of the room for even suggesting it.

"Well, Kathy, I think the first thing we need to do is find out the sex of the baby, before we go any further. I know we're all hoping for a little boy, but if it's a little girl, then we can go all pink and frilly. When do you find out?" Micah asked Kathy, noticing a little frown on her face.

Kathy looked guiltily at the swatches, moving some of them around nervously.

"Well, I went to this little place in the mall, and they told me the sex of the baby last Wednesday. I know you and Phillip really want a little boy, but, um, she's . . . not." Kathy said, looking up at Micah.

Micah grinned at her. "Well, congratulations, Kathy! A little girl! A little boy would have been nice, of course, but a cute little baby girl will be so much fun. Imagine doing her hair and picking out the laciest, frilliest dresses. A little sister—now that's nice," Micah said softly, smiling out the window at nothing in particular.

Kathy started crying softly into her napkin. Micah looked over at the noise and got up immediately, scooting in by Kathy on the chair next to her.

"Hey! What's the matter? Little girls are fun too. You'll see," Micah said comfortingly.

Kathy looked up with red, puffy eyes. "Oh, Micah, it's just your dad. He has his heart set on a little boy. What is he going to do when he finds out it's a girl?"

Micah looked down at the table and frowned. She knew why her dad wanted a little boy so bad. She didn't know if Kathy knew why though. Maybe it wouldn't hurt to tell her.

"Kathy, the reason my dad wants a little boy so bad is because he lost a little boy a long time ago. And ever since then, he's missed him. But if you plan on having more children, heck, the next two babies could boys. You'll see, my dad will be just fine. He's just happy that he has you and now a little baby on the way. You guys are going to be a happy little family," Micah said sadly, wishing she'd had a happy little family growing up. All of a sudden, she felt horribly jealous of the little baby inside of Kathy.

Kathy looked up at her hopefully.

"Really? Wow, I didn't know that. That explains a lot. Okay, I can deal with this. I think I'll tell Phillip tonight. Besides, he's already had experience raising a wonderful daughter like you. This will be great, won't it?" Kathy asked, smiling through her tears.

Micah did something that shocked them both. She leaned over and hugged her stepmother. "Yeah. It's going to be great," she said truthfully, putting her jealousy aside.

The two girls pored over the samples as they ate lunch, and by the end of the hour, they had become good friends. Micah no longer noticed the sleeveless tank top and short skirt Kathy was wearing. She saw the person underneath. And she liked her. But as a new Relief Society president, her mind was on saving souls and doing her part for the kingdom. As Kathy paid the check, Micah nervously gathered up all the samples for Kathy.

"Um, Kathy? Hey, I was wondering—has Dad ever talked to you about how families can be forever?" Micah asked nervously. She'd never been on a mission and had really never tried to talk religion with anyone other than other LDS people. This was a big first. And if she messed it up, she'd have her dad to answer to.

Kathy frowned and put the samples in her purse.

"No, not really. What do you mean?" she asked curiously.

"Well, I know you've seen the temples that our church has. There's one in Salt Lake, and there's one right here in Provo. Well, people who belong to our church go there to be married by someone who has the proper priesthood authority and they are sealed together forever. Not just for as long as they live but forever. Do you understand what I'm saying?" Micah asked.

Kathy nodded and leaned forward in her seat.

"You mean, if Phillip and I got married in the temple, then our baby would be ours, no matter what—forever?" Kathy asked breathlessly.

Micah nodded and looked into her stepmother's eyes.

"Yes, Kathy. That means that your family would be yours forever. Throughout eternity. There's something special about our church, Kathy. Why don't you ask Dad about it tonight? He can tell you a lot better than I could," Micah said, hoping Kathy would.

Kathy nibbled on her fingernail and thought about it.

"Phillip has been so embarrassed to go to church lately—what with how things happened and all. But if he knew I wanted to go, then I know he'd go back. He's so sad whenever I ask him why he doesn't go anymore. I know it would make him happy. He loves your church so much. He reads that little book every night, you know. Maybe I should. Maybe I will," she said, looking away.

Micah grinned to herself and got up from the table.

"Well, let's go, Kathy. Dad will be wondering where you are, and I have a ton of homework already."

Kathy dropped Micah off at the Wilkinson Center again, reaching over and hugging her before she got out of the car.

"Hey, thanks, Micah. Thanks for going to lunch with me. I really needed to be with another woman and just talk."

Micah hugged her back and smiled.

"Anytime, Kathy," she said. And she meant it.

Micah walked away, toward the library, and smiled to

herself. Life was so strange sometimes. If Kathy could just get her dad to go back to church, and if Kathy was baptized, then their family really could be together. And her with a new little sister! Who would have thought that that would make her so happy?

* * *

The next two weeks passed by quickly as Micah jumped into the new school semester with her emphasis on psychology. Her new calling as Relief Society president was met by her roommates with squeals of delight and surprise. Micah was glad when everyone in the ward seemed to accept it as no big deal. She still remembered when it was just a few weeks ago and she had sat in the back of the chapel wishing she could trade souls with any of the sparkling, beautiful girls who had instant access to all things good and wonderful in the world. And for once in her life, she was starting to feel like maybe her soul was good enough. Maybe there was some hidden spark in her after all. Maybe she was going to be just fine the way she was.

But getting used to being the Relief Society president was a big transition. April and Lisa insisted that they do scripture study and pray together in the morning and at night before they went to sleep. She grinned as she thought about it, though. April and Lisa were still acting awkwardly toward each other, but they were rock-solid together when it came to helping her out spiritually.

She had thought of just automatically calling April and Lisa to be her counselors, but when she had prayed about it, she had decided on calling two girls she didn't know very well at all. When she had told the bishop about it, he had smiled and told her that that was the Spirit at work. *The Lord knows people better than we do,* he had said. Micah was just happy that the first test was over. Now, all she had to do was get through the rest of the year.

She loved it when she went to church now though. No one even seemed to realize that she had hated church before and how insecure she had felt. Everyone accepted her—well, everyone except Jenny. Jenny had taken to coldly ignoring her ever since she found out about her dad's lifestyle. She blamed Micah for some reason. Bryce insisted she'd get over it soon, but Micah wasn't so sure. In the meantime, it made things very uncomfortable—especially when they all went to Bryce's mom's for dinner. Jenny frowned at her the entire evening, making her appetite completely disappear and making her more nervous and quiet around Bryce's mom than she normally would have been. It was only when Bryce's mom gave her a hug before she left that she felt better. She had whispered in her ear, "Don't worry about Jenny, she's going through a hard time. When she grows up a little, you'll see she's really a wonderful person. She's just doing a good job of disguising it right now."

Micah had hugged her back and had felt weightless. *Bryce's mom approves of me! Yeah!* The rest of the week had gone by smoothly and wonderfully. She and Bryce had gotten in the habit of going to the library and studying together. They were spending so much time together she was sure that he would ask her to marry him by Christmas. He was always talking about the future as if she were a big part of it. Micah smiled whenever she thought of Bryce. It was just her father who was determined to get in the way.

Phillip had come over to the apartment to confront her about staying out of his business. He hadn't brought up the word *religion*, but she knew what had gotten him so upset. Micah smiled grimly, knowing that Kathy wasn't about to back down about religion. Kathy called her almost every day to ask her something new about the Church. They even had a lunch date set up for next week. Micah was planning on taking her to The Roof in Salt Lake for lunch. It just so happened to be across from the temple. If they happened to go to the visitors center and talk to a couple missionaries, what was the harm? Her dad wasn't going to get his way on this one, she vowed.

Yep, everything was going wonderfully. Well—except April. April's dad could give Micah's dad lessons on being stern and strict. April's lunch date with her father had gone disastrously. April had come home crying and refused to come out of her room for the whole day. She hadn't seen as much of Joel, either. Something was going on, and Micah didn't know what. Apart from wrestling April to the floor and forcing her tell her, she couldn't do anything. Maybe she should ask Bryce? Maybe Joel had said something to him?

Micah parked her car and walked down the path to Bryce's apartment. They were meeting up to get something to eat for dinner, and then to go to the library to study. Micah grinned—she couldn't wait until they were married. Then she would cook him fabulous meals all the time. She laughed as she walked around the corner, knowing she'd need to take a cooking class first, but she stopped quickly as she spotted a tall, gorgeous redhead knocking on Bryce's door.

Micah watched curiously as Bryce opened the door. She was only a few yards away, but neither of the two people staring at each other even noticed her.

"Michelle!" Bryce said and swooped down to pick up the beautiful woman and twirled her around in circles. The girl's musical laughter filled the courtyard.

"Put me down, Bryce! Everyone's going to think you've gone crazy," she said flirtatiously.

Bryce set the slender woman down but kept hold of her shoulders, looking her in the face.

"I can't believe it's been a year and a half, Michelle. I think you've grown even more beautiful," Bryce said simply.

Michelle looked up into Bryce's eyes and stepped closer.

"Oh, Bryce, you don't know how much I've missed you. I think it was knowing that I was coming back to you that made it all worth it," she said—and then leaned up on her toes and kissed Bryce smoothly on the mouth.

Micah's mouth fell open as Bryce didn't seem to be pulling away very fast. Michelle obviously took Bryce's lack of reaction as acceptance and ran with it, wrapping her arms around Bryce's neck and deepening the kiss.

Micah felt a large slap of anger and jealousy hit her and jerk her forward.

"Hi, Bryce. Looks like you have some company," Micah said loudly and in a strangely high voice.

Bryce jerked Michelle's arms from around his neck and pulled quickly away.

He looked past the redhead's long wavy hair and saw Micah's eyes filled with shock and hurt.

"Micah, come here, sweetheart. I need to introduce you to someone," Bryce said firmly.

Micah felt tears pricking the backs of her eyelids but blinked them away furiously as she pasted a small artificial smile on her face. Fine, she would make nice, but he was going to get it when they were alone. *He let her kiss him!*

The redhead slowly turned around and glared at the intrusion. She'd been waiting for eighteen months for this reunion, and some idiot was ruining her reentry into Bryce's life.

"Michelle, this is Micah, my *girlfriend*. Micah, this is Michelle, an old friend of mine."

Micah saw the shock bloom on Michelle's face and felt more calm. At least he hadn't introduced her as just a friend. But as the horror continued to grow on the girl's face, she felt a small sliver of compassion sneak in. She obviously hadn't been expecting this.

"What are you talking about Bryce? *Girlfriend?* She's your *girlfriend?*" Michelle asked, ignoring Micah's out-stretched hand and turning back to face Bryce.

Bryce closed his eyes and looked at the ground.

"Michelle, look, you and I broke up a long time ago. Why should it matter to you if I have a girlfriend? We're just friends. That's the way it was before you left and that's the way it still is. Micah and I are together, and we're very serious about each other," Bryce said simply, looking warily at the girl, hoping she wouldn't make a scene.

Michelle looked back at Micah and practically snarled, "You're turning me down for her! Some stupid little blond! The only reason I went on a mission was for you. To give you more time to get used to the idea of us being together. I've learned so much, Bryce. I'm a different person now. Just give me a chance to show you. *Please?*" Micah's mouth fell open. Michelle was acting as if she wasn't even there, as if she were a speck of dust on her shoe. Of all the nerve!

Bryce cleared his throat nervously.

"Look, Michelle, why don't you come back tonight and I'll call Jenny, and you can show us all of your mission pictures and tell us about all of the people you met. I know Jenny is really excited to have you back. Why don't you come over about seven?"

Michelle looked slightly pacified. "Will *she* be here?" Michelle asked, not even looking at Micah.

Micah's mouth fell open at the insult but waited to hear Bryce's reply.

Bryce looked guiltily at Micah and then back to Michelle.

"Micah has a presidency meeting tonight, otherwise she would be."

Micah remembered her meeting and looked at her shoes. *Well, wasn't he lucky he didn't have to step into that one?* she thought crossly.

Michelle reached up and hugged Bryce one more time, kissing him noisily on the cheek.

"Fine. I'll see you tonight. You'll see, Bryce. Things are going to be different from now on," she said, finally looking at Micah with cold, blue eyes. She walked away with an obvious swing to her hips.

Micah looked down and noticed her hands were clenched into tight, white fists. With this new threat to her relationship with Bryce, her dreams of a perfect romance were starting to crumble at the edges. Why couldn't her life just be normal for once?

Bryce watched Michelle disappear around the corner and then turned to face Micah.

"Sorry," he said and looked at her solemnly, waiting for some kind of emotional explosion.

Micah looked at him without any expression on her face and stuffed her clenched hands into her pockets.

"She's very pretty isn't she?" she finally said, when she couldn't think of anything else to say.

Bryce looked down at his feet and nodded.

"Yeah. I guess so."

Micah was hoping secretly that he would deny it, but one of the things she had always liked about Bryce was that he never lied—ever. *Darn it.*

"I guess she's a pretty good kisser too," Micah said, looking away at nothing in particular.

Bryce leaned against the brick wall and looked bleakly at the sad girl standing in front of him.

"She's all right. Look, Micah. *She* kissed *me*. I didn't kiss her. I didn't enjoy it. I didn't feel anything. She might have it in her head that we're meant to be together. But it's in my head that you and I are meant to be together. Don't let what you saw become something bigger than it was. Okay?" he asked quietly.

Micah looked up at Bryce and felt a small tear slip from

under her eyelash.

"Why did you let her kiss you? I would never have let *anyone* kiss me. I'm committed to you. That means something to me," she said with a tremor in her voice.

Bryce sighed and ran his hands through his hair.

"Now, wait a second. Just because Michelle planted one on me doesn't mean I'm not committed to you. You know I am. You're the only woman I even think of, and you know that. *You know that, Micah.* I honestly didn't even see it coming. I was a little shocked. I should have pushed her away immediately, but now I'm glad I didn't. Because now I have rock-solid proof. I *don't* like kissing Michelle. I like kissing you. You're the one I'm in love with. I'm sorry you had to see that. But I'm glad you were here. Now Michelle will know that there is this gorgeous woman in my life and she has no chance—none," Bryce said emphatically.

Micah swallowed but still wished with everything she had that he hadn't let Michelle kiss him. She didn't know if she would ever get that image out of her head. And Michelle was coming back tonight to be with him. How was she ever going to concentrate at her meeting, knowing that?

"Yeah, well, have fun tonight with Michelle. Try not to experiment too much," she said and turned around, walking toward the parking lot.

Bryce kicked into motion immediately.

"Look, this is over. Let's turn the page and move on. Weren't we going to go get something to eat?" he said, grabbing her arm and turning her around to face him.

Micah felt miserable, but she knew she'd feel even more miserable if she stomped away childishly and went home alone. And she was hungry.

"I guess so," she said finally.

Bryce tilted her head up so he could look into her eyes.

"Please don't be sad. Don't let her ruin this. We didn't let my dad or your dad ruin our relationship. We're not going to let a crazy little redhead get in the way, are we?" he asked with a teasing smile.

Micah tried to smile back. "I'll agree to that as long as I don't walk in on you two kissing, ever again," she said darkly.

Bryce laughed and leaned down to kiss her. Micah pushed him away, though, and used her hand to wipe the red smear of lipstick off his mouth. He winced at the lipstick he saw on her hand and shook his head.

"Better," Micah said and reached up to kiss Bryce.

He let her kiss him quickly on the lips but didn't release her when she pulled away. "Now, this is how I kiss the woman I love," Bryce said and cupped her face in his large hands. He kissed her tenderly for a long moment before pulling away.

"See. I'm yours. No contest," he said kindly, still holding her.

Micah sighed and let the jealousy she was holding onto slip away.

"Come on, I'm starving," she said and pulled him toward her car.

As they pulled out of the parking lot, Micah turned her head and saw a tall, slender woman with red hair leaning up against a tree, staring at them drive away. Michelle hadn't gone anywhere. She had been eavesdropping the whole time! Micah frowned. Bryce thought this was over with Michelle. Micah knew differently. Michelle wanted Bryce. She was sticking around.

chapter thirty-four

April stared out the window of the bus as she rode slowly home from school. Her classes were over, and she didn't have a yoga class until Wednesday night. That meant she could go home and study. *Hooray.* April sighed and knew she was miserable.

Her dad's last words to her kept banging around in her head: *We've sold the house, and we're moving down to Utah. There's nothing for us in Rigby anymore. We're tired of being shut out. That's why I came down here—to look for a house. It's time we were a family again. And that means you're going to straighten up and start living right. No more crazy rebellions. No more talking back to your mother, no more talking back to me, and no more crazy boys who already have children. It's time to remember who you are—you're my daughter.* April sighed and rested her head on the window. She'd been on her own for a while, and now to have her family just around the corner was going to be a big adjustment. Her father had made it clear—crystal clear. Joel was out of the picture. And that thought made her completely miserable. Joel had been calling her for the past couple of weeks, but she kept putting him off. She was running out of excuses. She needed to make a decision. Did she get rid of Joel like her dad wanted her to, or did she make the decision that would make her happy?

April groaned. But wouldn't being an accepted part of her family again make her happy? She knew it would. Why couldn't she have both? April got out at the next stop and decided to walk home. The fresh air would help her clear her mind. She needed to think. She needed to decide what was best for her. April walked with her head down and decided to say a quick little prayer.

Dear Heavenly Father, what should I do? I love Joel, but I love my family too. Which is the right path for me?

It was a short prayer, but it was all she could think of to say. She walked slowly down the street, ignoring the passing cars and the students walking in giggling, chatting groups past her. Why couldn't life be easy? Black and white. Yes or no.

"Hey, want a ride?" someone called from a car driving up next to her.

She tilted her head up, prepared to yell for help if she needed to, but grinned when she saw who it was—*Joel.* He was her answer. She'd known it all along.

"Yeah, as a matter of fact, my wimpy little legs were just getting ready to collapse. Would you please give me a ride?" she asked as she stepped toward the car and opened the door.

"Wimpy legs? I'm dating a yoga instructor for heaven's

sake. You could probably crush me in less than five seconds," Joel said, driving away from the curb and smiling at her.

"Oh, Joel, it's so good to see you." April said emphatically.

Joel looked over at her and smiled. "Well, you're a hard woman to get together with, that's for sure. I don't think we've even gone out in two weeks. I *know* we haven't. What's up?" Joel asked point blank.

April looked out the window and thought of making up an excuse, but she was too tired to think of any. She didn't want to anyway. She needed to be completely honest with Joel.

"My dad is what's up," she said simply and looked back at him. Joel nodded his head and pulled into the parking lot of Wendy's.

"Do you want a hamburger or anything?" he asked as he pulled up to the drive-through.

April shrugged. Why not?

"Sure. Could you get me a salad? If Lisa even thinks I've been eating junk food, she'll skin me alive," April said seriously.

Joel looked at her curiously. "You're teeny! Come on. Try a hamburger. You'll love it," he urged her.

April laughed. "Fine, but I'm blaming you when Lisa finds out."

The two took their food to a park and sat down at a bench. They munched away quietly for a few moments before Joel looked up and pinned her with his smoky gray eyes.

"Spill it, April. What has your dad said to make you so unavailable?"

April groaned and took a sip of her drink before answering. She was so torn up about the whole stupid situation.

"My father informed me a couple weeks ago that he's selling the house and farm and everything and moving my family down to Utah. He was down here looking for a house.

He also informed me that he will accept nothing but perfection from me from now on, and that means no boyfriends who already have children. He stated that the only acceptable boyfriend for me would be a young man from a good family who was a returned missionary and who would support me comfortably. Et cetera, et cetera," she said quietly.

She watched as Joel's expression went from kind and considerate to dark and unreadable. He looked as if his face had turned to stone. She'd never seen gray eyes blaze before, but now they looked like hot metal.

"And so that's why you've been so busy lately that you couldn't even spare me fifteen minutes? So that's it. That's it," he said tightly.

April felt like pulling her hair out. Yes, she had stayed away from him but only to figure out what she was going to do.

"Joel, listen to me. Let me just explain how I feel and what I've been going through this last couple of weeks. My family means everything to me. But for the past few years, because of a stupid, childish mistake, I have been estranged from the people who have meant the most to me. I haven't even seen my younger brothers or sisters in years. I've been the prodigal daughter who wasn't welcome home. So now my father shows up and offers me a way back and all I have to do is give you up. That's it, and I can have my family back again. But I want you to know something. I haven't called my parents and told them to kill the fatted calf. I haven't been obedient. I haven't because I can't. Every time I think of it, I feel physically ill. My father asked me to do the one thing I can't do—give you up." April's voice trembled.

Joel's eyes softened and his face relaxed as he watched April pour her heart out. He reached over and took her hands in his and kissed her knuckles gently.

"April," was all he said, and then he leaned over the table and kissed her.

April pulled back after a moment and smiled.

"You know, this is the best I've felt in two weeks. Just being with you makes everything else okay. You know, I was praying about what to do when you drove up. And when I looked up and saw you, I knew that Heavenly Father was giving me my answer. I think you're the answer, Joel. So what do you say to that?"

Joel grinned and pushed April's bangs out of her eyes.

"I think any girl who would go against her family's wishes to be with me is someone I'm never letting go of. So, let's do this, April. I'm not even prepared, and I don't have the ring on me, but what do you say? Would you like to be sealed to me and Garrett for time and all eternity?" he asked quietly and sincerely.

April's mouth fell open. *Holy cow!*

"But, Joel, we've only been dating for such a short time. I haven't even met your family. I might be really weird. You don't know me that well. I mean, I totally love you, but I don't even know anything about you. Are you serious?" she asked in a shocked voice.

Joel laughed and got up from the bench and walked around to kneel in front of her.

"You silly, beautiful, wonderful girl. I love you. We don't have to know all of that stuff right away. That's what eternity is for. We can be engaged for a while. We don't have to get married tomorrow. Come on, you know this is right. You can feel it—I can feel it. We are meant to be together. You can't deny that. So, for the second time, April, will you marry me?" Joel said, still kneeling looking searchingly up into her eyes.

April blew the hair out of her eyes and looked up into the blue sky. She smiled as she felt the sun warm her face. She needed love. She needed to be happy, and she needed Joel and his son.

"Yes, Joel. I will marry you," she said and laughed when

he jumped up and did a back-handspring and two cart-wheels.

"Yes!" Joel shouted to everyone in the park—not a few people were staring at him.

April thought about trying to outdo Joel with one of her most complex yoga positions but thought better of it and just threw her arms around his neck, laughing with happiness.

"Come on, April. You are meeting my mom and dad and all my brothers and sisters tonight. I'm taking you home," he said and pulled her toward the car.

They jumped into the car, grinning at each other. He pulled out into the traffic and headed straight for the free-way.

"Wow, I can't believe this," she said, shaking her head. "I can't believe I'm engaged to be married. To you! There were so many times I would just sit in church and stare at the back of your head, thinking you were the most gorgeous guy I'd ever seen in my whole entire life and knowing that you would never even look at me," April said.

Joel grinned and looked over at her.

"You think I'm the most gorgeous guy in the whole world? Seriously? That's perfect. Hilarious but perfect. And what do you mean I never looked at you? What about all those times I asked you to pass me a hymnbook or to borrow your pencil? What did you think I was doing?" Joel asked with a laugh.

April's eyes went large. "I had jet-black hair and outra-geous makeup and you were interested in me? I don't believe it," she said.

Joel smiled at her. "Why can't you believe that I've always been able to see the real you? From the moment I first laid eyes on you I knew that you were amazing. Believe it—because it's true," he said sincerely.

April leaned over and kissed Joel's cheek. She couldn't resist running her hands through his hair.

"I've been wanting to do that for over a year. I love your hair," she said.

Joel laughed. "Man, I already love being engaged. We should have done this a long time ago."

April laughed and drew her knees up with her arms, still smiling at Joel.

"Compared to how I was feeling, I might as well be in heaven. Do you think Garrett will be okay with me being his new mom though? It's not just the two us. I'm going to be a mom," she said in almost a whisper.

Joel looked over at April and grabbed her hand with his, steering with his left hand.

"You're going to be a great mom. And don't worry about Garrett. He hasn't stopped talking about you ever since he met you. Every time I see him he asks if we can go get more cookies and see April. It's going to be great, April. You'll see. We'll be a family," he said with hope and wonder in his voice.

April felt nervous at the thought, knowing in her heart that being Garrett's mother was going to be a big part of her life—and one of the best parts too.

"And my family, Joel. How am I going to break it to them that we're getting married? They probably won't even come to the wedding," she said sadly.

Joel frowned and shook his head.

"You know what? Let's worry about that tomorrow. If you want, I'll call your dad myself and tell him the good news. But tonight is a night for celebrating. Forget the fatted calf—you haven't tasted anything until you've tasted my mom's enchiladas. Come on. Put your smile back on and kiss me again. Life is good and wonderful," he said.

April leaned over and kissed him on the cheek.

"You're right, Joel. Life is good," she said and sat back with a smile on her face and a warm feeling in her heart. Life was good.

chapter thirty-five

Micah walked down the pathway toward her apartment smiling. The meeting had gone wonderfully. She loved her two counselors. She had chosen Keeley Shaw and Renee Cannon. They were both so smart and so nice. They acted like it made perfect sense that she was the new Relief Society president. And they had all gotten along together as if they had known each other their whole lives. And they had gotten everything done on the list Micah had made. It had been the perfect meeting. And she hadn't thought about Bryce and Michelle the entire time. Micah knew the prayer she had said to start the meeting was why. She had prayed that they would be able to concentrate on the Lord's business and leave the world behind for the meeting—and it had worked! She had to hand it to Lisa and April. Talking to Heavenly Father just made life easier—well, easier to handle, anyway.

She fixed her purse on her shoulder but stumbled when someone bumped into her from behind.

"Hey!" she said and turned around to see April sitting on the ground, giggling.

"Micah, I'm so sorry. I didn't even see you. Help me up," she said and grabbed Micah's outstretched hand.

"Well, you sure look happy. Is it safe to say that you're through being depressed now?" Micah asked curiously.

April got up and dusted her pants off, still smiling.

"Yep. It's safe to say that I'm the happiest person in the world. Micah, you will not believe this because I still don't, but Joel asked me to marry him today and I said yes!" April said, giggling and jumping up and down.

Micah jumped up and down with her, laughing and smiling too.

"April, that's fantastic! Tell me everything! How did he do it? What did he say? Where were you guys? Does Bryce know? Does your dad know?"

April stopped jumping up and down and pulled Micah over to a bench in the main courtyard to sit on. It was almost ten o'clock, but the courtyard was well-lit by all of the lamps.

"He asked me at the park, and it was kind of just a spur-of-the-moment kind of thing, but he did get down on his knee to ask me. Well—the second time anyway—and then he took me home to meet his mom and dad and his brothers and sisters, and Garrett was there, and it was just the most wonderful moment of my life. His mom was so nice! She gave me a hug and told me I was perfect for Joel and Garrett, and Garrett wanted to sit on my lap the entire time I was there. He was so sweet. And his dad was awesome.

Did you know he's a doctor? I had no clue his family was wealthy. His house is like a mansion. But anyway, his mom made us enchiladas for dinner, and I swear I've never tasted anything so wonderful in my life, and Micah, I am just so happy and so in love and life is just so wonderful," she said all in one breath.

Micah laughed and grabbed April's hands. "April, you deserve to be happy. You deserve this, and you deserve to have Joel and Garrett. I think this is wonderful. Congratulations," Micah said and gave her roommate a hug.

April and Micah talked for another twenty minutes before going inside the apartment. Both of them stopped in surprise when they found Lisa sitting on the couch, watching TV by herself.

"Hey," Micah said.

Lisa smiled at both of her roommates and turned the TV off. She got up and walked into the kitchen to join them.

"Hey, guys. I thought I'd wait up and see how you're doing. I haven't really seen much of you two lately," she said.

Micah shrugged and put her purse on the counter. That's when she noticed the large bouquet of white roses.

"Hey, who are these for?" she asked, looking at April and thinking they must be from Joel.

April shrugged and looked at Lisa.

"They can't be mine. I'm not expecting flowers until tomorrow," she said with a happy grin.

Lisa took the card out and handed them to Micah.

"They're for you, Micah. Read the card," she said.

Micah frowned, thinking they were from Bryce. He was probably trying to make up for the kiss.

"To Micah. Sorry for being such a pain. I hope that we can be friends. Love, Rod," she read out loud.

"No way," she said, staring at Lisa. "Did he drop these by or were they delivered?" she asked.

Lisa blushed and looked down at her feet.

"Well, he brought them by himself. And he was so nice, Micah, you wouldn't have believed it. I think we've been wrong about Rod. Maybe in the beginning he had the wrong idea, but underneath it all, he's kind of sweet. He stayed for a while, and we talked. He's really embarrassed about the way he acted. He really does just want to be friends with you. I promise. And aren't these flowers just beautiful? I wish they were mine," she said, leaning over and smelling the flowers.

Micah's eyebrows shot up. Rod was here. And Lisa had let him in. *Scary.*

"Um, Lisa, I don't think letting Rod into the apartment was a good idea," April said slowly, sharing a raised eyebrow with Micah.

Lisa frowned and turned away, walking back toward the couch.

"You're the one who's always telling me that people can change, April. I really think Rod has. He was so nice tonight. I'm sorry if you guys are freaked out, but I enjoyed his company. There—I said it. I enjoyed talking to Rod," Lisa said firmly, staring Micah and April down.

Micah cleared her throat and sat down on a stool, staring at Lisa.

"Did Rod ask you out, by chance, Lisa?" she asked cautiously.

Lisa blushed even brighter and studied a fingernail before answering.

"Micah, don't be weird about this. I know he liked you first, but yes, he did ask me out and I said yes. Okay—I have a date Friday," Lisa said guiltily.

Micah covered her eyes with her hands, and April groaned out loud.

"What? You guys date. Isn't it okay if I go out every once in a while?" Lisa said, raising her voice defiantly.

Micah lowered her hands and stared at Lisa helplessly.

"Lisa, we don't care if you date. We do care if you date a psycho. I'd rather you went out with Corbin than Rod. And I can't stand Corbin. Look, you have always said that you would only date returned missionaries. Guess what? Rod isn't even a member of the Church. Did he mention that?" Micah demanded.

Lisa picked up a throw pillow and rearranged it nervously on the couch.

"Well, actually, he did mention that your stepmother, Kathy, has been talking to the missionaries and that he was interested in talking to them too. He might take the discussions, Micah. He could join the Church," she said.

Micah's mouth dropped open. She didn't believe it—Rod might take the discussions. *Rod.* She shook her head. It was too much to take in.

"Look, Lisa, I can't make your decisions for you, and I'm too tired tonight to try. April, you try and talk to her. I'm going to bed," Micah said and walked down the hallway toward her bedroom. She could already hear April talking in soothing tones and smiled. She shut her door firmly and lay down on the bed fully clothed. She wondered if Michelle was still at Bryce's apartment. *She better not be,* Micah thought darkly.

She got out her scriptures, turned to her bookmark, and began to read. Whatever was happening in her love life, her spiritual life came first now. She kicked off her shoes and got comfortable. Life was going and coming and whipping around her so fast and furious that being centered in the gospel became more and more important to her every minute. She sighed, content to know that whatever happened in the future, she was determined to have the Spirit with her.

chapter thirty-six

Micah got home the next day from her classes and opened the front door wearily. She walked over to put her books on the counter. All of her new classes weren't as easy as they had first sounded. Switching majors meant switching her whole brain around, and she was exhausted from the effort. She walked over and collapsed on the couch, wondering where her roommates were off to. April was probably off looking for rings with Joel, she thought with a smile. And Lisa—what would Lisa be doing? Probably shopping for a new outfit to wear on her date with Rod.

Micah winced at the thought and had to wonder if this was just some sick and twisted way Rod had thought up to get closer to her. *Ick!* She shuddered. Hopefully April was able to talk some sense into her last night. She had been too exhausted to even try. But if something were to happen to Lisa, if Rod ever hurt her, then she didn't know what she'd do—she just didn't know. Was Rod really a nice but misunderstood guy, or was he some psycho stalker? That was the question. She hoped for Lisa's sake that he really was nice. That, or that Lisa was asked out by someone decent in the meantime.

Micah flicked her hair out of her eyes and scooted down into the cushions, getting comfortable. Now to think about Bryce. She'd been putting that off for hours. What was she supposed to think? He hadn't even called her last night. He had probably been having too much fun with Michelle and Jenny.

Micah frowned and closed her eyes. She hated feeling jealous and unsure of her relationship with Bryce. Lucky April! There was no one else for Joel but her. But this Michelle, this gorgeous returned missionary was bound and determined to have Bryce, regardless of what he wanted. How could he not be tempted? Michelle looked like a model, for heaven's sake. Who wouldn't want to go out with her? If she could only set up Michelle with Rod, then her life would be perfect. She giggled at the thought. Too bad life was never that easy.

The knock on the door had her getting slowly up from the couch. What she needed was a nap before she started her homework. She peeked through the peephole just to be careful. If it was Rod, she wasn't answering it, no matter how nice Lisa said he was.

The man standing on the other side of the door didn't look like anyone she knew. She opened the door cautiously.

"Hi," she said politely as she checked the stranger out. He was tall. Probably as tall as Bryce—and just as muscular too, she couldn't help noticing. And his hair was dark blond with light blond sun-streaks running through. His light blue eyes were crinkled up in a friendly smile. He was drop-dead gorgeous. She might be in love with Bryce, but she wasn't dead. He must be some model, lost and needing directions.

"Micah?" he asked.

She nodded her head, puzzled. She would have remembered if she had ever met this guy.

"I'm Brian Procter. I work for your dad at the law firm. He wanted me to come over and meet you. I guess you and I will be working together during the next little while. He's transferring your trust fund over to you now—something about you wanting to be independent, and it was time for you to make your own decisions. We have a lot of paperwork to go over and decisions to make. So if you have some time now, we can get started, or I can come back later, or you can just call me and set up a time. Whatever you want," he said, smiling down at her with the whitest teeth she had ever seen.

She shook her head in confusion. Her dad thought it was time she was independent? It was time for her to make her own decisions? Uh uh—she wasn't buying it.

"Um, were you looking for Micah Rawlings? Because that doesn't sound like something my dad would say," she said with a frown.

Brian laughed and looked at the paperwork he was holding.

"Micah Rawlings. Right here in black and white. You're actually quite a wealthy young woman. Your mom's life insurance has been sitting in a bank, growing every day. That's why we need to discuss what you want to do with it. There are investments you can make, and I can help you with that, or we can go over other options. I'm afraid we're going to be spending a lot of time together over the next month or so. I hope that's not a problem," he said, smiling flirtatiously down at her.

Micah blushed at the thought. How could she spend all this time with this gorgeous blond? What would Bryce think? She frowned, thinking of the kiss she had witnessed just yesterday—and the no phone call last night.

"It sounds great, Brian. Come on in and we can get started. I'm through with classes for the day so time isn't a problem right now," she said, moving aside so he could walk in.

He smiled down at her and walked inside, putting his briefcase on the table and opening it up. He pulled so many papers out of his briefcase that Micah suddenly felt tired again. She might have thought he had been flirting with her a little out on her front step, but now he was all business, and most everything he said went over the top of her head. She did a lot of nodding and saying yes. She knew she'd be up late reading all the small print and using a dictionary to help her figure out all of the legal terms. Why hadn't her dad just done all of this for her? she wondered as she looked at the clock and realized that Brian had been sitting at her kitchen table for almost two hours. She stifled a yawn and smiled as he finally closed his briefcase.

"Now we're not done, so don't look so relieved," Brian said, teasing her. "We still have a lot to do. Why don't we meet up again in few days?" he asked, standing up.

Micah stood up too and walked around the table.

"Okay, I'm usually free after two o'clock. I don't think I have anything important going on this week. Just call me later and we can set it up," she said.

Brian walked to the door but turned before opening it.

"I can't believe a beautiful girl like you doesn't have three dates a night. You must be lying. I bet your social calendar is stuffed," he said, definitely flirting with her now.

Micah laughed. She'd never had a stuffed social calendar. And now that she had started dating Bryce, a beautiful redhead seemed to be taking up his time.

"Sad, isn't it?" she said, smiling up at Brian.

Brian leaned against the door and raised his eyebrows. "Well, maybe we should do something about that. Why don't we mix business and pleasure and do some of this paperwork after dinner Friday night?" he asked.

Micah stuck her hands in her pockets and bit her lip nervously. What had she just gotten herself into? Would she be cheating on Bryce if she said yes? *And would he even care?* she wondered ruefully.

"Oh, Brian, I don't know. I just started seeing someone. We probably shouldn't mix the business and pleasure thing too much," she said apologetically.

Brian frowned and looked very disappointed. "I see. Well, I'm sorry if I made you feel uncomfortable," he said, still not moving.

Micah winced, feeling horrible now. "Look, if I wasn't seeing anyone right now, then I would love to go out with you. Absolutely, but since I am, I just couldn't go out to dinner with you and feel good about it. I'm sorry," she said sincerely.

Brian smiled at her. "Well, if things change in that department, I'll be waiting," he said, and opened the door. Before walking out though, he grabbed her hand and held it for a moment.

"I'm looking forward to spending a lot of time with you, Micah," he said with a wink and then turned around—and bumped into Bryce.

"Bryce!" squeaked Micah guiltily.

Bryce glared at Brian, who had stepped back and smiled in apology.

"Sorry there. Didn't see you," he said with a friendly grin.

Bryce frowned even more. "I know you didn't. You were too busy staring at Micah. Micah, who is this?" he demanded.

Before Micah could even get a word out of her parched throat, Brian stepped in smoothly.

"So this is the someone you're seeing. Well, now I know you weren't making him up just to get rid of me. Listen, I'll let you explain our relationship. I've got a meeting I'm late for. Bye, Micah," he said and walked confidently away.

Micah cleared her throat and moved over to let Bryce into the apartment.

"Hi, Bryce," she said quietly, looking slightly guilty.

Bryce ground his teeth and looked over his shoulder at Brian, who had just walked nonchalantly around the corner.

"Who the heck was that Micah, and what kind of *relationship* exactly do you have?" he demanded in a furious voice.

Micah sighed and shut the door quickly, before Bryce could go after Brian.

"Bryce, don't get upset. He works for my dad. He's a lawyer. My dad sent him over today to help me with some paperwork. My mom left me some money when she died. It's a *business* relationship. He did ask me out on a date, but I told him no, of course. There's no reason to snarl. It's not like you walked up on us kissing or anything," she added, feeling bratty.

Bryce looked up at the sky and put his hands on his hips. Micah stared at him, wondering what he was thinking. He didn't look very happy at all.

"Sorry, Micah," he finally said and looked at her. "For some reason, when I walked around the corner and saw that guy looking at you like you were dessert or something, I just wanted to punch him out. Sorry. I shouldn't have acted that way," he said and walked over and kissed her lightly on the lips.

Micah smiled and relaxed, knowing that although Brian was beautiful, Bryce was the one she was in love with.

"All is forgiven. Come in and tell me how your date with Michelle went," she said teasingly.

Bryce frowned again but walked into the apartment and went right for the couch.

"Ha ha. You're funny, Micah. And it didn't go all that great. Imagine being in love with one girl and having another girl sit there and flirt with you all night long. It's not as fun as it sounds. It's very uncomfortable. I think I had a migraine after she finally left. And Jenny, the little stinker, wasn't much help. *Oh you guys are so cute together. You guys look like you were made for each other.* On and on and on. It was enough to drive me crazy. And Joel wasn't even there to buffer the situation. I'm sorry, but it was pure torture. The whole time I was wishing I was with you," he said soulfully.

Micah melted and sat next to him on the couch, leaning her head on his shoulder.

"Well, you poor thing. You almost have me feeling sorry for you," she said, kissing him on the cheek.

Bryce smiled at her and put his arm around her shoulder.

"You better feel sorry for me. But now that I've done my duty, I am free from Michelle. We'll send her an invitation to the wedding and hopefully that will be the next time I see her," he said, his eyes sparkling down at her.

Micah grinned but shook her head.

"You're always talking like that, Bryce. When this happens and that happens. If you ever do ask me to marry you I won't even believe you. Did you know that Joel asked April to marry him last night? For real."

He sat up and turned to look at her fully.

"You're kidding me. Joel asked April to marry him? Like, with the ring and the words and everything?" he asked.

Micah laughed at his shocked expression.

"I'm not kidding you, Bryce. Some guys don't just talk

about it, they do it. You might want to ask Joel for some pointers," she said, still giggling at his expression.

Bryce sat back on the couch, his eyes wide and his jaw slack.

"I can't believe it. He didn't even tell me, and I'm his roommate."

Micah reached over and smoothed Bryce's dark, wavy hair away from his face.

"From what I hear, it was very spur-of-the-moment. Don't worry about Joel. They're going to be great," she said.

Bryce looked at Micah and pulled her in close.

"Hey, I'm sorry if I'm always talking about the future. That's the way I am. I'm a dreamer. But that doesn't mean I'm not a doer. I can't say it's going to happen as soon as Joel and April, but you know that I love you and that I want to be with you forever. How do you feel about me?" he asked very seriously.

Micah caressed his cheek and looked deeply into Bryce's eyes.

"Bryce, I don't even think I was alive before you came into my life. I'm finally me. You give me the courage to be someone that I like. And I'm completely me when I'm with you. Of course I love you. I was born to love you," she said simply.

Bryce sighed and shook his head. "I think I knew the minute I saw you. Honestly. And then when you were so cold to me, it made me furious. How could my future wife not even like me? I couldn't figure you out. But in the end, the only thing that matters is that we're together. If people would just stop getting in the way—fathers, redheads and surfer dude lawyer models," he said with a grin.

Micah snuggled closer to Bryce and reached for his hand.

"Don't worry about the surfer model. I could never fall

in love with a lawyer," she said.

Bryce laughed. "Why not?"

Micah sighed. "I grew up with a lawyer. It's impossible to have a normal conversation with a lawyer without having everything analyzed or being given the other side's point of view. It's exhausting. Nope. I would have to say that I would be mostly interested in, say, a journalist. Someone with an inquisitive and bright mind, with a love for truth. That suits me perfectly," she said.

Bryce laughed and hugged her tightly.

"You suit me perfectly, Micah." And he kissed her.

chapter thirty-seven

"So what's your plan?" Jenny asked as she took a bite of her pizza.

Michelle smiled at the pretty young brunette and flipped her long red hair carelessly.

"You're worrying too much, Jenny. You saw Bryce. He was hanging on every word I said last night. I give it two weeks, and he's breaking up with Micah. We'll be sisters-in-law within the year. You have my word," she said seriously.

Jenny took a sip of her soda and frowned.

"You sound so sure, Michelle. But I've never seen Bryce like this. I've told him over and over that I can't stand her, but he doesn't even care. We used to be so close, and she's ruined everything. Bryce doesn't even have time for me any-more. We used to eat dinner together all the time. Now he's always with *her*. And I hate her father," Jenny said angrily.

Michelle sat up, knowing this was something impor-tant.

"What, Jenny?" she prodded gently. "Why don't you like Micah's father?" she asked softly.

Jenny banged her cup on the table and shook her head furiously.

"He's horrible. He's mean and hateful and I can't stand the thought of Bryce marrying her someday and having that man for his father-in-law. It's just not right. I mean, it would be so perfect if he would just marry you. Then my best friend could be my sister," Jenny said with real tears in her eyes.

Michelle swallowed her frustration.

"Micah's dad—what did he do?" she asked more firmly.

Jenny looked guiltily down at the table, not meeting Michelle's eyes. She hated Micah and her father, but she didn't want to have to put into words what she now knew about her own father. That, and she didn't want to ruin Bryce's chances with Michelle. What if she found out about their dad and didn't want to be with Bryce anymore? She hated even thinking about her father now. And all because of Micah.

"Oh, he was just rude to Bryce. Saying things like he wasn't good enough for his little princess," she ad-libbed.

Michelle laughed cruelly.

"Bryce isn't good enough for Micah? What a joke. Bryce is the most perfect man in the world," she said fervently.

Jenny looked at Michelle quizzically. Bryce—perfect? She loved her brother more than anyone, but she knew for a fact that Bryce was far from perfect.

"Anyway, what are you going to do, Michelle? I mean, he could propose to her any minute. That's how much he likes her. It scares me to death to think that she might be my sister-in-law some day. It's a total joke that she's even the Relief Society president," Jenny said cattily.

Michelle laughed and patted Jenny's hand.

"Just leave it to me. Bryce won't know what hit him. If he thinks he's getting away from me now that I'm home, he's kidding himself. I remember when he told me that he could only love someone with a tender heart and beautiful spirit. So I go on a mission—just for him. I had to give him proof that I'm exactly what he needs in a wife. There's no way that I went on a mission to North Dakota for nothing. No, Bryce better come through, or he's going to be sorry," she said viciously.

Jenny squirmed uncomfortably. This was sounding kind of scary.

"What are you talking about, Michelle? What do you mean, Bryce is going to be sorry if he doesn't marry you?" she asked worriedly.

Michelle looked back to Jenny and smiled brightly.

"Oh, I was just kidding, Jenny. Don't take everything so seriously. Just relax. Soon Bryce and I will be together, and everything will be perfect. We just have to get rid of Micah. She looks like a wimp to me. You should have seen her when she walked in on me kissing Bryce. *Hi, Bryce, looks like you have some company.* I about laughed myself sick. She probably wears pearls to clean the floor. A prissy little blonde—that's my competition!" Michelle said with a sneer.

Jenny cleared her throat nervously. Michelle was acting very strange. And Micah saw Michelle kissing Bryce? She must have been crushed. How horrible. She caught herself feeling sorry for the girl who refused to stop liking her brother no matter what her father wanted. Could she have been wrong? Jenny frowned and shook her head.

"Well, I hope that it works out soon. I can't wait to be one of your bridesmaids," she said, smiling.

Michelle laughed and got up from the table.

"Jenny, you're the only friend I have. Of course you'll be my bridesmaid. See you soon. I've got some business to take care of," she said and walked away without a backward glance.

While Jenny finished her lunch she did some hard thinking. Since her dad had been gone most of her life, Bryce had meant everything to her. And for him not to be with someone *she* had picked out and who *she* loved had put her back up like nothing else. But what if Bryce knew what he was doing? What if her pushing Michelle on him would only make him miserable? Jenny did some soul-searching but couldn't come to any decision. She had wanted this for over four years and now it was within reach. She couldn't turn her back on all her plans now. No, Micah was out and Michelle was in. Whether Bryce liked it or not.

chapter thirty-eight

Phillip watched his young, beautiful wife waddle over to the chair in front of his desk and collapse in exhaustion.

"Hey, sweetie, what are you doing?" she asked tiredly.

Phillip put his papers down and walked around to kneel by his wife.

"I'm just finishing up some paperwork from the office, but I can do this later. How are you feeling? You're looking too tired. What does the doctor say?" he asked in concern as he laid his hand on her stomach protectively.

Kathy laughed and patted his cheek.

"Oh, Phillip, you say that every time you see me. I'm pregnant. I'm going to look and act like this for a long time.

Get used to it, buddy. It's very normal. Not fun but normal," she said with a slight laugh.

Phillip relaxed and kissed his wife's cheek. He couldn't help being nervous. If anything happened to her, he didn't know what he'd do.

"Have you thought of any more names?" he asked as he rubbed a circle on her stomach.

Kathy frowned. "You know, it's kind of hard to pick names out. Nothing feels right. I was thinking of Angela, but then I remembered I hated this girl in high school named that. So then I thought of Rachel, but that doesn't feel right. So, what do you think of Beatrice?" she asked seriously.

Phillip laughed and sat back on his heels.

"Definitely *not* Beatrice. Let me think about it, and I'll get back to you. Have you asked Micah? I bet she'd love to help you look up names," he said, looking at his wife carefully.

Kathy brightened up immediately. "Oh, she's already on it. We're going to lunch this Friday, and she's bringing me this huge printout she got off the Internet. I'd do it myself, but I still can't figure out the computer. Micah is so great. You know she bought me a book on designing nurseries? In a couple weeks, we're going to go pick everything out at the store together. It's been so much fun. I just love her," Kathy said, smiling.

Phillip relaxed and smiled, thinking of his daughter. He loved her too—enough to make sure she made the right decisions in her life.

"I'm glad you two hit it off. Hey, I have a great idea," Phillip said, trying to sound spontaneous. "There's this huge banquet I have to go to Friday. What do you say we call Micah and see if she can come too? It's going to be a lot of fun. There will be live music and dancing. They're giving out a few awards, but that shouldn't last too long. Why don't you two go shopping for dresses together? What do you say?" Phillip asked, knowing his wife loved shopping above just about anything.

Kathy's face glowed with excitement.

"Phillip, do you mean it? Oh, I would love that. And I am starting to feel a little better. I haven't been dancing in so long. I'll call Micah right now." She allowed Phillip to help her out of the chair.

Phillip watched her leave the room and smiled grimly. Micah would be there. And so would Brian. Telling Micah she couldn't see Bryce anymore had been the wrong move, he admitted to himself. Showing her a better choice—now that was brilliant. And all he had to do was keep throwing the two of them together, and it would be so easy. Brian was perfect for her—bright, ambitious, and from a good family. A wealthy family. And most importantly, a family with no ugly skeletons in the closet, he thought grimly.

Phillip pulled his cell phone out of his pocket and dialed Brian's number. He better let Brian know he had plans Friday. Nothing was going to get in the way of his daughter's happiness. *Or his.*

chapter thirty-nine

Lisa looked through the peephole and saw that it was Rod. She pulled back and bit her lip nervously. April had told her in no uncertain terms that she was not to ever let him in their apartment again. He could be very dangerous. Lisa looked down at her new jeans. A size ten. She hadn't been a size ten since she was sixteen. Rod had been so nice to her the last time he had come by. What would it hurt? She slowly opened the door and looked at Rod cautiously.

"Um, hi, Rod," she said, not opening the door all the way.

Rod smiled at her and moved in closer.

"Hey, cutie. I was hoping you would be home. I was just

working in the area, and I thought about you. I was wondering if you would like to go see a movie or something," he asked almost nervously.

Lisa opened the door even further and looked at him carefully. A movie? That was definitely a date.

"Oh, I don't know, Rod. I told you last time you called that I can't go out with you. And besides, I've got a lot of homework tonight. I don't think so," she said, with a touch of disappointment in her voice.

Rod heard it and grabbed onto it.

"Lisa, a gorgeous girl like you can't sit home every night. Do your homework tomorrow and come have some fun with me. I haven't had a piece of eye candy like you on my arm in a long, long time," he said, winking at her.

Lisa giggled and opened the door a little bit further.

"I don't know, Rod. Really. I mean, we all thought you were, like, obsessed with Micah or something. We were even close to calling the cops on you one time. April and Micah wouldn't like it if they knew I was going out with you," she said and closed the door a little bit.

Rod frowned and rubbed his chin, which was already showing a five o'clock stubble.

"Well, I guess I did act pretty crazy there for a while. I was going through a rough time though. I had just lost my job, and my girlfriend of two years had just dumped me. But now that I have a good job and I know there are beautiful girls like you out there, what would I want with Micah?" he asked with a grin.

Lisa laughed and opened the door a little further.

"Well, she's so pretty and thin and everything. Everyone thinks she's almost perfect," Lisa said with a twinge of jealousy in her voice.

Rod leaned on the doorjamb and ignored the fact that the door was still only opened halfway.

"Nah, she's okay, but you're something special, Lisa.

And look at you. Who would want to look at Micah when you're around?" he said, looking sincere.

Lisa opened the door a fraction more but still looked torn.

"I don't know, Rod. If April ever—" Lisa stopped suddenly, seeing April standing right behind Rod.

April moved carefully around Rod and opened the door, making Lisa walk backward quickly. April looked mad. She set her books down and then turned to look at Rod, who was now standing at attention in the doorway, trying to look as innocent and unassuming as possible.

"Rod, I'll let this go this time, especially since Lisa is feeling vulnerable right now, but I promise you, if you come back here even once more or call, I'll have Micah put that restraining order on you. The only reason she hasn't is because of your sister. But I'll call Kathy up myself right now and get that out of the way if I have to. Back off and stay away," April said in a deadly serious voice.

Rod glared at her menacingly.

"You can't tell me what to do. Besides, Lisa and I were just getting ready to go on a date. Weren't we, Lisa?" he said, trying to see her over April's head.

Lisa peeked over April's shoulder and shook her head sadly.

"I'm sorry, Rod, I don't think so. You better find someone else to ask out," Lisa said quietly.

Rod stood there for a moment, looking like he would explode, but then he changed his mind when a few girls from the next apartment walked by. He turned and walked away without saying another word.

April shut the door firmly and then turned to face Lisa. Lisa looked pale and guilty. April knew that if she hadn't gotten home when she did, Lisa would have gone out with him. She didn't even want to begin to think what that would have started. She walked over and put her arms around Lisa and held her for a moment. When she pulled back, she was surprised to see tears in Lisa's eyes.

"I'm sorry, Lisa, but Rod is kind of dangerous. He's not safe."

Lisa nodded and wiped a tear away that had slipped down her cheek.

"I know. I know. I was there. I remember what he was like when he tried to get Micah to go out with him. It's just . . . it's just that you're right. I think I am vulnerable right now. I've lost all this weight, and still no one has asked me out on a date. It's just so depressing," she said quietly.

April frowned and pulled Lisa over to their couch.

"Lisa, the right guy for you is out there. Dating really horrible guys in the meantime is no way to pass the time. Hey, look at me. I didn't even date for practically three years and then I found Joel. Just keep doing what you're doing— studying, working out, and being a wonderful person. He'll come along sooner or later, but getting hurt in the meantime just because there's no one else isn't something anyone should do," April said carefully, not wanting to offend Lisa but caring too much not to say anything.

Lisa nodded and reached for a tissue on the end table. She blew her nose quietly and looked at her lap.

"Thanks, April. I guess I am kind of relieved you came home when you did. It was really weird because something in my head kept telling me, *No, don't go out with him. Don't do it. Shut the door.* But he was so persuasive. It was like he was pulling me in with his words. I don't even know how to explain it," Lisa said, shaking her head morosely.

April cleared her throat and grabbed Lisa's hand to get her to look at her.

"Lisa, honey, that was the Spirit trying to protect you. Dangerous situations can be very tempting and hard to resist, but in the end it is your decision."

Lisa bit her lip and nodded. "I know. But when you're

right there, going through it, it's hard to make the right decision. Well, for me, anyway. But from now on, if I see him through the peephole, I promise I won't answer the door," Lisa said firmly.

April squeezed her hand and let go, getting up from the couch.

"Good. Now that that's over, grab your purse. Micah is meeting us at this bridal boutique just down the road. You have to pick out your bridesmaid dress," she said with a grin.

Lisa jumped off the couch. "Really? You mean it? You want me to be your bridesmaid?" Lisa asked breathlessly.

April laughed and grabbed Lisa's purse for her. "Of course, you idiot. Who else? Joel wants a Christmas wedding, and since my father refuses to have anything to do with the wedding, Joel's parents are paying for everything. And they're insisting on me having at least four bridesmaids. Joel's little sisters will be the other two. So come on. You're driving," April said, opening the door for Lisa to walk through.

Lisa laughed happily and led the way, taking her keys out of her purse.

"I love weddings," she said to April as they drove toward the boutique.

April smiled with her. "You and me both. And just as a side note, Joel has this gorgeous cousin a year younger than him, who is one of his best friends too. I'm definitely introducing you to him. He's a few years older than you, a returned missionary, and only a few credits away from graduating. He's going to the University of Utah though. I think he's going into medicine," April said, looking over at Lisa to see her reaction.

Lisa smiled widely. "Sounds perfect, April," she said and shrugged off all of the bad feelings she'd had because of Rod.

chapter forty

The two girls joined Micah, who was already there with Kathy. Micah introduced Kathy to Lisa and April and watched closely to see her roommates' reactions to her stepmother. Kathy, although pregnant, still enjoyed a fashion that had more to do with teenagers than expectant mothers. And even though her tank top covered her bulging stomach, it was pretty low-cut and very sleeveless. Micah had gotten past the fashion differences they shared to see the real person. But she didn't know how her roommates, especially Lisa, would treat her stepmother. She was feeling kind of protective toward Kathy, so she hoped she wouldn't have to step in and knock any heads around. But she would if she had to.

Lisa was the first one to offer her hand.

"Oh, so you're Micah's new stepmother. I've heard nothing but good things about you. It's nice to meet you finally," she said kindly.

Micah smiled over her stepmother's head gratefully at Lisa. Lisa had her moments, but she really was awesome.

April stepped around Lisa and shook Kathy's hand too.

"Hey, Kathy. I'm glad you're here. You can give me some advice on weddings," she said and pulled Kathy toward a rack of white dresses where the two talked as if they were reunited best friends.

Micah stared in awe. She had really lucked out when it came to her friends. Sometimes she took them for granted, but when it came down to it, they were two of the best people she knew.

Lisa grabbed Micah's hand and pulled her toward the bridesmaid section, where they pulled out ten dresses each.

Micah laughed when she saw the dresses Lisa was choosing.

"Um, excuse me Lisa, but these dresses might have looked good on the *old Lisa*, but the new Lisa is way too cool and way too thin to wear those tents. Try this one on instead," she insisted and pushed a gorgeous green velvet into Lisa's hands.

Lisa looked down at the dress and checked the size.

"No way can I pull this off, Micah. You could, but no—not me. Not in a hundred years," Lisa said sadly.

Micah frowned at Lisa and pushed her toward the changing rooms.

"If it doesn't fit you, I'll do an advanced yoga class with you tomorrow."

Lisa looked hesitantly at the dress. "Fine, but no excuses when I drag your rear end to the gym tomorrow. And no whining afterward either," she said firmly.

Micah grinned as Lisa disappeared through the doors. Lisa had turned into a yoga fanatic. Micah had to admit that she would stay happily at the amateur level for the rest of her life. The advanced yoga set could contort their bodies into the strangest positions. She just wasn't that ambitious—unlike Lisa and April.

She busied herself trying to find herself two dresses. One for April's wedding and the other for Friday night. Kathy had called the night before and practically begged her to go. And then her dad had called twenty minutes later and practically ordered her to go. Bryce had to do some work for his journalism class Friday, so she was free and her dad was picking up the tab, so it was better than sitting at home all alone.

Ten minutes later though, April and Lisa found her staring at a beautiful white wedding dress with a square neck and a long, flowing skirt.

"Um, you're the bridesmaid, not the bride quite yet," April said, teasing her friend.

Micah put the dress back sadly.

"I know, I know. But I just wish we were *both* getting married. Bryce isn't in a position to ask me right now, I guess. I wonder how long I'll have to wait?" she said.

Kathy looked at the dress and at her stepdaughter.

"Wow, you're really serious about this guy, huh? But I thought Phillip said that was all over," Kathy murmured.

Micah looked up, her eyes narrowing. "Well, I hate to break it to you, Kathy, since you're a newlywed and all, but the thing about my dad is, he likes to think he rules the world. Fortunately for the rest of us, he doesn't. I will choose who I love and who I marry—not my father," she said in a quiet and very firm voice.

Kathy's mouth formed a perfect O. "Interesting," was all she said in response.

April looked back and forth between the two girls and

pushed them toward the changing rooms to try everything in their arms on. As they reached the doors though, Lisa emerged, looking stunned and flat-out breathtaking.

"Tell me this is really me. If this is some dream, I don't want anyone to wake me up. Holy cow, Micah, this is a size 10! And it zipped up easily. Please tell me this is not a dream," she said again in shock.

April and Micah walked around Lisa critically, murmuring to each other in soft tones.

"You know what, Lisa? It's official. You are hot," April said very seriously.

Micah nodded her head sagely. "I think April's right, Lisa. You're going to knock 'em dead in that dress. Back me up, Kathy. Hot or not?" Micah asked, turning to Kathy.

Kathy grinned at the group of girls and laughed. "Of course she is. Why wouldn't she be? We all have eyes. Heck, we're all hot. Come on, let's try these dresses on," she commanded and whooshed into the dressing room to try her formal on.

Micah, April, and Lisa giggled together for a minute and then spent the next hour and a half trying on dozens of dresses.

April decided that she would put one of the dresses on hold because Joel's mom wanted to take her shopping at a boutique in Salt Lake. But Micah and Lisa were set on the green velvet bridesmaid dresses. The dress Micah picked out for the banquet for Friday was the exact opposite. It was more sophisticated and understated. It was an off-white silk skirt and top that seemed to flow around her whenever she moved. She absolutely adored it. She just wished Bryce would be there to see her in it. Kathy, on the other hand, had picked a sleeveless black form-fitting formal that was more suited for the prom. The owner of the store was having it altered to allow for Kathy's stomach. So all in all, it was a successful shopping spree.

Kathy pulled out a Visa card and had her own and Micah's dresses paid for in a flash. April also had a Visa card.

She handed it to the lady at the counter and blushed when she turned and caught Micah and April staring. They'd never seen their friend with plastic.

"Joel's dad insisted. He's put a limit on it of course, but since my dad refuses to help out with the expenses, he wants me to feel like I can make my own choices and that they're not taking over the wedding just because they're paying for it," she said.

Micah and Lisa exchanged smiling glances.

"Joel's family sounds awesome, April. You are one lucky girl," Lisa said in awe.

Micah nodded her head in agreement. "You know what, your family is going to regret this someday. But in the meantime, it sounds like you have an awesome family just waiting to spoil you rotten."

April smiled and took the bags from the clerk.

"I know. I just don't get it though. Joel and I are getting married in the Salt Lake Temple. We're both worthy temple recommend holders. Why can't they approve of my marriage?" she wondered sadly.

Kathy stepped into the circle of girls and reached out a hand to April.

"You know, I was scared to death that Micah wouldn't approve of me. She's all the family Phillip has. But she accepted me, and now we love each other like no other. I'm so sorry, April. I hope your family comes around," Kathy said.

Micah felt bittersweet as she put an arm around Kathy's waist and hugged her. She hadn't felt very accepting of Kathy at all in the beginning. It all came down to giving people a chance.

"Wow, Kathy, you're not like Rod at all," Lisa said matter-of-factly.

Kathy's head whipped up from Micah's shoulder, and Micah cringed, while April bit her lip and looked away. That was not supposed to have been said.

"What did you say?" Kathy demanded, looking white and pinched around the face. "You know my stepbrother, Rod? You've met him?"

Micah put a hand on her stepmother's arm. "It's okay, Kathy. He's come by the apartment a few times is all. It's no big deal."

Kathy frowned blackly. "It is a big deal. My stepbrother is bad news, and I don't want him anywhere near you girls. He's mean, vicious, and completely without a conscience. He's been in prison twice for armed robbery and assault and battery. I need to call Phillip. This is not good," Kathy said, hurrying toward the door.

"Bye, Kathy!" Micah called before she disappeared.

"Oh, my," Lisa said in a small, scared voice.

April put an arm around Lisa's shoulders and ushered her to the door.

"Everything's fine now. Nothing to worry about," she said in a very worried voice.

Micah followed her roommates out the door and couldn't help sending a grateful prayer up to heaven that Rod hadn't been allowed to cause any serious havoc in her life.

chapter forty-one

Micah spent the rest of the week getting used to her new homework overload and spending as much time as possible with Bryce. He was funny, romantic, considerate, and the perfect boyfriend. But every time she was with him, she felt as if his mind was on something else—as if he were only using half of his mind to pay attention to her. Something was going on, and she hoped with all her heart it had nothing to do with Michelle.

She'd decided to cancel lunch with Kathy, since they were going to be seeing each other that night at the banquet. She came home early from campus and put all of her books away. She didn't even want to look at them for at least a day. She spent an hour taking a bath and doing her hair. She hadn't spared herself much attention lately and it was beginning to show. Her hair was dry, her skin was looking dull, and she was looking like what she was—a tired college student. But for tonight, she wanted to relax, enjoy her new dress, and eat foods that would have Lisa throwing a fit. It would be perfect—if only Bryce could go. She hadn't dared ask her father for another ticket for Bryce, and Bryce had mentioned offhand that he had to cover a story that was a quarter of his grade in one of his journalism classes.

Two hours later, even without the massage, she felt like she'd just stepped out of the best spa in the country. All she had to do now was focus on hair and makeup. She paid attention to every detail, and when she was done, she smiled in satisfaction. She looked great. She slipped the blouse over her head and pulled the lightweight skirt over her narrow hips, turning to see how it moved and shimmered. She sighed in happiness. Dressing up was so much fun—especially when she was the one who got to pick the clothes.

The knock on the door had her hurrying through the apartment to see who it was. She hoped it was Bryce coming by to say hi, but she paused to check the peephole just in case it was Rod. She looked—and then she looked again in horror. *Michelle*. The pesky redhead! What on earth was she doing here? Micah squared her shoulders and took a deep breath. She could do this. She opened the door and smiled brightly.

"Well, hi, Michelle," she said.

Michelle looked Micah up and down and wrinkled her nose as if she smelled something bad.

"My goodness, Jenny was right. You really are a pampered princess. May I come in? I think you and I have a few things we need to talk about," Michelle said and walked past Micah before she could say anything.

Micah felt like breathing fire. She, a pampered princess?

Well, maybe a little bit, but it wasn't all it was cracked up to be.

"Okaaay. Why don't you have a seat," she said as Michelle walked over to the couch and sat down, elegantly crossing her ankles and clasping her hands on her knees.

"To begin with, I just want you to know that this isn't personal. Bryce feels absolutely horrible about the whole situation, but what's he to do? I'm sure you're a wonderful person. I don't care what Jenny says, you look very sweet. But sweetness doesn't cut it when it comes to love. And that's why I'm here. Bryce and I have decided that now that I'm home from my mission, he and I are going to start seeing each other again. I know that he felt some true and genuine feelings for you, but as he told me just last night, he now realizes that those feelings were feelings of a deep friendship and nothing else. I told him he needed to tell you this himself, but he just couldn't bring himself to hurt you face-to-face. So that's why I'm here. I'm sorry, Micah, but it's over," Michelle said with a tender look of sympathy.

Micah, who was still standing, crossed her arms over her chest and tilted her head to the side as she studied Michelle. She didn't believe any of it for a second. She had been with Bryce the night before until ten o'clock and the way he had kissed her good night had been anything but friendly. Michelle was loco. Better to play along though— she could be dangerous.

"Wow, Michelle. Thank you for being so kind. Coming over here to break the news to me must be so hard on you. I really appreciate it," Micah said, for lack of anything else to say. If she confronted her and told her she was cracked up, who knew what she'd do?

Michelle smiled in surprise, happy that things had gone so well.

"Well, good. I'm glad you're taking this so well. I was a little nervous that you would fall apart on me and start crying hysterically. Oh, and by the way, Bryce asked me to tell you that he'd appreciate it if you didn't call him anymore. It would just make things uncomfortable," Michelle added, getting up from the couch and walking past Micah to the door.

Micah smiled understandingly and nodded. "You're so right, Michelle. It'll be easier to get over Bryce if we just make a clean break of it."

Michelle opened the door and smiled victoriously at Micah. "You're so wise and so mature, Micah. I don't know what Bryce is thinking, dumping you for me, but that's men for you," she said with a tinkling laugh.

Micah nodded her head and laughed along with her and watched as Michelle walked quickly down the path, swinging her arms happily and practically floating on the air.

"Lunatic," Micah muttered and shut the door firmly. Poor Bryce—and she had thought she'd had it tough with Rod! Michelle made Rod look like a Sunbeam.

She finished getting ready, but then she couldn't resist. She had to call Bryce. She rang his apartment and let it ring ten times. But when someone finally answered, it was Michelle's voice on the other line—and she had obviously been laughing as she had picked up the phone. It almost sounded like a party in the background. Micah lowered the phone slowly and stared at it. It couldn't be true—could it? No. She wouldn't believe that of Bryce. Michelle was just very, very good at manipulating people and situations. *This is just a mistake*, she told herself, breathing hard.

She had plans to see Bryce the next day for a picnic in the mountains. They'd had it set up three days ago. He was supposed to pick her up at noon. If he didn't show up, then that would be her answer, and Michelle was right. If he did show up, then life was exactly as it should be. Bryce was hers.

She picked up her car keys and purse and headed out

the door. She was supposed to meet her dad and Kathy at the Springville Art Museum, and she didn't want to be late. Her dad had been very clear that he wanted her there with Kathy, since he would be busy mingling with his business associates. He didn't want his wife left alone and feeling out of place. And neither did Micah. She tried to put Bryce out of her mind but found it was almost impossible. Bryce was there to stay.

chapter forty-two

Bryce pulled into the Chili's parking lot and leaned his head against the steering wheel of his car. His dad had called him three days ago and had told him to meet him here. The phone conversation had been short and to the point, and Bryce had ended up agreeing to the meeting. His dad was flying all the way from California just to talk to him; the least he could do was give him fifteen minutes of his time. Bryce shuddered. What was he going to say to his dad? How could he face him after finding out all these horrible things? It had been easy when his dad had been a few states away. He could despise him from a distance. But how would he feel, seeing him face-to-face after all this time? He didn't know, but after slowly getting out of the car and walking to the front door, he knew he already had *ill* down perfectly.

He opened the door slowly and was immediately met by the hostess, a cute little brunette. He mentioned he was meeting his dad, and she led him right around the corner where his dad was sitting, flirting with their waitress. His mouth dropped open when he realized that the woman was handing his father her phone number on a piece of paper. *Unbelievable,* he thought, shaking his head. That was his dad, the player. He looked at his dad and tried to see him as everyone else did. Tan, tall, good-looking. Wicked green eyes and a ready joke for everyone. He was the type of guy that everyone wanted at their party. Everyone wanted a part of Troy Jorgenson—especially his children. Bryce felt his heart break even more as he realized that wasn't the case anymore.

Bryce noticed the table was already packed with every appetizer the restaurant offered. His dad was obviously planning on more than fifteen minutes of his time. His stomach turned over at the sight of the fried food, and he wasn't sure he'd even be able to make it ten.

Bryce waited for the waitress to walk away before he walked forward.

"Hi, Dad," he said quietly, startling the older man.

Troy Jorgenson stood up quickly and grabbed his son in a huge bear hug.

"It's so good to see you, Bryce. You look great. You working out still? Fantastic. Man, if I could look as good as you, I'd be the number one box office star."

Bryce looked down and pulled away from his father slowly but surely. He knew what kind of box office stars his dad knew. Thank you, but no.

Bryce sat across from his dad and stared into the face of the man he had spent his whole life idolizing. He had loved this man like no other. And now what did he feel for him?

He wasn't sure, and that was the most upsetting part.

"Look, Bryce, I know you're not here for small talk. The reason I flew all the way out here is to make you understand. I know you're judging me harshly, but if you just knew the circumstances . . . . It wasn't like I woke up one day and said to myself, 'Great, I'm going to write scripts for pornos.' It just happened. I had been in L.A. for a few years, and I was dead broke. It wasn't like the jobs were flying in, you know. And I was on the verge of just packing up and flying back to Utah to pick up where I left off with your mom. But I couldn't go home a loser after all the promises I had made to everyone. I had to be successful for you kids. I had to be someone you could look up to. So a buddy of mine told me of some quick money I could make just writing a B movie script. Well, it turns out it was rated X, but I did it, and it was so easy. I'm not proud of it. But I was finally able to make my child support payments. I didn't want to be a dead-beat dad. I loved you guys too much," Troy said soulfully.

Bryce cleared his throat and pushed the plate of deep-fried whatever the heck they were out of his line of sight. The smell alone was about to push him over the edge.

"So instead of coming back to your family—to your wife and children who needed you—you decided to go into the porn industry. You didn't want to be a loser, so you went into the porn industry. You didn't want to let us down, so you became the man you are today," Bryce said softly, looking out the window.

Troy sat up straighter and frowned at his son. "You're twisting my words on me, Bryce. It wasn't like that. You know I love you kids. Who bought you that Jeep for your sixteenth birthday? Who sent you to Italy for your graduation present? Who's paying all your stinking bills for school? Me, that's who. *That's* love, Bryce."

Bryce shook his head and looked at his dad finally.

"That's love? Really? Who was at my first football

game? You? Who was there when I was ordained an elder? You? Who was there when I broke both my legs in my car accident? You? No, not someone as successful as you. It was our home teacher, Brother Mills. And you know what, I never once thought of him as a loser for being there for me. You don't know what love is, Dad. Love isn't money. Love is honorable and respectable, and it's being there. You aren't any of those things. Why don't you go back to L.A. to all of your little girlfriends and stay away from me and Jenny. You broke her heart. Please, just go back Hollywood and the life you chose over us," he said and got up from the table, walking away.

Troy watched his son disappear and realized that he was walking away from him in more ways than one. He hadn't been able to charm his son like he had in the past. Something was different. He couldn't put his finger on it, but Bryce was different. And he had been dead serious. He'd seen it in his eyes. He had meant every word. What did that mean? Troy wondered.

The waitress came back to the table, hoping to earn a few more compliments and a bigger tip, but he waved her away with his hand. He had to think. He'd always been able to get out of tight squeezes. His nickname in L.A. was *Slick* for a reason. But this felt different. This didn't feel right. Bryce telling him to stay away from Jenny? His own daughter? His little girl, and now she knew about him. Well, forget that. He was here to see his family, and his family was going to see him. Business was business and family was family. He just had to make them understand.

Troy threw down some bills and left the restaurant. He pulled a piece of paper out of his pocket and looked at the address. He was going to see his daughter. He wasn't losing both his kids today. Bryce would come around eventually. But if Jenny refused to see or talk with him—well, he didn't even want to think about that.

He drove the rental car quickly out of the parking lot and down the road. For some reason, his neck felt tense and he was sweating. He paused in his thinking to wonder why his body was acting this way. His mouth went slack with surprise when he hit on it—he was upset. He was worried. This whole situation was stressing him out, and he wasn't used to feeling that emotion. He was used to popping out the scripts and lying back and enjoying all the cash that flowed in. That was what he was good at. Enjoyment.

He shook his head, wishing for a cigarette. He hadn't had one since that morning. He didn't want his kids to know he smoked. He pulled into the small apartment complex and hopped out, shading his eyes from the sun as he looked for the right apartment building.

The sign pointed him in the right direction, and he found her door almost immediately. He knocked three times hard on the door and stood back with a large smile on his face. Two minutes later, Jenny answered the door, looking as if she had just woken up from a nap.

"Dad!" she exclaimed, looking at him in dismayed shock. And then she frowned and looked down at her bare feet.

Troy lowered his arms and cursed softly. So Bryce was right. Jenny knew. And she looked just as happy about it as Bryce did.

"Hey, honey. I'm in town for a few days, and I wanted to take my best girl out for dinner and a show. What do you say? Do you have a few hours you could spare your old dad?" he asked, smiling charmingly.

Jenny stood back in the doorway, staring at the man she had loved so much and had craved attention from for as long as she could remember. If he had stopped by even a month before, she would have jumped in his arms and gone wherever he asked. But it was different now. Now, she knew who her father was. Her mom had told her and Bryce had confirmed it. And they had never lied to her. This man did though—this man who was her father. She felt something cold slip down her spine and freeze in her heart.

"I don't think so. I have plans," she said without any expression on her face or in her voice.

Troy blinked in surprise. Whenever he had thought of his daughter—and it wasn't often, but when he did—he always pictured her as a little puppy, always jumping up and down, begging for love and attention. Who was this cold young woman staring at him as if he were a worm? No, this could not be happening.

"Look, Jenny. I know what your mom told you. But that doesn't matter. Why should it? I'm your dad. I'll always be your dad. I love you. You know that, Jenny. Now, grab your purse and let's go. We have a lot of catching up to do," he said, using his best dad voice.

Jenny stared at him silently, not even blinking.

"Good-bye, Dad," she said and shut the door, leaving Troy looking stunned and crushed.

He walked back to his car, looking back over his shoulder every few seconds, expecting Jenny to come tearing out of her apartment and running after him, telling him that she was sorry and that she hadn't meant it. But she didn't.

Troy drove back to his hotel and called the only person he had left to call—his ex. She had some explaining to do. Poisoning his children's minds against him—the nerve of her! And after all he had done for her! He'd paid off her mortgage so she didn't have to work two jobs now. He sent her jewelry on her birthday every year. And he paid for her kids' college educations. Now how he was suddenly the bad guy, he didn't know, but earning a decent living wasn't a crime. At least, not where he was from.

No, forget the phone, he wanted someone to sit and listen to him, and if it had to be Amelia, then that might be the best, anyway. She'd talk to the kids. They'd calm down and next time he was in town, then everything would be back to normal. He'd take his kids on a cruise for Christmas. That's what he'd do. A little trip down to the Bahamas. That was the ticket, he thought with a grin and headed toward Bountiful. He'd get out of this one. They didn't call him Slick for nothing.

chapter forty-three

Micah walked into the large art museum and swiveled her head around, looking for Kathy. She spotted her almost immediately, standing in front of a large potted plant, looking pale and slightly intimidated.

"Hey, Kathy. You look great. How are you feeling though?" Micah asked, giving her stepmother a quick hug.

Kathy looked relieved and hugged Micah back extra hard.

"Oh, I'm so glad you're here. I was about to go find the bathroom and hide. I don't know any of these people, and they're looking at me as if I were some bug. And I am hungry. I'm starting to feel a little weak. If they don't serve the food soon, then I'm a goner," she said, looking helpless.

Micah frowned, turning around to glare at anyone who dared to look at Kathy as if she were a bug.

"Well, first things first. You are going to come sit in this nice chair over here, and I'm going to go grab you a little snack. They probably have to give out the awards before they serve dinner, so we better hurry and get something inside of you," Micah said, ushering Kathy quickly to a nice, comfortable seat in a corner. She even pulled a chair over for Kathy to put her feet up on.

"Thanks, Micah. You are an angel of mercy," Kathy said, still sounding weak.

Micah smiled grimly and ran off to find the caterer. Where was her father, she wanted to know? Leaving Kathy all by herself like that. *Men!*

It took a lot of smiles and dimples to get it, but she got a full plate. A roll, some salad, and the main course in small portions. She rushed it back to Kathy and made sure she ate everything. She was amazed as the color returned immediately to Kathy's face. Pregnancy wasn't for wimps, Micah thought nervously, thinking of her own future.

The two women talked and chatted as the crowd of people got bigger and bigger. As their conversation about names for the new baby wound up, Kathy cleared her throat nervously.

"Micah, I need to talk to you about something," Kathy said, her voice sounding squeaky.

Micah smiled. "Sure, what's up?"

"Well, remember when Lisa mentioned Rod and I kind of flipped out? Well, I went home and talked to Phillip about it. And he said that Rod has been bugging you for a while but that neither one of you wanted to mention it to me because you didn't want me to be upset," she said.

Micah looked away at the crowd of well-dressed people, and sighed. Too late—Kathy was upset.

"I'm afraid so, Kathy. Are you and Rod close?" she asked.

Kathy shuddered and shook her head. "No! He's my stepbrother from my mom's third marriage, and he's just the most horrible person you'll ever meet. He's the reason I moved out when I was seventeen," she said, her eyes dark with the memory. "Please, promise me that you won't have anything to do with Rod," Kathy said.

Micah nodded her head quickly. "Of course, but he keeps showing up on our doorstep. We've threatened to call the cops on him a couple times, but he keeps coming back. Now he's trying to get Lisa to go out with him," she said.

Kathy's grip on Micah's hands grew tighter and tighter, and Micah noticed her stepmother's face grow paler. She was deadly serious. What had Rod done to make Kathy act this way? Micah wondered.

"Maybe you girls should move into a different apartment. I want you to get an unlisted phone number and don't tell anyone where you've moved. I'll have Phillip find you girls a nice place. I won't let him hurt you," Kathy said quietly.

Micah gave Kathy a hug. "Listen, it's okay. Bryce was there twice and scared him away from me, I think. And April showed up and was able to get rid of Rod one time. I think he's finally getting the message. Don't worry about us. We're big girls," she said with a laugh, trying to get Kathy to relax.

Kathy shook her head sadly. "That doesn't matter to Rod, Micah. Just be careful."

"What are the two most beautiful women here doing hiding in a corner?" Phillip asked, interrupting the conversation, to Micah's relief.

Kathy looked up and smiled. Kathy took Phillip's extended hand and pulled herself up.

"Hiding. That's exactly what we're doing. Are they getting ready to start?" Kathy asked hopefully.

Phillip leaned over and kissed Micah on the cheek.

"They are. Let's go find our seats. They'll serve dinner right after, and then there'll be dancing. Come on, you two," he said and escorted the two women quickly to their table.

"Brian. There you are. I was wondering when you were going to show," Phillip said testily.

Micah looked around her father to see Brian already sitting at the table, deep in conversation with a man next to him. He got up quickly though and helped Phillip pull out chairs for the two women.

"Business, Phillip. Always business. Hi, Katherine. Hi, Micah. You look stunning," Brian said, switching seats so he could sit next to her.

Micah smiled in surprise. "I didn't expect to see you here tonight," she said,

"These awards banquets are a pain, but they come with the territory when you work with the big names," he said, leaning over to whisper intimately in her ear. "But now that you're here, I'll be able to enjoy myself," he said, scooting his chair even closer.

Micah cleared her throat nervously and looked up to see her dad smiling at the two of them. And that's when it hit her—this was all her dad. Her dad had foisted Brian off on her so she would magically fall in love with Brian and get rid of Bryce. She frowned at her father and moved to the farthest side of her chair, away from Brian.

"Well, actually, I can only stay for the dinner," Micah said repressively, hoping that Brian didn't think that the two of them were going to dance the night away.

"Can I get a shot of you two?" asked a man from across the table. He was holding a camera in front of his face, but the voice sounded oddly familiar. The lights were low, and the music loud enough to make her unsure though.

Brian leaned over even closer. "You'll get used to it.

With a beautiful face like yours, it's bound to end up on the front page."

Micah tried to smile for the camera, but after the flash faded, she blinked her eyes to find Bryce standing in front of her, glaring, with a camera in his hands.

"Bryce!" Micah yelped, leaping up from the table and walking quickly around to grab Bryce's clenched fist.

"Micah, please take your seat, dear. We're about to begin," Phillip commanded in a deep voice.

Micah ignored her father and pulled Bryce out of the room and into the hallway.

"What are you doing here?" she asked breathlessly.

Bryce stared at her, his eyebrows clenched together and his shoulders very stiff.

"What is this, Micah? A date? Tell me I didn't just catch my girlfriend on a date with someone else," he demanded.

"No!" Micah said shaking her head back and forth quickly. "You know I'm not on a date. I told you my dad insisted I come to watch out for Kathy. I didn't even know Brian was going to be here. He came and sat down next to me. Please trust me. Don't assume the worst, Bryce. This is me. You know me, and you know I love you. And why didn't you tell me you were going to be here tonight?" she asked.

Bryce's shoulders relaxed, and he grabbed her hand, leaning his head gently against her hair.

"Oh, Micah, I've just had the worst day of my life. What do you say I take a few more pictures, grab some quotes, and then we ditch this place? I just want to be with you. I feel like I'm about to crack."

Micah put her arms around Bryce's waist and held him for a moment.

"Let me eat dinner, or my dad will have a fit. But when the dancing starts, I'll meet you at the front door. Okay?" she asked, looking up to see that he really did look hammered.

Bryce nodded and leaned down to kiss her quickly on the lips.

"I'm sorry I overreacted in there. It just looked like you two were the perfect couple or something. Not what I needed today," he added with a chuckle.

Micah smiled up at Bryce and pulled him back toward the banquet.

"Come on. Let's get through the next hour and then we'll escape. Remember, this is a quarter of your grade," she added, squeezing his hand and leaving him at the door.

She rejoined her dad, Kathy, and Brian at the table as the announcer walked up to the podium. She knew her father was staring at her and that Brian was looking at her curiously, but she ignored them both and clapped when she needed to and laughed when she should. But she couldn't get Bryce's tragic expression out of her mind. Something bad had happened today. Did it have something to do with Michelle? She couldn't help wondering.

The next hour passed by so slowly, she felt like pulling her hair out. Every now and then she spotted Bryce smiling and talking to tuxedo-clad men and beautifully dressed women. She hoped he was getting all of the information he needed. She tried to pay attention to Brian out of politeness, but he could sense that her mind was elsewhere and turned to his dinner partner on his right-hand side, leaving Phillip fuming. Micah knew why her dad was sending her cold looks, but they didn't have the same power over her that they used to. She pushed them aside, enjoyed her prime rib dinner, and waited as patiently as she could.

As soon as the band began to play, she got up from her chair, kissed Kathy on the cheek, and waved at her father. As Phillip got up to go after his daughter, Kathy pulled him back with a slight moan.

"Oh, Phillip, I don't think I feel so good," she said.

Micah whipped her head around, but Kathy's wink had

her grinning. Kathy was the best.

She hurried toward the exit and ended up running as she saw Bryce's profile.

"Hey," she said breathlessly as she reached out a hand to him. He smiled and pulled her into a tight hug.

"Thanks for leaving the party early for me. I feel bad stealing you away. You look so beautiful in that dress. But I just need to be with you right now."

Micah nodded and pulled him out the door, leaving the party and the music without any regrets.

"I'll follow you," Micah said and slipped into her car. The ride back to her apartment didn't take long, but she had so many questions for Bryce that every moment seemed an eternity.

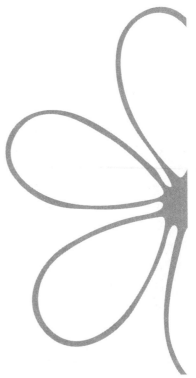

chapter forty-four

She pulled into a parking space and got out, locking her car. Bryce pulled up and rolled the window down.

"I don't feel much like talking to your roommates tonight. I'll wait outside while you go change. We can go look at the city lights and talk in private."

"I won't be long," she promised and hurried toward her door.

She opened it to a party. April and Joel were dancing and Lisa and some guy were talking over a bag of chips and salsa.

"Hey, there you are!" April said, laughing, and stopped dancing. "We're celebrating! My dad and mom stopped by, and they've had a change of heart. They're coming to the wedding!"

Joel hugged April from behind, smiling just as big. "Of course they did. They love you. Celebrate with us, Micah," he added.

Micah smiled and gave both April and Joel a hug.

"Oh, I'm so glad for you guys. You deserve the perfect wedding, and now it will be. I'd love to stay and celebrate, but Bryce is waiting for me in the car. We have to take care of some things, but hopefully the party will still be going when I get back," she said.

April nodded happily and started dancing again. Micah laughed and walked over to grab a chip and to say hi to Lisa and her friend.

"Hey, Lisa. Introduce me," she said.

Lisa smiled glowingly at Micah and made the introductions.

"Micah, this is Preston, Joel's cousin. He's going to the U, but he wanted to come down and meet April."

Micah shook Preston's hand and smiled. He was just as cute as Joel, but he was shorter and with light blue eyes.

"It's nice to meet you. Did you know that Lisa is one of the best dancers I know? You guys need to join April and Joel," she added, laughing at Lisa's expression of acute embarrassment.

Preston grabbed Lisa's hand and pulled her toward the family room. "Come on, Lisa. They can't be the only ones making fools of themselves."

Micah hurried to her room, stripped off her skirt and blouse, and pulled on a pair of jeans, a T-shirt, and some flip-flops. She ran back through the apartment, waving at everyone, and went straight to Bryce's car. She opened the passenger door and jumped in.

He grabbed her hand immediately but drove in silence up the canyon. Micah was still curious, but he seemed to be dealing with something painful. She didn't want to push him. When he was ready to talk, he would. Her just being there was what he needed right now.

Bryce came to a stop and shut the lights to his car off and turned the key in the ignition switch. He sat for a minute, staring out at the valley, and sighed. He turned his head and finally met Micah's eyes.

"I met my dad for lunch today," he said quietly and leaned his head against the seat.

Micah looked at him and noticed the strain around Bryce's eyes. It had obviously taken a lot out of him to do that.

"How did it go?" she asked softly.

Bryce closed his eyes before answering. "Horrible, I guess. He was expecting everything to be the same between us, as if it didn't matter that I knew. He's so used to his life that he can't even understand why it would bother me so much. As long as he gives us money every now and then, then that automatically makes him a great father. It's just so sad. I got up and walked out on him, Micah. I walked out on my father. I didn't know what else I could do. I know I need to forgive him and love him and everything, but right now, I can't even stand to look at him. How do you accept a father who is unacceptable?" he asked, opening his eyes to look at her pleadingly.

Micah reached over and caressed his cheek.

"I'm so sorry you have to go through this, Bryce. And I don't know. I don't have any answers for you. I only have my own experience to draw from. When I finally realized that being some soulless clone for my father, just to make him happy, wasn't right, I had a lot of hateful, angry feelings about him. And he keeps making mistakes. Look at the way he keeps throwing Brian in my face. He's still trying to manipulate my life, but you know what I realized? I love him. He's not perfect and sometimes he's just plain annoying, but he's my dad, and spending my whole life hating and resenting him would only make me bitter and miserable. So I deal with him the best way I can and live my life in a way that is hopefully acceptable to my Father in Heaven, if not my earthly one. And that's pretty much one day at a time. Maybe right now you do have some hard feelings about your dad, but in time, you'll remember that you love him," Micah said.

Bryce looked at the city lights and shook his head.

"That's the worst part. I know I love him. That's why it hurts so bad. You know, he's the reason I went into journalism. I wanted to be a writer just like him. Now I have to reassess my whole life. I was going to be a writer just to impress him, I think. Growing up, I would do anything to impress him, just to get his attention. Just to have a reason to call him or to get him to fly out and see us. Who am I? Am I my father's son? I feel like I have to scrape him off and try to figure out what's left behind. Heck, maybe I'd rather be an accountant—? I don't know. But without his influence, what decisions will I make because *I* want to make them? I just feel so lost," he said brokenly and leaned forward, resting his head on the steering wheel.

Micah reached over and rubbed his back. Bryce would have to go though what she had already been through, but to a greater extent, maybe. It wasn't easy, and no one could do it for him. Bryce had a lot of soul-searching ahead of him.

"You know I had a life makeover myself, and I have to say I've kind of enjoyed it. But I'll give you one piece of advice. If you want to find out who the real you is, ask your Father in Heaven. He knows you better than you do. He knows if you should be a writer. Maybe instead of following in your dad's footsteps, maybe you're supposed to write great magazine articles for the *Ensign* or work for the *Deseret News.* If you have a talent for writing, then you have to know that

that's a gift from God. It's what we choose to do with those talents that makes us who we are. Don't throw everything away because it reminds you of your dad. You might end up throwing away something precious," she said softly, still rubbing his back.

Bryce lifted his head and leaned over to kiss her sweetly.

"I knew I needed to talk to you. I already feel better. You always do that for me, Micah. Thank you," he said seriously.

Micah smiled. "That's not what Michelle said," she said with a laugh.

Bryce snorted. "What were you doing talking to Michelle?" he asked as he started the car.

"Well, I didn't really have a choice. She kindly stopped by to inform me today that you had broken up with me and that you didn't want me to call you anymore. Or something along those lines," she said with a shake of her head.

Bryce stopped in the act of backing the car up and stared at her.

"What?" he said with his eyes practically popping out of his head. "Say that one more time. I know I didn't hear you right," he said in a clear, hard voice.

Micah shrugged her shoulders. "You heard right. It's not like I believed her. Well, I did wonder when I called your apartment this afternoon and she answered the phone," she said.

Bryce growled in his throat and continued reversing the car. "She is something else. Jenny probably let her in. She thinks by dumping my girlfriend for me, that I'm going to go running to her? What a joke. You know, she pulled some pranks on this girl I went out with my senior year. Marcy wouldn't have anything to do with me after Michelle scared her half to death. I was so glad when Michelle decided to go on a mission. I thought, 'Finally! She'll grow up and straighten out.' I guess we have our answer. The only way to get her to back off is to get married, I guess," Bryce said with a smile to Micah.

Micah laughed and turned the radio on softly. "Yeah, yeah. You and me married. I've heard it a million times. I don't think I'll believe it until we're on a honeymoon somewhere, sitting on a beach," she said with a smile.

Bryce looked thoughtful for a moment. "Is that right? You think Joel is the only one who can do things spur-of-the-moment?"

Bryce stopped the car halfway down the canyon and pulled off to the side of the road. He turned the key, put on the emergency brake, and got out of the car. Micah stared as he walked around the car and opened her door, reaching for her hand. He pulled her to her feet and shut the door.

Micah laughed. "Okay, enough with the joking, Bryce. Let's go home. April and Joel are expecting us," she said nervously.

"Uh uh." Bryce kneeled on one knee and held her hands, looking up into Micah's face with the stars as a background.

"Micah Rawlings, will you do me the greatest honor and agree to be my wife?" Bryce asked in a voice that was strong, smooth, and sure.

Micah stared down at Bryce. He was so beautiful and so sincere. She knew he wasn't kidding around. But did he mean it? Or was he just so emotionally worn out that he didn't know what he was doing? She closed her eyes and tried to feel the Spirit. Was this right? She knew she loved him and that he loved her, but should she say yes right now? She tilted her head up to the sky and felt the warm breeze drift over her and felt a bursting of joy inside her heart. *It is right. This is right.* She opened her eyes and looked down at Bryce, still kneeling in the dirt.

"Yes, Bryce. I will be your wife," she said, and leaned down to kiss him.

He kissed her back and then leaped up from the ground and twirled her around in circles.

"How perfect is this, Micah?" he exclaimed, holding her and looking out into the star-filled night. "I'm closing one chapter of my life and opening up a new one, with you by my side. I couldn't ask for anything else," he said and kissed the top of her head tenderly.

Micah wrapped her arms around Bryce's waist and fit her head under his chin. He was right—it was a new chapter for both of them.

"Come on, Bryce. Let's go tell April and Joel and everyone the good news. They're back at the apartment, dancing already. They're going to love this," she promised and pulled Bryce back toward the car.

They drove down the canyon and back home, smiling, laughing, and making plans for their future. But before they made it back to the apartment, Bryce turned serious once more.

"Micah, you need to know something. If we get married, we'll be on our own. I'm not going to accept money from my father anymore, now that I know where it comes from. I can't. I'll have to get a job to support us, and I'll have to take night classes or something. It won't be forever, just for another year or so. But at least we'll be together," Bryce said.

Micah nodded her head. "Bryce, I understand that you feel the way you do and I'll support you in that decision. But I think you should focus on school. Working to support the both of us isn't necessary. My dad has been kind enough to give me my inheritance from my mother now, instead of making me wait until I'm twenty-five. His plan was for Brian to sweep me off my feet. But instead, he's making it possible for us to be together and finish up school too. Isn't my dad wonderful?" she asked, laughing at Bryce's expression.

"Your dad is wonderful," Bryce agreed, still in shock. "I'm marrying an heiress. How cool is that?" he asked and laughed with her.

The two of them reached her apartment, where the dancing was still going strong. Bryce and Micah announced their engagement and were met with hugs, kisses, and enough congratulations to have the tenants in the apartment upstairs banging on the floor.

Micah was twirled around her family room so many times she grew dizzy. She paused for a moment to catch her breath and looked around her apartment at the people surrounding her. She felt so happy she could burst. This was everything she had dreamed of—being loved and loving others. If only her father could understand.

She rejoined the dancing and her fiancé and put all thoughts of her father behind her. This was her night. And she'd never forget it.

chapter forty-five

Troy Jorgenson cursed in frustration. The one time he tried to see his ex, and she wasn't home. Well, he would just wait her out. *Where could she be?* he wondered over and over, checking his watch every few minutes. He looked at the house that had once been his. He sneered. His condo with a view of the ocean had this beat. Man, he was glad he escaped when he had. Mowing lawns, casseroles, and the same old thing every stinking day—it had driven him crazy then and just the thought of it drove him nuts now.

He looked at his watch again. Nine o'clock at night and the woman still wasn't home. Where could a middle-aged woman be this time of night? She was probably playing bingo, he thought with a laugh. *That's as exciting as it gets here in Bountiful, Utah*, he thought pityingly. He got back in his car and leaned his seat as far back as it would go. He turned some music on and had decided to close his eyes, when headlights loomed down the street, coming his way. He sat up quickly, squinting to see if it was her.

Hallelujah! he thought as the sporty car pulled in the driveway. Troy frowned in confusion. He had bought Amelia a boring little Volvo a few years back. She must have traded it in for something with a little more pizzazz, he thought in surprise. He watched as a man got out of the driver's seat and walked around to open the door for Amelia.

A date! The woman had been on a date, of all things. He chuckled. He would have never thought it of her. He shrugged mentally, not caring one way or another. He watched as the two kissed briefly, and she waved him away. As soon as the car was down the road he got out of the car and walked to the front door. This was it. He rang the doorbell and stood back with a polite smile on his face. Amelia opened the door and stared at him with a surprised frown.

"What? That's the greeting I get? Come on, invite me in. We gotta talk—and I mean now," he said.

Amelia sighed but moved aside for her ex-husband to walk into her home. She hadn't seen Troy since the day he had walked out on her. All of their interaction had been on the phone. She'd drop the kids off at the airport and pick them up a week later, worried sick and hoping that her kids would be the same kids she had dropped off. And when he came to town to see them, she insisted on taking Bryce and Jenny to Troy's parents' home in Farmington.

She studied the man who had broken her heart, and now her children's hearts. She couldn't hate him. He had given her her children. But she did despise his choices, and she resented his being there in her home.

Troy walked around the family room, smiling smugly

at the French country decor and looking curiously at the pictures of the kids scattered everywhere there was a free surface. Jenny had been into gymnastics? He looked more closely and realized she was holding a trophy. *No kidding*, he thought proudly. He hadn't known. He looked at the picture of Bryce, wearing a suit and a name tag over his left breast, with his arm around a similarly dressed man. He had known Bryce had served a mission. He couldn't remember where though. All he knew was that he had paid for it. Troy turned around at the polite cough Amelia made.

"Beautiful kids, aren't they?" Troy said.

Amelia smiled and picked up their most recent family picture. They had gone to the mountains with the photographer to get a natural backdrop. It had turned out beautifully. Her children were wonderful, she had to agree with him.

"You're right, Troy. They are beautiful. They're the one good thing you've done in your life," she said honestly and sat down in her favorite chair to hear what this man had to say, now that everything wasn't going his way. She was kind of curious.

"Beautiful but ungrateful. You know they don't even want to see me? I just don't get it. I'm their *father*. I've given them everything they could ever want, and now they think they can turn their backs on me just because I write scripts for the racier movies. It's not like I'm proud of what I do, but if it pays the bills, then it pays the bills," he said defensively.

Amelia sighed and clasped her hands, wishing this was over.

"You're wrong, Troy. You haven't given them everything they wanted. You gave them everything but what they wanted most—a father. The one thing you weren't willing to give them. Do you blame them, Troy? Really? They're wonderful, good kids who have strong testimonies of the gospel. Bryce served a mission, and Jenny's already planning on doing the same. Do you blame them for being repulsed by you?" she asked curiously.

Troy glared at his ex-wife, wishing he could divorce her all over again.

"Listen, you tell those kids of yours that if they want even one more penny from me, then they'll have to treat their father with some respect. They either accept me and my money, or they can do without both," he said, shoving his hands in his pockets, pleased with his ultimatum.

Amelia smiled faintly and smoothed her skirt over her knees. Poor Troy. He was in for a shock.

"I hate to break it to you, Troy, but Jenny and Bryce have both asked me to close the account you opened for them at the bank. Neither one of them wants any more money from you now that they know where it comes from and what you have to do to earn it. They can't do anything about the past, but from now on, they refuse to live off the profits of evil," she said quietly but firmly.

Troy growled and turned around to face the wall. He was so furious he felt like punching something. He had to or else he would explode. He pulled back his fist and let it fly into the wall, making all the pictures shake and tremble and leaving a large, ugly puncture wound in the wall.

Amelia shot up from her seat and walked to the phone. She picked it up and then walked over to face her ex-husband.

"You're leaving right now. If you don't, I'm calling and filing charges against you. Go," she ordered him.

Troy stared his ex down but knew she wasn't bluffing. He had lost it and now he was out of options. He walked slowly to the door and opened it.

"Just one question before I leave. When did you find out? Have you been accepting my dirty money all these years happily, but now that the kids know, you're too good for it too? How long have you known?" he asked softly.

Amelia looked down at her feet but then straightened her head proudly.

"I found out six months ago from your parents. They called me, crying and heartbroken. Some friends of theirs who were serving a mission down in L.A. were teaching the discussions to some acquaintance of yours. They were shocked to say the least. Six months ago was the last time I cashed one of your checks. Ask your accountant. I'm free from you too, Troy. Good-bye," she said and motioned for him to leave.

Troy turned and walked out of the house, knowing he'd never set foot in her home again. There was nothing for him here anymore. He headed back to his hotel room. He would pack up and catch the first flight back to L.A., *his home.* His bridges were all burned behind him, and there was no going back now. He stared at the dark night and felt just as dark on the inside. He had a lot of thinking to do. Too bad he thought better with a cigarette and a bottle of scotch. He smiled sadly at the thought. His family wouldn't approve of that either. Nope, his family didn't approve of him at all. He was gone, and they were all glad to see the back of him. *Well, I won't trouble them anymore with my annoying presence.* Troy almost groaned with the misery that thought brought him. He looked at the blinking lights of the city as he drove down the freeway and wished for the first time in his life that he had made different decisions. But it was too late for him. Too late.

chapter forty-six

Jenny stared off into space as she waited for Michelle to join her. Michelle had called and left a message on her machine to meet her at Panda Express for lunch. Jenny frowned—it was more like she had ordered her to show up, as if she were some silly puppet or something. Jenny sighed and looked out the window. Nothing was going the way it should. Her dad dropping by unexpectedly yesterday had depressed her horribly. She had shut the door on someone she loved very much. But she hadn't seen another option available to her. She had called Bryce, but he was so excited about getting engaged to Micah, he acted like he didn't even care. She had called her mother, but her mom had just told her to come home this weekend so they could talk about it.

She sighed and pulled all of the salt and pepper packets out of the holder and attempted to stack them. They all fell over almost immediately. Just like her life. Her dad was gone. Her brother was soon to be gone, lost in the land of happily married college students. And her best friend, Michelle, was not very friendly and a little strange. Maybe she should drop out of school, run away to Hawaii for a year, and then come back, tan and happy, next year. She smiled faintly. Nope, she shook her head. That wouldn't work either. She'd told her mom to close up her bank account that her dad put all of her money for school and living expenses into.

She was on her own. Heck, instead of waiting here for Michelle, she should be down at the financial aid office trying to get a student loan—or better yet, a job. She tried to smile at the thought that she would be just like everyone else on campus now. But she couldn't. Life was going to be very different from now on. And she knew already she didn't like it.

"Jenny!" Michelle called from across the restaurant.

Jenny turned and waved for her to join her. Michelle walked over and glanced down at the table.

"Where's the food? I'm at least ten minutes late. You could have had lunch ready," Michelle said in a pouty voice.

Jenny looked up at Michelle and frowned. She didn't like what she was seeing. Michelle always expected Jenny to pick up the bill wherever they went, which was always where Michelle wanted to go, for some reason. Maybe that was why she wanted to be friends with Jenny—to sponge off her.

"Sorry, Michelle. It's your turn to pay. I'm broke," Jenny said, watching Michelle's expression.

She looked shocked and annoyed. "Whatever," she said and walked off with a glare.

Jenny shook her head and wondered what she had been

thinking, trying to shove Michelle on her brother. That was her problem—she hadn't been thinking very much at all, except about herself. Micah had been so nice to her too. Even when she treated her horribly, she never retaliated. She just took it and kept trying. *Something to think about,* Jenny thought guiltily.

"Fine, here we are. Enjoy," Michelle said nastily, plopping down two waters, two of the free fortune cookies, and one measly egg roll.

Jenny's eyebrows rose, but she didn't say anything. She took her water, a fortune cookie, and broke off half of the egg roll and took a bite, trying not to laugh at Michelle's fuming expression. Michelle had assumed that Jenny would hop up and buy something just to appease her. Not today.

"So what did you want to see me about, Michelle?" Jenny asked, glancing at her watch. She had a class in an hour, so she needed to hurry.

"What do you think? Bryce, of course." Michelle sipped on her water and sneered at the egg roll.

Jenny smiled and shook her head at herself. Of course Michelle wanted to talk about Bryce. Bryce had been the basis of their friendship from the very beginning. What would happen if Bryce were taken out of the equation? Would there even be a friendship left? She was curious to find out.

"Well, if you want to know what's going on with Bryce, I'll tell you. I talked to him late last night, and it turns out that he and Micah are engaged to be married during Christmas break," she said confidingly.

Michelle reared her head back, and her nostrils flared in shock.

"No!" she screeched, causing everyone in the diner to turn and stare.

Jenny ignored everyone and nodded her head.

"Yep, it's the truth. I think Bryce and Joel are taking

Micah and April ring shopping today. It sounds pretty serious," she added, watching as Michelle's face went from red, to white, and back to red again.

"That little witch," Michelle muttered under her breath. "You know, I went over to see Micah just yesterday to tell her that it was over between her and Bryce, and she acted like she believed me. She agreed that a clean break was the best," Michelle said in a strangled voice. "But she was lying to me the entire time!"

Jenny's eyebrows raised again. Michelle, who had lied to Micah, was mad that Micah had gone along with her. This was too much.

Jenny got up from the table and grabbed her backpack.

"See ya, Michelle. I gotta go. Take care," she added, thinking she wouldn't be seeing much of her friend anymore.

Michelle didn't even look up, she was so lost in thought. Jenny shrugged and grabbed her fortune cookie and walked away. She broke it open and tossed the cookie in the garbage but kept the tiny paper. She needed good fortune today. She read, *Friendship, prosperity, and love are waiting just around the corner for you.*

Jenny turned her face up to the sky to feel the warmth of the sun, and smiled just a little. She hoped so.

chapter forty-seven

Micah picked up a ring with a marquise-cut diamond in a platinum setting and showed it to April. "What do you think of this one?" she asked with a frown, looking at it from different angles.

April shook her head. "Uh-uh for me, a big yeah for you," she said and turned back to the glass-encased display. She pointed to a square-cut diamond that must have been at least two carats and had the man who was helping them set it in front of her.

"I love this one," she murmured softly, staring at it.

Micah grinned and knew her friend had found the ring for her. Too bad she wasn't having such good luck. She couldn't seem to find anything that called out to her and shouted, *I'm yours! Take me.*

She looked over at Bryce and Joel and smiled happily. They were picking out their wedding bands together. Their heads were together, and they were talking about the pros and cons of silver, gold, and platinum. They were both supposed to pick out their three favorite rings and then decide together. April already had her three picked out. Micah had zero.

April was so excited about finding the perfect ring, she called out to the guys.

"Okay, we're done. Let's see what good taste you guys have."

Bryce and Joel looked over and grinned. They talked to the young lady helping them and had her walk the rings they had chosen over to join the girls. Micah took Bryce's hand as she looked curiously at the rings he had chosen. She frowned in surprise. He hadn't picked out a single ring that had even one diamond on it. They were all three just plain bands. One was silver, one was platinum, and one was gold. Huh. She didn't know what to think about that.

She looked over at Joel's selections and saw he had done the same thing. She exchanged a look with April but didn't say anything. So their guys weren't into the flash and dazzle of diamonds. That was okay with her.

Bryce and Joel were admiring April's choice of ring. And since Joel could afford just about any ring there, price wasn't an issue. Joel didn't even blink an eye when he leaned over and asked the salesman the price.

"We'll take it," he said. They busied themselves with measuring April's finger and started the paperwork.

Bryce turned back to Micah and placed his hands on her shoulders.

"Where are the rings you like?" he asked, looking back and forth on the glass counter.

Micah bit her lip and turned to look Bryce in the face.

"Nowhere. Bryce, I don't know what's wrong with me, but none of these rings are *my* ring. I don't know how to explain it, but none of them are right. They're all pretty, but just not for me," she said lamely, hoping Bryce wouldn't be mad.

Bryce nodded his head, grinning. "You're not going to believe this, but I was hoping you were going to say that. I wanted to give you the chance to pick out a ring that you liked, but I was going to give you another option. This," he said and pulled a small box from his pants pocket. He opened it slowly and pulled out an old-fashioned ring with a large pear-shaped diamond in it.

"This was my great-grandmother's, and my family would be honored if you would wear it," he said.

Micah's mouth opened in surprise. It was perfect. She held out her hand, and Bryce slipped it on her finger. It fit perfectly too. It was her ring!

"Bryce, I don't know what to say," she said and stood up to hug him.

Bryce couldn't stop grinning. "Say you love me. That's all you ever have to say."

"I love you, I love you, I love you!" Micah laughed.

"Now we need to pick out a wedding band to go with it, and we need to have it cleaned," he said, holding her hand up to admire the way it looked on her small, elegant hand.

Micah grinned and went right to the wedding band section. She picked out a thin gold band that would go perfectly.

She walked over and showed April her ring, and April laughed and hugged her. The two girls had grown even closer due to their almost simultaneous engagements. They both couldn't have been happier for each other.

The two couples left the jewelry store twenty minutes later, each of the girls wearing their engagement rings proudly, holding their hands up whenever they talked.

"Stop, stop!" Bryce cried theatrically. "You're blinding me!"

Micah giggled and put her arm through his.

"Listen, Mom wants you up to the house Sunday for a big celebration dinner and a planning session. She is so excited. She already has a lot of ideas for the wedding dinner, but she wants to run them past you," he said.

Micah grimaced. "I don't know if I'll survive giving my lesson this Sunday though. If I don't make it, just tell your mom that she would have been a great mother-in-law. I just know it," she said.

Bryce laughed. "You'll be great. I just wish I could be there to hear it," he said and opened the car door for her.

"Micah, by the way, have you told your dad yet?" he asked as she sat down.

Micah looked up at him and nodded but didn't say anything. He walked quickly around the car, waving as Joel and April zoomed away and got in quickly.

"Well, what did he say?" Bryce prodded as he started the car.

Micah sighed and picked a piece of lint off her pants.

"Oh the usual. Congratulations, we're so happy for you, you're a big disappointment to me. You know, all the usual," she said, looking out the window.

Bryce smiled and then frowned. He drove quietly for a few minutes and then hit his hand on the steering wheel.

"This is ridiculous!" he exploded.

Micah winced and hoped he didn't ask her any other questions about her father's reaction.

"He's disappointed in you? I don't believe it. So what's the deal, are they going to support you or not? We can do a reception ourselves in the church gym. We'll just combine the wedding dinner with the reception and invite fewer people. Don't worry, Micah. It will still be wonderful. I promise," he said.

Micah laughed and leaned over, kissing his cheek as he drove.

"You are so sweet, but I don't think we need to go that far. Kathy took the phone away from my dad, and she's the one who is overjoyed for us. You wouldn't believe how excited she is to help me put my wedding reception together. She says it will take her mind off her pregnancy. She's even going to get a wedding planner. I don't think Kathy is going to let my dad spoil my wedding. I have a feeling it's going to be great," she said with a laugh.

Bryce grinned over at his future wife and kissed her hand. That was Micah—always positive and always willing to look for the good in any situation. Why was he so lucky?

Micah's stomach rumbled loudly and unexpectedly, sending them both into a laughing fit.

"Why didn't you tell me you were starving?" Bryce said and turned his car in the direction opposite of Micah's apartment. He drove into the parking lot of the Olive Garden and turned to look at Micah.

"How does bread sticks, soup, and salad sound? I'd offer you more, but without my dad bankrolling everything now, I'm on a tight budget."

Micah smiled and got out of the car. "Hey, it's my treat this time, anyway. Let's celebrate and order that new shrimp dish," she said, tempting him.

Bryce shrugged happily and grabbed her hand as they walked into the restaurant.

"You're the boss, sweetheart."

They were seated immediately and held hands as they waited for their orders.

"You know, I'm so glad that April's parents ended up changing their minds like that. I think it made her life knowing that she finally had their approval," Micah said, grabbing a bread stick from the basket.

Bryce raised his eyebrows and took a bite of salad.

"Well, let's just say that Joel's dad isn't the kind of guy to sit back and watch any injustice go by unchallenged. He's like a modern-day Moroni with no hair. From what Joel said, his dad drove up to Idaho and had it out with April's mom and dad. He's a stake president you know, so he's used to being kind and loving but at the same time brutally honest. I'm sure he had them begging for mercy within an hour."

Micah looked in awe at Bryce. "Really? That's so funny because April's dad is a stake president too. Wow, I would have loved to be a fly on the wall for that conversation."

Bryce frowned and grabbed the last bread stick. "Well, don't say anything to April. I think it would mean more to her if she thought that her parents had come to their senses on their own," he said.

Micah nodded and moved her salad plate so the waiter could place a large steaming plate of shrimp, mushrooms, and noodles in front of her.

"Are we in heaven or what?" she asked Bryce as her mouth watered at the sight and smell of her lunch.

Bryce lifted his fork in a salute to her.

"Anywhere you are is heaven," he said with a wink and took the first bite.

After lunch, Bryce dropped Micah off at her apartment. She had tons of homework and a lesson to prepare for Sunday. She walked into her empty apartment and went straight to her bedroom to put her purse away. She didn't feel like schoolwork, so she opened the latest conference issue of the *Ensign* and skimmed through it, looking for a talk she could base her lesson on.

She leaned back on her pillow and got comfortable. Wouldn't it be great if Kathy could come and listen in on her lesson? She knew Kathy would come if she asked her. If only her dad would come too. He could go to priesthood meeting with Bryce. She knew from Kathy that he was on probation with the Church for his premarital indiscretions. It would be hard for anyone to say no to the sacrament with everyone watching. But at least he hadn't been excommunicated.

She continued looking through the *Ensign* and finally picked a talk by Bruce C. Hafen on the Atonement. Then she picked up the phone and dialed Kathy's cell number. She had it on speed dial.

"Hello?" came Kathy's voice immediately.

"Hi, Kathy. It's Micah. How are you?" she asked.

Kathy laughed on the other line. "Well, I'm here at the Joseph Smith Memorial Building, of course. Remember when you took me to The Roof for lunch and how you said that when you got married you wanted your reception here? Well, it's yours, honey. I've got my deposit down, and it's all set," she said breathlessly.

Micah jumped up off the bed and jumped up and down, shouting in happiness.

"Kathy! You did? I love you, Kathy, you're the best!" Micah practically screamed, hopping around her room like a crazy woman.

Kathy giggled happily. "I knew you'd be happy, Micah. I would have waited and gone with you, but they're so busy during Christmas, I had to hurry or we wouldn't have gotten a reservation. Phillip and I want to take you and Bryce out to dinner at the Roof in celebration of your engagement. We do need to make an appointment soon with the reception coordinator to pick out the food and the colors and the centerpieces and everything. They take care of it all, you wouldn't believe how nice it is. It makes me want to do my wedding all over again," Kathy said.

Micah smiled into the phone. Well, when Kathy joined the Church someday and she married her dad in the temple, she would make sure that Kathy had the reception of her dreams.

"That wish just might come true someday, Kathy," was all Micah would say.

Kathy talked to her for a few more minutes about the wedding's date and time but then gasped. "I'm sorry, I've gone on and on, and I haven't even asked you why you called."

Micah sat back down on the bed and held the phone tightly to her ear. She didn't want to mess this up.

"Well, I just have a big favor to ask you. Remember I was called to be Relief Society president in my ward? Well, I have to teach the lesson this Sunday, and I was wondering if you would come and give me some moral support. I just get so nervous talking in front of crowds," Micah said.

There was a pause on the other line, but then Kathy's voice came over strong and clear.

"I would be honored, Micah. Just tell me when and I'll be there," she promised.

Micah smiled happily and lay back down on her bed, talking to Kathy for a few more minutes.

She hung up the phone and grabbed the *Ensign*. This had better be the best lesson ever. She'd never had the urge to go on a mission, but for some reason, the thought of doing a little missionary work on her stepmom had her wishing for a little previous experience in that field. Well, all she could do was try her best and hope that the Lord would make up the difference. Micah said a quick prayer in her heart and then grabbed a highlighter pen. Doing her part was going to be a lot of work.

chapter forty-eight

Micah's breaths came fast and short, and she knew she was starting to hyperventilate. Sacrament had gone by smoothly, with not even one butterfly making its presence known. Sunday School was different though. She sat next to Kathy and her dad, with Bryce on her other side, who was flanked by Joel and April. Lisa was sitting on a different row with a friend of hers but kept giving her the thumbs-up sign every time she caught her eye.

She watched the clock's hands move ever closer to the time when Relief Society would start, and knew she was about to have a panic attack. She couldn't stand up in front of all of these wonderful girls and preach to them. Half of them were returned missionaries. They'd laugh her out of the room. She closed her eyes as a wave of nausea rolled through her stomach and felt tears prick behind her eyelids. This was going to be a total disaster. Why had she invited Kathy? Why? She'd never want to go to church again when she saw what an idiot her stepdaughter was.

But at least her dad had come too. She had been hoping but not expecting him to show. So when he picked her up for church with a corsage in his hand and told her how proud he was of her, it had made her day like nothing else. She didn't want to let him down. Especially when he was being so brave in coming back to church. She had watched as the sacrament was passed, and when he passed the sacrament plate to her without taking a piece, she could tell that it pained him. She realized right then that repentance was hard-core. People willing to do whatever it took to get back in the good graces of God and the Church were amazing. She was so glad that her father had taken the first step.

And Kathy had been wonderful. She had even shown up in a dress that went past her knees and had sleeves. Micah was so proud of her. And she had listened carefully to every word spoken during sacrament meeting, leaning over to ask Phillip questions every now and then.

It was all going so well. If only she could just get through the lesson without collapsing, then the day wouldn't be ruined. She looked at the clock again and realized that she only had five minutes left. Her shoulders slumped, and she wondered if anyone would notice if she crawled for the nearest exit.

Bryce leaned down, pushing her hair out of the way, and whispered in her ear.

"Relax. You were set apart for this calling. That means that Heavenly Father is obligated to support you if you do your part. If you've prepared, then you'll do fine. Say a quick prayer and then let the Spirit take over. You're going to be great, Micah," Bryce said encouragingly.

Micah looked up at Bryce gratefully. He had said exactly what she had needed to hear.

"Thanks," she whispered back and bowed her head to say a quick prayer.

Dear God, please help me. Please help me to stand in front of all of these incredible, beautiful people and teach them what thou would have them know. Please bless me with thy Spirit. In the name of Jesus Christ, amen.

She looked up as the closing prayer was started and bowed her head again. The countdown had begun.

She stood after the prayer and hugged her dad and Bryce before they walked out of the room together. Her dad hadn't been exactly friendly to Bryce, *resigned* was maybe a better word. But it was a start.

"Come on, Kathy. I want you to sit in the front row with April and Lisa. I'll just look at you the whole time so I won't be so nervous," Micah said and grabbed Kathy's hand, leading her to the front.

Kathy followed her lead and sat down in front, and was immediately joined by April and Lisa. Micah smiled as some of the girls in her ward walked up and introduced themselves to her stepmom. She loved returned missionaries. They were never shy when it came to welcoming someone new to the ward.

She busied herself with making sure everything was in place, talking to the music person, making sure someone passed out the hymnbooks and that the roll for attendance was ready to pass around. She paused when she realized that some of those dreadful butterflies had flown off. She was still nervous, but she could handle it now, she realized.

She smiled her thanks to heaven and kept moving. She had a job to do.

Her first counselor conducted the meeting, so Micah sat down in a chair facing the room and watched everyone in the small Relief Society room, some of whom were still trickling in slowly.

The song was almost done when Jenny walked in and sat down in the far back. Micah frowned, worried about her. Ever since she had found out about her dad, she hadn't been the same bubbly, cheerful girl everyone loved so much. But then again, Jenny had been much kinder to her in the last week. When Bryce had fixed her dinner Wednesday, Jenny had stopped by and hadn't run at the sight of her. She'd even sat down and joined them. She hadn't talked much, but then she hadn't glared much either. Maybe she was softening toward her. Micah smiled and hoped she was right. Everyone deserved a chance. Maybe Jenny was ready to give her one.

"Micah? You're up," Keeley said, laughing as Micah just sat there.

Micah started and blushed. She had been zoning out and hadn't realized that she had been announced. She grabbed her notes and her picture of Christ and walked quickly to the podium, which was sitting on the table.

"Good morning, everyone. I don't know if everyone got the chance to meet my stepmother, Kathy, but she's here with me today for moral support. Kathy, stand up so everyone can see you," Micah urged, grinning at Kathy's surprised expression.

She stood up shyly and waved at everyone before sitting down quickly and giggled as April put an arm around her shoulders for a quick hug.

"Today, I'd like to talk about the Atonement," she said as she put her favorite picture of Christ up on an easel so everyone could see. It was a picture of Christ walking over rocks in a stream, holding out a hand. The caption underneath read *Be Not Afraid*. It always gave her courage and the knowledge that Christ would always be there to help her.

She dove into her lesson and was surprised when she

got a lot of hands shooting into the air. It seemed like everyone had a personal story of how the Atonement had touched her life. She glanced down at one point in her lesson and was surprised to see Kathy weeping into a tissue.

She looked at the clock and realized they only had five minutes left to the meeting, and she felt like shouting for joy. She was almost done. She had made it! She was about to close with her testimony when one last hand was raised in the back. It was Jenny's.

"Yes, Jenny?" she asked nervously. She had been wondering if Jenny was going to sabotage her lesson. Now she would find out.

"What do you do when you've been taught your whole life about the Atonement and that we're supposed to forgive others so that we can be forgiven, but you just can't? What if somebody you love very much has done the most horrible, sickest things in the world, and you just can't get past it? How do you forgive someone something like that, and how do you keep loving them?" she asked with tears in her voice.

Micah's heart broke for Bryce's sister, knowing exactly what she was talking about. How could she help Jenny understand?

"Jenny, that's a good question," Micah said, walking around the podium to stand by the picture of Jesus.

"Look at this picture, Jenny. See how hard it is for this person to walk and not fall? But Christ is holding his hand out. In your life right now, you're on this rocky path. You could fall. You could get hurt spiritually. Not forgiving and not loving people damages our spirits. But see, this person is reaching out to Christ. If you go to Christ and tell him how you feel and how impossible this task is for you, he will first comfort you and then he will help you. Some of the things we have to do, like forgive others, may seem impossible. But God is a God of miracles. Nothing is impossible for him—especially when it comes to healing hearts. Pray, Jenny. Pray for help, and you'll get it," she said.

She swallowed and hoped that what she had said could help her in some way. She closed the meeting with a short testimony, and since they were over their time limit, they went right to the closing prayer.

Micah looked up after the prayer and started to shake. She had survived! She had done it! She looked around the room happily and noticed many young women were making their way to her side.

"Thank you so much. I loved your lesson. You did such a great job," one girl said.

"Beautiful job, Micah. I'm so glad you're the Relief Society president. Thank you for your lesson," a girl named Beth said.

Micah was in awe as girl after girl came up and thanked her. She couldn't believe it.

When the crowed dispersed, Jenny walked up to her with tears streaming down her face. She walked up to Micah and put her arms around her, sobbing.

"I'm so sorry, Micah, for hating you. I'm so sorry. Please forgive me for being such a brat. I know you love Bryce and that he loves you. I'm glad you're getting married," she said, and then ran out of the room.

Micah collapsed into a chair, stunned by Jenny's confession. She hadn't seen that coming.

"Come on, Micah, let's go get your dad," Kathy said, grabbing Micah's hand and leading her out of the room.

"Well, what did you think?" Micah asked as the two women squeezed down the halls, looking for Bryce and Phillip.

Kathy, still holding Micah's hand, looked at her stepdaughter seriously.

"It was all so interesting, Micah. I feel so energized. I don't even know how to explain it. It's like when your dad reads the Book of Mormon to me. I just want to know more and more. Can I come back next week?" she asked hopefully.

Micah grinned and put her arm around Kathy's shoulders.

"Of course you can. But don't you want to go to your own ward? It's just around the corner from your house," she said as they found her dad and Bryce, talking to the bishop.

Kathy smiled and asked Phillip immediately about next Sunday, causing him to turn red in the face and usher her quickly out of the building, waving good-bye.

Bryce and Micah looked at each other and smiled. Phillip was well on his way to coming back to church.

Jenny joined them shortly, and they all got in Bryce's car to go to Bountiful. Amelia Jorgenson was planning a good old-fashioned Sunday dinner for her children, and none of them wanted to disappoint her. Micah was worried about the planning meeting Amelia wanted to have after dinner, but it turned out to be fun. They played Monopoly and ate apple crisp for dessert. When Amelia did mention the wedding dinner, all she did was ask if they liked chicken or steak.

Bryce and Micah both agreed on chicken and that was the end of the discussion. Micah went home that night feeling as if a great burden had been lifted off her shoulders. She wouldn't have to teach another lesson for four more months, Jenny was being nice to her, and she was about to get the nicest mother-in-law in the world. Life couldn't get any better.

chapter forty-nine

Two months passed by quickly, filled with school and preparations for the wedding. She and April were planning on being married in the Salt Lake Temple but on separate days—April on Friday and Micah on Saturday. But they were spending their honeymoons together in Sydney, Australia. Micah couldn't wait. A whole week of white sandy beaches, hanging out with her new husband and their friends. She couldn't imagine anything more perfect.

She looked over at Bryce licking an envelope and couldn't help noticing his look of distaste.

"I'm never going to lick another envelope in my life," Bryce swore and picked up one more.

Micah laughed. "Well, that's what you get for having so many friends. Your pile is twice as big as mine," she pointed out. She didn't have any relatives besides her dad and Kathy. Her dad's business associates and a few neighbors comprised Micah's entire list.

Bryce put down his envelope and picked up his list, scanning down to the next name: *Troy Jorgenson—?* He frowned and looked away. His mom had made the list out for him, but she had put a question mark by his father's name, leaving the decision up to him.

"I have to invite him," he said, mostly to himself.

Micah looked up from her list with her eyebrows raised questioningly.

"Who, Bryce?" she asked.

"My father," Bryce said quietly. "I don't really want to, but it's my wedding. Regardless of his choices, he's my father, and he should be invited. I don't think we'll be able to accept his wedding gift, but he should still be able to come," he said, looking at Micah for her reaction.

Micah smiled and handed Bryce an invitation.

"Of course he's coming," she said simply.

Bryce took the invitation and leaned over to kiss her on the nose.

"How did I get so lucky?" he asked, smiling, and addressed his wedding invitation to his father.

"We better hurry though, Bryce. We're supposed to meet my dad and Kathy at The Roof in an hour and a half, and you know my dad does not accept excuses for tardiness," she said, grabbing her pile of invitations and placing them in a large box.

Bryce put a stamp on the envelope and placed it on top of the rest before standing and holding out a hand to Micah.

"Okay. Let me run home and change, and I'll be back in twenty minutes to pick you up. I wouldn't want to miss this dinner," he said dryly.

Micah ignored the hint of sarcasm and pushed him out the door. Bryce and her dad still didn't get along perfectly. Their time together was spent mostly with Bryce being grilled by her father on everything from his political views to his grades. Bryce usually ended up with a headache afterward.

Micah smiled grimly. Her family was her family, and they were all going to get along—someday. She just had to be patient, that was all.

She changed quickly and opened the door before Bryce could ring the bell. They drove to Salt Lake in comfortable silence, listening to soft music on the radio and holding hands.

They only had four short weeks until their wedding. Thoughts of their future filled both of their minds.

They reached the parking lot with fifteen minutes to spare. They met Kathy and Phillip at the doors to the restaurant, and Micah couldn't help noticing that Kathy looked pale and tired.

"Kathy, are you okay? You look like you're not feeling very well," Micah asked with concern in her voice.

Phillip looked at his wife sharply and nodded in agreement.

"You're doing too much, Kathy. I've told you to slow down. You'd think this wedding is the most important thing in the world. I keep telling you the wedding planner is there for a reason. Let her do the running around," he said testily.

Kathy laughed and rubbed her stomach.

"You two need to stop worrying so much. I'm having the time of my life. If I want to make sure the flowers are perfect and that the lace on the table is hand-crocheted, then I will. It makes me happy," she said truthfully and then reached out for Bryce's hand.

"Come on, Bryce. Let's leave these two worrywarts and

go get something to eat," she said.

Bryce grinned and took her hand, following the host to their table.

Micah and her father shared a look of amusement and followed their loved ones into the restaurant.

The two couples spent an evening of good food and polite conversation, to Bryce's amazement. He'd been expecting the third degree again but hadn't even been asked any question that hadn't related to his dinner or to their upcoming wedding. He began to relax during dessert and even enjoyed himself.

Micah sighed as she looked out the window at the temple. It was so beautiful at night. She couldn't believe she would be inside the temple in less than a month, making sacred covenants to God and her husband. It took her breath away to just think about it.

"Um, Micah, Kathy and I wanted to tell you something," Phillip said, interrupting her thoughts.

Micah looked at Bryce and then at her father. *Uh-oh. What now?*

"Kathy and I have been going to church for a while now—well, ever since you invited us to your ward. And we just want you to know that Kathy has decided to take the missionary discussions," he announced, kissing his wife's hand tenderly.

Micah squealed in delight and rocketed up from her seat to run around the table to kiss Kathy and hug her dad.

She took her seat, still grinning and clapped her hands in happiness. "Oh I'm so happy. I just knew you'd join the Church someday!"

Kathy smiled up at Phillip and reached for his hand.

"Well, I'm not baptized yet, but I hope when the time comes, that Phillip will be the one to baptize me," she said solemnly.

Phillip cleared his throat but looked at his daughter

with dignity as he said, "I won't be able to be in the temple with you when you get married, Micah, but hopefully in a few months my probation will end. When the time comes to baptize Kathy, I will be worthy to do my priesthood duty," he said with a catch in his throat.

Micah felt tears come to her eyes as she realized how determined her father was to become worthy once again.

"I know, Dad, and it's okay. Our bishop will be there for me. I wish it was you, but just knowing that someday you and Kathy will be married in the temple makes up for everything," she said.

Phillip reached over and in a rare show of affection, patted his daughter's cheek.

"I love you, Micah," he said gruffly, and then looked away in embarrassment.

The conversation moved on to less serious matters, and they decided to end the evening with a toast.

Phillip held his water glass up and waited for everyone to join him.

"To Micah and Bryce, may your future be as bright and good and wonderful as my daughter's heart," he said tenderly.

Bryce smiled and drank to the toast. At least he and Phillip could agree on one thing.

Kathy held her glass up too, not to be outdone.

"To the Rawlingses!" she said simply, and laughed as she clinked her glass with everyone else's.

Micah grinned and raised her glass. "To the Jorgensons!" she said and smiled at Bryce.

He grinned and clinked his glass to hers and Kathy's. Micah and Bryce reached their glass over to clink against Phillip's but he had lowered his glass with a frown.

"Sorry, Bryce, but you know I want you to change your last name. I can't seem to get over it," he said, looking down at his plate.

Micah and Bryce lowered their glasses in embarrassment.

Bryce's face turned to stone, and Micah knew immediately he was deeply hurt and offended.

"Phillip, please. Please don't ruin the evening," Kathy
pleaded as she looked down at her plate sadly.

Phillip shook his head, frowning, and turned to look out
at the window.

"No, Kathy. I've let you have your way on just about
everything. But there's no getting over this. I have had to
accept the fact that my daughter has chosen to marry someone that I didn't necessarily approve of in the beginning. I
will not, however, be happy about certain family relations
that come along with the marriage. The only comfort I have
is knowing that that man won't be at the wedding."

Micah and Bryce exchanged a quick look.

"Actually, Dad, he will be," Micah said softly.

Phillip turned his head slowly to stare at Bryce with
cold anger.

"I've pretty much already paid for the wedding. But so
help me, if that man shows his face at my daughter's reception, I will leave. It's either him or me. And if you had any
respect for my daughter, you wouldn't want your father
anywhere near her," he sputtered, getting angrier by the
second.

Micah bit her lip unhappily. She didn't know what to do.
Her dad was about to explode and was refusing to go to her
wedding reception, and her fiancé, the man she loved, was
sitting next to her, hurt, angry, and humiliated. And she
was stuck in the middle. She looked at the temple one last
time and then said a quick prayer for help. She needed it. She
took a deep breath and broke the cold, heavy silence.

"Dad, attacking Bryce because of his father's choices
isn't fair. It was Bryce's decision to invite his father, and I
stand by him. We can't all have perfect families. It's not like

our family is the typical LDS family, either. A wedding is a special time when families put their differences aside and come together for the sake of their loved ones. This is *my* wedding, Dad. Please just let it go—for me?" she asked, her voice quavering.

Phillip's stern face relaxed a fraction, but he shook his head.

"Micah, you have a decision to make," he said and grabbed Kathy's hand, pulling her up, while throwing down a generous tip. Kathy turned to wave but was rushed out of the restaurant before Micah could wave back.

Micah sighed and turned to look at Bryce. He was completely silent, sitting in his seat and looking down at his napkin. Micah felt a chill run down her spine and knew absolutely the evening had been completely ruined. *Whoever said weddings were fun must have been insane*, Micah couldn't help thinking.

"Bryce, it's going to be okay," she said, trying to get him to look at her.

Bryce looked up slowly and put his napkin on the table.

"You know he's right, Micah. About everything. What are you even doing with me? Maybe I *should* change my last name. What did your dad say—I don't have respect for you? Yeah, that's just great. Come on, Micah, let's go," Bryce said and got up quickly from the table, throwing his napkin down angrily.

Micah followed Bryce out of the restaurant, practically running after him. He acted like he didn't even want to be with her.

The car ride home was silent, horrible, and very long. Micah knew that nothing she could say right now could help make Bryce feel any better. He dropped her off at her apartment and didn't even bother to kiss her good night. She watched the car as he drove quickly away from her. She clasped her arms around herself and felt tears of frustration and sadness course down her cheeks. What if dealing with her father was just too much? What if Bryce asked for his ring back? What if this was it and he dumped her? Micah cried outside in the empty parking lot for a few more minutes and then wiped her eyes. She didn't want her roommates asking any questions. Telling them that her dad was trying to ruin her wedding was too embarrassing. She walked toward her apartment but slowed down when she realized that there were policemen walking out through her doorway.

She went from a walk into a sprint, running past an officer who was talking into his radio. She ran through the door and saw April and Lisa sitting on the couch, talking to a policeman who was writing what they were saying down on his pad of paper.

"April, Lisa! What happened? Are you okay?" she asked, running to her friends and grabbing both of their hands.

The policeman stood up, and before April and Lisa could say anything, he took control of the situation.

"Miss, are you Micah Rawlings?" he asked in a strong but kind voice.

"Yes," she said uncertainly. "What was going on here?"

"Miss Rawlings, your apartment has been broken into and vandalized. We need to have you check your room for any missing items. Please go with Officer Tanner. He'll escort you and write down the information," he said, motioning for another officer to lead her away.

She looked back at April and Lisa and saw shock on their faces. She felt ill all of a sudden. This was all too much. Dinner turning into a fiasco and now a break-in. Everything had been going so well. Too well, she now realized. She should have known she wasn't this lucky.

Officer Tanner went before her into the room, and as she stepped in behind him, all thoughts of anything else left her head. Her room had been ransacked and destroyed! All of her new clothes were on the ground, ripped up and covered in what looked like grape juice, ketchup, and molasses. Her pictures had been torn off the wall and smashed, leaving glass everywhere. Her sheets and bedspread had been ripped off her bed, and her mattress had been slashed with an ax or something. But it was what was on the empty walls that had her going dizzy. Officer Tanner grabbed her arm, before she could collapse. He led her to a chair in her room that hadn't been completely destroyed. The words on the wall were spray-painted in large block letters—horrible, *vile* words that seemed to cover her in filth. She felt violated just being in her room. She looked at the walls and then at Officer Tanner and broke down weeping. He escorted her out of the room, where she went right to her friends, who put their arms around her and tried to comfort her as best as they could.

"Miss, I know you're upset, but we need to know if anything is missing. We'll give you a few minutes to calm down, but we need a list. If we're going to catch the person who did this, we need to have the details," Officer Stevens, the first policeman, said to her in a gentle voice.

She turned her head away and cried harder on April's shoulder. She'd never had anything like this happen to her before. Ever. She felt as if someone were trying to destroy her life. Who would write such hideous things about her and destroy her clothes? Who would hate her that much?

She lifted her head up and looked at her roommates. "Did you see my room?" she asked with tears in her voice.

April and Lisa both nodded. "What did they do to your rooms?" Micah asked as April handed her a tissue.

"Nothing," April said quietly, looking at Lisa and then away.

Micah sat up straight. "What! Someone broke into our apartment and did that to *me* but didn't do anything to you guys? Somebody hates me," she said in shock.

"Miss Rawlings, do you know of anyone who is capable of doing this to you? Do you have any enemies? Someone who's mad at you and might want revenge?" Officer Tanner asked softly, trying not to upset the girl any further.

Micah sniffed and lowered her eyes. "Yes," she said so quietly they could barely hear her.

"Who would that be?" Officer Stevens asked, reaching for his pen.

Micah looked at April and Lisa and then sighed, knowing her dad wasn't going to like this.

"Rod. My new stepuncle," she said and then started to cry again.

April wiped her own tears away at the pain she felt for Micah.

"Officers, I think I can give you some information. Why don't we give Micah a few minutes," she said and motioned for the officers to join her in the kitchen, where she gave them Micah's dad's phone number and told them about all of their previous run-ins with Rod.

Micah felt so numb. She sat there with Lisa's arm around her shoulders, but she felt nothing. She felt cold and so lonely. Someone *hated* her enough to do this. She shook her head. This couldn't be happening to her.

A few minutes later, her eyes abruptly focused on Bryce kneeling in front of her; she was jolted out of her paralysis.

"Sweetie, come on. Let's go look through the room one more time. The officers need to know what's been stolen."

April must have called him, she thought as she stood up and was hugged for several long minutes by Bryce. She laid her head against his chest and felt safe for a moment. All thoughts of their horrible dinner date were gone. He was here.

He held her hand and gently pulled her toward her room, with an officer following closely behind.

She swallowed and tried not to see the scarlet words

written everywhere. She crunched through the glass and picked through her room, looking everywhere. She had to be certain. Ten minutes later, she lifted her head from looking under her bed and stared at the officer and Bryce in surprise.

"Nothing's gone," she said. "They didn't steal a thing. It's all here." She got up from the floor, careful not to get glass in her hands and walked over to Bryce, who put a protective arm around her shoulder and led her out again.

Phillip arrived fifteen minutes later, breathing fire and condemnation down on anyone who would dare do this to his daughter. Micah watched from the couch as her father and Bryce cornered all of the officers separately and talked to them endlessly, it seemed.

"What am I going to do? Where am I going to sleep tonight and tomorrow night and the next?" Micah asked April and Lisa sadly.

April shook her head.

"Everything you have is destroyed. You don't even have a pair of pajamas to sleep in. Thank heavens you didn't pick up your wedding dress this week. If they'd destroyed that, I would have died," April said.

Micah's eyes went large at the thought.

"Yeah, I guess I'm pretty lucky," she said in a small, depressed voice.

Lisa winced and patted Micah's knee. "Don't worry, Micah. You can borrow a pair of my pajamas, and you can sleep on the couch. It's pretty comfortable. And tomorrow, we'll help you clean up this mess. We can have your room repainted by tomorrow afternoon if we work hard," she added.

Micah sighed. All of this destruction because someone hated her. *Could it have been Rod?* she wondered. *What if it was someone else? Someone from our ward? What if it was Jenny?* she thought, guiltily looking at Bryce, who was in deep conversation with Officer Tanner.

She didn't want to think something so horrible of his sister, but Jenny had been very open and passionate about her dislike for her.

"Come, Micah. I'm taking you home. I'll have some people here tomorrow to clean this mess up. The insurance will pay for everything. Kathy can help you get some new clothes tomorrow. It's okay, dear. Let's go," Phillip said, more kindly as he finally noticed all of the tears on his daughter's pale face.

She looked at her roommates but got up and followed her dad.

"Bye, guys. I'll see you tomorrow," she said and looked at Bryce. He was too busy talking to notice her so she followed her dad outside.

The drive home was quiet, and Micah was grateful for it. She leaned her head back and didn't open her eyes until she heard the garage door close on them. Kathy, although younger than she, clucked over her like a real mother and even tucked her in.

Micah fell asleep immediately, exhausted and sad. Her life wasn't as perfect as she had thought it was. Fairy tales were called fairy tales for a reason. Real life just never turned out the way you wanted it to.

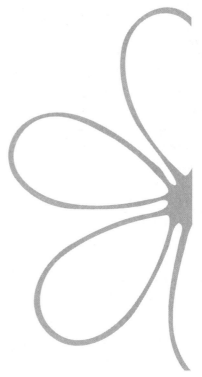

chapter fifty

Bryce finally let Officer Tanner go and got into his own car. He glanced at his watch and winced when he saw it was almost 1:30 in the morning. Good thing it was Saturday. He was going to be dead tired. But at least he'd convinced the police officer to check out Michelle.

When he'd gone into Micah's room with her to check for theft, he was almost knocked off his feet with déjà vu. The damage, the destruction, the horrible words—it was all the same. Years and years ago when he had asked Jennifer Rosenthal to senior prom, she had cancelled at the last minute because someone had broken into her home and vandalized her room. She had been so traumatized she hadn't felt like going to the dance. Bryce had completely understood and had gone stag to the party with a few of his friends who hadn't bothered to get dates. Michelle had been there. She hadn't come with a date. It was like she had been waiting just for him. He danced most of the night with her and had driven her home, ending the night with a kiss. He'd always known that she'd had a crush on him, so it was almost natural to start dating. But there was just something off about Michelle. Something wasn't right behind those diamond-hard blue eyes. After a few months of miserable dating, filled with screaming fits, jealous rages, and temper tantrums, he had broken up with her. But she hadn't been able to accept it. And now he finally understood—she was flat out crazy.

He couldn't get Micah's shattered face out of his mind. She had looked so broken and sad that anyone would hate her enough to destroy her room. He'd wanted to bundle her up and take her away from it all. He had to admit that he had been furious after he had dropped her off at her apartment. He was angry at her dad, at her for even having Phillip for a dad, and at the world in general. But when April called and told him to come quick, there was trouble, he had run. He'd never been so terrified in his life. Just the thought that something could have happened to Micah put ice in his blood. And that's when he knew. He knew that it didn't matter what her dad said to him. He was going to love Micah for eternity, and nothing was going to get in the way of that love. Nothing and *nobody*.

 chapter fifty-one

"Kathy, just go to the mall and leave me in peace," Phillip bit out angrily at his wife.

Kathy backed up a step but didn't retreat.

"I know how upset you are, Phillip, but threatening to kill Rod is only going to get you in trouble. Please calm down and just let the police do their job. Micah is okay. She's not hurt," Kathy said, intuitively knowing that if anything happened to Micah, Phillip wouldn't be able to handle it. Losing his wife and son had made him a very controlling and protective parent—but only because he was terrified of anything ever harming his child or taking that child away from him.

Phillip threw some papers down on his desk and turned his back on his wife.

"I know she's okay, Kathy. I have eyes. But something *could* have happened. What if she had been home instead of out with us? She could have been hurt—or worse," he muttered darkly.

Kathy walked over to Phillip and put a hand on his arm.

"Please don't get so upset, Phillip. It's not healthy. Micah is strong. She's going to be fine. I'll take her shopping and out to lunch while you have her room cleaned up and everything will go back to normal," she said soothingly.

Phillip turned his head to look at his wife. "Rod is going to pay," he vowed and left the room, leaving Kathy worried and frightened. She felt a sharp pain in her stomach and had to sit down, breathing heavily. She'd been having them regularly since the night before when Phillip had half-dragged her out of the restaurant, furious and upset.

She got up from the chair as soon as the pain disappeared and sighed in relief. She had a few hours at the mall with Micah to get through and then she could put her feet up and rest. That's all she needed, a little rest and quiet. She waddled down the hall to see if Micah was ready. She knocked softly on the door before opening it. There was Micah, sitting on the edge of the bed, weeping softly. Kathy walked in the room and closed the door. She walked over and sat on the bed next to Micah and put her hand on her stepdaughter's knee.

"Micah, please don't be sad. This will all be over soon," Kathy said softly.

Micah didn't even look up.

"Oh, I know. I think I'm just a little stressed out with everything happening all at once. And I don't think Bryce is very happy with me or Dad right now. I don't even know if I'm still getting married," she said, looking up at Kathy with red-rimmed eyes.

Kathy smiled and hugged her.

"Now you're being plain silly. Bryce loves you. Do you think he would have put up with your dad *this* long if he didn't love you more than anything? Come on, let's go have some fun, spend tons of your dad's money, and get our minds off all of this depressing stuff for just a little while. By the time we get back, your apartment will be back to normal and so will your life. I promise," Kathy said.

Micah smiled and took Kathy's hand. "You know what, I don't understand it. You're younger than me. You've only been married to my dad for a little while, but sometimes I get the weirdest feeling that I've been waiting a long time for you to be my mom," she said with a short laugh.

Kathy threw her arms around Micah and held her tightly. It was Micah's turn to put a comforting arm around Kathy this time.

"I'm sorry, Micah," Kathy said with a sniff. "I've just been so emotional lately, and you don't know how much that means to me to hear you say that. When I first married your dad and he told me he had a daughter, I hoped that someday we could come to love each other in a sisterly kind of way, you know. But it's like you said, I love you like you're my daughter," she said and hugged her one last time.

Micah sniffed, wiped the tears off Kathy's cheeks and helped her stepmother off the bed.

"Come on, Kathy, let's go shopping. I think we need to buy you some things too. After you have the baby, you're not going to want to see maternity clothes for the next ten years," Micah said with a laugh.

Kathy tried to laugh too but grabbed her stomach in pain as Micah disappeared out the door. *Those darn Braxton-Hicks contractions.* She paused and tried to catch her breath, but they were getting more and more painful. She prayed she could get through the afternoon. If she could take Micah's mind off this horrible situation, then she would do whatever it took, even if that meant trying not to double over in pain when it felt as if a slash of lighting was rippling down her stomach.

She hurried to catch up with Micah and smiled. She loved Micah. She couldn't have asked for a better older sister for her daughter. Kathy rubbed her stomach nervously though. She wasn't supposed to have the baby for three more months. But if she didn't know better, this felt like real labor. Kathy pushed the thought away and eased herself into her tiny car, wishing now she had a large minivan. *Everything is going to be okay,* she thought. *At least it better be.*

chapter fifty-two

Micah watched as Kathy drove away in the cute little sports car. She frowned in concern though when the car turned a corner and went out of sight. The poor thing had looked so drained and tired at the mall. She smiled and laughed a lot, but underneath the happy face, Micah could see the strain. She had ordered Kathy to go home and put her feet up.

Micah shook her head and turned toward the apartment complex. She was curious to see her room now that her father had called in a small army to put everything back to normal. It was hard to believe her dad could really pull it off.

As she walked toward her apartment, her cell rang. She paused to answer it while she waved at a few girls in her ward as they walked by.

"Hello?" she said, not recognizing the number.

"Miss Rawlings? This is Officer Tanner. We would like you to come down to the police station. Your father is already here. We've arrested the person who broke into your apartment last night. We need you to come down and fill out some paperwork."

"Um, okay. Just tell me where you are and I'll come right now," she said.

She wrote down the information down as best as she could and walked quickly back toward the parking lot and her car. She made it downtown in ten minutes.

Micah parked next to her dad's car and walked into the large building, feeling strange and out of place. She spotted her dad almost immediately. He must have been waiting for her.

"Micah, dear. I'm glad you came quickly. Let's just sign the papers and leave. I don't want you here any longer than you need to be," he said, taking her by the arm and leading her over to an office.

She sat down in front of a large, ugly, paper-strewn desk and looked at her father. He looked tense but relieved—kind of how she was feeling, she thought. She just sat there as her father and the officer talked back and forth and gave her a paper to sign every now and then. But when they were through and standing up, she continued to sit.

"Hold on," she said, raising her hand. "Who did it? Was it Rod?" she asked curiously.

Her father shook his head. "No, thank heaven. He's down in Las Vegas working as a valet. Since he's on parole, he had to get special permission to go. He's innocent. It was some girl named Michelle Bertrand. I guess the police got a tip last night that she was the one. The officers went to her apartment and found proof all over the place. Spray cans, scissors, and clothes covered in paint. She even had paint under her fingernails. She's guilty. She hasn't confessed yet, but her lawyer is hoping for a plea bargain," Phillip said with a haughty sniff.

Micah walked in a daze out of the building and toward her car. *Michelle.* So her gut feeling had been right. The girl was nuts for Bryce—so much so that she was going to have a permanent record now, even if she didn't serve jail time. *Too weird.*

She kissed her dad on the cheek and waved good-bye before driving home. Her life was turning into a soap opera. But at least it wasn't Rod. Kathy would have felt so bad if it had been.

She walked into her room ten minutes later with April and Lisa right behind her and gasped. Her room didn't look the same. It looked ten times better. All of the furniture had been replaced, the walls repainted a soft, buttery cream color. There were new curtains and even a throw rug. And now all she had to do was hang up her new clothes.

"You are such a daddy's little girl, Micah," April said with a laugh.

Micah blinked in surprise. She'd never once thought of herself that way. But maybe all along, she had been.

"Yeah, I guess so," she said.

She felt so much better about everything that she made everyone dinner that evening and gave them all the juicy details of her police station visit. April and Lisa hung onto every single word that came out of her mouth.

April shook her head and stabbed a tomato. "If I were you, I'd move as far away from Michelle as I could. If she's crazy enough to do this, what else is she capable of doing?"

Micah shrugged. "I'm not going to live my life in fear because her obsession with Bryce went over the top. Besides, my dad is putting a huge restraining order on her. If she comes within fifteen feet of me, she's in jail."

Lisa ooohed and aahed. "I can't believe how boring my life is compared to yours," she said. "Getting engaged, getting vandalized. Holy cow," she said.

April laughed and threw a tortilla chip at Lisa, who ducked and threw one back.

"Don't let her fool you, Micah. This girl has been on the computer for hours at a time e-mailing Preston. I think there might be a new and exciting romance right under our noses," she said, smiling at Lisa.

Micah laughed and listened to all of the details, enjoying her roommates' company, but she couldn't help looking at the clock every twenty minutes. She hadn't heard once from Bryce that day. Before long, she might be able to add one more exciting thing to her list—getting dumped.

chapter fifty-three

Kathy gasped in pain and rolled clumsily out of bed. Phillip was fast asleep, and she didn't want to disturb him, but she was in so much pain, she couldn't hold back her moans any longer. She went to the bathroom, and noticed a trickle of blood making its way down her leg.

"No," she whispered and grabbed some tissue.

This couldn't be happening. She couldn't be having the baby right now. But as she sat on the edge of the tub and shivered in fear, she knew that to help her baby, she needed to get to the hospital as fast as she could. Waiting was putting her baby at risk. She had to wake up Phillip.

She pulled herself up and walked slowly and painfully

back into the bedroom.

"Phillip? Please wake up. Something's wrong. I think the baby's coming now," she said, shaking his shoulder.

Phillip woke up immediately and stared at Kathy in surprise.

"The baby's not due for a few more months. What's going on?" he asked as he jumped out of bed and grabbed a pair of slacks and a polo shirt. He kept asking her questions as he ushered her out of the house and into the car within minutes.

The constant talking from Phillip calmed Kathy like nothing else, especially since she wasn't expected to answer. He sped down the empty roads to Provo Regional Medical Center. He ran in and got her a wheelchair and was back in seconds. She closed her eyes and clenched her teeth in agony as another contraction ripped through her body, harder than even the last one. By the time it was over, Phillip had her up on the third floor. A nurse took one look at her and had Phillip wheel her into an examination room.

Kathy ignored everyone as the pain became too intense and let Phillip answer all the questions. But she did catch one sentence from the nurse that caused a large wall of fear to crash down on her.

"It's too soon for this baby to come. Get the on-call doctor here right now—it's too late to stop the labor."

The nurse hadn't said anything she didn't already know, but just having her thoughts confirmed had her searching for Phillip's hand. After the next contraction ended, Kathy looked up, panting, with perspiration covering her forehead. Phillip stood next to her quietly, with a good strong grip on her hand. But it was the look on his face that caught her off guard. He looked defeated. He had already given up. He was already in worst-case-scenario mode.

Kathy wanted to reach out and comfort Phillip, but she couldn't. She was too busy dealing with contractions that were skyrocketing upward every few minutes.

Before she knew it, she was dressed in a light blue dressing gown that was backless and receiving pain medication through an IV. The nurse told her sympathetically that it was too late for an epidural. The baby was coming right now.

The doctor, whom she'd never seen before in her life, took charge while issuing orders to get everything ready for the newborn intensive care unit. Having a baby three months early was not good. There were so many things that could go wrong. Lung development, eye development, organ development—everything.

She looked up at Phillip and motioned him to lean down.

"Phillip, I'm scared," she whispered and then bore down with another contraction.

Phillip looked down at his young, frightened wife and felt his heart break. *Not this time. Not this time.* He couldn't stop saying it over and over in his head. He watched the doctors and the nurses work together competently and wished he could do something. He felt so useless. So powerless. He bowed his head and said a silent prayer for help. With his eyes still closed, he felt an impression come into his heart.

Turn to the one who can heal.

Phillip felt his breath catch as he realized that the Spirit was communicating with him. It had been so long since he had felt the Spirit in his life that it took him by surprise. What did it mean though? *Turn to the one who can heal.* He couldn't do anything—he was on probation. *If only I could give my wife a blessing,* he thought with regret sitting heavily on his shoulders.

The doctor looked intently down at Kathy and urged her on. "One more push, Kathy, and your baby's here. Come on, one more big one. Yes! Here she is." He pulled the infant from her mother's womb.

Phillip looked on in amazement at how tiny and yet how perfect their little baby was. The doctor didn't waste any time with ceremonial cord-cutting. He quickly severed the connection between mother and child and placed the baby in the hands of a waiting nurse, who then placed the baby in a small cart and wheeled her immediately out of the room. The baby hadn't made even one little noise. Phillip's heart sank at what that could mean.

"Is the baby okay? Will she be all right?" Phillip asked the doctor.

The doctor was busy delivering the placenta but looked up at Phillip with kind eyes.

"The on-call pediatrician will be taking care of your daughter now. I'm going to make sure your wife is okay, and then we'll see what's going on," he said, turning back to Kathy.

Phillip had never seen Kathy so exhausted and so white-faced. Her eyes were closed, and her lips were almost gray. A cold shiver of dread trickled down his spine. He couldn't lose Kathy. She was his life now. She loved him. No, he would not let her go like this and leave him all alone. *Again.*

He leaned down, kissed her gently on the forehead, and told her that he'd be right back. Her eyes barely flickered as he let go of her hand. He walked quickly out of the room and down the hall to a courtesy phone. He picked it up and looked at it for a second but then frowned with resolve. Forget pride. Forget everything he had said. His wife and new baby needed help, and if it meant humbling himself, then he would do whatever it took. There was one who could heal. He knew it and he knew his wife and child needed that help right now.

He dialed the number quickly and waited. "Hello? Micah dear. I know it's three in the morning. I—*we* need help. Will you please call Bryce and come down to the Provo Regional Medical Center? Kathy just had the baby. They both need a priesthood blessing. Hurry, Micah. I don't know how much time we have," he said, his voice breaking.

He hung up and ran back down the hall. A weight had been lifted off his shoulders. If his wife and child could receive a blessing from a worthy priesthood holder, then everything would be okay. He just knew it. *It has to be,* he thought desperately.

chapter fifty-four

Micah stared at the phone and then threw her covers off. She quickly pulled on some sweatpants and a new T-shirt Kathy had helped her pick out and then grabbed her car keys. She didn't waste time calling Bryce. She would just go get him.

She slammed out of the house, sprinting for her car, and peeled out of the parking lot—every second counted. Her car squealed going around the corners and she probably peeled at least ten layers off her tires, but she made it in half her usual time.

She jumped out of her car and ran for Bryce's door. She pounded with both of her fists and rang the doorbell too.

"Come on, Bryce!" she couldn't help yelling, feeling that every moment that passed was one too many. Her dad's scared voice had frightened her more than anything else ever had. Her dad was never scared, but she knew he was terrified now. He couldn't lose another baby. That would be too much for him to bear.

Bryce opened the door with Joel standing behind him, disheveled and grumpy.

"What—" Bryce began, but Micah interrupted him.

"Come with me right now! My dad's at the hospital. Kathy went into labor early, and the baby needs a blessing. He's scared he's going to lose her. Please help him," she pleaded, grabbing his hand and trying to pull him toward her car.

"Wait, Micah," Bryce ordered and ran back into the apartment, coming out with a small vial of oil.

"Joel, since you're up, do you mind?" Bryce asked.

Micah realized as they ran for the car that they needed Joel too. It took two worthy priesthood holders to give a blessing of healing. Joel didn't even say anything, he just ran with them.

She drove quickly and silently to the hospital, parked the car, and ran with Bryce and Joel through the hospital to the elevators. They made it to the third floor and spotted Phillip immediately. He was pacing outside a closed door and rubbing his hands through his hair, making it stick up in all directions. The cool, calm, sophisticated lawyer was gone. A desperate man stood in his place—a humble man.

He spotted his daughter and waved them over.

"Bryce, in here. I have special permission for the blessing. It's not good. Her lungs aren't developed enough to sustain her, and they don't know about her heart yet. They think it might have a hole in it. Please, just bless her that she'll be okay," Phillip pleaded.

Bryce grabbed Phillip's shoulder. "We'll give her the

blessing the Lord wants her to have, Phillip. That's all I can do. What is the baby's full name?"

Phillip looked taken aback. "I don't know. Kathy was still thinking about it. We thought we had three more months to decide."

Bryce nodded his head. "Okay, no problem. Baby Rawlings it is then," he said and walked into the room with Joel, leaving Micah and Phillip behind. The two stared through the window as Joel poured a tiny bit of oil on the head of the infant lying in the incubator, with tubes coming out every which way. Their hands were too large to lay on her head, so they used their fingers. Micah and Phillip couldn't hear what was said, but Joel finished and then raised his fingers, and then it was Bryce's turn to seal the blessing. Micah watched the earnest face of the man she loved and felt a feeling of gratitude in her heart that she loved someone worthy and honorable. She couldn't imagine not having the gift of priesthood in her life.

They finished and were ushered immediately out of the room. Phillip shook Joel's hand and then looked searchingly into Bryce's face.

"Bryce, I'm sorry for all of the things I've said about you and your family. If you're a worthy priesthood holder and you honor that priesthood, then that's good enough for me. Please forgive me, Bryce. I had no reason to treat you so horribly, especially when I'm not worthy right now to help my own family." His voice broke.

Bryce took Phillip's outstretched hand and shook it but then reached in and gave Phillip a one-armed hug.

"All is forgotten, Phillip. Besides, I knew I'd grow on you someday," he said with a smile, trying to lighten the moment.

Phillip looked doubtful but smiled back.

Micah, with tears in her eyes, walked up to Bryce and hugged him.

"Thank you," she said and relaxed as she felt his arms encircle her in return.

Bryce held Micah and looked again into the room holding the tiniest little baby he'd ever seen. He had been scared to death to even touch her little head. It had felt so smooth and fragile. In his blessing he had been impressed to bless her with total recovery. It seemed impossible, but nothing was impossible with the Lord. *Even getting along with Phillip,* he thought.

After giving Kathy a blessing too, he and Joel stayed with Phillip and Micah, bringing them drinks and snacks from the machines. Phillip was able to go in and see Kathy after a while. She had begun to hemorrhage right after the delivery, but the doctor caught it immediately and was able to stop the bleeding. She was receiving transfusions of blood, and the color was returning to her face.

Phillip looked down at his sleeping wife and felt a moment of peace in the storm. Everything was going to be okay. He bowed his head and said a silent prayer of thanks. From now on, he would dedicate his life to God and to being a better man, a man worthy to hold the priesthood. He would never take that special gift for granted again. He now realized that his life had been dedicated to himself and his needs and wants for so long that he had turned into a hard, proud, and selfish man. No more, he swore. Life was going to be different from now on.

* * *

Micah drove Joel and Bryce home just as the sun was making its way over the tops of the mountains.

"Hey, how about I treat you two to a breakfast at IHOP? You look like you could use some pancakes," Micah offered.

"Pick up April, and it's a deal," Joel said, yawning so

wide that his jaw cracked.

Micah called April on her cell and had her waiting outside in the parking lot within minutes.

The two couples ordered large, insane breakfasts and talked and laughed and ate until they were so full they could barely move.

"Life is amazing, isn't it?" April said, leaning into Joel's arm.

Micah agreed as she paid the bill. "I have a tiny little sister in the hospital right now. I can't believe it. Life really is amazing. It's crazy, it's hard and impossible sometimes, but then it's full of joy and miracles the next. I think life is wonderful," she said seriously, blushing at her speech.

Bryce leaned over and kissed her cheek.

"Yeah, I know what you mean. One minute your future father-in-law wants to kill you and hide the body somewhere, and then the next, he's offering his complete and total approval. Today is definitely a day of miracles," he said, grinning.

"Let's do it then, Bryce," Micah said with a laugh. "Let's get married."

Bryce took Micah's hand and helped her up from the table.

"That's just what I was going to say," he said and walked out into the sunlight with the woman he loved.

chapter fifty-five

Wedding Day, One Month Later

Micah walked out of the Salt Lake Temple, holding Bryce's hand and smiling as the flash of cameras went off everywhere she looked. She was freezing, but she was happier than she'd ever been in her whole entire life.

The light snow drifting around the small crowd of people didn't dim any of the happiness. It was Christmastime, a time of joy and peace and love, the perfect time to get married.

Micah leaned over and received a kiss from her father and Kathy. She wished her new little sister, Sophie, could have been there with them, but at least she was coming home from the hospital in a few days. She had grown so much and put on so much weight, the nurses were starting to call her chubby. Kathy was already planning for a family portrait to be taken in the spring.

Micah looked around at their friends and family and took it all in, knowing she would always remember this day and this feeling. Even Bryce's dad, Troy, being there was okay now that her dad had called him up and made peace with him. Troy had informed Phillip over the phone that there was no need to apologize. He had decided to quit the pornography business and go legitimate. He really was going to write for a sitcom now.

With Bryce's arm around her, they were ready to begin their new life. Together.

about the author

Shannon Guymon lives in Alpine, Utah, with her husband and four children. She enjoys spending time in the mountains, gardening, being with her family, and, of course, writing. She is the author of *Never Letting Go of Hope, A Trusting Heart, Justifiable Means,* and *Forever Friends.*